DAR & EARTH
ORACULI

ATHENA M. KAIMAN

ATHENA PRODUCTIONS INC.

Distributed by Book Publishing Company, 415 Farm Road, PO Box 99, Summertown, TN 38483, Phone: 931-964-3571, Fax: 931-964-3518, Toll-Free: 888-260-8458, info@bookpubco.com, or sales@bookpubco.com.

Cover illustration, cover design, and book designed by Kent Hernández.

The Library of Congress Cataloging-in-Publication Data is available upon request.

ISBN 978-1-7339828-0-1

For my Oraculi, Sabarah Sabin
A great civil rights leader

You were right, Sabarah
about everything
and I miss you

DAR & EARTH
ORACULI

CONTENTS

1

The Mission

AELISH STOOD IN the Great Rotunda of Peace before the Head Council of DAR. The Rotunda was as imposing as the first time she had entered it, so many years ago. The marble dome's hand-carved, historical scenes depicting the legendary figures of DAR towered above her.

The Head Council was seated on the elevated U-shaped dais known as the Arc of Leadership. Aelish remained poised before them, a solitary figure with at least five thousand citizens of DAR in attendance. The citizens at her back observed the proceedings from marble benches in the multitude of tiered, curved rows under the monumental dome. Her brocade gown was partially obscured by her green velvet cape. Her long red hair was secured by her signature fishtail braid and hung down the back of her cape.

"Congratulations on attaining the position of Oraculi," said the Council Chair, with a bit of whimsy in her voice. She smiled toward the citizens upon hearing the appreciative low murmur of laughter echoing throughout the Chamber. It was rare for them to witness a living legend before the Head Council.

Aelish bowed her head and smiled at the Council Chair. She had the greatest respect for Melanthia, since first meeting her as a child—their bond now unbreakable.

The Council Chair continued in a more serious tone, "Have you been keeping a steady watch over the twelve-year-old Human female child named Isabela? The Council has observed she is in rapid decline both in attitude and motivation."

"Yes, Council Chair. I can see that the obstacles confronting her are beginning to overwhelm her. I feel we have miscalculated the appropriate time for she and I to meet. With the Council's permission, I feel it is in her best interests if I leave when the sun is directly overhead," suggested Aelish.

"Hmm . . . do we all agree?" asked the Council Chair.

Seated in the center, most powerful position on the dais, Melanthia looked left and right toward the other Council Members. The eight other females that comprised the Head Council of DAR nodded in unison.

"Very well, then. Do you fully understand the gravity of what we are attempting to achieve through your responsibilities as an Oraculi to a Human child?" asked Melanthia.

Aelish firmly nodded and continued to pay close attention to the Council Chair.

"We cannot afford to lose this young girl as she is presenting an extraordinary aptitude for science. You must nurture and imbue the child with the necessary confidence for her to succeed in this branch of knowledge. You must prevent her from becoming consumed by the severe obstacles in her life, which in turn could derail her from reaching her fullest potential. She also demonstrates deep compassion, an attribute we always cherish.

"Your supervision of the Environmental Commission and their most recent report, demonstrates that the Earth is nearing devolution. This has caused consternation for the Head Council. As an Oraculi, your primary responsibilities are to the Human child. But it is crucial you report to the Head Council any transformations you observe since your last trip to Earth. The Council must be prepared for the impending crisis. We need dedicated Human scientists that are not only highly educated, but are also emotionally capable of withstanding the repercussions of this turning point. We must never again be caught off-guard, as we were in the last millennium. Based on this report, we expect to be facing even greater devastation," said the Council Chair.

"I understand the importance, Council Chair," said Aelish. Aelish felt her stomach flutter with nerves and anticipation. But she was confident the unprecedented policy she was about to initiate would be successful.

"Excellent. The Head Council wishes you safe travels and the best of magic. Please let us know if there is anything you need while you are in the Human world. If you encounter any problems, we will of course send assistance," concluded the Council Chair.

Aelish nodded, signaling her understanding that her audience with the Head Council was finished. Demonstrating the utmost of respect, she began walking backward. When she was the proper distance from the Council she turned around and faced the audience. She heard a groundswell of applause and made her way up the steep aisle to the exit. The Guards of the Rotunda opened both sets of enormously heavy wooden doors. She walked past them, outside, into the sunlight.

Once back home, Aelish packed her supplies and stuffed them into her flypack. She carefully retrieved the most important item from its place of safekeeping. The white linen pouch had yellowed over the years, but the item was still secure. She tucked it inside the bodice of her traveling gown, keeping it close to her heart.

She took a last look through her Earth Capsule Viewer. She watched Isabela's father and brother gently lower her mother onto the hospital bed in their new home. Aelish deeply sighed, as tears streamed down her face. She wiped them away with the back of her hands and pushed the Viewer deep inside her flypack. Her mission was going to be very hard, indeed.

2

SKIPPING CHURCH

ISABELA WOKE UP and was momentarily disoriented. As reality replaced her dreams, she felt sad. *Will I ever get used to waking up in my new room in this new house? Oh, no . . . and tomorrow, a new school. This is never going to feel like home.*

Abuela's cooking seemed to refute her thoughts, as the familiar aroma of beef enchiladas enveloped her bedroom. Then she remembered why Abuela was cooking at eight in the morning—there was a festival at their new church today after mass.

Isabela was desperate to skip church today. She was not allowed to, unless she was very sick. With the exception of her mother, her family had attended mass for the first time at the new church last Sunday. Nothing about it felt remotely similar to the one she had left behind in the city where she was born.

She turned over onto her side and looked at the beautiful picture window in her room. It had plantation shutters, which were now closed, allowing only the smallest amount of light into the room. Her bedroom faced the backyard and had a view of the pool. She had always dreamed of having an in-ground pool, but somehow it did nothing to alleviate her sadness.

Her old room was definitely not as grand, but she missed it terribly. She closed her eyes and tried to remember L.A., but the sounds were different. Other than Abuela making noise in the kitchen, it was so quiet.

Her family had spent most of the last week in a hotel by the Nashville airport, while they waited for the moving truck to arrive. Her father had been distressed because the physical accommodations had been very hard on her mother. For that reason alone, Isabela was relieved to finally be in their new house and out of that depressing hotel.

There were boxes everywhere, but at least the tall wardrobes with metal rods had been easy to find. They contained her hanging clothes, which had gone straight into her closet. Unfortunately, she had to search all over the house for the boxes that harbored the rest of her clothes that belonged in her dresser. She spent all day yesterday unpacking—carefully hanging up and refolding everything. Her clothes were wrinkled and smelled of cardboard, but if she held them up against her nose, they still smelled of home.

She couldn't believe how fast Abuela had unpacked, washed, and put away all the kitchen items. There were so many boxes labeled KITCHEN that the movers had to stack them to the ceiling. But Abuela had finished it all in two days. She had even found time to go to the grocery store and last night she cooked the family's first dinner, in their new house. And now she was cooking trays of enchiladas for the church festival.

Isabela marveled at Abuela's strength, energy, and focus. She knew she was going to get quite an earful about not wanting to go to church today. The priest had come by yesterday to bless their new house, but Isabela did not feel blessed. She knew she should be grateful for her family arriving safely after their cross-country move, but she just felt sad and exhausted. She could have stayed in bed the whole day.

She was repositioning her covers to try and sleep a little longer, when Abuela cheerfully burst into her room, "Buenos días, nieta, estás bien?"

"Sí, Abuela. Your cooking smells so good," said Isabela, stretching.

Abuela opened the plantation shutters as Isabela hid under the covers from the light and the day to come. Abuela began looking for her under the covers. It was a game they had played since Isabela was very little.

"Dónde estás, Izzy?" laughed Abuela.

Isabela kept squirming and going deeper and deeper under the covers. She also began laughing, as she ran out of mattress and began falling onto the floor. She had played this silly game with Abuela since she was in her first real bed. Despite now being twelve, it always brought a smile to her face.

"Ay! I found you!" exclaimed Abuela. She began kissing Isabela's face all over. Abuela sat on the floor against the bed with Isabela. She turned to look at her granddaughter. "You look so tired, nieta—and you look like you want to tell me something. Qué pasa?"

Isabela could never understand how her grandmother always knew when she was worried about something. Isabela sighed.

"I don't want to tell you because you are going to get angry and I love you and I don't want you to get upset."

"Let's go, tell me," instructed Abuela.

"I don't want to go to church today," said Isabela, not looking at Abuela's face.

When there was no response she turned and saw Abuela rubbing her face. Abuela always rubbed her face when something was troubling her.

Please don't be angry and let me stay home.

"Por favor, Abuela? I am so tired and nervous about my first day of school tomorrow. I want to be with Mom and just stay home. I know you will be at the festival all afternoon. I could get dinner ready for us?" pleaded Isabela, trying to sweeten her request.

"You know I don't like us to miss church, nieta, especially with your mother so ill," said Abuela, tears forming in her eyes. "I feel it is very important we demonstrate our devotion to God by attending church each week. We've had so much upheaval in the last month and we need Padre and the members of our new church to pray for us."

"I understand," sighed Isabela, resigned.

"Let's sit on the bed and talk, before I'm not able to get up from the floor."

Abuela extended her arm so Isabela could help pull her up. It was moments like this when Isabela realized Abuela was getting older. She couldn't bear to think of it. Abuela had always been the constant presence in her life and she could not imagine living in a world without Abuela by her side. They settled themselves onto the bed and Abuela held Isabela's face in her hand.

"All right, mi amor. Only this Sunday, okay?" said Abuela, as she kissed the top of Isabela's head.

"Gracias, Abuela," said Isabela, hugging her grandmother. "I love you so much, thank you for letting me stay home."

"I need you to do some other things while I'm gone, besides preparing dinner," said Abuela, in a serious tone. "Can you change your mother's sheets and give her the medicines at the right time? I also need you to finish unpacking your mother's things. Your father did not get to it yesterday. I want their room to be finished by tonight, so he doesn't have to worry about it. I think he is also nervous about starting his new position tomorrow."

"Yes, of course," agreed Isabela. She couldn't believe she was free from having to face all those nosy people at church, who already knew of her family's circumstances.

"I mean it," Abuela said sternly. "I will not be happy if you do not finish everything I have asked you to do."

"I will, I promise," said Isabela.

"Okay, go wake up your brother and tell him to be ready to leave for church with me and your father in thirty minutes," instructed Abuela. "I have to go and check on your mother and make sure your father is awake as well."

Isabela gave Abuela a big hug and a kiss, before going to wake up her brother. She was relieved and almost felt the stirrings of normalcy, as she gently knocked on her brother's bedroom door.

She opened it slowly and peered around the door whispering, "Javier? Javi? Are you awake?"

Javier moaned and began to yawn loudly.

"What is it, Izzy? What time is it? I keep waiting for the traffic sounds to wake me up, but there aren't any," complained Javier.

"I know. The quiet is so loud, I can barely sleep," Isabela agreed. She pushed opened the door and stood inside Javier's bedroom.

"Why aren't you dressed for church?" asked Javier, looking at her pajamas.

Isabela took a moment to consider how to answer him. Javier had recently turned eighteen and looked like a grown man, but he could still act like a baby.

"Abuela said I don't have to go to church today," said Isabela.

Javier sat straight up in bed and yelled, "What? Why not? Why do I have to go?"

"I promised Abuela I would make dinner, change Mom's sheets, give her the medicines, and finish unpacking Mom's things," Isabela stated firmly, ready for him to sabotage her arrangement with Abuela.

"I would rather go to church," groaned Javier, as he

flopped back onto the bed.

Isabela came over to the bed and sat down on the edge. Javier turned on his side to look at her.

"Are you as sad as I am?" asked Isabela. She could feel herself getting warm as she tried to stop the tears from coming.

"Of course, Izzy. I was supposed to be settled in at UCLA by now. Instead, I'm starting my training as a barista tomorrow—how do you *think* I feel?" asked Javier.

Isabela knew the money Javier was going to earn from his job would help defray the extra costs not covered by the family's health insurance for their mother's new medical treatments.

"I know, Javi, but UCLA will hold your place. It's going to be so weird for me, starting a new school in the beginning of *October*. I'm actually glad you are still home with me. I know that's very selfish, but it's the truth," sighed Isabela. "I would miss you so much."

"Me too—come here." Javier extended his arms beckoning Isabela for a hug.

As she hugged Javier, Isabela thought about all the sacrifices he had made for the family. Javier had packed up their old house with barely any help, he had deferred college for a year to take their mother for her treatments, and now he was lagging behind all his friends who were already ensconced at their new universities.

Javier remained with his family, trapped in this nightmare, when he could have been free. He was a very special person, an outstanding athlete, and had received a full baseball scholarship to UCLA. Isabela hoped she could be as amazing as her brother by the time she turned eighteen.

Their private moment of comforting each other was interrupted by Abuela shouting from the kitchen, "Javier! Come and eat something before we leave for church!"

"Ay," grumbled Javier. "Let me get ready, Izzy. You better do all the things you promised Abuela or she is going to be so mad. Do *everything* she told you to."

"It's a lot of things. I hope I can finish them all," said Isabela.

"Well you better, otherwise she is never going to let you miss church again," warned Javier.

"I know, I know," Isabela replied, already overwhelmed at what she had promised Abuela.

Isabela left the room so Javier could get dressed. She had looked up to her brother all her life. He was a talented and generous person. Despite being incredibly busy during high school with sports and his schoolwork, he had always made time for her, taking her bike riding or surfing. Isabela knew the one thing she and her brother would miss the most were the sunsets over the Pacific, after a day of getting knocked off their surfboards. She sighed and went to the kitchen to make her breakfast.

3

MAKING MOM'S BED

ISABELA SAID GOODBYE to her father, Javier, and Abuela and began cleaning her cereal bowl. She went into the laundry room and grabbed a pair of jeans and a long-sleeved top folded in a laundry basket. After dressing, she gathered up the clean sheets for the hospital bed and headed toward her parents' bedroom.

She was beginning to feel like the hospital bed had always been in her parents' bedroom. It was becoming hard for her to remember a time when it *wasn't* there. Her mother had gotten sick around her tenth birthday and the last two years felt like her whole life.

She quietly opened the door and dropped the pillowcases and sheets on the bench at the foot of her parents' bed. Her mother was sleeping, but began to stir as Isabela approached the hospital bed. Isabela rested one hand on the rail and used the other to gently stroke her mother's face. She was careful not to disturb the woolen cap Abuela had knitted for her mother's bald head.

Her mother slowly opened her eyes. She turned her head and saw Isabela and began to smile.

"Hi, Mom, how are you feeling?" Isabela sweetly whispered.

"Better now that I can see my angel's face. Why aren't you dressed for church, sweetheart? I thought I heard everyone leave?" asked her mother, her breathing labored.

12

"Abuela let me stay home today so that I could spend some time with you. I need to change the sheets on your bed and give you your medicines after I'm finished," replied Isabela, still stroking her mother's face.

Her mother said with a weak laugh, "Well, at least you got something out of taking care of me."

"I really didn't want to go to church today, Mom. All those new people . . . and I'm nervous about starting school tomorrow."

"I understand, sweetheart. I'm sorry you've had to make so many changes and leave all your friends and cousins behind. Do you at least like your new room? I thought you'd like facing the pool. Can you believe we could afford a house with a pool?" asked her mother.

Isabela noted her mother's speech was sluggish. She was so ill.

"The houses are much less expensive here in Brookdale than in L.A. I'm glad you finally got your pool. I hope we can go swimming together soon," said her mother, weakly.

Isabela knew how unlikely that was to happen. But she was determined to be strong and not let her mother see the tears welling up in her eyes. She turned her head away from her mother, toward the bench where she had dropped the clean pillowcases and sheets.

"Are you ready to change the sheets now, Mom?" asked Isabela. She was anxious to begin Abuela's list.

"Yes, my angel," answered her mother.

"Let me get your pillowcases. We can start there," directed Isabela.

Before getting the pillowcases, she moved the rolling hospital table away from the bed. Then she removed her mother's cell phone from a small pouch that hung on the right rail of the hospital bed. She didn't want it to get damaged during the process. Abuela had designed and sewn the pouch so her mother's phone would always be securely accessible. The pouch prevented the phone from falling off the bed or hospital table. Isabela temporarily stuck it in the back pocket of her jeans.

There were many pillows on the bed. A nurse at the hospital in L.A. suggested they be put around her mother's shoulders and arms so she wouldn't hurt herself on the rails of the hospital bed. It was a wonderful suggestion and had made her mother much more comfortable.

As Isabela began pulling out the pillowcases tangled in the sheets, she asked her mother, "Do you need help getting to the commode before we start?"

"No, sweetheart. Your father helped me to the commode before he left for church. Then he helped me put on an adult diaper, since I thought you would all be gone for the day—with mass and the festival afterward. Who knew I'd be in diapers before Abuela?" asked her mother, with a faint laugh.

Isabela started laughing. Her mother had always been the funniest person in the family and Isabela was happy she still had her sense of humor.

Isabela began removing the pillows and changing their cases one at a time, leaving her mother's head pillow for last. She temporarily placed them all on her parents' bed. Then she gently lifted up her mother's head and slid out the pillow.

"I know you're uncomfortable, Mom. I will change the sheets as fast as possible."

"Don't worry, honey. Let me know when you're ready and I will help as much as I can," said her mother.

Isabela had watched how the nurses at the hospital changed the sheets, while her mother remained *in* the bed. She'd asked them to teach her how to do it and was proud she had learned, as it was not easy. But it made her feel useful to her mother.

When she finished changing the case on her mother's head pillow, she gently removed her mother's blanket and top sheet, tossing them onto her parents' bed.

"This won't take long, Mom, I know you're cold," comforted Isabela. "Okay—you need to roll onto your right side and grab the right rail with your left arm. I will help you roll. You need to hold onto the rail and stay in that position, until I can pull off this side of the fitted sheet. Ready?"

Isabela helped her mother roll onto her right side, while at the same time pulling the elastic of the fitted sheet off the mattress. The mattress was about the same size as Isabela's bed. Once all the elastic was loose, she began scrunching the first half of the fitted sheet up against her mother's back.

"Okay, Mom, are you ready to turn toward the other side?"

This was the hardest part. Her mother had to roll over the scrunched up sheet against her back, so Isabela could pull it out from under her mother, onto the other side.

"Yes, sweetheart," said her mother.

Isabela helped her mother roll to the other side so her mother could grab onto the left rail. As her mother rolled over the fitted sheet, Isabela simultaneously pulled the sheet out from under her mother and detached the elastic from the mattress.

"Stay like that, Mom, and let me get the clean sheet hooked onto this side of the mattress," Isabela instructed.

She grabbed the clean sheet from the bench, secured the elastic, and scrunched up the balance against her mother's back.

"Okay, Mom, last time."

She helped her mother turn over one last time, as she pulled the clean sheet from underneath her mother. Her mother had lost so much weight that pulling the sheet out from underneath her wasn't very hard anymore. Isabela finished securing the clean fitted sheet onto the mattress and told her mother she could lie flat again. She briskly returned to the hospital bed with her mother's head pillow.

"Whew, that was exhausting," said her mother. "And to think I used to run half marathons."

"You did great holding the rails, Mom. I couldn't have done it without your strong arms," complimented Isabela.

Isabela got the clean top sheet from the bench and began tucking it under the mattress. She grabbed the blanket she had thrown earlier onto her parents' bed and placed it gently over her mother, also tucking it under the mattress. She knew her mother was cold and needed to warm up. Isabela finished the final step of repositioning all the extra pillows against the rails.

"I'm going to get your medicines now," said Isabela. "But first, can I press the button that raises your head up? I always worry you'll choke when you swallow your medicines if your head isn't high enough."

"Yes, my angel," whispered her mother.

Isabela lifted up the head portion of the hospital bed. She could see her mother was utterly exhausted from the ordeal of changing the sheets. She rolled the hospital table back alongside the bed, checked to see that her mother's cell phone was fully charged, and set the volume on the loudest setting. Then she placed the phone back inside the pouch.

By the time Isabela had returned with the medicines, her mother was asleep. Isabela pulled a chair over to sit with her. She would let her rest for thirty minutes since it was too early for her medicines anyway. She stared at her mother and couldn't believe this was the same person she had gone to Disneyland with for her tenth birthday. It had been the best vacation they ever had, and now it meant so much more.

4

AELISH REACHES THE PORTAL

AELISH WATCHED THE extraordinary composure of Isabela as she tended to her mother through her Earth Capsule Viewer. She had decided to check on Isabela while she sat on the ground resting, before continuing on to the Portal. The compassion and love demonstrated by this young girl made her remember why DAR was completely devoted to protecting the Human world. It was so often through the Human child that those in DAR could observe the best of Humanity. Certainly there were children who were mean-spirited and unkind, but Aelish believed that Human children, who were cruel, had been taught to behave that way. It was a learned behavior and not the normal nature of the Human child.

As she stuffed the Viewer inside her flypack, she reflected on her own life. She remembered caring for her parents in much the same way Isabela was now caring for her mother. It had been almost impossible to endure, feeling utterly powerless against the sickness, and the inevitable outcome. She hoped Isabela's mother's fate would be different. She marveled at Isabela's ability to change her mother's sheets, with her mother *in* the bed. Aelish was truly impressed at the level of maturity possessed by this twelve-year-old child.

Aelish stood up, determined to succeed as Isabela's Oraculi. She could see how special and deserving this young girl was. But she had no illusions of how difficult it was going to be to convince Isabela that not only was she real, but also that her attributes and abilities were desperately needed by DAR.

She continued on and realized she had been lost in thought, for when she looked up, she had arrived at the gate of the Portal. It had been five years since she had last stood in this same place and she wondered if Earth would *feel* the same. She was excited to find out.

"Aye! Aelish! Mah favorite DARling! It has bin too long since I last laid eyes on ye! How ur ye mah, lassie?" exclaimed the troll Hamish, in his unique Scottish-English dialect. His brogue was as thick as ever.

"Greetings, Hamish! It's so good to see you are still here!" exclaimed Aelish, with a grin from ear to ear.

"Now where else wid I be, lassie?" laughed the troll, banging his rod against the gate.

"I see you're still as funny as ever," laughed Aelish.

"And I see ye haven't aged a day in nearly five hundred years, lassie," winked Hamish, ridiculously flirting.

"You've always been a bad liar, Hamish, but you will always be my favorite Gatekeeper," chuckled Aelish.

She remembered shortly after her arrival to DAR that Hamish and his brother Artagán had petitioned the Head Council for the position of Gatekeeper of the Portal. The Portal separated the dimensions between DAR and Earth. The brothers pointed toward their lengthy troll ancestry in the Scottish Highlands where most had served as Gatekeepers. They had promised to protect and serve DAR, rotating shifts between each other.

Aelish was pleased when the brothers had secured the position, as she frequently passed through the Portal to observe and report ongoing environmental changes on Earth. In the process, she had developed quite a soft spot for Hamish. He was a charmer and she was thrilled he was on duty today rather than his brother.

"And did ye remember tae bring yer favorite Gatekeeper his favorite goodies?" asked Hamish, naughtily. He rubbed his gnarled hands together in anticipation.

"Of course!" laughed Aelish. She took off her flypack and placed it on the ground. She knelt beside it and reached inside to retrieve a pink box with a purple bow.

"Are thay whit I think thay are?" asked Hamish. He was already starting to drool a bit down his wart-covered face.

"They are . . . I made you twelve lavender sweetcakes and even added a special ingredient to the icing," winked Aelish. "So don't eat them until you are off-duty, *promise?*"

She would not give him the box until he agreed to her condition. She could always turn the tables on Hamish. It was he who was supposed to dictate the terms, in order for her to pass through the gate. But Aelish was cunning and knew that all she needed were her sweetcakes to bring Hamish to his knobby knees.

"I promise! Ah lassie, ye always know th' wey tae mah heart!" exclaimed Hamish, as he massaged his distended belly.

"I do, don't I?" laughed Aelish.

"You're lucky Artagán wasn't 'ere instead o' me! He's getting crankier with each passing decade," said Hamish, shaking his contorted head.

"How can you tell the difference?" asked Aelish, sarcastically. Hamish burst into hysterics.

"He is a bit o' a dolt, isn't he? Whit are ye goin' tae do, lassie, it is whit it is," continued Hamish, still doubled over in laughter.

He was always somewhat doubled over, but Aelish loved to get him laughing to the point where he was nearly level with the ground.

Hamish and Artagán were literally the definition of polar opposites, like night and day or black and white. Hamish was always smiling and laughing, whereas Artagán was a cantankerous, cranky pain. They were both excellent at their job, but Aelish dreaded having to deal with Artagán. Yet they came as a package, and Hamish more than made up for Artagán's miserable demeanor.

"So, I assume yer on a secret mission fur th' Earthlings again?" asked Hamish. He grabbed his clipboard and began making the necessary notations before he could open the gate.

"I am. Will you wish me luck?" asked Aelish.

"Ye'll be needin' no luck from me, lassie. Ye know yer job very well. Ur ye lookin' forward to seeing home again?" asked Hamish.

"I am, indeed," sighed Aelish.

"Och! As fur me, I'm happy here 'n' prefer tae remember th' Highlands in mah heart. No need tae see it again," replied Hamish.

Aelish nodded. She understood that for certain magical creatures there was no going back to Earth once they had decided to leave. Choosing to live in DAR or in one of the other magical dominions often became a permanent transition. They were happier in the magical world. Those that chose to live in DAR often expressed the feeling that they finally had a sense of *belonging* and would never go back to their original birthplace—whether in the Human world or in one of the other magical realms.

"Well, ur ye ready, lassie? Gather up yer things, don't forget anythin' now," instructed Hamish.

Aelish lifted her flypack from the ground and secured it snuggly to her back. She locked the clasps to prevent them from opening during her time in the Portal, between dimensions. She secretly checked to make sure that the linen pouch was still secure in her bodice while Hamish continued his note taking. Depending on the time of year, the pressure through the Portal could be excessively forceful and this was *definitely* that time of year.

Aelish approached the gate and said, "I'm ready, Hamish! Let's do this!"

Hamish opened the gate and she took three steps past the threshold and stared at the grayish vibrating blur in front of her—the Portal.

"Brace yerself fur th' noise 'n' th'pressure. I wish ye th' best o' magic 'n' safe travels. Make sure ye come back tae us now, fur thare is no other DARling like ye, Aelish. Be careful wi' those Earthlings. I don't envy ye traveling thare," said Hamish, with a shudder. "Ye know whit tae do next."

"Be well, Hamish!"

She took three more steps forward. There was a simultaneous bolt of lightening, which instantly blinded her, followed by a huge crash of thunder, which instantly deafened her. Her senses were completely disoriented, but it didn't last long.

When it was quiet again, Aelish opened her eyes and was on Earth. It was more beautiful than she remembered. She could look at it anytime through her Viewer, but the Viewer could never truly capture the essence of Earth. She closed her eyes and took a deep breath, inhaling that distinctive woody scent of the moss on the forest floor. She looked up at the trees, ebullient with the colors of autumn. They were so tall, they nearly blocked out the sun. It would always be home.

Using the Panoramic spell, Aelish lifted high above the trees and began taking it all in—the oceans, the mountains, the plains, the canyons, the moors—it was so green and so blue. She could never understand how Humans took their birthplace for granted, as if no matter what, it would always be there.

For nearly five hundred years, she had watched Humans persist in treating the Earth with a carelessness that was astonishing. They continued to mine mountains until they disappeared, taking the wildlife and trees the mountain had supported along with them. They continued to dump toxic waste and chemicals into lakes, rivers, and streams, and every sixty seconds they dumped one garbage truck of plastic into the grandeur of the oceans. They continued to pollute the air that literally sustained Human life and they continued to create weapons of mass destruction that could destroy it all.

She marveled at the strength of the Earth, enduring the endless pillaging and polluting of its natural resources. When would Humans finally evolve and understand that they needed to put the Earth before their own greed?

It wasn't the poor who promulgated the pillaging. It was done by those of great means, in their unquenchable thirst for more and more money. Her family had owned mines. She understood firsthand what great wealth meant on Earth and the power, prestige, security, and lavish lifestyles it afforded Humans. She understood it because she had been born a child of privilege. But there had to be a balance. The Earth needed to survive until the last ray of sunlight was gone from its brilliant sun. DAR was beautiful, but Earth was magnificent.

As she perused the different landscapes, she noticed extraordinary changes, specifically in the Arctic and Antarctica. She could see that some of the glaciers in the Arctic were much smaller and huge chunks were actively falling into the surrounding water.

In Antarctica, Aelish noticed rapidly growing banks of moss on its northern peninsula. She had never seen anything like it. She was horrified that a huge ice shelf had also broken off from the peninsula.

She observed in both the Arctic and Antarctica that the permafrost was actively melting and the sea ice extent had been severely diminished. Water was now visible between sections of the sea ice that was still frozen. How had it changed so rapidly, since her last visit, only five years ago?

She felt despondent. She understood the consequences these changes would bring to the Earth and its inhabitants. Deadly diseases, buried for years under the frozen ice and snow, could once again become active, threatening Humanity. Rising sea levels would bring economic devastation to once thriving coastal cities that would soon be underwater. She knew her report on these observations would mandate some form of immediate action from the Head Council—the Earth was already in devolution.

With a heavy heart, she took out her magical compass, got her bearings, and began the journey to Isabela's house. She chose to go the long way in order to continue logging her observations. The beautiful, brilliant sun, high in the sky, made her discoveries that much sadder.

5

THE THREE VISITORS

AELISH ALTERNATED BETWEEN flying and walking as she journeyed on to Isabela's house. Walking enabled her to see things on Earth up close and to take little mementos. She would put them in her house in DAR upon her return. She did this each time she visited to remember home.

Each memento brought back vivid memories. Holding some lavender, she remembered her own life, when she too was twelve years old, like Isabela. She would never forget the day she looked down at her hands and noticed the pigmentation of her porcelain skin changing to lavender. It was terrifying. She didn't understand what was happening. She had never met or heard of anyone in Ireland with lavender skin.

She tried concealing her changing skin color by wearing gloves and long-sleeved dresses with high necklines. She even made her own homemade face powder from cooking flour, but she only got away with that for a few months. Mrs. Doherty, the household cook, finally caught Aelish taking flour from the pantry.

She'd snuck up on Aelish and yelled, "What do ya' think yer doin' in me pantry, Lady Aelish?"

Aelish was so startled she dropped the sack of expensive flour all over the floor. Mrs. Doherty was prone to forgetting she was a servant in her father's household and demanded an explanation. But Aelish ran out of the pantry, upstairs to her bedchamber. She stood against the bedroom door crying, listening to the echo of Mrs. Doherty continuing to yell. She didn't feel badly for ignoring Mrs. Doherty, but she greatly regretted that the scullery maid, Catríona, was going to have to clean up the mess she had made.

Catríona was not much older than Aelish. They could have been friends if not for their class divide. Aelish liked chatting with Catríona on the rare occasions when she snuck downstairs into the servants' quarters, as she was very kind. Aelish pitied Catríona having to endure the endless tirades of Mrs. Doherty.

She might have been the lowest-ranking servant in the household, but she was also the smartest. Aelish never could figure out how Catríona had managed to sneak a small sack of flour upstairs into Aelish's bedchamber when Catríona was never allowed out of the kitchen. She had found it on her bedside table and knew it was Catríona who had done that for her. Aelish repaid the kindness with a beautiful sampler she had sewn. She hid it under Catríona's blanket, on the pallet she slept on, in the servants' quarters.

After the flour incident, she became desperate to find an alternate way to conceal her lavender skin. Once she ran out of the flour from Catríona, it became nearly impossible to camouflage. It got to the point where she no longer wanted to venture outside her bedchamber. Her changing skin color was making life very difficult.

Aelish often accompanied her father to Dublin. He traveled there to manage the commerce he was responsible for as the

Earl of Brólaigh. When his schedule permitted, her father would take her to visit the seamstress for a new frock or her favorite bakeshop—the same bakeshop where she obtained the recipe for the lavender sweetcakes Hamish loved so much. She and her father loved spending time together and when she began to beg off going, she knew it was only a matter of time before her parents became suspicious.

Aelish was born in Ireland, in 1546, to noble parents. Her father, Cian Carrigan, was Earl of Brólaigh and her mother, Saoirse Mulcahy Carrigan, was Lady of Brólaigh. They owned vast acres of land, had tenant farmers, owned copper ore, zinc, and silver mines, and were responsible for employing nearly the entire village.

She grew up at Brólaigh Castle, her family's ancestral home. It was a tower house structure more than four stories high. The fortified residence was built from cut stone. In between the stones was lime-based mortar, which contained straw and animal hair. Having mortar between the stones demonstrated great wealth, while providing its occupants with insulation that helped keep out the cold and rain. The entire exterior of the tower house was covered with a lime plaster, which was then whitewashed. The stark white served as a warning to strangers approaching the tower house and was meant to be off-putting. The nobles of Ireland built these tall tower house castles amongst sparse forest cover, which made their severe white color stand out like imposing fortresses. She could see her house from miles away.

The main rooms for the family had leaded, diamond shaped, crown glass windows. The interior walls were the flip side of the mortared cut stone on the exterior. They had large hand-sewn tapestries hanging on them. The tapestries depicted various historical scenes and landscapes, as well as the family's coat of arms. The tapestries provided warmth and vivid colors, although many had faded over the years. In the drawing room and great hall were large iron candelabras laden with dripped candle wax. Some of the rooms had iron candleholders affixed in sockets carved into the stone.

She was lucky to have grown up with stone floors instead of the hardened dirt floors found in the servants' quarters. In wintertime, she remembered how cold and slippery the stone became, despite the servants' best efforts to keep them dry by laying down layers of rush matting. The rush was plaited by hand using a nine end flat weave, into lengths three inches wide. These sections were then hand sewn together with jute twine. Often a layer of straw was placed underneath the rush matting to further absorb the moisture from the cold.

She loved the custom-made stone spiral staircase. It spanned over four stories—leading up to the bedchambers or down to the servants' quarters. With nothing more than a rope for a railing, the diagonal stone steps were quite hazardous. But Aelish fondly remembered playing on them as a child. The staircase in Brólaigh Castle was built with the rope railing on the left walls. This enabled the Lord to defend his castle from the top of the staircase, with his sword in his right hand.

In the servants' quarters below, the windows only had wooden shutters to keep out the cold and rain. There were huge fireplaces in the great hall and in the kitchen area—large enough for a man to stand inside, under the mantle. The fireplace in the kitchen was used for cooking and also provided much needed warmth for the servants who slept in the same room on pallets on the dirt floor. The drawing room and bedchambers had smaller fireplaces. Aelish loved to snuggle in her canopy bed during the winter, with a roaring fire, under numerous fur covers.

Inside Brólaigh Castle, she was tutored three days a week by Miss O'Boyle. The butler was also teaching her proper decorum and the responsibilities of becoming an Earl's wife. Mr. MacSweeney was stern and strict with all of the servants and was very serious about the management of the household. He was an excellent butler, but he was an awful teacher.

When it came time for her lessons on the proper placement of tableware for elaborate evening supper parties, it was clear he had absolutely no patience, whatsoever, for children. He tolerated instructing her, but she knew he despised her lessons.

She felt the panic and terror afresh, as she remembered her last lesson with Mr. MacSweeney. Her magical abilities had begun to emerge on their own—she had no control over them. Learning to properly arrange a table became a harrowing experience, as the tableware began to set itself! She had quite a time running around the large table trying to hide what was happening.

"Lady Aelish, what in the name of Providence are ya' doing?" exclaimed Mr. MacSweeney, on more than one occasion. "A Lady does not run in the great hall, *ever*!"

During her lessons with Miss O'Boyle, books that she needed would fly off the shelves and arrive at her writing table. Miss O'Boyle usually had her back turned toward the large piece of slate that was installed in the lesson room and thankfully didn't see this phenomenon. But it made concentrating nearly impossible for Aelish.

Miss O'Boyle would say, "Turn to page twenty-one." And the book would turn on its *own*, to page twenty-one. Her ink, parchment, and quills would independently fly through the air and arrive at her desk along with anything else she needed.

At first she thought a house elf or faerie was toying with her. But she finally realized that when she *thought* of what she needed, her magic would engage and it was *she* who was actually causing the mayhem.

Everything changed, however, on that fateful day in the early morning, when there was unexpected knocking on the heavy wooden front doors of the tower house castle. Her family had recently returned from morning prayers at Brólaigh Church and was being served breakfast by the footmen in the great hall.

She and her parents simultaneously looked up from their food aghast that an unexpected caller was casually knocking on the front doors of the Earl's castle. Unexpected callers were fraught with danger, as they could be robbers or enemies of the Earl. Mr. MacSweeney apologized to her father for not knowing who the unexpected caller was. He waited until her father gave the order to open the doors.

Mr. MacSweeney walked toward the front of the great hall to open the doors. Her father followed his butler, lagging behind with his sword drawn, hidden at his side. She knew her father was very concerned and irritated at the ill-mannered visitor who was intruding upon the family's breakfast, without an appointment.

Ignoring the whispering pleas from her mother to stay seated, Aelish quietly crept behind her father through the great hall. She hid behind a long tapestry until the doors were opened. She peeked out from behind the tapestry and saw three people—two women and one strikingly handsome young man, all dressed like Irish nobles.

"Good morning, may I help you?" asked Mr. MacSweeney.

"We have come to speak with Lord Cian Carrigan, Earl of Brólaigh and Lady Saoirse Mulcahy Carrigan, Lady of Brólaigh," replied a commanding woman in a stunning hat.

"What is this concerning?" demanded Mr. MacSweeney. "You do not have an appointment and the Lord and Lady are *very* busy."

"We have come to speak with them about their daughter, Lady Aelish," continued the woman.

Her father pushed past his butler and in the authoritative

tone of an Earl asked, "And what business do you have with my daughter?"

Aelish could see he was getting his Irish up, his face red with annoyance, verging on anger.

"I think it would be best if you left your name so we could schedule a proper appointment," scolded Mr. MacSweeney.

"No! I would like to know immediately what this is about," demanded her father.

"Lord Brólaigh, we mean no disrespect to Your Lordship and Your Ladyship. We are here on behalf of your daughter's welfare. Time is of the essence and if you would permit us inside to explain, we know that you will be thankful we have come," stated the woman in the stunning hat.

Aelish's mother, always a kind and gracious person, had by now also joined her father in the forward portion of the great hall. She gestured for him to sheath his sword and spoke softly into his ear.

"Cian, let them come in and say their piece. Perhaps it is very important," appealed her mother.

Aelish wanted to kiss her mother right then for intervening. She knew her mother was hoping these strangers would provide an answer to the mystery of Aelish's lavender skin color. It had been two weeks since Aelish had shown her skin, only to her mother, crying and hysterical. Of course her mother was startled and alarmed, but her inherent composure took over. She led Aelish to her bed and told her to lie down and compose herself.

After she had calmed down, Aelish remembered removing all her garments so her mother could see if the lavender color covered her entire body. She knew her mother was hoping it was some kind of rash or exposure to an exotic plant, but upon inspection, she could see her mother was just as confused and concerned as she was.

"Perhaps you've had a spell cast on you by one of the faeries that live on the hill, past the mine," said her mother, thinking out loud.

Faeries were very prevalent in Ireland. It was common knowledge that if you inadvertently annoyed one, they could exact their revenge in any number of ways. It was the first thing Aelish had considered, but then her magical abilities began emerging. She knew a faerie would never cast a naughty spell that would also grant her magical powers that could rival their own.

She and her mother discussed a myriad of scenarios that might be the cause of her skin color turning lavender. Ultimately, they agreed that for the time being, Aelish would use her mother's face powder to conceal her skin color. Face powder was something her mother used only on the rare occasions when she met with the wives of other Irish nobles.

"We must pray very hard for God to reveal the cause of this mystery, Aelish," stated her mother. "In the meantime, we will tell everyone, including your father, that you are unwell and must be confined to the tower house. We will temporarily cancel your lessons with Miss O'Boyle, and you are not to accompany your father to Dublin until we understand what is going on."

"All right, Ma," sniffled Aelish, wiping her tears.

Aelish already understood that she was different from her parents and she was frightened of losing her mother's love. Therefore, she disclosed only her changing skin color and kept her magical abilities a secret. She gauged it was too much information to divulge at one time. She didn't want to overwhelm her mother, who in turn could tell her father everything. And Aelish was *petrified* of the consequences of her father finding out.

Aelish wore the face powder on the exposed parts of her body when she joined her family for meals, but all lessons and trips were suspended for the immediate future. Even prayers were conducted inside the tower house. Aelish wondered if she would ever leave Brólaigh Castle again. It was a terrible feeling to be so confined and she empathized with those who were truly ill and could not leave their homes. It gave her an understanding and compassion she would need later in her life.

Remembering this, as she journeyed on to Isabela's house, Aelish thought, *God only lets us see just so far down the road, otherwise we could not endure what is to come.*

Her mother was at long last successful in convincing her father to allow the three strangers to come inside. Her father instructed Mr. MacSweeney to seat them in the drawing room and ordered tea and scones be served. He might have been utterly annoyed, but he was still a nobleman with proper manners.

Once inside the drawing room, Aelish and her family sat on one settee and the three strangers sat across from them on the other settee, with a tea table in between.

"Please allow me to introduce myself and my companions, Lord and Lady Brólaigh," said the woman in the stunning hat. "My name is Melanthia and this is Lady Antonia Harrington Stonebridge." She gestured toward the most beautiful young woman Aelish had ever seen. "And this is Thagar." She pointed to the handsome young man who had caught Aelish's eye.

"We understand Lady Aelish has not been feeling well for the last few weeks and we are here to hopefully assist in her rapid recovery," said Melanthia, with a glint in her eye, as she stole a quick glance at Aelish.

Aelish smiled to herself at the memory. Melanthia, now the Council Chair in DAR, had that same glint in her eye today in the Rotunda, when she congratulated her on becoming an Oraculi, as she did when she offered to "assist in her rapid recovery" on the settee, so long ago. From that one subtle expression on the settee, Aelish knew Melanthia would always be there for her and she had immediately relaxed. Her father's reaction, however, was *quite* different.

"How do you know anything about the health of Lady Aelish?" demanded her father. "Who are you people? What part of Ireland do you come from? I don't detect any brogue I am familiar with. Well?"

"Lady Antonia was born in England," stated Melanthia. "She grew up at the Court of King Henry VIII and knows your new rulers, the Tudors, quite well, Lord Brólaigh."

"Whether the Tudors remain the monarchy over Ireland, is something yet to be determined," scoffed her father, having lived through the ever-changing rulers of Ireland.

"Indeed," agreed Melanthia.

"And are you and this gentleman also from England? Speak up, man! Do you normally let women do all your bidding?" chided her father.

"Actually, yes, Lord Brólaigh," replied Thagar. "Where we are from, a man knows his place."

"Ha!" cried out Aelish's mother, who burst out laughing. "Well that's the most interesting thing I've ever heard." Her mother was laughing so hard she had to retrieve a handkerchief from her dress pocket to hide her face. Her father, however, was not amused.

He began inching toward the edge of the settee. "You, Sir—"

"Lord Brólaigh," interrupted Melanthia, before things escalated, "Thagar meant no disrespect, I assure you." But despite her reassurance, Aelish observed that Melanthia was thoroughly enjoying her mother's laughter.

"We come from a distant land whose customs you are not familiar with, as this place is not near to Ireland," said Melanthia. Aelish knew she was easing in to revealing something that was going to change their lives forever.

"What is the name of this distant land? I do know world

geography for heaven's sake," said her father, indignant.

"Your Lordship, have you noticed any changes recently with Lady Aelish, other than her lavender skin color?" inquired Melanthia.

Aelish gulped. She knew *this* was not going to end well. She and her mother had kept the secret of her skin color between them and her father would now be caught unaware. She and her mother stared at each other for a brief moment before her father exploded.

"Aelish! Have you been actin' the maggot about being sick? What is this woman talking about regarding your skin?" yelled her father.

He stood up, maneuvered his body around his seated wife, nearly knocking over the tea table, and stood in front of Aelish. He aggressively reached down, grabbed her arm and began rolling back the long sleeve of her dress.

"Da! No!" screamed Aelish. But it was too late.

"God save us!" cried her father.

He stepped back from Aelish, stumbling backward over the tea table between the settees. Thagar caught him before he landed on Melanthia and Lady Antonia. Upon hearing the clatter of tableware, Mr. MacSweeney came running into the drawing room.

"Take your hands off His Lordship this *instant*," he yelled at Thagar.

Once her father had regained his balance, Thagar let go and resumed his place on the settee. Her father maneuvered his doublet back onto his shoulders, smoothed out the sleeves, and remained standing.

Mr. MacSweeney righted the tea table, reassembled the service, and her father said tersely, "Leave us!"

Aelish remembered Mr. MacSweeney looking askance at the tone her father had used. She was secretly glad he had finally experienced the same tone he had always used with her, during their lessons.

"Lord Brólaigh, you have been very blessed," said Melanthia, soothingly.

"*Blessed?* I have a daughter whose skin is the color of the lavender growing on my land! Who put this curse on her?" screamed her father at the three visitors who remained seated.

"She is not cursed, Your Lordship. She is a magical being," stated Melanthia.

Aelish gasped simultaneously with her mother, who looked like she was going to faint.

"What malarkey is this!" yelled her father.

"I am the same as your daughter, Lord Brólaigh," stated Lady Antonia. She briefly closed her eyes and when she opened them, her exposed skin had turned from porcelain to lavender, exactly the same color as Aelish's.

"Good God!" cried out her father.

He walked away to his writing table, clearly shaken, where he collapsed onto the accompanying chair. Aelish was truly worried about him. He was pale and looked affright. But her attention was on the fact that only *one* of the three visitors had lavender skin.

"May I ask a question?" asked Aelish.

"Of course, my dear. I imagine you have more than one," said Melanthia, with an encouraging smile.

"Why is your skin color porcelain and Thagar's is bronzed? Why don't you all have lavender skin?" asked Aelish.

"Lady Aelish is as smart as we hoped," said Melanthia, turning toward Lady Antonia.

"You and Lady Antonia share a great rarity. My actual skin color is this," said Melanthia. She briefly closed her eyes and turned her skin color olive green. "I change it to whatever Human skin color is appropriate whenever I visit Earth."

"Ohh," whimpered Aelish and her mother.

"Good God," gasped her father. Aelish knew her father had been listening intently from the vantage of his writing table chair, and she'd seen him turn to witness Melanthia's transformation.

"I'm very confused," said Aelish. "Are you all from the same place and where is this place?"

"Let me start at the beginning. We are from a land in the magical world known as DAR," said Melanthia, glancing at Aelish and her mother on the settee.

Aelish watched as Melanthia turned to look at her father, but he was oblivious to Melanthia's attempt to draw him into the conversation. Aelish was concerned for him, as he had sequestered himself at his desk, staring blindly at the loft ceiling. She looked away from her father and back toward Melanthia.

"DAR," Aelish repeated.

"Yes, DAR," said Melanthia. "It is really an acronym for how we feel the world's beings, both Human and magical, should treat each other. DAR stands for Dignity, Acceptance, and Respect. It is a commonwealth in the magical world that accepts those who have been ostracized, persecuted, tortured, or simply not accepted, based on their attributes and physical appearance. It is a peaceful place, opposed to war, which is quite prevalent in the magical world."

"It is quite prevalent in the Human world, as well," sighed her mother.

"Indeed, Lady Brólaigh," agreed Melanthia. "Those of us originally born in DAR, disgusted with endless warfare, decided to utilize our magical abilities to create a peaceful dominion. Magical beings from other realms that share our devotion to peace may also join our commonwealth. They must accept our tenets of treating others with dignity, acceptance, and respect, and must ultimately take the Oath of Peace to permanently live in DAR."

"Saoirseee, I feel insaaane," bellowed her father. His head was bent backward against his chair, his arms resting on its sides, and he continued to stare at the loft ceiling. "Am I to believe that the three strangers on my settee, are in fact, magical beings?"

"We know this is extremely difficult, Lord Brólaigh," said Melanthia. "But we are, in fact, magical beings and need to speak with Your Lordship and Your Ladyship about your daughter, who is one of the rarest finds on Earth."

"Cian, we must listen, as Aelish has been suffering with the secret of her lavender skin for some time. Originally, I thought she was cursed by an elf or a faerie, but I have prayed to God long and hard these last few weeks for an answer. We must accept God's will, even if we do not fully understand it yet," comforted her mother. "Please come and sit back down on the settee with us, my love."

Her father rose from his chair shaking his head and solemnly resumed his place on the settee next to her mother. Aelish remembered how he had glared at the three visitors, knowing he wished he had never opened the doors of Brólaigh Castle *that* day.

"How could Aelish's provenance be of DAR, if she was born on Earth from Human parents?" asked her mother.

"It happens at most, three times, every one hundred years, Lady Brólaigh," answered Melanthia. "DARlings born on Earth from Human parents are exceptional in every way. They have lavender skin that often emits the aroma of lilacs."

"An' here I thought you were stealing me fancy sachets," chuckled her mother, looking at Aelish.

"I actually can't smell it," said Aelish.

"No, we are the lucky ones who get to be around such sweet-smelling beings," said Melanthia. "We believe that the sun's proximity to Earth causes DARlings born of the Earth, like Lady Aelish and Lady Antonia, to have lavender skin that emits the aroma of lilacs. You see—the sun is much closer to Earth, than it is to DAR.

"Your unique lavender skin color is highly regarded by the inhabitants of DAR, as it exemplifies exceptionalism and rarity. Because those with lavender skin have been born of Human parents, they also possess Human traits—traits not found in any other magical being. Possessing Human traits in addition to growing up around Humans, allows for the development of an extraordinary compassion and deep understanding of Human beings. For reasons unknown, this combination allows DARlings born of the Earth to reach the highest level of enlightenment and magical endowment. They afford the Head Council of DAR with guidance that those born in DAR could never know or understand."

"Why does DAR involve itself in the business of what happens here? Why should they give a whit about us?" questioned her father.

"Although the magical world is in a different dimension than the Human world, Lord Brólaigh, we share the same sun," explained Melanthia. "DAR is dependent on the sunlight that is reflected off the Earth. Without the Earth, both of our worlds would cease to be.

"We have watched the endless wars and conflicts amongst Humans over these past millennia. Therefore, the inhabitants of DAR decided to amend the Doctrine of DAR to include the core principle of furthering the evolution of Humanity and serving as its protector. Sometimes this amendment to our Doctrine causes conflicts within DAR, but we have always managed to overcome them by conducting ourselves as one commonwealth. By staying focused on the broader view of protecting Humanity, it is our hope that Humans will ultimately learn the importance of protecting the Earth. This in turn, will ensure the survival of DAR."

Lady Antonia added, "Those like Lady Aelish and myself, can travel between the dimension of the magical and Human worlds with great ease. We provide the Head Council with crucial information on the progress of this amendment."

"Oh, no!" Aelish's mother suddenly cried out. "Have you come to take Aelish away with you to DAR?"

"No, Lady Brólaigh," smiled Lady Antonia. "DAR would never cause that kind of pain to a Human family. DARlings born of the Earth may stay until their family has passed and they have transferred their affairs appropriately. They then journey to DAR and live approximately two millennia."

"Well, a long life to ya', love!" exclaimed her mother, kissing Aelish's cheek.

Aelish wiped her mother's tears off her cheek. She knew her mother was crying from relief that the three strangers were not here to take her away.

"What about her lavender skin color?" asked her mother. "She can't leave the house anymore or walk around the village, and I'm running out of face powder."

"We knew the situation was becoming untenable," smiled Melanthia, "which is why we are here today—to teach and protect this rare gem. With Your Ladyship and Your Lordship's permission, Lady Antonia will be staying on at Brólaigh Castle as Lady Aelish's Oraculi, a magical mentor, to further Lady Aelish's magical education. Her first lesson will be to learn how to change her skin color back to Irish porcelain, so she can resume her Human life, while she is still on the Earth."

"Aelish! How long have you been doin' magic?" accused her father.

She remembered feeling so badly for him. He was hurt that she had not taken him into her confidence. As an Earl, he was used to being in charge of everything—in Brólaigh Castle and especially in the village. She knew he had already internalized that her magical gifts surpassed his level of authority. But she had a deep love and respect for her father. In an effort to assuage his hurt feelings, Aelish just spoke the truth.

"At first, Da," began Aelish, "I didn't understand how objects were moving on their own, and I desperately tried to hide it from Miss O'Boyle and Mr. MacSweeney during my lessons. By the time I told Ma about my skin, I was already gaining the ability to control things from flying around the room."

"Is this why you haven't been accompanying me to Dublin recently, my love?" asked her father, still looking aggrieved.

"Da, I'm sorry that I didn't tell you everything," Aelish said sweetly. "Please know how much I love and respect you. I didn't really understand what was happening to me and even Ma knew nothing about the magic, until today."

She hugged her mother and whispered, "I'm sorry I didn't tell you, Ma. I was afraid."

Her mother hugged her tightly and said crying, "Aelish, you are my sweet baby girl—porcelain or lavender, magical or Human."

Her father got up from where he was sitting and motioned for her mother to scoot over so he could sit next to Aelish on the settee. He hugged her and then put her face between his hands.

"Aelish, you will let Lady Antonia help you with the first lesson. I want my girl back in my carriage, so I can still take you to the bakeshop and seamstress. I've missed you," said her father, as tears rolled down his cheeks.

This startled Aelish. She had never seen her father cry before.

"You've always been my amazin' daughter and it looks like you're going to be even more amazin' than Ma or I ever thought ya' could be."

Aelish looked toward Melanthia, who nodded, confirming

Lady Antonia would be staying to help her. Relieved she could once again spend time with her father, Aelish hugged him and began crying.

"I will hurry and learn the first lesson, Da. I have missed our trips together, too."

Looking back on the day, it amazed Aelish how accepting her parents were. It still seemed implausible that her parents would continue to love her just the same, if not more, once they were told she was a magical being, who would one day live in the magical world. They accepted it, tolerated her magical education, and were even excited for her future.

Aelish, however, found being different more difficult than her parents did. It took a long time for her to finally accept who she was. At times it was desperately lonely, but eventually she learned that being different would ultimately enable her to do wondrous things.

As she picked up her flypack from the ground, she hoped she would be as effective an Oraculi with the Human child, Isabela, as Lady Antonia had been with her. She began flying, as the autumnal sun was already low in the sky.

6

THE DIFFICULT CONVERSATION

As her mother slept, Isabela began thinking about her mother's life. Until she had gotten sick, she had worked as an auditor. Isabela had a basic understanding of what an auditor's responsibilities were and knew it involved an abundance of math. Her mother had worked since Isabela was a baby. Abuela had been responsible for Isabela's care during the day, as she had been for her brother. Her mother had told Isabela that she trusted Abuela more than anyone else in the world. When Abuela had volunteered to care for her children, she was thrilled. Despite working a full-time job, her mother was completely devoted to Isabela and her brother.

At night, she helped them with their homework, took Javier to all his practices, and her family never missed one of Javier's baseball games—with Abuela cheering the loudest. When Isabela was little, her mother always read at least one story to her before bed, two if she whined enough. On weekends they would all spend a lot of time outdoors—hiking, surfing, and sometimes even camping.

Her mother was the planner-in-chief of all outings and adventures and she arranged the most awesome vacations in the summertime. Their vacations were always different and she pushed Isabela to be more adventurous. She loved doing things with a bit of danger, like skydiving, which terrified Isabela, as she was afraid something would happen to her mother.

And something did happen to her mother, but not from jumping out of an airplane. It came from inside her and Isabela feared she would not survive. But her mother was not a quitter and treated her illness the same way she approached anything challenging—like something to be conquered. And they all followed her lead.

The family had decided to move across the country so she could take part in a clinical cancer trial being done at the Wainbridge-Archer Cancer Center in Nashville. They had made this decision as a family, knowing their lives were going to change significantly.

Her father had to arrange a transfer to the regional office of his company located in Nashville; Abuela had left behind Abuelo's grave and their church, along with her sisters, their families, and all her lifelong friends; Javier had deferred going to college for a year and would be responsible for taking their mother to her new treatments; and Isabela would be starting seventh grade in a new school, in a new town, in a new state. Isabela's mother had always been devoted to the family, but even she was shocked by the sacrifices they all had been willing to make, in an effort to try and save her life.

It had been two years of surgeries, radiation, and chemotherapy and she was not improving. She was getting weaker with each passing month. Isabela was losing faith in everything, as she watched the disease transform her mother. And Isabela had become angry—angry with God, angry with the doctors, angry with the hospital staff, and strangely, even angry with her mother. Isabela just wanted her mother to get better, so they could all go back to the way things were before. She didn't care that they had moved, and she would move again, if it meant her mother could get well.

A dog began to bark outside, startling Isabela out of her reflection. She got up from the chair and stroked her mother's face.

"Mom, I need to give you your medicines. It's already past the time. Can you wake up for a minute?"

Her mother's eyes remained closed, but her mouth began to smile. "You're still here with me?" she whispered. "My angel."

"Do you think you can wake up a little more, so you can take your medicines now?"

Her mother slowly pushed herself up on her elbows and asked Isabela to raise the top part of the hospital bed even higher. Nearly level with Isabela's face, her mother stared at her.

"You are so beautiful, mi amor. Please get my cup on the hospital table. I think I need more water."

Isabela took the cup and went to fill it in her parents' bathroom. When she returned, she handed her mother the pills, and then she helped her mother hold the cup of water. Her mother swallowed the pills and deeply sighed. Isabela went back into the bathroom to refill the cup and returned it to the hospital table.

"Thank you, angel," said her mother. "Can you sit with me for a bit? I'm sure Abuela gave you a long list of things to do today, but I want to talk with you about something."

"Yes, she did," reflected Isabela, realizing how much time had already passed. "Of course I will stay with you, Mom."

"You are very young, Isabela," began her mother, "and have had to deal with so much since I've gotten sick. Not just with the recent move, but before, when we were still in L.A. I'm so sorry I'm ill, angel, please forgive me."

Isabela could feel herself getting ready to start bawling, but she kept it together and said, "I love you, Mom, I just want you to get better."

"I know you do, sweetheart," said her mother. "I want to talk to you about the new treatments. They are *very* new and in fact, I will be one of the first patients to receive them. The doctors call these kinds of treatments *experimental* because nobody knows yet if the treatments will actually help me. Do you understand?"

"But Dad said it was a miracle that he was able to find a clinical trial so near to one of his company's other locations. What are you saying, Mom, they aren't going to work?" questioned Isabela.

"I'm saying that I will do all I can to endure the treatments in the trial, but no one knows if my illness will respond with a positive outcome. They told me I may have no more than a ten percent chance of it working," said her mother, gently.

"Ten percent!" exclaimed Isabela, louder than she intended. "You must have a better chance than ten percent, Mom. Please! *Por favor*, no me dejes. *Por favor*, don't leave me."

Isabela buried her face in her mother's neck. She was devastated that her mother confirmed what she already knew from her own research on clinical cancer trials.

"It might be better than ten percent," soothed her mother. "I just want you to be prepared if they don't work, sweetheart. I wanted to tell you the truth, difficult as it may be to hear, so your expectations are realistic. The clinical trial is a long process and we won't know for some time if the treatments are working."

Isabela remained buried in her mother's neck, desperately trying not to cry.

"It will give me strength to fight very hard, if I know you will also try very hard in your new school to make friends and do well with your studies. Do you think you can do that for me?" asked her mother.

"I will be right back, Mom," Isabela said evenly, lifting her head up.

She burst into tears as she ran toward her parents' bathroom. She needed to put some cold water on her face, and take a minute alone to compose herself. She could not cry like this in front of her mother. Abuela would be *furious*.

After a few minutes, Isabela returned to find her mother falling asleep. She leaned over and whispered in her mother's ear, "I will be the best I can be, Mom. Don't worry about anything. I love you and I know you are going to be okay."

Her mother said nothing, but Isabela could see a weak smile. Isabela knew she was about to start crying again. She closed the curtains and quietly closed the door, as she left her mother. She had to get out of this house.

7

MA & DA

AELISH PUT HER Viewer away and began sobbing. She could feel Isabela's agony in accepting that her mother only had a slim chance of survival. Isabela was watching her mother suffer and die slowly over the last two years. Aelish's parents both took less than five days to die.

Despite all her new magical abilities, they died like everyone else who contracted bubonic plague. They developed swollen lymph nodes in their armpits and groin—better known as buboes—that were the size of chicken eggs. They both had agonizing headaches and their high fevers made them shake uncontrollably with chills. It was unbearable to watch. It was a horrible death and in a convoluted way, Aelish felt it was a blessing they had died so quickly.

All she could do magically was utilize certain spells and potions to make them more comfortable. As she sat on the ground thinking about it, she tried to compose herself, but was unable to stop crying. Her empathy for Isabela had brought her grief back to the surface.

The tragedy of losing her parents began five years after Melanthia, Lady Antonia, and Thagar had visited Brólaigh Castle. Aelish had resumed her normal tutoring lessons with Miss O'Boyle, after Lady Antonia taught her how to change her lavender skin color back to porcelain. Lady Antonia had been tutoring her in magic over the last five years. She intermittently stayed with Aelish's family, as she was also needed in DAR.

Aelish was a rapt student of magic and occasionally got very frustrated with her spells, but Lady Antonia had tremendous patience and was also fun to be around. They enjoyed each other's company immensely. Nearly five hundred years later, she and Aelish remained the best of friends. She was one of the greatest joys of Aelish's life, and she would never forget how Lady Antonia had helped her when her parents got sick.

Lady Antonia had returned to DAR, and Aelish and her family were going on holiday to London. Her parents had been planning the trip for a year, to celebrate her seventeenth birthday. It would be a tiresome voyage, but she didn't care; she was so excited to be going to England. Lady Antonia had taken her back in time through magic, showing her the Court of King Henry VIII, where she had grown up. But now, she was actually going to be there in real time.

Her father took advantage of the trip and had scheduled many commerce appointments months ago. He also planned to visit his only brother, Eamon, who was two years younger, and had moved to England shortly after Aelish's parents were married. Similarly, her mother had a younger sister, Bronwyn, who had also moved to England before Aelish was born. She was excited to finally meet her Uncle Eamon, her Aunt Bronwyn, their respective spouses, and their children. While she was definitely eager to meet her first cousins, she was more excited for a British haberdashery and seamstress to fashion her an ensemble.

Over the last year, she had already begun having more mature dresses designed at the seamstress in Dublin, during trips with her father. She had grown tall and was quite trim. These mature dresses increased her confidence about her appearance. Her long red hair still remained a challenge in choosing suitable fabric colors, but now that she was heading to London, the choices would be vast.

Once they arrived in London, her family settled into a pleasant routine. Whenever her father had a meeting, she and her mother would head over to the haberdashery and the seamstress. She actually chose the hat first and the seamstress designed the frock around its style. She modeled her hat after the stunning one Melanthia had worn on that fateful day. She was thrilled to be out of bonnets and to be able to select from the great variety of Ladies' hats.

She and her mother often enjoyed afternoon tea with Aunt Bronwyn and her three daughters. Her cousins were all a few years younger than Aelish. On the rare occasions when they had tea with Uncle Eamon, her father would also join them, along with Uncle Eamon's three sons. The oldest boy, Declán, was a year older than Aelish and was already working in his father's trading business. He was very handsome and extremely kind. Declán provided her family with the best suggestions of places to visit while in London. Her cousins on both sides would often accompany them on sightseeing adventures.

Being an only child, Aelish loved the bustling households of her first cousins. But sometimes she would catch a glimpse of sadness on her parents' faces during their visits. Her parents had lost two sons before Aelish was born. Both of her brothers had been under the age of five. She didn't know how her parents had withstood the loss. Her mother always referred to her brothers as "the children God took home" and for her father it made primogeniture a serious situation—he no longer had a first-born male heir. Since the reign of Queen Elizabeth I, however, her father felt more confident he would be able to pass on his estate to Aelish, but the title of Earl would not transcend. He often teased Aelish that by the time they had to worry about it all, Aelish would be "long in the tooth" with a head of gray hair.

She adored the London house Mr. MacSweeney had arranged for them. It belonged to one of her father's business associates. The gentleman was most generous in allowing her family to use it during their stay and also provided them with the use of his household staff. The house was in a posh area and was newly built, reflecting modern Tudor architecture. The exterior of the house had both vertical and diagonal black timbers that gained notoriety under the reign of Queen Elizabeth I.

The loaned house was in the middle of a main road and was attached to seven other similar homes. Smaller side streets ran in between each grouping of eight attached homes. The main road contained a significant amount of these attached houses and the side streets lead to nearby shops. This area of London was not as extravagant as the manor houses built along the Thames River, but the people who owned them were just as wealthy. The location of the house was ideal—it was easy to walk to all the shops, which she and her mother found quite convenient. Aelish observed that most of the shopkeepers lived above their businesses, in much smaller dwellings than the house her family occupied.

The loaned house had a high chimney, an overhanging second floor, dormer windows, and a thatched roof. A portion of the second story that hung over the first floor, contained a small balcony, surrounded by an iron railing. It was barely large enough to step onto. The balcony distinguished the house amongst the other attached houses, as it was the only one like it on the entire main road. The double doors of the balcony were made of a heavy leaded glass that was far more contemporary than the leaded glass windows of Brólaigh Castle. Due to the construction of the second-story overhang, she could easily see out onto the street below.

When her mother first opened the doors to step out onto the miniscule balcony, Aelish gasped, concerned that the iron railing wouldn't hold and her mother would fall. But after watching her mother experience it unharmed, she was eager to try it herself. Ultimately, it became her favorite thing to do first thing in the morning. She would open the doors, step onto the balcony, and inspect the sky for rain. Looking left and right afforded her a long view of the happenings on the main road below.

It felt wonderful to be free of lessons and explore the city on foot alone during the afternoons when her mother would rest. Since discovering she was a magical being, her parents gave her greater freedom, worrying far less for her welfare. And while in London, she took exceptional advantage of this leeway. She adored her visits to Dublin with her father, but London was an entirely different experience. Aelish walked all over the city and visited all the unique shops London had to offer. She adored the hustle and bustle of this large city, with one exception—she despised the rats she often saw running through the streets.

Two weeks after their arrival, her father and mother had left early in the morning for an appointment, providing Aelish with the luxury of sleeping late. She forgot to look out the balcony doors, as the cook had prepared a delicious late breakfast for her. When finished, instead of waiting for her parents to return, she quickly got dressed. She was anxious to get her day started and decided to walk over to the seamstress to inspect the progress of her new ensemble.

The minute she stepped outside, she noticed panic all around her. There were men shouting and horse-drawn carts passing her with corpses piled on top of each other. She had never seen anything so horrible. Suddenly her dream trip had turned into a full-fledged nightmare. She was terrified and could not understand what was happening.

Why are there so many dead and why are they disposing of them in such an inhumane and disrespectful manner?

She walked up the road and stopped to ask one of the men in charge who was shouting instructions to the laborers handling the carts.

"Why are there so many dead and why do you treat them like animals? These are Human beings with families!" she frantically yelled above the fray.

"That may be, Miss, but I'd stay away from them death-carts if I were you. You can still catch the Black Death from the dead. Now get out of me way. I have to direct me men to the plague pits, so the bodies can be buried," he said gruffly, pushing her out of his way.

She couldn't believe how he had spoken to her. And his push landed her in a puddle ruining her fancy new shoes. She had nearly fallen to the ground.

"You're a despicable man!" she yelled after him. He looked backward and with a wave of his hand, dismissed her outrage.

Recovered from the altercation, Aelish suddenly realized what he had said—*plague pits*! She had studied the Black Death of the 1300s with Miss O'Boyle, but she had no idea the dreaded disease had made a resurgence. There was no mention of it in her village, or in Dublin, or on the ship crossing the Irish Sea to London.

How could this be?

She began to panic. She decided to return to the house, anxious for her parents to come back from their appointment. Walking the streets of London had lost its allure.

Lady Antonia had taught her that magical beings could never contract or pass on any Human sickness. She was not afraid for her own life, but if the plague was this rampant, she feared for her parents.

Back at the house, the hours dragged on for what felt like days. She stood on the balcony watching the men drive cart after cart past the house, with the dead stacked one on top of the other. It was positively gruesome.

After a few hours, her parents still had not returned. She decided to see for herself where the death-carts were headed and how the bodies were going to be buried. She told the housekeeper, who seemed oblivious to what was happening, that she was leaving for a bit.

She went downstairs to the front door, which was on the street level. Standing in the entryway, she checked to make sure none of the household staff was nearby and utilized the Invisibility spell. Now she could go and investigate wherever she wanted. Once outside, she flew upward and peered through the second story windows of the row houses and saw sickness in every home. In one of the houses, three doors down from her own, she saw a terrifying sight—a plague doctor. She remembered Miss O'Boyle describing these doctors and how they dressed, during one of her history lessons on the plague.

The doctor was dressed in an ankle length overcoat made of waxed leather, as were his leggings, gloves, and boots. On his face, he wore the most alarming mask shaped like the long beak of a bird. The beak had glass spectacles inserted, so he could see out. He wore a wide-brimmed hat, which completed his protective covering from head to toe.

She watched as he used his cane to point to the buboes and other infected areas on the sick, so he didn't have to touch his patients. Aelish knew these doctors were paid by the city when outbreaks occurred and were often second-rate doctors who charged those with means, extra money for false cures. She knew he would be well paid today, as this posh area was filled with people of means.

She shuddered and continued flying unseen, along the route of the death-carts. When she located their final destination, she gasped. There were so many laborers digging graves at least twenty feet deep. The bodies of the dead were wrapped haphazardly in whatever shroud must have been available in their homes when they died. The laborers threw one body after another into the pits. Hovering invisibly above this ghastly scene, she heard the voice of the man who had pushed her. He was arguing with another man she assumed was his superior.

"Sir, we have to pay these death-cart laborers today! There may be no tomorrow for the lot of us and that's what we agreed upon. We will take the drink that you're offering, but in addition to the wages, not in substitution," he demanded.

"Fine, fine," said the neatly dressed man. "Be sure to dig those pits twenty feet deep and forty feet wide. They're dropping dead faster than we can move them and we don't want to leave the dead for a week in their houses with their families—then we will have even more dead."

"There's where you're wrong, my fine sir," continued the man who had pushed her. "We Watchmen have new orders to lock the families in together from the *outside,* to prevent them from leaving and spreading the disease. They've already caught it, aye? We are to board up the doors and lock them all inside until everyone is dead."

"That's barbaric," said the neatly dressed man, shaking his head.

"It may be, but it's what the orders are and that's how it's goin' ta be, gov'nor," snapped the Watchman.

Aelish watched this exchange in horror.

Who had ordered such a thing—to sentence an entire family to death just because one family member became ill?

Having seen enough, she flew back to the house. She reversed the Invisibility spell in the entryway and began climbing the stairs. When she reached the top, the housekeeper was waiting for her.

"What is it? What's troubling you?" asked Aelish.

"Come m'Lady," said the housekeeper. She led Aelish toward her parents' bedchamber. At the doorway of the bedchamber Aelish saw her parents, still dressed in their clothes, lying on the bed.

"The Lord and Lady came home severely fatigued and now they both have fevers, as you can see, plain as day," remarked the housekeeper.

Aelish could see sweat droplets on their foreheads and instantly knew they had contracted the plague.

"The rest of the staff has already gone. Cook and I are goin' to have to leave ya' now, Lady Aelish, before the Watchmen lock us in here. Cook left food for you and your parents, but I doubt they are goin' to be eatin' much. We filled a large basin with water and set it there on the bedside table, so you can tend to their fevers. I'm so sorry for you m'Lady," said the housekeeper. She turned away from Aelish and began running down the stairs toward the front door.

"Wait!" cried out Aelish, running after her. "I saw a plague doctor at the house, three doors down. Do you think you could locate him and ask him to come to this house? I don't want to leave my parents," Aelish said crying.

"We will try to find him on our way out, but you better have lots o' money to pay him. They're supposed to tend to the rich and poor alike, but most times they don't," she stated flatly.

"Tell him I have money, *please*," said Aelish.

"All right, then. If they know you have money, they will come," said the housekeeper. "We will pray for you m'Lady." Grabbing her shawl, she left the house with the cook and slammed the front door.

Aelish stood in the entryway in a state of shock. She knew her magic could not cure sickness. She hoped the housekeeper could locate the plague doctor, as she couldn't bear to leave her parents unattended.

She turned away from the front door and went back upstairs to her parents' bedchamber. They were both thrashing on the bed, delirious with fever.

She held her mother's face and spoke softly into her ear, "Ma, I love you and everything is going to be okay. I'm going to move you into my bedchamber, so you will be more comfortable, all right?" asked Aelish.

"Help us, Aelish," begged her mother.

Her parents' anguish was unbearable. Aelish rolled up her sleeves and went into her own bedchamber to prepare her bed for her mother's arrival. She recited a spell that allowed her mother to float through the air and fall gently onto the bed.

Aelish decided that the first thing she needed to do was to get them out of their clothes. She went to the kitchen and found a strong pair of scissors. Then she retrieved as many rags and cloths as she could find. She needed to wipe them down to try and control their fevers.

She returned to her mother with the scissors. She began cutting away her mother's beautiful dress and kirtle, until she lay in her linen chemise, the undergarment that lay against her skin. It was soaked from her fever. Aelish took it off her mother, temporarily, so it could dry. Then she went back to her father and cut away his clothes until she was at his undergarments. She was embarrassed to see her father naked, but this was no time for modesty. She removed his soaked linen shirt and hung it on a chair to dry.

Leaving both her parents momentarily disrobed, she went back to the kitchen to find another pot or basin. She needed to divide the water the housekeeper and cook had left for her in her parents' bedchamber. Once she had divided the water, she returned to her mother and began wiping her naked body from head to foot. And that was when she saw them! Buboes filled with pus oozing in her armpits. In her groin area, the buboes were already beginning to turn black. Aelish screamed and began sobbing.

Remembering the moment, as she sat on the ground before continuing on to Isabela's house, tears fell down her face. Aelish now knew that if the buboes burst or were drained, plague victims could sometimes survive. But left unattended, the victims were dead in days.

If I had only known then, how to drain the buboes, they might have survived.

For two days and two nights, she neither slept nor ate. She stayed by their side, going back and forth between the bedchambers, using every comforting and pain-relieving spell she knew to ease their agony. The chills were the worst. They racked their feverish bodies to the point where the bed was shaking, which in turn made the floor shake.

On the morning of the third day, there was a knock on the front door. She ran downstairs and when she opened it, she gasped at the sight of a plague doctor. She allowed him to enter and led him upstairs to the bedchambers where her parents were.

He examined them with his cane and flatly said, "They will be dead in two days."

Aelish stared back at his beaked face and said nothing.

He gave her some laudanum for their pain, along with herbs she was to mix with water for their fevers. Then he requested payment. She knew her spells were more effective than anything he had given her, but she just wanted him to leave. She went to her father's possessions and found ten shillings and gave it to the doctor. It was an astonishing amount of money and she imagined he had made out quite well these last few days, tending to the sick in this posh neighborhood. She hated him.

Shortly after he left, she heard the voice of the despicable Watchman who had pushed her in the street. She went to the balcony doors and could see he was standing on the main road right in front of her house. It seemed like years, since she had first heard his horrible voice. She ran downstairs and stood in the entryway. She readied herself to open the door and yell at him to get away from her house.

With her hand poised on the iron door latch, she heard him shout, "Lock this up so no one can go in or out!"

She slid the latch across forcefully and opened the door.

He screamed at her, "No one is to enter or leave this house! We will give ya' bread and raise it up to yer balcony in a basket from the road."

She looked down the main road and saw that nearly every house had boards across their front doors, nailed from the *outside*. Men were literally boarding people up inside to die, along with the sick.

"You can't lock people inside!" she screamed at him. "Not everyone is sick!"

She could hear the terrified cries of people inside their homes, as the Watchmen continued hammering their nails onto the boards covering the front doors.

"Orders, Miss," he stated flatly. He turned away and walked down the road shouting at the laborers to work faster.

After she was locked inside, she recalled the feeling she had experienced when she and her mother had agreed she could not leave Brólaigh Castle, until they understood why her skin had turned lavender. It was that same hopeless feeling of being utterly trapped. Of course she could get out using her magical skills, but she would never leave her parents. Listening to the cries of the people sentenced to die in their own homes was abhorrent.

She sighed and went back up the stairs to her parents. Her spells were working, as they were both sleeping peacefully. Knowing they were temporarily out of agony, Aelish took the opportunity to think and come up with a plan for getting her parents back to Ireland for a proper burial by their priest at Brólaigh Church. Aelish's parents were still devout Catholics despite the Tudors' attempts to force Ireland to become Protestant.

There was no way she would allow her parents to be thrown into a plague pit. They were going to be buried in the Brólaigh Church cemetery, with the proper blessings from the priest who had married them. Aelish would have it no other way.

She could not believe a week ago, she was sightseeing, shopping with her mother, and having an ensemble designed. How trivial and meaningless that all seemed now.

Are Aunt Bronwyn, Uncle Eamon, and all my cousins going to die as well?

How had this happened? Her beautiful, kind, and accepting parents would be dead in two days. She put her face in her hands and sobbed uncontrollably. She cried for what felt like hours and then she remembered—Lady Antonia!

She had to get a message to her immediately. She needed help to execute her plan of getting her parents back to Ireland. Lady Antonia had taught her how to get a message to her in DAR, but Aelish had never needed to use this magic before. She hoped she remembered the lesson.

She could hear Lady Antonia's voice in her head. *'Now, Aelish, if you need me at any time, you must summon a Sylph to deliver a message to me. If it is urgent, you must relay that to the Sylph.'*

A Sylph! What were they?

She again heard Lady Antonia's voice. *'They are Air Faeries. They may be tiny or large and they come when you mentally contact them, in the same manner in which you pray. They are the freest of all the Faeries and can be found anywhere. They are kind and good and specifically help children. They can travel very quickly through the portal and deliver a message to me in DAR if you are ever in trouble.'*

Aelish stood in the drawing room and urgently began concentrating. Within minutes, a tiny green-colored Sylph appeared with large see-through wings. She said nothing, awaiting Aelish's instructions.

"Thank you for coming to help me," said Aelish, smiling. She was shocked she had been able to conjure one. The Sylph fluttered in the air and returned the smile. The Sylph pushed her long blonde hair away from her eyes so that Aelish could see her face more clearly.

"Please take this message right away to Lady Antonia Harrington Stonebridge in DAR. Tell her Lady Aelish is in London with her parents, who are dying of plague. I need help getting my parents back to Ireland for a proper burial. The Watchmen have locked me and my dying parents inside a loaned house," stated Aelish.

The Sylph batted her eyes three times confirming she understood and flew out of the room as quickly as she had arrived.

Aelish began pacing wondering if the message would ever get to Lady Antonia. Night was falling, so she began lighting candles throughout the house. The house felt desolate with the staff gone and she noticed the hammering outside had stopped. The Watchmen must have moved on to another road. But she could still hear the death-carts rolling past the house.

What if the message doesn't reach Lady Antonia?

Trying to calm herself, Aelish went to the bedchambers to

check on her parents. They were both mercifully still asleep. But when she touched her mother's forehead, Aelish realized she was burning up. She wiped down her mother and then went to her father and did the same. While her No Pain spells were ineffective in alleviating the symptoms of plague, at least they were not suffering.

She must have fallen asleep sometime in the night, on the chair by her father's bedside. When she opened her eyes, it was almost dawn. Her father was shaking with fever and she began wiping him down. She continued this process throughout the day and the following night for both her mother and father. She had never felt so alone in her life.

Finally, the sun began to rise. She went to the balcony doors to look out at the beginning of what she knew would be her parents' last day. She wondered if Lady Antonia had ever received her message. There was nothing to do but wait and have faith in her magical abilities. She sighed and went back to check on her father who was still burning with fever. As she was wiping her father's forehead, dripping with sweat, he suddenly opened his eyes.

"Da! I'm here!" cried Aelish. "Do you see me?"

"I love you, my treasure. Please never forget that," he whispered. He smiled at her, closed his eyes, and gasped his last breath.

"No, Da! Stay with me, *please!*" cried Aelish, sobbing with her head on her father's chest.

As she lay with her head on his chest, she realized his heart had ceased to beat. He was gone. She let out a wail of agony. She closed his eyes, which had remained open, and pulled the sheet over him with utter love and respect.

"I love you, Da. Thank you for loving and accepting me for who I am," whispered Aelish to her father. She promised herself that she would carry the attribute of acceptance with her until the day she died.

She walked into her mother's room and pulled the chair closer to the bed. She held her mother's hand against her face. She was so sorry her mother never got to say goodbye to her father, but she knew they would be together again shortly.

"Ma, can you hear me at all? I want to say that I love you and that you have been the most amazin' Ma anyone could ever ask for. Thank you for loving your lavender-colored daughter and thank you for accepting me for who I am," she said softly. She continued pressing her mother's hand against her face, as she wept.

She thought she detected a brief smile on her mother's face, but then she heard her mother's death rattle. It would not be long now. She continued holding her hand until her mother's last breath.

Knowing she was gone, Aelish lay down in the bed alongside her mother. She held her tightly, sobbing in anguish, as she remembered all the times she would climb into bed with her as a child. Her mother never once told her to go away. Her mother loved her unconditionally, and Aelish knew she had been so blessed to have a mother like this.

After a while, she got out of the bed and covered her mother with the bed sheet. She couldn't believe her parents had died within an hour of each other. Cian and Saoirse were no longer of this Earth, but she knew they were together.

She left their bedchambers and walked into the drawing room. She looked out the balcony doors toward the road and watched the never-ending parade of death-carts passing the house.

My God!

"Aelish, dear, we are here."

8

A Fortuitous Encounter

ISABELA MADE SURE all the doors were locked and put the volume of her cell phone on the loudest setting. She tucked it into the back pocket of her jeans. She grabbed the set of house keys hanging by the door that led into the garage.

She flipped on the garage lights praying Javier had found the box containing her bike. She couldn't believe it—her bike was against the far wall and her helmet hung from the handlebars.

Thank you, Javi!

She opened the driver's side door of Javier's car to retrieve the garage door opener. She pressed the button and stuck the opener into her other back pocket. She intended to reverse all these steps upon her return, to conceal the fact that she had snuck out of the house without telling anyone.

Once outside, she strapped on her helmet in the driveway and took a deep breath, trying to stop the next round of tears from coming. She had to keep track of the way back to her house, as she had never ridden her bike before in her new neighborhood. She began pedaling and took a right out of the driveway and rounded the corner.

She rode slowly on the sidewalk looking at the homes. They were all very similar to one another. This neighborhood was so different from the one she had left in L.A.—especially the lawns—they were so green.

There must be no drought here.

There were lots of hills too, which was also different. And it was so *quiet*. Being Sunday, she assumed everyone was at church, but still, not one car. And there were certainly no buses. She remembered her parents calling their new neighborhood a "subdivision"—and there were many of them in Brookdale, each with a different name. The names were always on both sides of the stone or brick walls that marked the entranceways into the subdivisions. Once inside, there were no bodegas, coffee shops, or grocery stores—just houses.

The observations of her new surroundings had briefly distracted her from the desolating conversation with her mother. But her tears immediately returned when she saw a mother jogging while pushing a stroller with bicycle tires. She could hear the child inside the stroller laughing.

She stopped her bike and berated herself for not bringing some tissues, as tears streamed down her face. Her sleeves would have to do for now.

How did I get here? Why did Mom have to get sick? This place is very beautiful, but very strange. I wish I could ride over to Gabby's house. Isabela looked at her phone and calculated the time difference. *I can't call her now. She's at the fellowship lunch after mass.*

She missed her best friend so much it made her insides ache. She checked her phone again to make sure the volume was still on the loudest setting, in case her mother needed her.

She wiped her eyes and began riding again, leaving the safety of the sidewalk for the street. There were no cross streets for what felt like miles. The street meandered up and down hills for so long, she thought it might be the longest street in the world. Finally, she saw a cross street and turned left down a big hill. She was about halfway down the hill when suddenly a brown dog came running out of nowhere. She squeezed her brakes hard, trying to stop before she hit the dog. Because of the steepness of the hill, it was difficult to stop and she almost lost control of her bike.

"Cocoa! Cocoa, stop!" yelled the dog's owner. He came running across his front lawn into the street.

Isabela thought this dog was very fortunate because she'd been able to stop in time, and she had yet to see one car on any of the streets.

But the man is so frantic. There must be traffic at some point?

The dog began jumping on Isabela and she could see it was a chocolate-colored labradoodle, like her cousins' dog Lucy back home. Isabela pulled her bike to the side of the street while the dog continued jumping on her.

"I'm so sorry she ran at you like that. Cocoa, *down*! Thank you for stopping so suddenly. She's a puppy and is constantly trying to run out of the house," said the dog's owner.

I can relate to that.

"Did she hurt you?" asked the man, concerned.

Isabela realized her face was wet from crying and she became embarrassed. She quickly began wiping her face with the back of her hands.

"No, I'm fine," she reassured the owner. "She was only jumping on me. I'm glad I was able to stop. She is very playful—Cocoa is her name?"

"Yes, not that original a name considering her fur is the same color as hot cocoa," chuckled the owner, yet still looking very concerned for Isabela. "I've never seen you before, are you new to the neighborhood?"

"Yes, my family just moved here from L.A.," replied Isabela. She took a closer look at the man. He appeared older than her brother and his skin color was light brown, like hers. She also detected an accent.

"Will you be attending Brookdale Middle School?" he asked.

"Yes," said Isabela, brightening. "I will be starting there tomorrow."

"What grade are you in?" he inquired.

"I'm in the seventh grade," said Isabela.

"Ah! Well, allow me to properly introduce myself. My name is Dr. Hector Rios and I teach advanced science at Brookdale Middle School," said the man, extending his hand to shake Isabela's.

She reciprocated saying, "Oh, wow. I have been assigned to the advanced-level science class."

"Wait, is your name Isabela?" asked Dr. Rios.

"Yes, it is," replied Isabela. She was shocked and excited that he knew her name.

"Perfect," said Dr. Rios. "I have been awaiting your arrival. How amazing we met this way. Would you like to take a break from riding and have some sweet tea on my porch? My wife just made some."

After growing up in a major city, Isabela's first instinct was caution, but there was something familiar about this man. She felt their meeting was somehow meant to be. She was also very curious as to how sweet tea would taste.

"Yes, I would like that very much," smiled Isabela.

Isabela got off her bike and walked it behind Dr. Rios, up the front pathway of his house. She laid her bike down on the grass and followed him up the steps leading to his porch, while Cocoa walked-jumped with them the whole time. As they were ascending the steps to the porch, a woman came out of the house scolding Cocoa.

"Bad dog, Cocoa! One day you are going to get hit by a car!" She looked at Isabela and Dr. Rios and smiled. "And who do we have here?"

"This is my new student, Isabela, from L.A. She will be starting at Brookdale Middle School tomorrow and is in my seventh grade advanced-level science class. Isabela, this is my wife, Marielena," said Dr. Rios.

"It is a pleasure to meet you, Mrs. Rios," said Isabela, extending her hand.

"And you, Isabela," said Mrs. Rios, shaking Isabela's hand. "Vamos—let's sit down and talk—you speak Spanish, sí?"

It felt so good to hear Spanish spoken in this new place by people other than her family.

"Yes, but in the week since I've been here, other than the movers and my family, you are the first person to speak Spanish to me," said Isabela, to Mrs. Rios. "It feels like there aren't many people here that look like us."

"Ay!" Mrs. Rios burst out laughing.

"That is true, Isabela," chuckled Dr. Rios. "But I'm seeing a few more students each year that do."

"Marielena, do you think you could bring us some of your delicious sweet tea? I promised Isabela," Dr. Rios asked sweetly.

"Sí, sí, of course," said Mrs. Rios. She got up and turned to walk back into the house. "You come with me, Cocoa—bad perro."

The dog obediently followed Mrs. Rios into the house.

Isabela nestled into the cushion of the wicker porch chair and stared out at the street. It was very lovely on their porch and she felt calmer since the conversation with her mother. Almost like maybe everything could be okay.

"So, Isabela, when did you first discover that you liked science?" asked Dr. Rios. "Because you obviously excel in it to be placed in my advanced class."

Her mother's illness returned to the forefront of Isabela's mind. She had always loved science, but after her mother's diagnosis, she had read everything available on the Internet and in textbooks from the library. In doing so, she had gained quite an aptitude for science. She would have preferred not to discuss her mother's condition, but she assumed Dr. Rios, like everyone at her new church, already knew about her family's situation.

"Do you know why my family has moved here?" asked Isabela.

"Well, I know that your mother is not well, and I am so sorry for what you must be going through," Dr. Rios replied with compassion.

"Yes, she is very sick. We moved here so she could participate in a clinical cancer trial at Wainbridge-Archer Cancer Center in Nashville. We hope she will improve. But the reason I was out riding my bike was because my mother just told me that the treatments have only a ten percent chance of helping . . ." Before Isabela could finish the sentence, her voice caught and tears began pouring down her face.

"Pobrecita," said Dr. Rios. He wiped away a tear from his own eye, and then handed Isabela a handkerchief from his pocket. "But at least with the trial, your mother has a chance that she did not have before you moved here. You must think positively and hope the science has advanced enough to help her."

Isabela nodded her head. It felt reassuring to hear someone finally say it was science that could save her mother and not some miracle from lighting a candle in church every week.

"I imagine you have a doctorate degree—in what specialty?" asked Isabela, wiping her tears.

"I have a Ph.D. in Microbiology and Immunology from Georgetown. I worked in a lab for about a year. Then I saw a posting for an advanced-level science teacher in the Brookdale school district. I decided to try my hand at teaching young minds. I also teach the AP science classes at Brookdale High School."

"Oh, cool—so you would also be my teacher in High School?" asked Isabela.

"Exactly," stated Dr. Rios.

"Was it hard getting a doctorate?" asked Isabela. She was relieved to be talking about something other than her mother.

"Some of the coursework was very challenging," replied Dr. Rios, "but I always wanted to study science. I'm now finding teaching very gratifying, as my students are quite intelligent."

Mrs. Rios reappeared carrying a tray filled with glasses of sweet tea, along with a variety of cookies stacked on a white plate. She graciously said nothing about Isabela's visible upset. Isabela eyed the cookies on the plate and realized she was starving. She quickly wiped her face with Dr. Rios' handkerchief.

Mrs. Rios put the tray down on the wicker coffee table with the plate of cookies closer to Isabela than to Dr. Rios. She passed a glass of sweet tea to both Isabela and her husband. Isabela thought she detected a cautionary look from Mrs. Rios to Dr. Rios, regarding the cookies, which made her smile.

Isabela took a long drink of the sweet tea. She grabbed a napkin off the tray and wiped her mouth before exclaiming, "This is delicious! It's the first time I've ever had sweet tea. Thank you."

"De nada," smiled Mrs. Rios. She lifted the plate of cookies. "Here, Isabela—try some—I baked them this morning."

Isabela chose a chocolate chip cookie, always her favorite, and chewed rapidly. Then she drank nearly the entire glass of tea at one time.

"May I try another?" she asked politely.

"You may have as many as you like, mi querida," replied Mrs. Rios.

Dr. and Mrs. Rios sat with Isabela on their porch for quite some time talking about L.A., the South, and their respective ancestries, which had quite a bit of overlap. Dr. Rios told Isabela about the different types of science projects they were going to be doing this year and she found herself getting very excited to go to school tomorrow. She couldn't believe she had met her science teacher and that he lived in her *own* subdivision—considering how many there were.

She was finally relaxing when she noticed that the sun was starting to go down. And then she remembered all the things she had not finished on Abuela's list—especially having dinner ready for them when they returned home from the festival. She quickly glanced at her phone and could not believe it was four o'clock! Isabela started to panic, but hid it well from the Rioses. Since her mother's illness, she had to learn to hide her feelings a little too well, with the exception of today's tears.

"If you will both excuse me, I need to get home and check on my mother," Isabela said abruptly.

"Oh, of course," said Dr. and Mrs. Rios, simultaneously.

"Thank you so much for the sweet tea and cookies. They were absolutely delicious. And I greatly enjoyed our conversation and can't wait to start school tomorrow. Thank you so much for spending time with me this afternoon," said Isabela.

"Please know you are welcome anytime, Isabela," said Mrs. Rios.

"And thank you for your help earlier with Cocoa," said Dr. Rios, rolling his eyes.

Isabela descended the porch steps and put her helmet back on. She checked her phone again—still no messages. She lifted her bike up from the lawn, gave a final wave to the Rioses, and began pedaling home. She needed to remember the way back and get dinner prepared, before everyone returned.

She began to pedal as fast as possible, as the sun was nearly down. With the help of the longest street in the world, she thankfully remembered the way. She rounded the corner that led to her house and slammed on the brakes. Her father's car was already in the driveway.

Oh, my God—Mom!

9

GETTING HOME

A ELISH TURNED AROUND to see Lady Antonia, Thagar, and a man she had never met before. She ran to Lady Antonia and collapsed in her arms. She had only slept a few hours and had not eaten anything for the last two days.

"They are dead," wailed Aelish, sobbing. She could barely stand.

"Come, dear," said Lady Antonia, sweetly. "Lie down on the settee and let me get you something to eat. Thagar, please introduce your second-in-command, while I prepare something for Lady Aelish. She needs to rest before we begin our journey."

Thagar pulled three chairs away from the dining table and set them in front of the settee. He sat down and gestured for the other man to do the same.

"Lady Aelish, this is Sartaine," Thagar said in a compassionate tone. "He is the Lieutenant Commander of the S.E. quadrant of DAR where the capital city of Bencarlta is located. He has come to assist us in transporting your parents back to Ireland for the proper burial you requested. You can trust him with your life, as I do, each and every day."

"It is a pleasure to meet you, Lady Aelish, although I wish it were under entirely different circumstances," said Sartaine, as he bowed his head in respect. "I am terribly sorry for your loss. I wish I could have met Lord and Lady Brólaigh. Commander Thagar has told me how exceptional they were."

"Thank you so kindly, Sir," said Aelish, quietly weeping. "They were indeed . . . and I will miss them forever."

Lady Antonia reappeared with a tray of food and told Aelish to sit up so she could put the tray on her lap.

"Eat something, please," she instructed.

Aelish reached for a piece of bread. Taking a bite, she realized she was starving. Lady Antonia, Thagar, and Sartaine sat in the three chairs that Thagar had placed in front of the settee. They said nothing, allowing her time to process her loss and concentrate on eating.

When she was finished, she collectively asked them, "How are we going to get them back to Ireland without bringing the disease back to the village and Brólaigh Castle? How are we going to get past the Watchmen, load them onto the ship, and what in heaven's name will we tell the servants and the villagers about how they died?" Aelish felt like her head was underwater.

"We will take each step, one at a time," soothed Lady Antonia. "Thagar and Sartaine have already made arrangements at the port for the Nereides to accompany the ship back to Ireland.

"The Nereides?" asked Aelish.

"We spoke of them only once in our lessons, dear," said Lady Antonia. "The Nereides dwell in the sea and ride creatures called hippocamps, which are part horse and part dolphin."

"Oh, I remember. They wear headdresses made of shells and have often been accused of luring sailors to their death, when in fact, they actually protect sailors," stated Aelish, reciting the lesson.

"Exactly," said Lady Antonia. "We will need their magic to ensure a safe and uninterrupted passage back across the sea to Ireland."

"But how are we going to get Ma and Da out of England, without infecting anyone else? No one at Brólaigh Castle can know that they that actually died of plague, and we certainly can't bring the disease back with us to Ireland," pressed Aelish, who began crying again.

"Aelish, dear, you are utterly exhausted and nearing a breaking point," calmed Lady Antonia. "Thagar, Sartaine, and I will take care of all the details and necessary magic needed to ensure your parents contaminate no one, and are buried properly in the Brólaigh Church cemetery."

"We must get them out of the house or the Watchmen will bury them in the plague pits with thousands of victims," cried Aelish, on the verge of hysteria. "My God, they pile the bodies one on top of the other. It is disgusting and gruesome. They are my Ma and Da and I will not allow it!"

Thagar reached his hand across and took hers in to his. He looked into her green eyes and asked her, "Lady Aelish, do you trust us?"

Aelish was suddenly lost in his eyes. Memories flooded her mind: seeing him for the first time while hiding behind the tapestry in Brólaigh Castle; how he had stopped her father from falling over the tea table; how he had respected her father when her father was about to scream at him. His steady composure was always present. It momentarily reassured her.

"Yes, Thagar, of course," she said softly, without breaking eye contact.

"Then you must allow us to handle all of the arrangements. We will apprise you of them as needed, all right?" he asked firmly, seeking her agreement.

"All right," she agreed.

Suddenly, the sound of the Watchman's voice that she despised rang out through the balcony doors.

"Come and get yer bread, lassie," he yelled from the street.

Aelish stood up from the settee in a panic and headed toward the balcony doors.

"They will be raising bread in a basket to these doors. If I don't answer, he will think everyone has died. They will then break down the front door, load Ma and Da onto the death-carts, and take them to the plague pits!" she exclaimed.

"I suggest we make ourselves invisible until Lady Aelish has received the bread," Lady Antonia said to Thagar and Sartaine.

By the time Aelish had reached the balcony doors, the three chairs were empty. She opened the doors and looked down at the face of a man she would never forget.

"Ah! You're still alive, then," he said, laughing at her.

What a cruel and horrible man.

"Yes, I am, with no help from you," snarled Aelish.

"Take yer bread. It'll probably be yer last meal, so enjoy it," smirked the Watchman.

Aelish took the piddling loaf out of the basket and pushed the basket away in disgust. She turned her back on the Watchman and slammed the balcony doors.

"Aelish, dear, you need to lie down and sleep for a bit," said Lady Antonia, who had reappeared with Thagar and Sartaine. She took the loaf from Aelish. "We are going to be busy preparing your mother and father for transport. The only thing I need you to do, before you lie down, is select the clothes you wish them to be buried in."

"All right," said Aelish. She remembered feeling she would never get through it. But she had to, for Ma and Da.

"Sartaine and I are going to secure horses, a carriage, and a cart for the coffins. We will make all the necessary arrangements for Lord and Lady Brólaigh to be transported on the ship back to Ireland. We should be back by the time you have finished preparing the bodies," said Thagar to Lady Antonia.

"Make sure you select Humans that are trustworthy and disclose nothing," instructed Lady Antonia. "Be sure to return with death certificates and burial permits. We need the necessary paperwork if we are questioned at the port in London or in Dublin."

"Understood," said Thagar.

Aelish watched as he and Sartaine simply vanished from the room.

"All right, then," said Lady Antonia. "Let's get started so you can get some rest."

Aelish walked with Lady Antonia to where her parents lay dead with sheets over them. Ordinarily, commoners were buried in a shroud. Those born into nobility were buried in their best clothing and coffins were reserved only for nobles or the very wealthy. These traditions would work in their favor. Thousands of people had died of plague since their arrival in London. Both nobles and commoners had been thrown into the plague pits in haphazard shrouds. If the authorities ordered the coffins to be opened, having two corpses dressed in noble finery would support the fictitious cause of their deaths—a carriage accident.

She selected her mother's most beautiful dress hanging in the wardrobe along with her father's finest doublet. Their other clothes would all be left behind in the disease-ridden city. Aelish packed up their jewelry, money, and her father's business papers, putting everything inside her father's leather satchel.

"All right, then. Go and lie down now, dear," instructed Lady Antonia. "I will prepare them. You need to rest."

Aelish nodded and went back to the settee to lie down. She instantly fell asleep.

‡‡‡‡

Aelish felt her face being gently stroked. She was completely disoriented and thought she was in her bedchamber in Brólaigh Castle.

"Ma?" she whispered.

"No, dear, it's Lady Antonia. Take a minute to wake up. You are in London and we are ready to leave the house with your parents," soothed Lady Antonia.

"Good God, they are *dead*," Aelish cried out in anguish. She began sobbing hysterically.

"Hush, my dear," said Lady Antonia. She sat on the edge of the settee. She reached down and lifted Aelish up until she could embrace her. She hugged and gently rocked her, whispering soothing alms in her ear.

After several minutes, she helped Aelish sit up on the settee. Aelish saw Thagar and Sartaine standing beside two beautiful mahogany coffins, with their lids open.

"Before I cast the final spell on their appearance, I wanted to make sure you are pleased with how they look," Lady Antonia stated calmly. "The spell will mask their true cause of death and encapsulate any possible contamination to others, in perpetuity."

She helped Aelish get to her feet and walked her over to the coffins.

"But how did you . . . where did you . . . oh, my goodness, thank you," said Aelish. She hugged Lady Antonia and smiled over Lady Antonia's shoulder at Thagar and Sartaine.

"They have been prepared according to Catholic ritual and we have the necessary paperwork for the authorities and the priest at Brólaigh Church," said Lady Antonia.

"How are we going to get them out of here?" asked Aelish.

"The same way we did everything, dear—magic," smiled Lady Antonia.

Aelish walked over to the coffins. She fluffed the collar of her father's doublet and kissed his forehead. "Goodbye, Da. I will love you, always," said Aelish. A single tear rolled down her cheek. She walked over to her mother and stared at her still beautiful face. She bent down and kissed her on the cheek, whispering something inaudible to the others.

"I'm ready," she stated, as she turned around toward Lady Antonia.

Lady Antonia went over to Aelish's parents and put the spell on them. The spell not only masked the physical symptoms of plague, but also encapsulated them in a clear casing, visible only to DARlings.

"All right. Close the coffins," instructed Lady Antonia.

Lady Antonia embraced Aelish, as Thagar and Sartaine closed and locked the coffins.

"Thagar and Sartaine will each fly with a coffin on their back to the cart waiting near the port. They will load the cart with the coffins and serve as undertakers accompanying the bodies back to Ireland. It will appear as if they have brought the cart through the city," explained Lady Antonia to Aelish. "We will meet them there shortly."

"All right. Thank you," said Aelish to Thagar and Sartaine.

Thagar, Sartaine, and the coffins, then vanished from the room.

"Do you have everything you need, Aelish? Go and do a final room check and then we will leave," instructed Lady Antonia.

Aelish walked back alone through the bedchambers, remembering her parents. She grasped the clothes still hanging in her parents' wardrobe, and held them against her face. She breathed in the last remaining scent of her parents. As she released the clothes, she mentally said goodbye and rejoined Lady Antonia in the drawing room.

"Please take me home," said Aelish.

Lady Antonia embraced Aelish who had her father's satchel slung over her shoulder.

"The next place we will be, dear, is a short distance from the port. I am using the Transporting spell so that we can avoid flying and simply arrive where Thagar and Sartaine are waiting," said Lady Antonia.

"Amazing. Will you teach me that spell one day?" asked Aelish, trying to smile.

"When you are ready," smiled Lady Antonia.

Aelish suddenly found herself on the streets of London and could smell the sea. There was a cart with two coffins pulled by a horse, which Thagar sat astride. Sartaine was atop another horse which had a small carriage attached. Both were dressed in funereal garb looking the part of authentic undertakers. Aelish and Lady Antonia stepped inside the carriage and sat across from one another.

They travelled for a short time in the carriage to the wharf, where the ship was docked. As they disembarked from the carriage, Aelish looked up toward the deck of the ship and saw an imposing man dressed in a decorative uniform, standing on the deck. She assumed he was the Captain, here to oversee the loading of her parents. Her heart began to race as she braced for trouble.

"Do you have the proper papers?" the Captain called out to Thagar. "Give them to my first mate."

Aelish saw the first mate, also in a fine uniform, standing on the wharf. She could hear Thagar's voice in her head. *'Lady Aelish, do you trust us?'* She tried to steady her breathing.

Thagar came down from his horse and took out a folio of necessary documents from his doublet, which he then handed to the first mate.

The first mate inspected the documents and yelled to his Captain, "It's all in order, Sir."

"Good! Load the coffins and assist the ladies to their

room," he instructed. "You gentlemen will be bunking together beneath the aft."

Aelish watched as they loaded the coffins onto the ship. She couldn't believe she was going home. Something in the water caught her eye and she knew it was the Nereides. Only visible to DARlings, she counted at least fifty all around the ship, waiting to ensure their safe passage back to Ireland.

As she flew on to Isabela's house remembering it all, Aelish could still feel the relief as she stood at her parents' funeral. It was attended by all the servants, the entire village, and was administered by the priest who had married them. They were placed in the burial plots reserved only for nobles in the Brólaigh Church cemetery. Her parents were finally home, and Aelish began to truly understand the power of the magic of DAR.

10

BIKE RIDE FALLOUT

ISABELA REMAINED FROZEN on her bike. Something had to be wrong with her mother; otherwise, why had they returned from church so early? She quickly checked her phone again for messages—still none—and she saw that the time was only four-fifteen.

She forced herself to confront the situation. She pressed the garage door opener and waited until she could squeeze under the door, as it rolled upward. She hastily removed her helmet, hung it back on the handlebars, and put her bike back against the wall. She clicked the garage door gadget one last time, closing the garage door, and put it back in Javier's car. Isabela braced herself before opening the door that led into the house.

"Ay, Dios mío!" exclaimed Abuela, clutching her chest, as Isabela entered the house. "Izzy está aquí!"

Her father and brother came running from different parts of the house.

"Oh, my God, Izzy!" exclaimed her father, echoing Abuela's words in English. "Where were you? I was just about to call you and if you didn't answer, my next call was to the police."

"Izzy, not cool leaving without telling anyone!" yelled Javier, who was visibly upset. "And we didn't know Mom was alone. We thought you were going to be here all day finishing Abuela's list. Why did you leave the house?"

Isabela said nothing. She let the relief wash over her, as she realized her mother was okay. She remained quiet staring at the three of them. Her feelings of rage and betrayal, suppressed all day, replaced her momentary relief and fomented into an emotional explosion.

"Why? I'll tell you why! Because Mom told me today what you all decided *not* to tell me—that she is most likely going to die! She told me there's only a ten percent chance of the treatments working. How could you all lie to me like that?" she screamed, as tears poured down her face.

Isabela yelled so forcefully, she felt herself close to collapsing onto the kitchen floor. She took a deep breath and decided to make a run for her room. As she pushed past Abuela, Isabela noticed she was hunched over, sobbing with her face in her hands. She couldn't think about that now—she just had to get away from all of them.

Basta! Enough!

She slammed her bedroom door and locked it, something she had never done in her life. She threw herself on her bed crying hysterically. Her heart felt like it was literally breaking. She was crying in anguish, not only from today's news, but also from the last two horrible years of her mother's illness.

Mom is going to die. How could they not tell me and then yell at me like that? We originally planned to leave Mom alone all day, anyway, to attend church and the festival. How dare Javi accuse me of intentionally hurting Mom by leaving her alone? And I was only gone for an hour!

Isabela heard someone knock and try to turn the locked door handle.

"Izzy, unlock this door right now," ordered Javier.

"No! Just leave me alone!" Isabela yelled back, her face still buried in her pillow.

"Izzy, please. I'm worried about you. Please open the door," pleaded Javier.

Isabela ignored his pleas, hoping her silence hurt him the way his words had hurt her.

How dare he insinuate I was selfish leaving Mom alone? I'm old enough to change her sheets, give her the medicines, but not old enough to be told the truth?

Isabela was so angry and distraught all she could think about was running away. She was so rage-filled she felt strong enough to *walk* back to L.A.—to home, to Gabby, to her extended family, to before her mother got sick.

But then she thought of her mother and remembered what Dr. Rios had said this afternoon. *'You must think positively and hope the science has advanced enough to help her.'*

She never wanted to face the truth and reconcile her own research on clinical trials with her mother's chance of survival. As much as she wanted to, she could no longer live in denial. If they hadn't moved, her mother would certainly die. She began to internalize that there simply was no other option than to be here, in this new place, with her family, and accept the scientific facts. It was her mother's last chance at life, her last ray of hope to survive. She buried her face deeper into her pillow and cried for hours.

‡‡‡‡

When she was finally spent, and had not one tear left to shed, she picked her head up off her pillow and sat up on the edge of the bed. Through the still-opened slats of the plantation shutters, she could see it was nighttime. The lights around the pool were on, but the house was devoid of any sound. She wondered how much yelling her mother had heard. She hoped her mother had slept through it all.

Where is everyone?

She turned on her night table lamp and checked her phone for messages—still none—and it was already six o'clock.

She sat there listening for noises, finally hearing a pot clatter in the kitchen. Isabela wasn't ready to speak to anyone, but she knew the more time that went by, the harder it would be in the long run.

She unlocked her bedroom door, feeling a moment of regret, and slowly opened it. She peered cautiously into the hallway—empty. She quietly walked down the hall to the bathroom, put some cold water on her face and looked at herself in the mirror. Her face was so swollen she looked like her friend Vanessa after an allergic reaction to shellfish.

I look awful.

She wanted to check on her mother, but her parents' bedroom was on the other side of the house, past the kitchen, where she knew Abuela was. Isabela bolstered herself and quietly entered the kitchen ready to face the inevitable backlash from Abuela. Abuela's back was to her, as she was facing the stove.

"Buenas noches, Abuela." Isabela's earlier rage was now gone, leaving only despair in its wake.

Abuela did not answer her. At first, Isabela thought maybe Abuela did not hear her. But then Abuela turned and faced Isabela without a smile. She was holding a spoon and was wearing an apron. Isabela's stomach flipped. She had never been on the receiving end of the expression on Abuela's face. She knew her only option was to apologize and do it quickly.

"I'm sorry I yelled at everyone before," said Isabela. "I'm sorry if I upset you and that I didn't get a chance to prepare dinner like I promised."

Abuela continued to stare at her.

Oh, boy. Isabela mentally went through the checklist Abuela had left for her.

"I'm sorry I didn't finish unpacking the boxes in Mom and Dad's room. I did change the sheets and I did give Mom her medicines at the right time," Isabela continued. "I know I should have let someone know I was leaving the house, but I was so upset by what Mom had told me, I just had to get out of here. I was only gone for an hour."

Abuela continued to stare at her.

"Why did you all come back so early from the festival and why was everyone screaming at me? Abuela, please speak to me!" pleaded Isabela.

"You snuck out of this house and you got caught," stated Abuela, in a tone that stunned Isabela. "I don't care what the reason was that made you leave, but there will be serious consequences if you ever do anything like that again. Comprendes?"

Isabela felt distraught and completely misunderstood. Based on what her mother had told her today, she couldn't understand why Abuela refused to show her any sympathy. She began to cry quietly.

"Those tears are not going to work on me, Izzy, so stop and listen," Abuela said sternly.

Isabela wiped her eyes and looked at Abuela.

"We came home early today because I felt I had given you too many things to do before your first day of school. We came home early so I could prepare dinner and make sure you were okay. But when we got here—where were you—out doing God knows what. You left this house, you left your mother, and told *no one*? We all have phones and we all know how to text each other, sí? Do you know how scared we were? We did not know what happened to you. We did not know if someone took you. We do not know *anyone* here! We have no family or friends here that we could call to try and find you. Don't we all have enough going on and a very big day for everyone tomorrow? What were you thinking, mi niña? How could you put your family through this when you know how much we love you? How?" questioned Abuela, her eyes were brimming with tears.

Isabela had never received a verbal lashing from Abuela in her life. She was afraid to say anything.

"You lock the door to your room? This is the kind of family we are now—since when? I sent your father and Javier out to get dinner, so they could calm down. You don't open the door for your brother who loves you and would do anything for you? Your father is so worried about your mother and starting his new position tomorrow and you don't even have the respect to apologize to him for making him worry like that? You lock yourself in your room away from everyone? We are all in this together, Izzy! Your mother is not only *your* mother, she is also *Javier's* mother and she is also your father's *wife*. Losing your mother means something to everyone—but for *me*—it means losing my child! My *only* child, mi amor," finished Abuela, sobbing into her apron.

Isabela ran over to Abuela and hugged her tightly, tears streaming down Isabela's face.

"I'm sorry, Abuela. Please forgive me for being so selfish. I never looked at losing Mom from your perspective. Please, por favor, forgive me."

Isabela and Abuela cried, hugging each other for some time.

Isabela had never seen Abuela this upset. She was terrified Abuela would get sick and leave her too.

Isabela gestured toward the table. "Come, Abuela. Please sit down. Let me get you some water and something to eat."

Abuela sat at the table while Isabela poured her a glass of water. She noticed a pot on the stove. She lifted the cover and stirred the bubbling leftover stew. She lowered the flame and began preparing a small dinner for the two of them. Isabela was so distressed she did not know how she would eat. But she knew Abuela was exhausted and had to eat something and go straight to bed.

Isabela decided *she* would be the one to give her mother the nighttime medicines. This way, when her father and Javier came home, they could also go straight to bed. She would wait up for her mother tonight.

11

PRIMOGENITURE

THIS POOR GIRL and her poor family—what they are going through.

Aelish put her Viewer back inside her flypack. It was a heart-wrenching exchange to witness between Isabela and her grandmother. Aelish knew how much Isabela's grandmother meant to her, especially with the death of her mother looming. She was nearly at Isabela's house when Aelish decided to check on her through the Viewer. The sun had been down for a few hours. She always forgot how quickly it became dark on Earth, during the autumn, like someone closing a window shutter.

Isabela's grandmother's anguish had a profound effect on Aelish. As she put on her flypack and resumed flying she couldn't stop thinking about the word "loss." Isabela's grandmother had so eloquently described how loss meant something different for everyone.

Aelish began to think about what she had lost after her parents' deaths. Hundreds of years later, it still felt like yesterday. After the funeral, the relief of getting them back and buried in Ireland began to fade and was replaced by a terrible despair.

She never imagined she would be leaving Ireland and the Earth less than six years after discovering she was a magical being. She assumed she would be a bit "long in the tooth" as her father had teased, not on the precipice of her eighteenth birthday.

Putting the affairs of the Earl of Brólaigh in order, took almost a year. It was exceedingly more complicated than she could ever have imagined. The plague had not only killed her beloved parents, but it had nearly wiped out her entire extended family residing in London.

Aunt Bronwyn, her husband, and two of their daughters had perished, as did Uncle Eamon, his wife, and two of their sons. The only reason the eldest daughter of Aunt Bronwyn had survived was because she was visiting a family friend in Cambridge. Likewise, Uncle Eamon's first-born son, Declán, had survived. He had been away in France, on business for his father. She wrote to her last two remaining cousins. Through their responses, she learned that her extended family that had perished, shared the gruesome fate of being thrown into the plague pits. The pits still brought a shudder to Aelish whenever she thought about them. She was grateful, to this day, for the magic of DAR affording her parents a proper burial.

Two weeks after her parents' funeral, Mr. MacSweeney came into the drawing room and announced that her father's solicitor had arrived at Brólaigh Castle with a legal team. The primogeniture her father had often worried about, because his only surviving heir was a daughter, was indeed problematic.

Although Aelish knew she would one day have to deal with the issue of her father's title and estate, she never anticipated it would be this soon in her life. She also wasn't emotionally ready to leave for DAR. She was frightened by the prospect of leaving Ireland, her home, her village, and her life on Earth. Despite the deep friendship and magical mentorship between herself and Lady Antonia, the forthcoming change was terrifying. She had just begun to acclimate to her magical abilities and she was most definitely *not* ready to live in DAR. It was all completely overwhelming.

Her father's solicitors had determined that Declán was the true and rightful heir to her father's title and estate. Her father's title was originally created with no special remainder clause for female heirs. Aelish, therefore, would inherit nothing—not the title or the estate. Aelish profoundly resented male primogeniture. She perceived it as an outrageously antiquated law of inheritance, especially while Queen Elizabeth I sat on the throne in England.

Ironically, it was Declán, the usurper of her inheritance, who got her through it all. Declán had no desire to become Earl of Brólaigh and resented the entire situation. When her father's solicitors sent word that he must come to Ireland immediately, he was quite put-off. He was busy trying to maintain the success of his father Eamon's trading business and resented the intrusion. His life and business was in London. He was not desirous of returning to a country he had no recollection of, since leaving as a small child. He was indignant over the entire situation. Thus, began their camaraderie.

Their camaraderie only deepened during the months it took to transition her father's title and estate. The process and time spent together enabled them to forge a great bond. If she wasn't a magical being destined to live in DAR, she imagined she would have accepted his marriage proposal. They, of course, would need a dispensation from the Catholic Church because they were first cousins, but dispensations were routinely given to noble families.

The solicitors informed them one afternoon that they were nearing the end of the process. They decided to take a much-needed break, with a walk through the gardens of Brólaigh Castle.

Aelish loved sharing memories from her childhood with

Declán. She also learned some humorous tales about her father as a young boy through the stories Uncle Eamon had shared with Declán. He began to fill a void and she grew to love him, in her own way, more as an older brother than a lover. In time though, she imagined she would have been very comfortable married to her first cousin. Many noble families throughout Europe were married to their first and second cousins. It wasn't something she considered odd or unconventional.

When Declán dropped to one knee during their walk in the gardens, Aelish was genuinely surprised. He produced a ring from behind his back and was gallant in his proposal. She was thrilled to have experienced a marriage proposal before she left her Human life behind. The memory provided her with great comfort during her first year in DAR.

She, of course, declined Declán's proposal, not only because she would be leaving the Earth, but also because she felt her heart may lay elsewhere. During the last year she had begun preparing a fictitious story for her remaining family, servants, and fellow villagers, as to why she would be leaving Ireland. Therefore, when Declán unexpectedly proposed, she was ready with an explanation that was partially fabricated and partially true. She was very gracious when she saw the ring. She was a Lady after all, and knew how to be respectful in such a situation.

"You are too kind, Declán," she smiled, "but I cannot marry you or anyone else at this time. Come, let us sit down on the bench."

After they were seated he took her hands in his and asked rather distressed, "But why? Why can't you marry me?"

"Because it is going to take me a long time to get over what happened in London. My heart is not healed. I never even completed my first originally designed ensemble from the dressmaker in London," she said wryly, shaking her head thinking about the fittings, left unfinished. "Strangely, I don't feel mature enough to marry, despite being almost eighteen. It feels like I was in bonnets only hours ago."

"But this is your home. I don't want you to feel as though you have to leave because of this ridiculous primogeniture law. I will take care of you for the rest of your life, Aelish. You can become Lady Brólaigh and help me make sense of becoming Earl and all that it entails. You understand it better than I do," he said honestly. "I need you. We can make a life here together."

She kept her eyes to the ground as he spoke, but at the mention of her becoming Lady Brólaigh, she looked up. When he was finished speaking, she could no longer hold back the tears for her mother. They came out in a torrent of anguish, her hands covering her face.

Declán reached across and drew her into his arms, "Shh, shh . . . all will be well, Aelish. Please don't cry, dearest."

He produced an elegant handkerchief for her tears. As she wiped her eyes, she tried to compose her grief, which always lay right below the surface. His arms around her felt so familiar. She had been cared for and loved her whole life by her Ma and Da. It was how she was raised, a child of privilege in every way.

It would be so easy to stay in his arms, stay in my home, and grow old and die on the land of my ancestors. But would he still love me if he knew the truth about what I was? Would he be so accepting of my lavender skin and magical abilities the way Ma and Da had been? I can't break his heart, but I must be firm.

"I need to live a bit more before I marry and have a family. This is all yours now," she said, extending her arm toward the acres of land in front of them.

"But it would be *ours*, Aelish," he pleaded.

"I can't stay here anymore, Declán. The memories are too painful. I need to move elsewhere and try to forget what happened to the two most loving people I have ever known. Their deaths were positively gruesome and I fear I will never get over it. If I don't leave Ireland, I am *certain* I will never get over it. I need to move forward so I can stop looking backward. Do you understand?" she asked, gently stroking his face.

"But where will you go?" he asked.

She could see he was genuinely panicked. Not only because she wasn't going to marry him, but also because she was leaving Ireland.

"As soon as we are finished with the solicitors, I plan to move to France where Lady Antonia has a vineyard estate in Bordeaux."

And that was the first time she tried out the lie. It went against her upbringing, but she felt relieved she had done it. The next time would be easier and the next even easier, until she almost believed it herself.

"France?" he asked confused. "Really?"

"At least they are still Catholic instead of the new Tudor Protestant," she said ruefully.

"Well, that is true," said Declán, shaking his head. "I suppose that will be another challenge I will have to face as the new Earl."

"Indeed it will, but you will handle it with the grace you handle everything, my dearest cousin," she said.

"There's no changing your mind, then?"

"I'm afraid not, but I will write and try to visit whenever I can," she promised, hoping she'd be able to see him again after leaving for DAR.

"All right, then," he said, resigned to her refusal. "Let's go back inside. It's getting chilly out here."

They both stood and he put his arm around her shoulders, shielding her from the north wind that suddenly began to blow, as they walked back toward the Castle. Aelish hoped he would find the happiness she knew she could not give him.

He is going to make some other girl so happy.

Declán had helped her mature since her voyage to London a year ago. She had endured the deaths of her parents. She had gained an understanding of the monetary responsibilities of an Earl. She had learned the importance of providing a livelihood for the families in the village that depended on the Earl. Had the title and estate passed to her, she now knew she was capable of handling those responsibilities with fortitude.

She had no idea how long it would take before a female would be permitted to assume the responsibilities of an Earl. But it gave her great confidence to know she could fill her father's shoes. Being *Lady* Brólaigh, however, or any nobleman's wife, was no longer her destiny. As far as she was concerned, her mother was the last Lady Brólaigh.

Although Declán never knew the true cause of her parents' deaths, their shared grief over losing one's parents, began to heal her heart. She grew stronger, more independent, and for that, she would always be grateful to Declán. The last year demonstrated she could move forward. After refusing Declán's proposal, she felt ready to embark on the adventure to DAR.

Declán was more than generous with his inherited estate. He went against the solicitors' advice and granted Aelish a large sum of money from her father's estate. It was enough for her to live on, without a husband, for the rest of her life. Knowing she would have no need for money in DAR, she decided to give a large portion away to someone she had never forgotten.

One afternoon, she asked Mr. MacSweeney to bring Catríona into the drawing room. He looked askance at the suggestion of the scullery maid being allowed into one of the Castle's formal rooms. The fact that Catríona cleaned the fireplaces everyday, in the formal rooms, mattered not one bit to Mr. MacSweeney. Catríona could come into the rooms to clean, but never for a visit. But he did as she requested. After all, he was still *her* butler until

Declán assumed his official role.

After she spoke with Catríona, Catríona left the drawing room in hysterical tears of joy. She ran past a startled Mr. MacSweeney on her way back to the kitchen.

"Is everything all right, Lady Aelish?" he inquired.

Aelish knew he assumed that she had taken it upon herself to terminate the employ of Catríona. It would never dawn upon him that his perception of the situation could be inaccurate.

He's such a smug, insensitive arse.

"Yes, everything is *fine*, Mr. MacSweeney," replied Aelish, somewhat haughtily. "Catríona will be leaving service for life. She has suddenly come into a vast sum of money from a distant relative."

She relished the look of shock and jealousy that came across Mr. MacSweeney's face, as he realized that would *never* happen to him.

"Please go about finding a new scullery maid immediately. That will be all, Mr. MacSweeney." Her dismissal of him was one of the most satisfying moments of her life.

She knew his position would compel him to be polite when he bowed and left the drawing room uttering, "Yes, m'Lady."

Declán's generosity had enabled her to bestow a vast amount of money for Catríona. The sum was in excess of what all the Brólaigh Castle tenant farmers would earn in their lifetimes—combined.

And that, is how much a small sack of flour costs.

When the process of transferring her father's title and estate was finally finished, she packed her trunk and bags. It was time for her to leave the Earth. She remembered waiting in her bedchamber in Brólaigh Castle for Lady Antonia to arrive. Her father's carriage had been sent to retrieve Lady Antonia, and that same carriage would then lead her to a new life in DAR. She was actually excited.

When the carriage arrived, Aelish ran outside to Lady Antonia, embracing her tightly.

"Lady Antonia! It's so good to see you. I've missed you during this past year."

"Now then, Aelish, don't you think it's time you called me, Antonia?"

Aelish tilted her head backward, laughing at Lady Antonia's mirthful demeanor. The footmen loaded her trunk and bags onto the carriage. Most of her belongings would be donated during their journey. Declán then came outside to meet Lady Antonia.

"Lord Brólaigh," said Aelish to Declán, using his official new title, "allow me to introduce, Lady Antonia Harrington Stonebridge. Lady Antonia, this is my dear cousin, His Lordship Declán Eamon Carrigan, the new Earl of Brólaigh."

"M'Lady, I have heard the most wonderful things about you," said Declán. He took Lady Antonia's hand and bowed. "It is my distinct pleasure to put a face to the name."

"The pleasure is all mine, Your Lordship," said Lady Antonia. "Thank you for looking after this treasure and I wish you nothing but happiness in your new title and estate. Rest assured, my family and I will take wonderful care of Lady Aelish."

"Your assurances are most appreciated. I don't know what I will do without her," he said wistfully, glancing at Aelish.

"Well then, I will wait in the carriage so you two may say your goodbyes," said Lady Antonia, bowing graciously. She winked at Aelish as she walked back over to the carriage.

"Thank you for helping me to move forward, Declán. I will never forget all the kindness you have shown me. I can't tell you how much it has meant to me. I wish you so much good fortune and happiness, cousin," she said, embracing him.

"Please know this will always be your home and you may live

here anytime if you change your mind. It will always be yours," said Declán. His smile conveyed sadness for what could have been, and acceptance for what would never be.

"Thank you, my dearest cousin," said Aelish. She hugged him one final time.

As she walked over to the carriage, Lady Antonia asked, "Are you sure you have everything, dear?"

"Yes, I do," smiled Aelish.

12

ISABELA MEETS AELISH

ISABELA AND ABUELA ate their dinner mostly in silence. When they were finished, Isabela began to clear the table.

"I will clean up, Abuela. Go get ready for bed and I will come in and kiss you good night," said Isabela.

"All right, nieta, gracias," said Abuela. Isabela knew she was emotionally exhausted and was very concerned about her.

Isabela rinsed the dishes. The warm, soapy water over her hands began to soothe her. She was thinking of absolutely nothing. She robotically loaded the dishwasher, washed the pot, cleaned the counters, wiped down the kitchen table, and shut all the lights, with the exception of the one above the sink.

She went down the hallway toward Abuela's bedroom and saw her standing beside her bed. She was in her nightgown, saying her prayers in Spanish. Isabela stood outside the doorway waiting, until Abuela was finished. She entered the room and helped Abuela get into bed, arranging her blankets.

"Buenas noches, nieta," whispered Abuela, who was lying on her side.

Isabela sat down on the edge of the bed and gently stroked Abuela's face.

"Make sure you apologize to your father and brother when they come home. And don't worry about your first day of school tomorrow. God will help us with everything, mi amor," continued Abuela.

"I know, Abuela. I'm so sorry I upset you like this today. I love you. Now go to sleep, and stop thinking about everything," said Isabela. She bent over and kissed her forehead.

She turned off Abuela's night table lamp and quietly closed the door. She heard the sound of the garage door opening and headed down the hallway to confront her father and brother's anger head-on.

"Hi," said Isabela, evenly.

"Where's Abuela?" asked Javier.

Her father said nothing and hung up his jacket on the hook by the door.

"I prepared a small dinner for us and tucked her into bed. She is hopefully sleeping," said Isabela, awaiting the scolding.

"Is she okay?" asked her father, not smiling.

"Yes. I think she just needs a good night's sleep to forget about today and the upset I caused all of you. I'm very sorry," said Isabela, tears forming in her eyes. "There's no excuse for my behavior."

"We didn't know Mom was going to tell you today about her chances with the clinical trials, Izzy," said her father. "Come here."

Her father embraced her in a loving hug and she knew all was forgiven. She exhaled a deep sigh of relief.

As they disengaged from their hug, Isabela looked up at

her father and said, "I'm going to wait up for Mom's nighttime medicines tonight, so you and Javi can go to bed, all right?"

Her father looked concerned. She knew he was worried about her getting up for school tomorrow.

"Please, Dad, let me do this for you," Isabela pleaded.

"All right, but promise you will go to bed right afterward, okay?" asked her father.

"Yes, Dad, okay," said Isabela, relieved.

"I will see you in the morning, Izzy," said Javi, as he reached his arms out for a hug. "Everything's okay, all right?"

"All right," she whispered into his shoulder, thankful for his forgiveness.

"I still have to shower, so I will shut all the lights before I go to bed," she said to them both.

"Okay, then. Good night, sweetheart," said her father.

"Good night, kiddo. See you in the morning," smiled Javier.

"Good night," said Isabela, returning his smile.

Her father and brother walked in opposite directions toward their respective bedrooms. She waited in the kitchen until she heard both bedroom doors close. She was going to end this day with almost all of the promises she had made to Abuela this morning completed. She headed down the hallway toward the bathroom to shower.

She turned on the water and stepped into the shower. She let the deliciously scalding water wash away this horrible day. She was just beginning to relax when she remembered that she'd forgotten to put on a shower cap. She hadn't intended to wash her hair, as she was unable to dry it properly on her own.

Would this rotten day ever end? How could I have forgotten?

Isabela had inherited thick, long, wavy, black hair from her Mexican heritage. If she didn't dry it properly, her hair ended up looking and feeling like cotton candy.

Oh, my God!

As she stepped out of the shower, she immediately wrapped her hair in a towel trying to buy time until she could figure out how to dry it. She dried herself off and wrapped her body in a bath sheet. She went to her room and put on her pajamas.

Leaving her hair in the towel, she pattered down the hall barefoot and went into the kitchen to prepare her mother's medicines. She walked toward her parents' bedroom and slowly opened the door. She was thrilled to hear the sound of her father snoring in a deep sleep.

Good.

She approached her mother who was also asleep in the hospital bed. She hated to wake her, but it was time for her medicines. She gently kissed her.

"Mom, I'm going to raise the bed so you can take your medicines," she whispered. "Don't speak, so you don't wake up."

Her mother swallowed them down, and Isabela lowered the bed back down to the position it had been in. She stroked her mother's face and watched her fall back to sleep. Pleased that she had fulfilled her promise to Abuela, her father, and Javier, she left the room and quietly closed the door.

She shut the kitchen light on her way back to the other side of the house where her bedroom, along with Abuela and Javier's, was located. She quietly checked on them and found them both sound asleep in their rooms.

Excellent.

Isabela went back to her room to retrieve her blow dryer from her closet so she could bring it into the bathroom. She was going to have to make an attempt at drying her hair. Abuela had been doing it since her mother had gotten sick. She opened the door to her room, which only had a nightlight on and she quietly closed the door, her back to the room.

As she turned away from the door, heading toward her closet, she thought she was having an apparition. Back in L.A., there was a group of old ladies in church, who were always talking about their visions.

This cannot be possible.

Leaning against her bed, was a tall, beautiful, lavender-faced being in a white, sleeveless, billowy nightgown. Her lavender feet were bare and her long red hair was pulled to one side in a fishtail braid.

Isabela blinked and rubbed her eyes trying to make the vision go away, but then it spoke.

"Hello, Isabela. I'm Aelish. I think I can help you finish your hair tonight," said the being cheerfully, with a big smile on her lavender face.

13

ISABELA DEBATES AELISH

"**A**M I DEAD?" asked Isabela.

"Oh no, sweetheart, far from it," gently answered Aelish.

"I need to sit down," said Isabela. She reached for her desk chair feeling faint. She put her head in her hands and began rubbing her face the way Abuela did.

I'm losing my mind. She cannot be real!

Isabela felt frantic. She lifted her head and stared at the lavender being, utterly at a loss for what to say. This was *all* she needed after this unbelievably rotten day.

"Who and what are you—and don't lie to me."

"Don't be afraid, Isabela. I'm not here to hurt you, but hopefully quite the opposite," said Aelish.

"What are you—some kind of angel or fairy?" asked Isabela. She was growing more terrified by the minute and just wanted to go to bed.

Wait! Maybe I'm already in bed and this is nothing more than a nightmare. She began trying to wake herself up, but it wasn't working.

"I am a magical being that has been sent to help you cope with the severe obstacles and difficulties in your life," stated Aelish.

"Seriously—a magical being? Oh, *come on!*"

"Yes, Isabela. I am a magical being," said Aelish.

"A magical being—like those created by talented writers—the same people who brought us the Tooth Fairy, Santa Claus, and the Easter Bunny? You actually expect me to believe that you are real, and that I am not going to wake up any minute from this dream where you will become nothing more than a memory, instantly forgotten in the daylight?" scoffed Isabela.

"I was prepared for skepticism, Isabela, but I detect an underlying bitterness. I would expect that inclination from an adult, but not from someone your age. I fear coping with your mother's illness has brought you into the adult world too soon, depleting your innocence and hope."

"Wait! What do *you* know about my mother?" Isabela snapped back. She didn't want to let on to the being that she was genuinely stunned it knew anything about her mother.

How is this possible? Oh, my God! She began rubbing her face again.

"I know she is very ill and that you have moved here so she may receive experimental treatments for her disease," Aelish said evenly. "I know you don't expect her to survive and that you are angry at your family for not telling you about her slim chance of survival, even with these experimental treatments."

"I *am* angry they didn't tell me!" yelled Isabela. "I have lived through this whole ordeal too and we moved across the country for only a ten percent chance of survival? Why didn't they tell me?"

Isabela began crying. She remembered afresh, the difficult conversation with her mother this afternoon, and the subsequent explosion she set off by leaving the house without telling anyone. She was still furious with her family, for not disclosing the truth about her mother's chances, since the day she was diagnosed.

"You feel betrayed by your family, don't you?" asked Aelish.

"Yes, I do," said Isabela. "I'm intelligent enough to understand that my mother will certainly die without these treatments, but they never told me the truth from the beginning. She's as good as dead." Isabela felt defeated, as tears streamed down her face.

"Your desolation has blinded you from the kindness your family has shown you by *not* telling you the truth, until you were older, and until your mother was almost out of time."

"They should have told me everything from the beginning," retorted Isabela. "I know she has already lived longer than most people with the same diagnosis. But they let me delude myself into thinking these clinical trials might actually give her a chance to go into remission. And today, I'm told the trials will, at best, give her only a ten percent chance of survival?"

"It was your mother's decision not to tell you, Isabela," stated Aelish.

Isabela opened her mouth, but was speechless.

"They honored your mother's wishes in allowing her to be the one to tell you when *she* felt the time was right. None of your family members knew the day she would pick, and they have kept this secret, out of their love and respect for both you and your mother."

Isabela just stared at Aelish. Her tears were flowing like an open faucet.

"She has so little control left over her life," said Aelish. "As your mother, she felt it was in your best interests to wait until you were older, to better process the reality that she might die. Could you have handled this when you were ten? I think your mother's assessment was correct because I can see the bitterness and loss of hope that has enveloped you. She didn't want you to lose even more years of your childhood than you already have because of her illness."

I had no idea, reflected Isabela. She could feel her heart opening—the anger at her family slipping away. She was beginning to accept the reality of her mother's situation.

"I did not know this. My poor mother, what she has been through," sobbed Isabela into her hands.

"Your mother is very brave, Isabela. Remember, this is the same person who likes to jump out of airplanes," smiled Aelish.

"How do you—I know how brave she is!" shot back Isabela.

"Do you? She continues to battle the disease, tries every medicine and treatment available, while none have worked, and she does all of this while being worried about what her illness is doing to you. She loves her family so much that she is willing to try one more time—to live—that takes great courage, Isabela. Most people would have given up by now."

Isabela said nothing and listened intently.

"Your family originally kept certain information from you because you were too young to contend with how quickly she might die. Your father began searching for a clinical trial immediately after her diagnosis, as your mother was given only six months to live. He would not give up until he found one. Her cancer is very rare and seldom has a good outcome. But she has already survived two years. Perhaps, long enough for her to participate in the trial your father has been searching for? The fact that the trial is located near one of his company's locations, and that your mother was accepted, is remarkable. Do you know how rare all of this is?"

Isabela sat there shaking her head, as she tried to process her feelings.

"These clinical trials help doctors and scientists learn more about her type of cancer. Participating in them is almost an act of altruism. Whatever is discovered in treating your mother, even if it does not help her, may one day assist doctors and scientists in discovering new ways to detect and treat her type of cancer for other patients. It is truly the bravest thing she could do, and you need to internalize that and stop being angry. She needs you to be even stronger going forward, stronger than you think you are capable of."

"But I *am* angry!" Isabela countered. "What kind of life is this for her? Lying in a bed all day, barely able to eat anything or hold her head up? This is ridiculous! I am angry with the doctors, I am angry at this disease, and most of all, I am angry with God. Why would He do this to her—to us—to our family? Why? Abuela says I have to pray more, light a candle each week at church—for what—a miracle that will never happen? I believe in science—only science will provide the cure for her cancer. There is no God."

"What you are debating within yourself, is how to maintain a semblance of hope and faith in the face of such dire circumstances," stated Aelish. "Even science requires an amount of faith, correct? I'm not referring to faith in a deity, but moreover, a scientist's faith in his or her own abilities. When they perform experiments while studying a disease, they must believe that what they are attempting may ultimately save lives.

"Even magic requires faith, Isabela. If I didn't believe in my ability to execute my spells, they would never work. It's the same with science. You must try to find some remaining hope within yourself that the experimental treatments have a chance, slim as it may be, to help your mother. Otherwise, what's the point in ever trying anything new or uncharted?"

Isabela slumped back in her chair and stared at Aelish. She could not believe she was debating with a magical creature.

Is she real? Why is she making so much sense and why does the room smell of lilacs?

14

FINDING A CONNECTION

"You've drawn me into this whole debate. But you've told me nothing about who you are or where you come from, yet you seem to know *everything* about me," Isabela said caustically. "Well?"

Aelish couldn't help but smile inwardly at Isabela's sass.

"Well, why don't I start at the beginning, when I, too, was twelve years old," stated Aelish.

"Fine. Let's hear it," said Isabela.

"All right, then. I come from a place in the magical world called DAR. But I was actually born on Earth in 1546," stated Aelish.

"So you're what, then, nearly five hundred years old? Yeah, right," scoffed Isabela.

"DARlings live approximately two thousand years, whereas Humans live about one hundred years. Since I have lived nearly five hundred years, I have lived almost a quarter of my life, which makes me nearly twenty-five years old," smiled Aelish. She remained undaunted by Isabela's attitude.

"I don't mean to be rude, but let's get to the point—can your magical abilities cure my mother or not?" interrupted Isabela.

Aelish stared at Isabela who was still sitting on her desk chair with her arms crossed over her chest. Her wet hair was on top of her head, wrapped in a towel. She was barefoot, in her pajamas, and staring at Aelish with her head cocked to one side, eyebrows raised, awaiting the answer.

It's not easy to pull off an attitude wearing that ensemble, thought Aelish.

"So, let me see if I understand this then, you *do* believe in magic?" asked Aelish, baiting her.

"If you can go right now into my mother's room, recite one of your spells, and cure her tonight, then yes, I believe in magic," retorted Isabela.

Lady Antonia had warned Aelish this might happen. Isabela was angry, distraught, and desperate to save her mother's life. Aelish knew her commanding attitude was nothing more than a pretense that belied the terror of her impending loss.

"It was my understanding that you believed only science could cure your mother," replied Aelish.

"Aren't you here tonight to convince me that magic is real? The same way my grandmother is always trying to convince me that God is real? And if I pray just a *little* bit harder and light just *one* more candle—then she'll be cured, right?" Isabela said sarcastically.

Aelish knew the bitterness and acrimony emanating from Isabela was unadulterated rage at being powerless to stop her mother from dying. She was testing Aelish, while at the same time, pushing her away to shield herself from further disappointment.

Aelish, on the other hand, was momentarily panicked about the best way to reach Isabela. She imagined she might fail as Isabela's Oraculi on her first visit. She took a deep breath and made the calculated decision that honesty was the only way to penetrate the wall Isabela had built around herself.

"No, Isabela. Magic cannot cure your mother. If it could, I would have cured my own parents who died of plague," stated Aelish.

"Well then, what good is it?" asked Isabela.

Aelish watched Isabela's bitterness burst into hopeless tears. She gave her some time to process the realization that there would be no miracle tonight. After Isabela had stopped crying, Aelish continued.

"I actually agree with you that science is the only way forward, with regard to disease and also with regard to the devolving environment of the Earth, which in turn will bring more disease," said Aelish.

"Whatever," said Isabela.

Aelish felt Isabela's disgust at her magical limitations in her gut. It was a fresh reminder of her helplessness in preventing her own parents from dying. She sighed and continued.

"Magic has a severe limitation, Isabela. We cannot cure illness. We treat those in the magical world with various spells, herbs, and plants for their symptoms. But magic cannot cure disease in the Human or magical worlds," said Aelish.

"Well apparently, we can't either," Isabela said scornfully.

"What do you mean?" asked Aelish, drawing her out.

"The only science we seem to be working on also involves symptoms. Have you ever watched television?" asked Isabela. "Do you even know what television is?"

"Yes, I do, but why do you ask?"

"Every third commercial is about some amazing new drug that treats the *symptoms* of a disease. But there's never an advertisement for a drug that can *cure* a disease. There's so much money being made in treating the symptoms of diseases that it has nullified the need for science to cure anything. And the best part is—many of the drugs being advertised—can actually *cause* cancer!

"I often accompanied my mother to the cancer center for her treatments in L.A. I overheard other patients complaining to one another. They described how they'd been taking a drug for a specific disease, usually an autoimmune one, and the reason they developed cancer was because it was a side effect of the drug. A *side effect*—are you kidding me—cancer is a side effect? This is science? This is progress? People are dying, but who cares? There's money to be made by the drug companies and the gorgeous cancer centers with their libraries and glass buildings. It's disgusting! There's no hope for my mother," said Isabela. She finished her rant with fresh tears down her face.

Aelish was amazed by the knowledge and understanding Isabela had obtained. Being immersed in the world of the sick and the dying had provided her with a ghastly education. Yet there could be a positive repercussion from this education—it could propel her in the future toward the direction of science. But if Isabela's despair were left unchecked, it would pull her irreparably away from this possibility.

"Your aptitude and appreciation for the importance of science has captured the attention of the Head Council of DAR, Isabela," stated Aelish.

Isabela looked up from the floor and stared at Aelish.

"Despite the fact that you are very young, they have surmised that your future could conceivably hold great promise for both Humans and DARlings," continued Aelish.

"Are you *kidding* me? Seriously? I'm twelve years old, I'm starting a new school tomorrow in a part of the country I'm not familiar with, and my mother is dying. My schedule's a little busy at the moment for the head leaders or whatever you called them," said Isabela, with less sarcasm and more exhaustion in her voice.

"What could they possibly want with me? And where is this place you are from? Is it a planet? Is it in our solar system—what?"

Even though she knew Isabela's heart was bereft of hope, Aelish could nevertheless see the exceptional intelligence and curiosity exuding from Isabela.

"DAR and the Earth share the same sun," said Aelish. "But DAR is in a different dimension from the Earth. The two worlds are much closer to each another than say, another planet like Venus or Mars."

"Where on the Earth were you born?" asked Isabela. "You sound Irish."

"Yes, I was born in Ireland."

"And how in the world did you grow up in Ireland with *lavender* skin?" mocked Isabela.

"Until I was twelve," responded Aelish, "my skin was the typical Irish porcelain color. I did not know I was a magical being. After I turned twelve, however, my skin color began changing and my magical abilities began emerging. It was an extremely difficult time and I had to be confined to the house for a while."

"I know a little bit about having different skin color. In L.A., where I was born—wait—do you know where that is?" asked Isabela, abruptly.

"Yes, it's in sunny California," smiled Aelish.

"Well, it's not always so *sunny* when you're skin color is brown and your family is of Mexican descent," said Isabela. "The fact that my father, brother, and I were all born in the United States made no difference. Our skin color defined us. We were all called the same derisive names of those born in Mexico, or those who cross the border trying to escape violent gangs, the drug cartels, or to find work.

"We received the same treatment as undocumented Mexicans. You know—the same Mexicans who mow the grass, cook the food served in restaurants, and work the fields picking the produce grown in *sunny* California. Growing up in L.A. taught me a lot about hate. I've been called every derogatory name used to describe Mexicans.

"I can only imagine what school is going to be like tomorrow. There aren't many people here that look like me or have hair like I do and—*Oh, my God*—I forgot about my hair! It's probably already half-dried!"

Isabela shot out of her chair, took off her hair towel and began furiously running her hands through her hair.

"Oh, no! It's half-dried," she said in a panic.

"I think I can help you with that," suggested Aelish, "if you would let me."

"What could you possibly know about Mexican hair? You're a magical being with lavender skin from a place called—what is it again?"

"DAR. Aren't you predisposing my ability to fix your hair, in the same way people predispose your abilities, simply by the color of your skin and the texture of your hair?" Aelish watched the shame cross Isabela's face.

"Fine. I suppose you won't dry it any worse than I would. Can't you recite a spell or something and magically make it look great?"

"I actually think I have everything I need right here. May I suggest we get started before it dries any further?"

Aelish stepped aside to reveal her flypack on Isabela's bed. She emptied it onto the comforter and asked Isabela, "Well, do I have the necessary supplies to properly dry your hair?"

"How did you know you were going to have to dry my hair?" asked Isabela.

"I didn't," answered Aelish, truthfully.

Isabela looked away from the supplies and stared at Aelish.

"Did you bring all this stuff with you or did you just now, magically put it into your backpack?" asked Isabela.

"I just now magically put it into my *flypack*—that's what we call it in DAR. I suppose magic can have a purpose?" chuckled Aelish.

Isabela looked at Aelish and scoffed, rolled her eyes, and let out a big sigh. Aelish stood against the bed and watched Isabela drag her desk chair over to the bed and then head toward the closet. Isabela walked back toward her holding a blow dryer.

As she handed it to Aelish, she instructed, "I'm very particular about blow dryers, so please use mine." Isabela then plopped into the chair.

"Of course," replied Aelish.

"This is going to take forever," groaned Isabela. "I'm going to be so tired for school tomorrow."

"Don't worry," replied Aelish. "Before the night is over, I'll put a spell on you that will make you feel like you've slept for a week."

"You're not going to put any other spells on me, are you?" asked Isabela. She swiveled in the chair to glare up at Aelish.

"No, of course not," smiled Aelish. "Don't you trust me?"

"No, I don't," replied Isabela, her head now facing forward again.

Aelish was relieved she had been able to skillfully deflect Isabela's request to magically finish her hair. Of course she could use magic, but doing it manually meant that Isabela would be a captive audience. Aelish hoped to make a connection with Isabela that would afford her the opportunity to begin repairing Isabela's deteriorating attitude.

Thank heavens that in all worlds, both magical and Human, females have difficulties with their hair, thought Aelish.

15

WHAT IS AN ORACULI?

"I ALSO HAD an unexpected visit at my home when I was twelve years old," said Aelish. "Three beings from DAR came to speak to my parents about who and what I am."

"*That* must have gone over well," said Isabela.

"At first, it was extremely difficult, especially for my father. I had been keeping my skin color hidden from everyone with clothing and cooking flour. But eventually, I had to show it to my mother. So when the visitors arrived, she was more prepared than my father," explained Aelish.

"Cooking flour? Did that really conceal your skin color?"

"It was becoming more and more difficult to hide. I only used it on my face and hands."

"What did your mom say when you showed it to her?" asked Isabela.

"She was definitely shocked, to say the least. But my mother was extraordinarily kind. We decided that until we understood more about what was happening, I was to be confined to the house."

"But what about school?" asked Isabela.

"We didn't really have *school* at the time. Noble families had tutors come to their homes to teach their children."

"You are of noble descent?" asked Isabela, turning to look at Aelish.

"Stop moving," said Aelish. "Yes, my father was the Earl of Brólaigh in Ireland."

"Well excuse me, fancy-pants," scoffed Isabela.

"It was my Oraculi who helped my parents accept that I was a magical being," continued Aelish, ignoring Isabela's comment.

Your Ora—*what*?" snapped Isabela.

"Oraculi. It is the Latin word for mentor. The language in DAR is ordinarily English, but some of the old spells, titles, and doctrines remain in the ancient language of Latin. It was a language I was already familiar with, having grown up Catholic.

"Hold on! You were also raised Catholic?" asked Isabela, who refused to sit still, and turned to face Aelish.

"Yes, I was raised Irish Catholic," stated Aelish.

"But once you became a magical being, you stopped being Catholic and stopped believing in God, right?" pressed Isabela.

"Actually, no. I do believe in God and you can occasionally catch me praying the rosary."

"*No way*! I imagine you can fly, perform amazing spells, and you live in a magical world, yet you still believe in God? Why?"

"Because I have lived in both the Human and magical worlds for nearly five hundred years, and have seen too many things that cannot be explained. I firmly believe there is a deity more powerful than magical creatures or Human beings."

"Wow, you need to meet my grandmother," said Isabela, as she turned back around in her chair.

"My existence would be very hard for your grandmother to process," said Aelish.

"You think? She would have a heart attack," stated Isabela.

Aelish knew she would eventually have to discuss with Isabela the importance of keeping DAR's existence a secret from everyone in her life. But this was not that moment.

"I seriously can't believe you think there is a God," said Isabela, clearly perplexed. "Don't tell me there are Catholic churches in DAR?"

"Many DARlings born of the Earth, who ultimately come to live in DAR, continue to privately practice their beliefs. Others abandon it completely. DARlings are not permitted by law to proselytize, worship in mass gatherings, or create churches, temples, mosques, or any other type of structure in which to worship.

"Because organized religion was deemed by the citizens and the Head Council of DAR to be the single greatest cause of conflicts and wars upon the Earth, worship of any deity is not permitted in public. Of course, we have the freedom to worship privately in our homes with friends and family. This practice is neither encouraged nor discouraged," explained Aelish.

"I wish I lived in DAR. Then I would never have to go to church again," stated Isabela.

"Although worship remains a private matter in DAR, the Head Council does acknowledge that divine beings have walked the Earth," stated Aelish.

"Come on! How did they come to that conclusion?" asked Isabela.

"They came to that conclusion based on research and evidence," answered Aelish. "Whenever a divine being emerges, they accumulate a great number of followers and positively impact Humanity, but only temporarily. The Council has yet to observe a divine being whose contributions permanently alter the most negative of Human traits, such as greed, warmongering, and a total disregard for the Earth that sustains Human life. Further, once the divine figure departs, Humanity remains mostly unchanged. The Head Council cannot fathom it."

"Maybe that's because they were never really *divine*? Did the Head Council ever consider that?" challenged Isabela.

"I'm sure they have. There are canons written about these divine beings and the acts they performed while on the Earth," stated Aelish. "There is one building in DAR that contains all such writings and information. It is called the Breanon."

"What sort of acts—like miracles? Oh, please," protested Isabela. "I don't believe in God anymore. God is supposedly benevolent, so why would a benevolent God allow this much suffering on the Earth? No way, I'm not buying it."

"I understand your analysis, but it may not be the way you always feel. Leaving one's mind open to new possibilities and discoveries, seems to me, to be the ultimate definition of science. Even closing one door in your mind, could potentially stunt you from uncovering much needed answers and revelations," argued Aelish.

"Point taken," conceded Isabela. "Why do I feel the heat of the blow dryer, but I don't hear it?"

"I put a Quieting spell on it, so we don't wake your family," said Aelish.

"That's cool," Isabela said calmly.

Aelish noted it was the first time Isabela had spoken without anger, sarcasm, or rancor. She could feel her finally beginning to relax.

"Finish the story about your O-r-a-c-u-l-i," said Isabela, emphasizing each letter in the word, as she tried it out for the first time. "Wait! You're not here to tell me that I'm a magical being, are you?"

"No, Isabela, you are Human," stated Aelish.

"Well that's a relief, although I would be totally open to visiting DAR," stated Isabela.

Aelish was amused by how casually Isabela conveyed her desire to visit DAR. It was as if she were making a request for the next family vacation.

Wishing to visit DAR and leaving all her problems behind must sound very appealing, thought Aelish, *but she has no idea how much she would miss the Earth.*

"My Oraculi's name is Lady Antonia Harrington Stonebridge," said Aelish.

"*Lady* Antonia? Was she also born of noble descent?" asked Isabela.

"Yes, she was. Lady Antonia was born in 1521 at the Court of King Henry VIII in England. King Henry VIII was the second monarch of the Tudor dynasty, succeeding his father, Henry VII. The Tudor family ruled England for over one hundred eighteen years.

"By the time Lady Antonia was twelve years old, her skin color also began changing from porcelain to lavender and her magical abilities began to emerge. It became very dangerous for her and her family—much more so, than it was for me," said Aelish.

"Why was it more dangerous for her?" asked Isabela.

"Lady Antonia lived at the King's Court with hundreds of other people. I lived in a private castle."

"You grew up in a *castle*?" asked Isabela, stunned. She swiveled around in her chair and stared at Aelish.

"Yes, Brólaigh Castle in Ireland. Turn around and try to stay still," Aelish instructed.

"Geez," huffed Isabela. "I have a regular princess doing my hair. Shouldn't it be the other way around where the Mexican is doing your hair?"

"That's horrible, Isabela," chided Aelish.

"Apparently, you are unfamiliar with the way Mexicans are viewed in the United States," said Isabela. "Go on with the story—I want to know what happened to Lady Antonia."

Aelish reflected on Isabela's comment about Mexicans and remembered how the British viewed the Irish. She felt the familiar pain from her childhood. She considered relating to Isabela on the issue, but chose not to minimize Isabela's experience.

"Lady Antonia's parents were aware of her lavender skin color and suspected she was a magical being. They kept her in their living quarters at Court, desperately trying to protect her. One day, a beautiful woman masquerading as an invited guest of the King, approached her father. She was extremely discreet and told him she was there to assist in his daughter's welfare.

"Spies were rampant at Court, so her father was extremely suspicious. When the beautiful woman asked how Lady Antonia was coping with her new skin color, her father grew alarmed. He couldn't ascertain if the woman was there to harm his daughter or if someone had discovered his daughter's secret and had revealed it to this woman," explained Aelish.

"My father would have been so afraid for me," said Isabela. "What did he do?"

"After speaking with the woman over the next several days, she finally earned his trust. He decided to bring her up to the family's quarters. Once they were privately gathered, she explained everything to Lady Antonia and her parents about DAR and what Lady Antonia truly was. She even did a demonstration for them and turned her own skin color from porcelain to its true color of olive green. They were all then convinced that she was in earnest."

"Olive green? Oh, my God!" exclaimed Isabela. "Why wasn't her true skin color lavender like yours?"

"Only DARlings born of the Earth have lavender skin color.

The beautiful woman, who was actually Lady Antonia's Oraculi, was born in DAR. Her name is Melanthia and she was also one of the three visitors that came to see my parents at Brólaigh Castle."

"Did she show you and your parents her olive skin color, too?" asked Isabela, turning to look at Aelish.

"Yes, she did. I thought my father was going to lose his mind. He did not take the visit well at all. But once he realized I had been suffering with the secret of my skin color, his love for me overrode any misgivings and fears he harbored."

"I'm trying to think how my parents would react," said Isabela, pondering the idea. "I think they would come around."

"I think love and the ability to accept those who are different from us, is key. My parents were so accepting of my differences, it amazes me to this day," said Aelish.

"After Lady Antonia's Oraculi explained everything to her parents, what happened next?" asked Isabela.

"Once Melanthia taught Lady Antonia how to change her skin color back to porcelain, Lady Antonia resumed her presence at Court. Lady Antonia's father was a key advisor to King Henry, serving on the Privy Council. He greatly relied on Lady Antonia for guidance and assistance. He took full advantage of her magical abilities, despite her youth. Serving King Henry VIII was a quagmire of power hungry Lords and Catholic Bishops all vying for the attention of the King. And once King Henry was denied an annulment of his first marriage by the Catholic Church, his ultimate departure from Catholicism changed the world," stated Aelish.

"Oh, right. The King with a ton of wives; I remember now, from history class," said Isabela.

"Yes, King Henry VIII had a total of six wives before he died," said Aelish.

"Didn't he chop off their heads?" asked Isabela.

"Yes. Two of King Henry's wives lost their heads on the chopping block. King Henry was furious that his first wife, Catherine of Aragon from Spain, was unable to provide him with a male heir. He requested an annulment so he could marry again. He was in pursuit of a new wife who could bestow him with a male heir.

"But he had a daughter from his first wife, right?" asked Isabela.

"Yes. Catherine of Aragon provided him with a daughter, Mary, who became the first reigning female monarch of England—Queen Mary I," stated Aelish.

"So then, why was he obsessed with having a male heir if his daughter was able to become Queen?" asked Isabela, confused.

"Ironically, because of something King Henry did shortly before he died in 1547. But prior to his death, only a *male* heir could inherit the throne. Let me come back to that part of the story.

"King Henry decided he wanted his marriage annulled so he could marry a younger woman named Anne Boleyn. It was his hope that Anne Boleyn would provide him with a male heir. But despite years of wrangling with experts on Catholic and English law; the Catholic Church refused the annulment of his marriage to Queen Catherine. She was beloved by the people and a devout Catholic.

"King Henry was cunning, however, and decided to break away from the Catholic Church entirely. He aligned himself with the Protestant Reformation. He declared himself the Supreme Head of the newly formed Church of England. This enabled him to receive his annulment. He subsequently moved Queen Catherine and their daughter Mary out of Court, to a distant residence, and he married Anne Boleyn," stated Aelish.

"So basically, he appointed himself Pope of this new religion," concluded Isabela.

"Yes, excellent analogy," agreed Aelish. "He married Anne Boleyn in 1533. Lady Antonia was twelve and had just learned she was a magical being. Things at Court were chaotic, but then they became dangerous. After three years of marriage, Anne Boleyn was unable to provide the King with a male heir."

"After all that?" asked Isabela, shaking her head. "What happened to Anne Boleyn?"

"The King wanted to be rid of her. He subsequently accused her of bewitching him in to marrying her in the first place. Anne Boleyn was accused of witchcraft, incest, adultery, and conspiracy against the King. She was beheaded on May 19, 1536. Lady Antonia was fifteen years old."

"I would have so left for DAR," stated Isabela.

"King Henry immediately began searching for another wife who could provide him with a male heir. He married his third wife, Jane Seymour, on May 30, 1536, only eleven days after Anne Boleyn's beheading," said Aelish.

"Oh, my God, he's disgusting," said Isabela.

"Interestingly," continued Aelish, "Anne Boleyn gave birth to a daughter during their three year marriage. Their daughter ultimately became Queen Elizabeth I. Her reign lasted forty-four years. She restored stability to England, after the brief and tumultuous reign of her half-sister Mary I, who tried bringing Catholicism back to England and Ireland."

"Oh, Bloody Mary!" exclaimed Isabela.

"Yes, exactly," chuckled Aelish. "She earned that epithet after ordering the executions of over two hundred eighty Protestants. She also imprisoned her half-sister Elizabeth I in the Tower of London, so she couldn't lead a Protestant rebellion. Mary I turned England Catholic again. She died though, before she could produce an heir to displace Elizabeth I, her Protestant half-sister who was next in line to the throne. Elizabeth then turned England back to Protestant."

"What a mess! So wait, Henry's first wife, Catherine of Aragon, gave him a daughter Mary, who became the first reigning female monarch of England, right? And Anne Boleyn also gave him a daughter, who became Queen Elizabeth I. So now, two Queens reigned after King Henry VIII. You have to explain how his daughters inherited the throne, since his desperation for a male heir changed the religion of an entire country," remarked Isabela, clearly drawn into the history of the Tudors.

"I will get there. Be patient," said Aelish.

"I'll try, but this story is insane," stated Isabela.

"King Henry VIII passed the Witchcraft Act in 1542, six years after Anne Boleyn was beheaded for witchcraft in 1536. He was the first monarch to define witchcraft as an act punishable by death. The Act transferred the trial of witches from church courts to courts overseen by the King," said Aelish.

"Oh no, here comes the witch-hunt," said Isabela.

"Indeed. And the strange thing," began Aelish, "is that hundreds of years *before* the Witchcraft Act of 1542, it was generally acceptable for women, usually older women with no families, to make their own medicines to help those who were ill. They were often referred to as mystical, wise women. But after the outbreak of plague in the 14th century, these women were now looked upon with great suspicion. The populace feared they had conspired with evil forces to create the plague and they were subsequently blamed for this atrocity. Additionally, they became the scapegoat for crop failures, famine, and all hardships of society. Literature and various art forms began depicting mystical, wise women as dangerous and evil.

"The plague had inadvertently started an avalanche of zealous misogyny. This new perception began a downward spiral not only for mystical, wise women, but also for all women on

Earth. Men from the commoners to the King became threatened by a woman's perceived ability to harness evil powers. Men have subjugated women since the beginning of time, but King Henry VIII sought to codify the persecution of women suspected of witchcraft with the passage of the Witchcraft Act of 1542.

"Mystical, wise women who had formerly practiced alchemy for the betterment of society were now brutally persecuted and murdered. Kings relied only on men with the gift for mystical advice and believed mystical, wise women possessed only *evil* magical abilities," concluded Aelish.

"This is all so unfair," stated Isabela.

"Now, can you imagine being Lady Antonia or her parents, harboring an *actual* magical being from the world of DAR?" asked Aelish.

"She must have been scared every day of her life," said Isabela. "Why didn't she just leave and go to DAR?"

"DARlings born of the Earth are not forced to leave their families. They stay on Earth until their family has passed and they have transferred their affairs appropriately. One of the Doctrines of DAR, forbids the families of Earth born DARlings to be broken up unnaturally, as it was deemed cruel to do so," stated Aelish.

"That's very compassionate," reflected Isabela.

"Yes, it is. The transition from Earth to DAR is not a simple thing and the Head Council deemed it too great a hardship for an Earth born DARling to be forced to leave their loved ones. However, if they wish to depart for DAR before their family has passed, they are encouraged to do so."

"But what happens if they leave Earth when they're like eighty years old?" asked Isabela. "Do they look eighty when they arrive in DAR? I wouldn't want to look eighty years old if I was going to live almost two thousand more years!"

Aelish chuckled at how quickly Isabela had figured out this particular predicament of the Earth born DARling.

"Because I left Earth right before turning eighteen, I did not share the experience of DARlings who stayed until they were quite old," answered Aelish. "When these DARlings ultimately journey to DAR and cross over into the magical dimension, their age and appearance resets back to age sixteen. At sixteen years of age, you are considered an adult in DAR. But the reset only occurs, if DARlings leave the Earth when they are at least twenty years past the age of sixteen, or around age thirty-six."

"Oh, my God! They get to be young again. That's so cool!" exclaimed Isabela.

"The DARlings I've known who've gone through it, say it's an incredible experience," chuckled Aelish.

"Did Lady Antonia experience that? How long did she stay at Court once she discovered she could leave and live in DAR?" asked Isabela. "I would have been too scared to stay and would have left my parents behind."

"Lady Antonia stayed at Court until both her parents passed away, but it all happened within four years of her discovering that she was a magical being," said Aelish.

"Then she was only sixteen when she left in . . . 1537, right?" asked Isabela. "So like you, her age didn't reset."

This child has got one quick mind, thought Aelish.

"Exactly. She was sixteen when she left Earth and sixteen when she arrived in DAR. Now getting back to King Henry— the transition to Protestantism was very difficult for many of the Lords on the Privy Council, but it was a mandate from the King. Thus began the torture and executions of heretics, people who refused to convert from Catholicism to Protestantism. Lady Antonia's father was unfortunately among them," sighed Aelish.

"Oh no!" cried out Isabela. "Was he killed?"

"After King Henry married Jane Seymour, his third wife, she finally provided him with a male heir named Edward VI," said Aelish. "But she died twelve days after giving birth from infection. The King was heartbroken and took his grief out on his advisers and other members of Court and began a systematic cleanout of all heretics.

"Lady Antonia's father came under suspicion through rumor and innuendo. One of the other Lords on the Privy Council coveted Lady Antonia's father's position. The jealous Lord began spreading rumors and brought great attention to the fact that Lady Antonia's father had not pledged a portion of his gold to the new Church of England. When this was brought to the King's attention, her father was immediately brought to the Tower, where all forms of torture in England were carried out. The Tower of London still exists to this day, but it is now a museum."

"Oh, my God, they tortured him?" asked Isabela.

"At first, no. But when the new Protestant religious experts were sent in to question him, it became clear he remained true to his Catholic beliefs. After a week of grisly torture, which I will not describe to you, her father refused to recant his beliefs, and was beheaded. Because of his noble birthright, King Henry commuted his sentence of death from being burned at the stake to decapitation by the headman's axe."

"Oh, how awful," said Isabela.

"He was beheaded before the Privy Council, the residents of Court, Lady Antonia, and her mother. Lady Antonia put a spell on the headsman's axe so that her father would receive a clean and deadly swipe of the axe on the first try. It was not uncommon for the headsman to fail after one attempt. Sometimes it took two or three times before he actually concluded the execution."

"Oh, gross!" cried Isabela.

"Two days after his execution, her mother became very ill

with fever. She died within a week. To this day, Lady Antonia says that her mother died from a broken heart after watching her beloved husband beheaded."

"That is the saddest story," said Isabela. "I don't understand why people didn't just lie about their religious beliefs. It's better than being beheaded or burned at the stake."

"Those accused of heresy had to swear against their conscience," explained Aelish. "Many felt it was better to suffer death for high treason, than be damned for all eternity. Sitting here it's easy to pass judgment, but there is an honor in dying for one's beliefs."

"I understand what you're saying. I just know I would have lied," said Isabela. "In theory, being a royal always sounded awesome. But after listening to this story, I think I totally prefer being a commoner."

"Everything I have told you about King Henry VIII came about because of his obsession with having a male heir, including the deaths of Lady Antonia's parents," said Aelish.

"Oh! I almost forgot about his daughters becoming Queens," exclaimed Isabela.

"King Henry finally had one male heir, Edward VI, from his third wife, Jane Seymour. But when King Henry VIII died, Edward was only nine years old, a few years younger than you are. Becoming King at such a young age required him to have numerous advisers to assist him. But then, Edward died only six years later, at age fifteen. He died of consumption leaving no male heir."

"Oh, my God, this family," said Isabela. "He died so young."

Aelish realized she had been able to momentarily distract Isabela that her own mother was dying.

"Yes, it was tragic, but King Edward VI's death changed history forever."

"How?" asked Isabela.

"Before King Henry died, he was very shrewd," said Aelish. "He prepared his last will and testament with a very specific provision, with no legal precedent. He wrote that in case Edward VI died before producing a male heir, his daughters Mary I and Elizabeth I, *could* inherit the crown. Continuing his bloodline of the Tudor dynasty was ultimately the most important thing to King Henry.

"So after marrying six times, beheading two wives—Anne Boleyn and Catherine Howard, who was his fifth wife—and changing an entire country's religion, the provision King Henry included in his own last will and testament allowed his daughters to reign as Queen."

"That is actually incredible," stated Isabela.

"And King Henry VIII is the perfect example of why the Head Council of DAR no longer allows male DARlings to serve on the Head Council," concluded Aelish.

"Wait—*what*? The Head Council of DAR is comprised of only females?" asked Isabela, astonished.

"Yes, it is. I actually feel it is somewhat unfair, as there are some exceptional male DARlings. But males had ruled DAR for thousands of years. And during those years, DAR was constantly embroiled in wars with other magical worlds. It was Lady Antonia who brought about this radical change in DAR," smiled Aelish.

"She did?" asked Isabela.

"Lady Antonia left England for DAR soon after her mother died. She couldn't wait to be gone from King Henry's Court. Accompanied by her Oraculi, Melanthia, she arrived in DAR and was immediately summoned to appear before the Head Council. She gave testimony on everything she had lived through during King Henry's reign. She provided them with her opinions on religion, Kings, and patriarchal societies. After months of testimony, the all-male Head Council decided to bring the policy changes she recommended to a vote.

"The citizens of DAR voted in favor of setting an example to all other magical worlds ruled by males, and DAR became a matriarchal commonwealth. This was also when houses of worship were banned," explained Aelish.

"Wow, and she was only sixteen," remarked Isabela.

"Yes. A sixteen-year-old female was the catalyst that ousted DAR's all-male Head Council in perpetuity. After the males lost their long-held positions of power, there was much upheaval in DAR. But ultimately, the changes were incorporated into the Doctrine of DAR. The magical dominion of DAR has always been different—it has never been ruled by a single head of state such as a monarch, president, or religious leader. DAR has always been an egalitarian commonwealth, with one exception, males were the only DARlings permitted to serve on the Head Council or become Council Chair."

"I can't even imagine something like that happening on Earth," sighed Isabela.

"It is exceptional," responded Aelish. "After all the changes were implemented, Lady Antonia was made the youngest Oraculi in the history of DAR, which is how she became *my* Oraculi. We were born, twenty-five years apart. She possesses exceptional wisdom from having lived under the brutal reign of one of the most infamous Kings in Human history.

"Lady Antonia was also fortunate in that she was assigned the most respected Oraculi ever born in DAR—Melanthia. Once the Doctrine of DAR changed, affording females the ability to lead on the Head Council, it wasn't long before Melanthia became a member of the Head Council.

"Even before she served on the Head Council, Melanthia's devotion to Earth was revolutionary. She made it her life's goal to truly understand Humanity by reading nearly every document kept at the Breanon. She followed every major event on Earth and ultimately gave a speech, which propelled her to become a beloved leader of DAR, and a member of the newly formed, all-female Head Council," said Aelish.

"What did she say that was so unique?" asked Isabela.

"She explained her theory that Humanity is only in its adolescence," said Aelish. "She proffered that Humanity's belief systems are still evolving and its destructive tendencies are still raging. Its judgment is impaired, as it has not yet fully matured. She went on to say that it was the responsibility of DAR to ensure that Humanity be afforded every chance to reach its fullest potential. She hoped this would inevitably benefit the commonwealth of DAR. But until that time, we must seek out exceptional Humans who will lead Humanity into adulthood, hopefully preventing its destruction."

"I have to mull that over," said Isabela. "What a concept, Humanity is in its adolescence."

"She's amazing. It is Melanthia that found you, Isabela. She believes you are one of those exceptional Human beings that will thrust Humanity into adulthood. And while you said earlier that you are too young, that is exactly why you have been sought out. The Head Council hopes that your current exceptionalism will evolve, as you grow into adulthood. And you may one day help Humans to not only survive, but to also overcome the traits that propel them toward self-annihilation," explained Aelish.

"Oh," Isabela said softly.

16

THE BLACK DEATH

ISABELA GOT UP from her chair and sat on the edge of her bed and stared at Aelish, who looked regal even when holding a blow dryer.

"Are you saying that DAR protects Humanity because without the Earth, DAR could not exist? Are both worlds interconnected?" asked Isabela.

Aelish remembered she, too, had difficulty understanding the reality of another world so closely connected to Earth.

"Yes, Isabela," said Aelish. "Without the Earth, DAR could not exist. Our magic and our lives are all sustained by the way the sun's light hits the Earth and reflects onto DAR. This reflected sunlight supports life in DAR."

"But you are magical beings. Why couldn't you go live in one of the other magical worlds if the Earth was gone?" asked Isabela, puzzled.

"Just as Humans cannot survive on other planets in the Earth's solar system," began Aelish, "despite our magical powers, our composition as DARlings and our magical abilities, all come from this specific sunlight. It sustains everything in DAR. We could, of course, use magic to venture into other magical worlds, but DARlings could not inhabit any of the other magical worlds for any serious length of time. Probably no more than one thousand years, about half the lifespan of a DARling.

"Remember, time affects our bodies differently in DAR. Despite the numerical year being the same on Earth, DARlings do not age like Earthlings. And additionally, there are disparities in aging between Earth born DARlings and those born in DAR.

"For those born in DAR, they rapidly mature in the first three hundred years of their life to age twenty-eight, so they may serve DAR. But after the first three hundred years, their age holds for the next three hundred years, or until they have lived six hundred years.

"For the Earth born DARling, their aging process is dependent on how old they were in Earthly years, when they arrived in DAR. Their age may stay the same for a long time. That's what happened to me. I arrived at age eighteen and stayed eighteen, until I had lived three hundred eighty years, and I finally turned nineteen.

"Because of all these disparities, it's easier to calculate the age of all DARlings, as the cumulative number of years we've been alive, divided by our total lifespan of two thousand years. The percentage of years lived, becomes our age. So if you've lived five hundred years, that's twenty-five percent of your total lifespan of two thousand years, making you twenty-five years old. In the case of those born in DAR, the cumulative percentage formula begins *after* they have lived six hundred years."

Isabela stared at the floor. Aelish surmised that Isabela's scientific mind was calculating the variety of formulas. Aelish recalled how she, too, had found it difficult to understand the time continuum between DAR and Earth. The protracted lifespans of

DARlings and the disparity of time with regard to aging, between those born in DAR and Earth born DARlings, had made her head hurt. But most importantly, she hoped Isabela was beginning to understand how important the Earth was to DAR's existence.

"Come and sit back down on the chair so we can continue the next step in styling your beautiful hair," said Aelish.

Isabela reached up and felt her hair. "It feels so smooth. It's never felt like this before." Aelish watched as she began to walk toward the mirror hanging above her dresser. Aelish cast a spell that prevented the mirror from reflecting an image.

"No, no, no," said Aelish, startling Isabela. Isabela turned around to look at Aelish. "You have to wait until we are finished before you can look, okay?"

Ignoring Aelish, Isabela continued toward the mirror. "Oh, come on, just one peek?" Realizing there was no reflection, Isabela cried out, "Hey! What happened to the mirror?"

"I adjusted its reflecting capabilities for the moment," Aelish responded slyly. "You have to be patient. It's good practice for any self-respecting scientist."

"You put a spell on my mirror?" accused Isabela.

"Just a tiny one. I will reverse it when we are all finished," chuckled Aelish.

"Fine," Isabela said irritated, as she resumed her place back in the chair.

"There was a time in DAR when literally no one had any patience," said Aelish. "The greatest minds in magic had been working tirelessly for decades trying to defeat the one thing that threatened to destroy Humanity—the plague—and I mean the plague in all of its mutations."

"You mean bubonic, pneumonic, and septicemic plague, right?" asked Isabela. "I found research on the three forms of plague while seeking information on my mother's illness."

"Exactly," exclaimed Aelish. "No wonder you are going to be in Dr. Rios' advanced science class."

"Wait—how do *you* know about Dr. Rios—I just met him today!" cried Isabela.

"It is my hope that Dr. Rios will become an important Human mentor for you. He's only thirty years old and you both share a love of science."

"He's only thirty? Wow, I thought he was much older," reflected Isabela.

"When Humans are young, adults always seem so old, when oftentimes they are only one or two decades older," said Aelish. "I thought today was the perfect day for you both to meet. But I definitely had a tough time getting Cocoa to run into the street. She wouldn't leave the kitchen because the cookies Mrs. Rios had baked smelled so good," laughed Aelish.

"What are you saying?" asked Isabela. She swiveled around and glared at Aelish. "*You* made Cocoa run into the street using magic? I nearly fell off my bike!"

"Like I said earlier, I have faith in my spells, but this one did land a *couple* of seconds too late. Sorry about that," chuckled Aelish.

Isabela raised one eyebrow and continued to glare at her. "Unbelievable," she huffed, as she turned back around.

"Frustration with spells is a common occurrence in DAR," said Aelish. "They can be so annoying, similar to science experiments. However, having the perseverance to see them through, often ends up becoming more important than performing the actual spell.

"The plague presented the greatest challenge the Head Council of DAR had ever faced. The magical powers of DARlings were useless in destroying the Yersinia pestis bacterium. The bacterium was named in honor of the French-Swiss bacteriologist, Alexandre Yersin, who discovered it in 1894. The bacterium lay dormant for centuries after the first pandemic of The Justinian Plague of 541. But it came back with a vengeance in China around 1334. It spread along the great trade routes that eventually brought it to Europe."

"Didn't the plague go on for centuries?" asked Isabela.

"It did," sighed Aelish, remembering the helplessness. "We now know the bacterium infects fleas that live on small rodents. Black rats were the most commonly affected. The hungry fleas feast on the blood of the rat, ultimately killing their host. They then jump onto Humans looking to continue their blood meal."

"Rats really are disgusting," stated Isabela.

"Not always," said Aelish.

"What?" scoffed Isabela. "They are the worst vermin. They've carried diseases throughout the history of Humankind."

"Hmm," muttered Aelish. She was deciding whether now was the time to tell Isabela about the rats she came to know and respect. She decided later would be better.

"Yet rats had nothing to do with the bacterium eventually transforming into alternate forms of plague," continued Aelish. "People began to get infected by breathing in airborne droplets containing the bacterium from a sick person's cough. Once it started to spread through the air, the panic it caused was unprecedented."

"Oh, when it morphed into the pneumonic plague," Isabela said self-assuredly.

"Exactly," replied Aelish. "As new outbreaks occurred, the plague became known as the Black Death. Cities most seriously affected by outbreaks, such as London, became desperate. They empowered certain individuals to enforce new policies created to combat the contagion."

"Were they like the police?" asked Isabela.

"They were called Watchmen," said Aelish flatly,

remembering the despicable man in London and the gruesome plague pits. "I suppose you could call them the plague police. They didn't create the policies, but they were barbaric in the way they enforced them."

"Why, what did they do?" questioned Isabela.

"The authorities running the government of London decided that if one person in a family caught the disease, the entire family would be forced to stay inside their home. The Watchmen locked the families in from the *outside* so no one could leave an infected house. The policy's intent was to stop the spread of the infection. But by locking them in together, it ensured the death of the entire family," said Aelish, bitterly.

"Oh, my God, that is horrible!" exclaimed Isabela.

"It was, indeed. By the end of the 1500s, the Head Council, the citizens of DAR, and myself included, felt we had tragically failed the Human world, as the Black Death had killed over half of Europe's population. We watched helplessly, as entire families, villages, and cities were destroyed. Our magical powers were useless. It was one of the darkest times in DAR," stated Aelish.

"Didn't you tell me earlier that your parents died of plague?" asked Isabela. She turned around to look at Aelish, who was wiping away her tears with the back of her hands.

"I wipe my tears the same way you do," said Isabela.

"You do? I never seem to have a handkerchief when I need one," chuckled Aelish. "Yes, my parents died of plague one hour apart from each other. I was helpless to do anything about it." Aelish stepped away from the chair and sat cross-legged on Isabela's bed unable to stop her tears.

"Oh, my God, I'm so sorry," said Isabela. "I can't imagine having magical powers and *still* not being able to stop my mother's death."

Isabela got up from the chair and stood in front of Aelish. She put a comforting hand on her shoulder. Although time separated them by nearly five hundred years, Aelish knew she had forged a connection with Isabela through the loss of her parents and by the impending loss of Isabela's mother.

"Don't you see how powerful Humans are?" asked Aelish. "They *can* discover cures and remedies to stop diseases. Humans can end the heartache of helplessly watching their loved ones die."

"I'm Human and I've been helplessly watching my mother's illness for two years. What makes you think Humans are so gifted?" questioned Isabela.

Aelish stared into Isabela's beautiful brown eyes. Her overall coloring reminded her so much of Thagar.

"Because magical beings will never have the ability to develop cures for Human diseases. It is our greatest shortcoming and one we have searched the millennia to overcome. But Humans *do* have this amazing capability, if they would just harness it and cure!" exclaimed Aelish. "Not possessing this ability has brought DARlings to their knees, especially when a pandemic of plague threatened to destroy life on Earth."

"I understand what you are saying. I'm so sorry about your parents," said Isabela. She gently removed her hand from Aelish's shoulder, but Aelish grabbed it and pulled it against her chest.

"We believe you are one of these gifted Humans, Isabela. One that can stop the suffering and destruction of families brought about by incurable diseases," said Aelish, her green eyes trying to bore through the wall around Isabela.

Aelish hoped their moment of empathy might afford Isabela the opportunity to begin expressing her walled-up emotions. She knew Isabela had built this wall around herself to endure the likely death of her mother. But as her Oraculi, it was imperative Isabela let her in.

"Let's continue your hair," said Aelish. She stood up from the bed and gestured for Isabela to sit back down again. "Thank you for your kindness regarding my parents."

Isabela resumed her seat. "But how did the plague finally stop?"

"Ironically, the gruesome quarantine measures enforced by the Watchmen were effective in slowing the spread of the disease. And those who were not yet sick, began voluntarily quarantining themselves in their homes. The bodies of the dead were burned or buried in deep pits. People began boiling water. They sought out clean air by sitting between two burning fires. When they ventured outside they put an oil-soaked handkerchief against their nose and mouth. All these clean air measures were effective in containing the disease, once the bacterium became airborne," explained Aelish.

"And there weren't any medicines," sighed Isabela. "Antibiotics are the most effective way to combat a bacteria like the plague. But there were no antibiotics until 1928, when Alexander Fleming discovered penicillin. His discovery really is one of the greatest scientific achievements of the 20th century."

"You are correct, there were no medicines. Rudimentary methods were the only things available to the people. Wealthy people fled the cities, which were filthy. Black rats ran through the streets with abandon. The authorities needed to take action, so they hired plague doctors. Most had subpar education and training. Plague doctors were supposed to treat the rich and poor alike. But they didn't, and the desperation of the wealthy afforded them the opportunity to use the pandemic to line their pockets. To this day, I find how these doctors dressed to protect themselves from the plague, positively terrifying," said Aelish, shivering.

"Oh, right! They looked like a walking bird!" exclaimed Isabela. "I remember finding drawings of them during my research for my mother. I would have screamed if my mother's doctors dressed like this."

"I had one come to try and help my parents," stated Aelish.

"You did?" asked Isabela. She swiveled in her chair and stared at Aelish. "Was it terrifying?"

"Completely—and he was utterly useless," said Aelish. She bitterly recalled the ten shillings wasted on the ineptness of the plague doctor.

"Like my mother's doctors, useless," said Isabela.

"Perhaps her doctors are not useless, Isabela. The treatments prescribed may be the reason she is still alive, two years later. Almost as if her doctors are the placeholders for the scientists who will develop more effective measures," said Aelish.

"I'll believe it when I see it," said Isabela.

"I understand how unlikely you think that is, because even the plague still exists."

"It does?" exclaimed Isabela. "Why did I think it no longer existed?"

"I feel like this bacterium has a thought process," said Aelish, frustrated. "After it had exhausted itself in the crowded towns and cities like London, it made its way into the rural countryside and had a resurgence. The bacterium found new hosts, like ground squirrels and other small mammals, and again, it spread through blood-sucking fleas.

"Between 2000 and 2009, over twenty thousand people became infected with plague worldwide. That's approximately how many people died in London during the outbreak of plague in 1563 that killed my parents," said Aelish.

"Wait, I thought you lived in Ireland?" questioned Isabela.

"We took a trip there to celebrate my seventeenth birthday," said Aelish.

"Oh, my God, how awful," said Isabela. She got up out of her chair and embraced Aelish. Aelish nodded her head in gratitude, greatly comforted by Isabela's compassion. Once Isabela resumed her seat, Aelish continued.

"The twenty thousand who became infected with plague between 2000 and 2009, contracted it from rodents, bad camel meat, and sick herding dogs. The largest number of cases was in Africa, in the Congo and Madagascar. And fifty-six people in the United State were also infected, resulting in seven deaths," continued Aelish.

"That's just incredible," remarked Isabela. "I don't remember reading anything about that. I thought the plague was eradicated because of the vaccine developed by Waldemar Haffkine."

"By the time Haffkine developed the first plague vaccine," began Aelish, "the plague was no longer the threat it had once been in the world. The curative serum he first developed to fight bubonic plague was considered unreliable. He then moved toward a preventative vaccine, using dead bacteria. After first trying the vaccine on himself, he began testing it on Human subjects in British India in January of 1897. He created the preventative vaccine in record time and was able to contain an outbreak of bubonic plague in Bombay, India.

"The British authorities that controlled India during this time period, provided Haffkine with this opportunity because of his success in controlling an earlier outbreak of cholera. His preventative vaccine for cholera, which he also first tested on himself, was successful during the cholera pandemic of 1892 that swept across Asia and Europe. He saved millions of lives. Yet even after achieving all these life-saving accomplishments, his reputation was severely impugned."

"I remember reading that he was born in Odessa, Russia, with an entirely different name," said Isabela. "But I don't remember how his reputation became tarnished."

"He was born Vladimir Aronovich Khavkin on March 15,

1860, in Odessa, in the Russian Empire," stated Aelish. "But he left Russia because his religion was stymying his career. The Russian authorities discredited his work because he was an Orthodox Jew, who refused to convert to Orthodox Christianity."

"Why is religion always a problem?" asked Isabela.

"Because to use someone's faith or belief system against them, is an easy way to cause conflict and promote warmongering—history bears this out time and time again," answered Aelish. "As a bacteriologist, he decided to move to Paris in 1889 where he studied at the Pasteur Institute just like Alexandre Yersin. The Institute is named after Louis Pasteur, the renowned chemist and microbiologist. Pasteur is famous for—"

"Discovering that germs cause disease, pasteurization, microbial fermentation, and the principles of vaccination," said Isabela, finishing Aelish's sentence.

"Exactly. But why isn't Waldemar Haffkine better known? You'd think the scientist who created a vaccine for the bubonic plague would be a household name, right?" questioned Aelish.

"I don't know," said Isabela, baffled. "I knew of him because of my research, but I did not learn about Haffkine in school. I guess once his reputation was tarnished, history did not properly honor his legacy?"

"I agree," said Aelish. "Haffkine found himself embroiled in a scandal over his bubonic plague vaccine that lasted for more than five years. Scientists like Haffkine are very brave because in the blink of an eye, people seem to enjoy discrediting their discoveries."

"Did people die from his vaccine?" asked Isabela.

"You are very intuitive, Isabela. Nineteen people did die from the vaccine. But they died from *tetanus*, five years *after* his bubonic plague vaccine was administered," answered Aelish.

"What—*tetanus*? I had a tetanus shot after I cut myself on

a metal fence in L.A. But what does tetanus have to do with the bubonic plague?" asked Isabela.

"After the nineteen people died, it took five years for it to be discovered that the field worker who had administered Haffkine's bubonic plague vaccine, had accidentally contaminated the inoculations. It had nothing at all to do with the vaccine itself, but in the *handling* of the vaccine. Ultimately, Haffkine was found not responsible for the deaths, but can you imagine how he suffered during this scandal?" asked Aelish.

"Wow, you create a vaccine for bubonic plague, some technician contaminates the shots, and all your work is discredited—what a nightmare," sighed Isabela.

"But scientists like Haffkine forge ahead with a bravery that is boundless," smiled Aelish. "They continue with their research and discoveries, regardless of the fear or disdain they generate in the general population or amongst their colleagues. They are so respected and admired in DAR."

"I think I would have given up," said Isabela.

"I don't think you would have," countered Aelish. "After doing all that work, saving all those lives in both the cholera and bubonic plague epidemics, Isabela would have given up? I don't think so. I think your integrity would have propelled you to restore your reputation."

"That's probably true when you put it that way," laughed Isabela.

"There's a famous quote by Louis Pasteur that is revered in DAR," said Aelish. "It reads:

'Science knows no country, because knowledge belongs to Humanity, and is the torch which illuminates the world.'

The quote is etched in stone inside the building where the Head Council of DAR meets. It is so profound and demonstrates how greatly DAR respects Earthly scientists."

"Imagine if Louis Pasteur knew his quote about science was

etched in the magical world?" asked Isabela. "He'd never believe it."

"Right?" laughed Aelish. "It's pretty amazing. Two of the world's most famous virologists, in Human history, are also revered in DAR."

"They've got to be Jonas Salk, who developed the polio vaccine, and Edward Jenner who developed the smallpox vaccine," said Isabela. "My grandmother has a scar on her upper left shoulder from her smallpox vaccine."

Aelish smiled at Isabela's exceptional intelligence.

"You are correct," said Aelish. "Jonas Salk was so impressive. In the early 1950s, we observed in DAR, how he began testing a vaccine with killed poliovirus on volunteers who had never had polio. Some of the volunteers included himself, his wife, and his children."

"I would totally test out a new vaccine on myself, if I thought it could cure my mother," said Isabela.

"You may one day get that chance, Isabela."

"I find Edward Jenner brilliant," said Isabela. "Think about what an astounding achievement the smallpox vaccine was for the time period—1796—that's over one hundred years before the discovery of penicillin. And the Variola virus is horrible."

"I agree," said Aelish. "His discovery was not only one of the greatest scientific achievements in treating a deadly virus, but by creating the smallpox vaccine, he basically founded the field of immunology. The smallpox vaccine worked so well, that in 1972 the United States stopped vaccinating the general population because the last known case was in 1949—the disease was no longer considered a threat. The last known case *worldwide* was in Africa in 1977. Therefore, in 1980 the World Health Organization announced that smallpox was wiped out—the first and only time in history that an infectious disease was declared eliminated on the Earth."

"Imagine if we could say that one day about cancer . . ." said Isabela.

"But this history demonstrates why you must not give up hope, Isabela. Do you think anyone thought smallpox would one day be eradicated, while the infections were rampant?" asked Aelish.

"No, of course not," agreed Isabela.

"Right now, scientists are working tirelessly to find new ways to treat all types of cancers. Have you read about the groundbreaking research where scientists are utilizing some of the deadliest viruses in the history of Humankind to try and cure cancer? Wouldn't Jonas Salk or Edward Jenner like to be working on *that* if they were still alive?" asked Aelish.

"I did read about it in the library—it's incredibly radical. I don't know what the experimental treatments for my mother will include, but I wonder if they will be using this new research? I plan on asking her doctors as soon as I get the chance to meet them," said Isabela.

"Good for you, Isabela," smiled Aelish. "There's one last story about the Black Death that I want to share with you. To this day, the plague has killed over two hundred million people worldwide. But by the 1900s, it was no longer considered a grave threat to Humanity. Localized outbreaks still occurred, as I mentioned earlier, but not on the scale seen in the previous centuries. You can research high and low for an explanation, but you will not find one *definitive* reason as to how it became contained," said Aelish.

"What are you saying?" asked Isabela, who turned around to face her.

"I think it's time to tell you more about my journey to DAR," said Aelish, as she gently moved a strand of Isabela's hair away from her eyes.

17

LEAVING FOR DAR

AELISH STEPPED UP into the carriage and sat across from Lady Antonia, who had her back to Brólaigh Castle. Aelish stared at her ancestral home towering in the background. She took a moment to consider how much her world had changed since the three visitors had knocked on its doors only six years ago.

"Are you ready, dear?" asked Lady Antonia, rousing Aelish from her reverie.

"Yes, we can leave," smiled Aelish.

Lady Antonia instructed the driver to begin their journey. The driver was new to Brólaigh Castle, but the carriage was the same one she and her father had used on their trips to Dublin. It seemed fitting this particular carriage had not only picked up Lady Antonia in the village, but would also be taking Aelish toward her new life. She felt like her father was sitting right beside her. It was comforting.

Aelish waved a final goodbye to Declán. He returned the gesture with a melancholy look on his face. Declán waited until the carriage was barely visible, before venturing back inside the Castle. As she watched him vanish, she mentally said farewell to everything she had ever known. Brólaigh Castle, tall and imposing, took the longest to disappear from sight, making her departure more bearable.

"Declán seems like a lovely person. I assume he asked you to marry him?" asked Lady Antonia.

"He did," said Aelish, smiling at the memory.

"Any regrets?"

"None," stated Aelish.

"Then you are leaving with a clean slate—excellent."

They headed toward the first village in the direction of Dublin Port. The plan was, arrive at the port, board the ship destined for Cherbourg, France, and travel to the vineyard estate in Bordeaux. The journey was pure fiction, but Lady Antonia's family truly did own a vineyard estate in Bordeaux.

"We are so fortunate my aunt and uncle own a vineyard estate in Bordeaux," stated Lady Antonia. "It provides the perfect cover for our true destination."

"I don't know where else I would have instructed Declán to send letters and other important information for me," agreed Aelish.

"My aunt and uncle left England for France long before my father's abhorrent execution. I'm glad my aunt didn't witness it, nor the subsequent death of her sister," sighed Lady Antonia. "They are elderly now, so I try to visit them whenever I'm on a mission to Earth."

"When you first told them you were a magical being, how did they react?" asked Aelish.

"After the loss of my parents, I think they were grateful to have any extended family left," said Lady Antonia. "They were never able to have children of their own. They accepted me as a magical being, as kindly as my parents did. They are extremely giving people."

"We've both been fortunate to have families who accepted us for what we really are. My parents loved me unconditionally, until they died," sighed Aelish.

"Agreed. I often wonder if I would be so accepting if the roles were reversed," said Lady Antonia. "To this day, my aunt and uncle remain fascinated that I am a magical being. And I know they will take my secret to their graves, after what happened to my parents. Did I ever tell you how I inadvertently discovered a way for them to get word to me in DAR?"

"No, do tell!" chuckled Aelish.

"I discovered the method during a routine visit to the vineyard, not long after my parents died. I was taking a casual walk through the vines and saw a vineyard worker performing magic over the grapes," chuckled Lady Antonia.

"Oh, my goodness!" exclaimed Aelish. "What sort of magical being?"

"I instantly knew he was a Rain Sprite. I realized he *had* to be the sole reason for the success of the vineyard, year after year! As I approached him, I made sure my skin was its natural lavender color before introducing myself. He was thrilled to meet another magical being and told me his name was Murt. Once he realized though, that his secret was out, he grew a bit concerned I might not keep his confidence. But after I told him about my own experience of being a magical being in England, a country fond of burning witches, he knew I would not betray him. He was very appreciative, as he and his family loved their life at the vineyard. In fact, he felt so indebted he asked if there was anything he could do for me in return. Knowing I needed to devise a way for my aunt and uncle to send me messages whilst I was in DAR, I asked if he was able to summon a Sylph. Once he demonstrated that he could, I knew I had found a safe and secure way for my aunt and uncle to contact me in DAR," smiled Lady Antonia.

"What a fortunate circumstance. But how in the world did you tell your aunt and uncle to utilize Murt, without revealing he was a magical being?" asked Aelish.

"As I walked back to the house, I gave this considerable thought," said Lady Antonia. "As I got closer to the house though, I realized they would never question my judgment, and they didn't. I simply instructed them to locate Murt whenever they needed to send word to me. My now aged aunt and uncle still have no idea how the messages are conveyed, but they remain very satisfied with the method. Every time they summon Murt, they hear back from me within a short time. Murt and I have developed a caring friendship over these many years and he was only too happy to begin taking on that same responsibility for you," said Lady Antonia.

"I am so lucky to have you, Antonia," Aelish said sweetly.

"And me, you, dear," replied Lady Antonia.

As the carriage traversed, Aelish felt at peace with the sun on her face and the smells of Ireland all around her. After what felt like days, they finally reached the first village. They checked in at the local inn where they dined and slept overnight.

The following day the carriage took them to the next village en route to Dublin Port. Very few people from the village of Brólaigh Castle would know anyone in this village. Therefore, Lady Antonia chose it as the perfect place to secretly depart for the Portal to DAR.

Aelish advised the driver that they would be staying in this village for a few days to rest, before continuing on to the port. She instructed him to return to Brólaigh Castle. When he looked concerned, she informed him that they had hired a private carriage to conclude their journey. She requested he unload all their trunks and bags and install them in their room. When he was finished, Aelish bid him farewell, and felt a tear roll down her cheek. She watched her father's carriage disappear into the landscape for the last time.

While Aelish handled these arrangements, Lady Antonia instructed the innkeeper to send a message to Brólaigh Castle. It informed Déclan that they had arrived safely at the second village and would be resting here for a few days, before continuing on to the port. This way, in the event something unforeseen should happen to the driver on his return trip, Declán would at least know they had made it this far. It would also explain the early return of the driver.

Lady Antonia had calculated the exact amount of time it would take for their fictitious journey to France to be concluded, extra rest days included. She arranged for a Sylph to deliver a sealed note to Murt at the vineyard. Murt was then to send that same sealed note, on a precise date, by conventional Human methods to Declán. This enabled the timing to be realistic. The sealed note would inform Declán that Aelish had arrived safely in Bordeaux, France. Through strategic planning, utilizing both magical and Human delivery systems, their departure to DAR appeared like any other voyage from Dublin to France.

The following morning after a restful sleep, they began preparations for their departure to DAR. They sorted through all their trunks and bags. They selected only the items to be taken through the Portal and packed them into their handheld satchels. Lady Antonia then magically donated most of Aelish's possessions to the vestibule of the local church.

After finishing their noon meal, Lady Antonia told the innkeeper they were going for a walk. He bid them a good day and they began walking toward a wooded area. The village was very small and there were very few people about.

Once they were deep inside the forest, they magically summoned their handheld satchels, from the room at the inn, to the forest floor. They magically made the room neat and tidy—ready for the next guest. By the time someone checked on them, it would appear as if they had departed, not disappeared. Lady Antonia had also paid for their one night stay upon their arrival.

As they stood together in the forest holding their handheld satchels, Aelish heard the wind rustling through the canopy of trees above them. She looked up and hoped she would remember the beauty of Earth.

Will DAR be this lovely?

"Aelish, dear, I will be using the same Transporting spell I used when we left the house in London. We will simply arrive at our destination," said Lady Antonia.

"When are you going to teach me that spell?" Aelish asked laughing.

"It will most likely be the first spell you learn once you resume your magical education in DAR," answered Lady Antonia.

"Will you continue on as my teacher?" asked Aelish.

"I will always be your Oraculi and provide you with guidance and assistance. But I have already enrolled you at the Institutum de Magicae. There is no better place of learning in the entire magical world. I'm so excited to watch you soar," beamed Lady Antonia.

"Well you certainly did a great job keeping that a secret!" exclaimed Aelish. "When do I begin my classes?"

"Not long after you arrive, dear. I'm so excited for you, but first we have to get there," laughed Lady Antonia. "Now then, we are going to transport to the Earthly side of the Portal. The Portal is in between dimensions. Even standing near it can cause you to feel very odd, especially the first time. Do not be alarmed. You will regain your senses completely once we have passed through the Portal and arrive in DAR. Are you ready?"

"Yes, just one moment," said Aelish.

She bent down and gathered some dirt from the forest floor. She took a deep breath, inhaling its woody smell. She then let the dirt fall from her fingertips back onto the forest floor.

She stood up, wiped her hands on her dress, and said, "I'm ready."

‡‡‡‡

Aelish was disoriented for a moment, but the sound of rushing water made her look up. There was a beautiful waterfall in front of her that flowed down from a tall mountain.

"Oh, how lovely," she exclaimed.

"It isn't real," said Lady Antonia.

"What?" asked Aelish.

"It's an illusion. The waterfall is actually the Portal," stated Lady Antonia.

Aelish gasped. She watched Lady Antonia walk over to a tree to the right of the waterfall's pool. The trunk of the tree was enormous and there was a hole situated at eye level. Lady Antonia reached inside the hole. Aelish watched her pull up a metal lever on the inside, left wall of the hole. The sound of water stopped and in its place was a grayish blur and an enormous iron gate appeared where the waterfall pool had been.

"Make yourself lavender and follow my lead," instructed Lady Antonia.

Aelish watched her stick her face right in front of the hole for about two minutes, her chin nearly touching the bottom of the hole. A flash of light flickered only for a moment from inside the hole.

Lady Antonia turned to Aelish and said, "Your turn. Be sure not to move until after the light has flashed."

Aelish did as she was instructed and put her lavender face in the same position as Lady Antonia had. She did not move until the flash of light, which startled her.

"Come over to me now, Aelish," instructed Lady Antonia, who was standing in front of the iron gate.

Aelish walked over and stood with Lady Antonia.

"Why did we just do that?" asked Aelish.

"When I pulled the lever inside the hole, a bell rang on the DAR side of the Portal," explained Lady Antonia. "The bell alerts the Gatekeeper in DAR, that a being is waiting on the Earthly side. You must always be lavender when you put your face in front of the hole, so the Gatekeeper can capture your visage. While we are waiting here, he is putting our faces through his magical facial recognition test. Some have tried to trick the Gatekeeper by using magic to change their faces. So now our eyes are permanently imprinted with a secret code at birth, known only to the Gatekeepers. If the code in our eyes does not match the Gatekeeper's files, we cannot pass through the Portal. Once he has done the necessary verification, the doors of the iron gate will swing open."

"But I have never been here before," said Aelish, concerned. "How does he know what my face looks like and when was the secret code imprinted in *my* eyes? How could I be in his files?"

"I installed the code in your eyes during one of our lessons," smiled Lady Antonia. "I took care of all your necessary documentation some time ago."

Aelish inadvertently began rubbing her eyes. Suddenly, the iron gate began to loudly creak open and she forgot all about the secret code.

They took three steps forward and stood in front of the grayish blur that was vibrating. Aelish heard the iron gate slam shut loudly behind them. Her body began to feel very odd. She had strange sensations and felt a bit unstable.

"You must prepare yourself for what is going to happen next, Aelish," stated Lady Antonia. "As we pass through the Portal, be sure to keep your eyes closed. We will hold hands when we enter, as the first time is truly frightening. You will hear loud thunder and there will be bright lightning strikes. Be sure to keep your eyes closed and don't let go of my hand. The noise and lightning will only last a moment. When it is quiet again, you can reopen your eyes, as we will be on the DAR side of the Portal. Do you have any questions before we go through?"

"Yes," whispered Aelish, as she leaned closer to Lady Antonia. "How do we know there isn't a Human watching us do this right now?"

"Because the Gatekeeper has relocated the illusion of the waterfall. It is currently behind us, now, blocking all from view," explained Lady Antonia.

"But why don't I hear it like before?" asked Aelish.

"Because we are literally standing on the edge of the dimension that leads to the magical world. All Earthly sounds can no longer be heard. Listen—do you hear any familiar sounds?"

"No, I don't hear anything familiar," said Aelish, frightened. She was really leaving Earth.

"Don't be frightened, Aelish. I am right here with you, dear. Are you ready to see your new home?" asked Lady Antonia.

"Okay, let's go," said Aelish.

Aelish exhaled a deep breath that she didn't know she was holding. They took three more steps forward and Lady Antonia told her to close her eyes. Aelish stood to the left of Lady Antonia, tightly grasping her left hand. They each carried their satchels in the other hand.

"Close your eyes now, Aelish," calmed Lady Antonia.

Aelish felt like she had walked into her very own thunderstorm. It was deafening and she saw the flashes of lightning from behind her tightly closed eyelids. She was completely disoriented. If not for the grasp of Lady Antonia's hand, Aelish was certain she would have fallen down. And then—it was over.

"Open your eyes, dear," Lady Antonia said gently.

Aelish opened her eyes to a light mist. A short creature was walking toward her. When it was closer, Aelish realized it was a real-life troll, holding a slate tablet.

"Welcome to DAR," said the troll to Aelish. "Welcome back, Antonia. Did you have a smooth journey?"

"Yes, Tengstaad," replied Lady Antonia, with a smile. "Allow me to introduce Aelish."

The troll extended his gnarly hairy hand with nails that more resembled claws. Aelish wasn't sure if his nails were going to cut into the flesh of her hand, but her manners propelled her to extend her hand, regardless. The troll's leathery, hairy skin and shake were surprisingly gentle.

"It's a pleasure to meet you, Tengstaad," said Aelish.

"Ah! I love a first-timer," laughed Tengstaad. "Always so polite and still in a bit of shock from the Portal. This will be the thing I miss the most, when I retire from my post in a few weeks."

"Ah! Has the Head Council found your replacement, then?" asked Lady Antonia.

"It appears so," answered Tengstaad. "They have their sights set on two brothers from the Scottish Highlands—always a good breeding ground for quality trolls. I'm sure you'll have an opportunity to make their acquaintance, before the Head Council makes their final decision."

"Well, I'm happy for you, Tengstaad, but I will miss you even more," said Lady Antonia. She extended her arms toward the gnarly troll and embraced him in a hug.

"Are you ready to see your new home then, Aelish?" asked Tengstaad, with a warm smile.

"Yes," Aelish answered tentatively.

"You'll like it, don't worry," assured Tengstaad.

He made some final notes on the slate tablet and Aelish saw a low gate appear.

Had it been there all the time?

"All right, off you go, Aelish," said Tengstaad. The low gate swung open and the mist started to lift.

"It was a pleasure meeting you, Tengstaad. If we don't meet again, I wish you only happiness," said Aelish.

"Oh, she's quite the charmer," smiled Tengstaad.

"She's a delight," beamed Lady Antonia.

Aelish walked through the gate alone, as Lady Antonia shared some additional pleasantries and farewells with Tengstaad. As Aelish stepped further away from the gate, the mist completely cleared. A flicker of light caught her eye. She looked up at the bright blue, late afternoon sky. There, high on a mountain, was the most magnificent building she had ever seen. It seemed to sparkle in the sunlight.

"Beautiful, isn't it?" asked Lady Antonia, sneaking up behind her.

"It's absolutely gorgeous, what is it?" asked Aelish, her eyes glued to the structure.

"It is the Great Rotunda of Peace. That is where the Head Council meets and it is the most beautiful building in all of DAR," answered Lady Antonia. "We are so lucky to live in Bencarlta, the capital city of DAR."

"I'm going to be living in Bencarlta? In the S.E. Quadrant?" asked Aelish, astonished. She quickly tried to conceal her emotions.

"Yes, dear. And yes, this is where Thagar is stationed," whispered Lady Antonia.

Aelish gasped. She opened her mouth, but no words came out. Lady Antonia burst out laughing.

"How did you know?" asked Aelish, blushing orange through her lavender skin. "Does *he* know?"

"Well if he doesn't, I think we have the wrong DARling serving as Commander of the S.E. Quadrant," laughed Lady Antonia. She was thoroughly enjoying Aelish's embarrassment, her feelings for Thagar revealed.

"Oh, my . . . oh, my . . ." babbled Aelish, who also began laughing.

"Let's start flying before we hit air congestion, dear," said Lady Antonia. "DARlings will begin heading home shortly for their suppers." She picked up her satchel from the ground.

"What is *air congestion*?" asked Aelish, repeating these unfamiliar words.

"When too many beings are in the sky flying, at the same time," smiled Lady Antonia. "Be careful up there. Try not to fly into any."

Aelish's eyes opened wide. She stared at Lady Antonia, who began laughing again.

18

A New Home

"**W**ELL DONE, AELISH!" exclaimed Lady Antonia, landing on a beautiful country lane.

"Once I got used to all the beings flying with us, I realized it was an easier ride, much smoother than on Earth," stated Aelish, who landed right next to Lady Antonia.

"That's because the air is thinner in DAR. We are above the Earth, which is why Humans cannot live in DAR; they would be unable to breathe. Once you develop confidence, you will want to try aerobic flying, it's very relaxing. Come, let's walk down the lane and see your new home," beckoned Lady Antonia.

They proceeded down the lane, which had lush vegetation that obscured other cottages nearby. A lovely piece of land accompanied each dwelling.

"Well here it is, 5 Thackery Lane, your new home," gestured Lady Antonia, toward the most adorable cottage.

Aelish stood on the gravel road and stared at a wood-framed yellow cottage with a beautiful front porch. The wood trim of the glass windows was white, but the porch posts and railings were purple, orange, and forest green. There was a hanging wooden swing affixed to the porch ceiling, which was also white.

As Aelish walked up the three stone steps to the porch, she realized the front door was a striking turquoise color. It had an iron number five affixed right below three windows located on the top portion of the door.

"Before we go inside, let's sit on the swing for a minute," said Lady Antonia.

Aelish had never seen a bench swing before and sat down gingerly on it, as it moved backward with her weight.

"Whoa," laughed Aelish.

"The first time I sat on mine, I fell flat on my backside onto the porch floor," chuckled Lady Antonia.

They sat together in silence for a few minutes, enjoying the warmth of the late afternoon. They gently glided the swing back and forth.

"I'm very proud of you, Aelish. The transition to DAR can be difficult. I want you to know that I am always here for you. If you get frustrated, confused, or basically want to leave DAR—you must seek me out immediately. Don't let things fester."

"I understand," said Aelish.

"Now, let's see if they've completed the work on the inside of the cottage. Do you like the colors I chose for the outside?"

"Very much, thank you. It's very cheerful."

Lady Antonia opened the front door and held it open for Aelish to enter first. Aelish walked inside and stood in the front entryway looking at the main salon. It was surprisingly large and airy. Her shoes resounded on the floors, which drew Aelish's eyes downward. She noted they were wooden! They were the color of fine furniture and the planks were five inches wide. Aelish had never seen anything like it.

"This is like walking on the dining table in Brólaigh Castle. They are positively spotless. Should I take my shoes off?" asked Aelish.

"If it would make you feel more comfortable. Let's sit on the entry bench and leave our shoes here," instructed Lady Antonia.

Once they had removed their shoes, Aelish was the first to stand up and exclaim, "The floors are not cold! Oh, what a luxury not to have to wear shoes inside the house for warmth!"

"It truly is. The temperature doesn't fluctuate very much in Bencarlta. In this Quadrant of DAR, we do not have the traditional four seasons you are used to. Other than the rainy season, which occurs at the same time spring does on Earth, the sky is always blue with those wispy, feathery clouds we rarely ever saw," laughed Lady Antonia. "You will get used to the weather here in about two days, positively lovely."

As Aelish walked further into the cottage, she noticed a long oak table for preparing food and a stone fireplace that resembled the one in the kitchen area of Brólaigh Castle. Against one wall was a mechanism she had never seen before—a long iron handle with a spigot attached to it. The spigot was positioned above a basin. The basin was attached to a countertop, on either side of the basin.

"What is this?" asked Aelish. She ran her hand inside the white basin, which was made of a very hard substance.

"Lift up the handle and see," suggested Lady Antonia.

As water began to empty into the basin area, Aelish gasped.

"It's water! *Inside* the house?" exclaimed Aelish.

"We live better in DAR than King Henry ever did in his castle," chuckled Lady Antonia. "DAR is quite advanced for 1564. Running water—inside a house!"

"Oh, my goodness, it's absolutely remarkable," declared Aelish.

"The Rain Sprites in DAR figured out how to collect the rain water into a well. They created a series of pipes from the well and developed a pump that pushes the water into our dwellings," explained Lady Antonia. "You can wash up right inside the cottage. And wait until you see the bathing room."

"Show me!"

Lady Antonia took Aelish through a hallway that led to a large room with a white and black marble floor. Once inside, Aelish saw the most beautiful, brass, bathing tub. It was literally fit for a King. The bathing tub also had a long iron handle with a spigot.

Aelish lifted the iron handle and watched the bathing tub fill with water.

"This is incredible," remarked Aelish.

While the water continued to fill the tub, she ran over to an additional iron handle with a smaller spigot. This spigot was placed over a smaller basin with a shorter counter, similar to the one in the kitchen. She lifted the iron handle and watched the spigot empty water into the basin.

"Oh, my goodness," exclaimed Aelish. Lady Antonia was smiling at her.

Aelish was suddenly startled by an image she was unfamiliar with, over the smaller basin. She turned around and looked behind her for the source of the image. Finding none, she turned back around and stared into the mirror.

"What is this?" questioned Aelish.

"It is called a mirror," answered Lady Antonia. "You were startled by your own reflection."

Aelish leaned forward toward the mirror and gasped, seeing her face clearly for the first time in her life.

"Oh, my! Is this what I look like?" she asked, incredulous.

"Yes, dear. Amazing, isn't it—and all without magic. DARlings are extremely inventive and they use magic to assist them, but first one has to have the *idea*, yes?"

"Can you imagine if these were on Earth? I don't think Humans would do anything except stare at themselves all day," laughed Aelish, still staring into the mirror.

"I have to admit, I stared into mine for about two days," confessed Lady Antonia. "As if all of this wasn't enough, DARling artisans are working on creating a new contraption to make *hot* water come out of the spigots. I feel it is unnecessary, since heating the water is easy enough to do with magic, but they are having fun working on their invention. When I think back to life in England, we were lucky to bathe every other month. Now we can bathe every *day* if we want. Oh! And take a look at this."

Lady Antonia walked Aelish over to a stone seat with a hole in it.

"Is that what I think it is?" asked Aelish. They both peered down the hole.

"It is. You simply press this handle, here, and water flushes the waste into a water source and it never smells, ever. There's fresh water in it anytime the *need* arises," laughed Lady Antonia.

"Now that, is truly magical," Aelish said laughing.

"Agreed! Come, let's see your bedchamber."

They walked through a second door located inside the bathing room to enter Aelish's bedchamber. At first Aelish was confused, but then she realized the bathing room was attached *to* the bedchamber. The bathing room had two doors; one that led to her bedchamber and one that led into the hallway.

As she entered her bedchamber she began to cry. Covering an entire wall was the most beautiful mural of Brólaigh Castle. The rendering was so accurate, for a moment she felt like she was back in Ireland.

"Antonia, how did you ever get this done for me?" asked Aelish. She walked over to embrace her Oraculi.

"Art is extremely valued in DAR. You will see this when you walk through Bencarlta. Sculptures, paintings, carvings, and murals are everywhere. I used my Earth Capsule Viewer and showed Brólaigh Castle to the artist, who is the most famous artist in DAR. I showed it to him only once. It took him less than two months to complete. I'm so pleased you like it, Aelish."

"I love it. Thank you, Antonia," said Aelish, wiping her tears.

Aelish turned around and saw the four-poster bed. It had sumptuous white bedding with so many pillows it was impossible to count them. Aelish moved the willowy white sheaths of fabric aside, which hung on the iron frame. She jumped onto the bed and stared at the mural.

"I get to wake up and look at home every day—what a wonderful surprise, Antonia." Aelish nestled into the bed and began to disappear amongst the luxurious bedding. "I fear I will never get up in the morning, sleeping in this grandeur."

"Come back into the salon; there's a being I want you to meet," said Lady Antonia, mysteriously, as she left the bedchamber.

"What? Who is here? Wait! Wait for me!" cried Aelish, as she struggled to get out of the deep feather mattress and all of its bedding.

She found Lady Antonia sitting on a lovely settee in the main salon. There were two chairs across from the settee covered in cheerful fabrics. Aelish plopped into one of them and put her feet up on the small ottoman at the base of the chair. A low wooden table was between the chairs and the settee.

"Drummond!" bellowed Lady Antonia. "Please come out now and meet Aelish!"

Aelish heard the clomping of short legs coming closer. She turned toward the kitchen and saw a real-life Brownie. He was quite muscular and looked like a tiny male Human. He had a wrinkled face and was mostly bald. Thatches of short, brown, curly hair covered the back of his head, along with tufts around his pointed ears. His face was covered with a thick, brown beard. He was dressed mostly in dark green and brown garb. The length of his pants ended right below his knees, his shirt had cap sleeves leaving his arms predominantly bare, and he held a conical hat in one hand. He dramatically bowed in front of Aelish, his conical hat just grazing the floor. He stood back up, his big eyes staring at Aelish, and he wore a big grin.

"Drummond is the reason your house is so clean and tidy," stated Lady Antonia.

"Oh," said Aelish, looking back and forth between Lady Antonia and Drummond.

"Drummond and his sister Drusilda cared for the home of a family in England. When they began to treat them unkindly, my dear Oraculi, Melanthia, suggested they accompany me to DAR. In 1537, when I left England for Earth, Melanthia escorted Drummond, Drusilda, and I through the Portal. Drummond and Drusilda have truly helped me make a home here. I can't believe it's already been twenty-seven years," said Lady Antonia, smiling at Drummond.

"But I don't want you to lose this precious being, Antonia," said Aelish, concerned.

"It's jolly good to be here, Aelish. I've lived with my sister for over one hundred years—time for a change, aye?" said Drummond. Aelish noted he was a comical character.

"Oh, I see," said Aelish. Drummond winked at her acknowledgment of his situation with his sister. "Well, I'm delighted, then, to have the company, as long as you're happy."

"I am indeed, Aelish. And may I say, ya' are as lovely as Antonia described," said Drummond, rather flirty. "Ya' won't see much of me, except at suppertime, unless ya' need me of course. I do most of me chores at night, while yer sleeping."

"But where is your room?" asked Aelish, more of Lady Antonia, than Drummond.

"Drummond lives beneath the house, where he is quite comfortable," explained Lady Antonia. "He has his own magical dwelling with all the necessary comforts. He will assist you with cooking, cleaning, and tending the garden," said Lady Antonia. "Did you see the garden, Aelish?"

"No. I was distracted by the bathing room and forgot to step outside."

"Ya' can see it through the window over the basin in the kitchen area," said Drummond. "Or ya' can go out the back door which leads to the garden. I've started ya' a lovely vegetable patch." He gestured for Aelish to follow him.

They walked over to the kitchen window that looked out over the garden. Drummond climbed onto the counter, next to the basin, to show Aelish all of his work. Besides the vegetable garden, there was also a lush flower garden, with species of flowers Aelish had never seen before. She noticed the vegetable garden had an enormous shade tree located above it.

"There's a family of Wee Folk that live in that tree, so be careful not to fly into it," cautioned Drummond.

"Oh, thank you for letting me know. The garden is lovely, Drummond, thank you," Aelish said sincerely.

"Come outside anytime when I'm working. I love the company," said Drummond.

"Magical beings such as Drummond need to work," stated Lady Antonia. "Tending to a house or cottage is where a Brownie finds their purpose, as long as the owners of that dwelling treat them kindly. I knew he was becoming unhappy at my cottage living with Drusilda. I think this is the perfect solution for everyone."

"I'm mighty grateful to ya', Antonia," said Drummond. He once again deeply bowed, his conical hat in his hand.

"Of course," nodded Lady Antonia. "I assume you have already prepared us a lovely supper?"

"I have, indeed. Let me know when yer ready to feast, and I'll serve ya'," replied Drummond.

Aelish was thrilled to have assistance in learning about the household methods in DAR. She knew Lady Antonia had other responsibilities and could not be here every day. It was comforting to have Drummond's company.

"You probably should resume your preparations then, Drummond," instructed Lady Antonia. "I will summon you when we are ready to eat, and thank you."

"As ya' wish," bowed Drummond. He headed toward the kitchen area, departing under the house, as quickly as he had appeared.

"Your head must be spinning, Aelish," stated Lady Antonia, "but we need to discuss tomorrow's plans."

"What are we doing tomorrow?" Aelish asked with anticipation.

"I will return in the morning to accompany you on a tour of Bencarlta," said Lady Antonia. "If we step out onto the porch, we can probably see the lights of the Great Rotunda, now that night is falling."

Outside, Aelish looked up and saw the Rotunda high on a mountaintop. From the vantage of her front porch, she realized her cottage and nearby dwellings were situated in a valley on the outskirts of the capital. She leaned against the porch rail and stared at the sparkling lights of the Rotunda that got brighter, as dusk turned into nightfall.

"I'm so pleased your cottage faces the lights of the city, Aelish. I knew you would love it," smiled Lady Antonia. "Let's sit on the swing and relax for a bit, before we dine together."

"That sounds wonderful," said Aelish. "Thank you for everything, Antonia."

"Of course, dear."

They sat together in silence, as they moved the swing back and forth. Aelish breathed in a deep sigh of relief. She was finally in DAR.

19

BENCARLTA

AELISH OPENED HER eyes and saw the beautiful mural of Brólaigh Castle. She couldn't believe this was her first morning in DAR. It all seemed surreal. She hadn't slept that peacefully since her parents had died. She felt hopeful and eager to start the day.

What is that delicious smell?

She pushed aside the covers and stepped onto the warm wooden floors in her bedchamber. She pattered into the bathing room and began to wash for the upcoming day with Lady Antonia.

Running water—inside the cottage—unbelievable! Ma would have loved this.

She was soothed by the sound of the fresh water running from the spigot and the soapy splashes of water falling from her face and hands into the basin.

What a way to start each day.

After she dressed, she walked into the main salon. Drummond had cleaned up the mess from the previous evening's meal and the house was gleaming. There on the kitchen table was the reason for the sumptuous smell in the cottage—fresh baked biscuits smothered in butter and jam, along with a steaming pot of tea.

Oh, how delightful!

She knew Drummond was asleep under the cottage. She tried out a spell Lady Antonia had taught her at Brólaigh Castle and conjured a large, floating, translucent scroll. Her finger worked as a quill, as she wrote a heartfelt thank you note to Drummond in pink. It floated in the air near one of the kitchen walls, so he couldn't miss it.

"Yoo-hoo! Aelish, dear—are you awake?"

Aelish ran to the front door and opened it. Lady Antonia was dressed in a lovely frock. Aelish realized she needed to go shopping for some new ensembles.

"Good morning, Antonia," said Aelish. She kissed Lady Antonia first on her right cheek and then on her left cheek.

"How did you sleep, dear?" asked Lady Antonia. She stepped inside the cottage entryway. "Oh, I know *that* smell!"

"Look at what Drummond has made for us," said Aelish, leading Lady Antonia to the kitchen table.

"Those are his famous biscuits and he makes the butter without magic. Shall we nibble before we set off for Bencarlta?" asked Lady Antonia, who had already taken a bite out of a biscuit, not waiting for Aelish to answer.

"Good God, these are delicious," said Aelish, uncouthly, speaking with her mouth full of biscuit. "Mmm, so good."

"And he did a wonderful job tidying the house last night. He's a very hard worker," said Lady Antonia, as she poured herself some hot tea.

"How are the biscuits still hot?" asked Aelish.

"Magic, of course," laughed Lady Antonia, who was also talking with a mouth full of biscuit.

Lady Antonia spotted the floating thank you note. "Nice

touch, Aelish. He will really appreciate that."

"Do you think? I hope so. Dinner was delicious and I haven't slept that well in ages. And now this heavenly breakfast—I want to let him know how much I appreciate him."

"That's pretty much all a Brownie needs, recognition and kindness," said Lady Antonia. "I thought we could start our tour of Bencarlta today at the Great Rotunda of Peace."

"That sounds perfect. Let me wash my hands and get my shoes on," said Aelish.

As Aelish tidied up the breakfast, she spotted Lady Antonia wrapping some of the biscuits up in a cloth and stuffing it into her dress pocket.

"In case we get hungry," laughed Lady Antonia, caught.

As they exited the cottage, Aelish paused after closing the front door.

"Do I lock the door with a key, magic, or leave it open?"

"No one ever locks their doors. But if you feel more comfortable, use the Fasten spell. It will lock all the doors and windows."

"But what if Drummond needs to go out back to tend the garden and the back door is locked?" considered Aelish. "I will leave the cottage open."

"There is nothing here that cannot be replaced with magic. I really wouldn't worry about it," reassured Lady Antonia.

"It's nearly incomprehensible to fathom that DARlings don't need to steal," said Aelish, shaking her head. "We always worried about robbers back home. My father kept the doors of Brólaigh Castle locked and bolted at all times."

"This is merely the beginning of many new concepts you will become accustomed to in DAR. Before you know it, you will feel like you have always lived here. Shall we ascend?" asked Lady Antonia. She began lifting into the air.

"Let's go," said Aelish, as she lifted upward.

As they flew up out of the valley, Aelish observed the variety of homes situated beneath the Rotunda mountaintop.

"Why do some DARlings have larger homes than others?" asked Aelish.

"In DAR, you are given what you need. If you have a large family with lots of little DARlings, you receive a much larger house. The Head Council is very generous with its citizens."

"And we don't need money to buy *anything*?" asked Aelish. She was trying very hard to wrap her head around this concept.

"Each DARling is encouraged to work at what they love or are magically gifted to do. For example, the artist who did the mural in your bedchamber, he has amazing artistic abilities. He designs art installations throughout the commonwealth. We will see one of his most famous works inside the Rotunda. His work is manifested through his magical abilities, but his artistic visions come from within," explained Lady Antonia.

"Are there shopkeepers here? I was thinking of getting some new frocks. But I can't imagine going into a shop and not needing money to pay the dressmaker," said Aelish.

"The tailor or dressmaker is gifted and expresses him or herself through their designs. The materials they utilize are all created through magic. Each month we have demonstrations of their new designs. The shows are such fun and the ensembles have never been seen before—complete originals. When you go into their shops, they design something especially for you. That is their contribution to the commonwealth—making us all look fabulous," laughed Lady Antonia.

"They create the fabric, thread, buttons, hats, etcetera, all through magic?" asked Aelish.

"Exactly. Their magical gifts allow them to produce all that is needed to design the most beautiful, and sometimes, outrageous ensembles. We pride ourselves in being the best dressed beings in the magical world," stated Lady Antonia.

"What about food?" asked Aelish. "DARlings still need to grow crops and catch fish, correct?"

"Do you remember at Brólaigh Castle when Melanthia showed you and your family her true olive green skin color?" asked Lady Antonia.

"Of course. I thought my father was going to collapse onto the floor," replied Aelish.

"Melanthia's family is from the S.W. Quadrant of DAR where all of the agricultural needs of DAR are located. Our food is actually grown in the soil and is not created through magic. However, those who farm in DAR have amazing magical abilities used to: prepare and fertilize the soil; control the proper amount of rain needed; manage the sunlight necessary to nurture the crops; and have bountiful harvests. Farming is what DARlings from the S.W. Quadrant excel at and we are blessed with an abundance of food," explained Lady Antonia.

"So there are no droughts or bad harvests in DAR?" asked Aelish.

"Precisely."

"How different life on Earth would be without food shortages," noted Aelish.

"Truer words were never spoken, Aelish. You see, although DARlings are predominantly Humanoid in appearance, the most distinctive characteristic that differentiates us from one another, is the color of our skin—as you are well aware," laughed Lady Antonia.

Aelish rolled her eyes. "How could I ever forget?"

"The different skin color of DARlings is created by how the sunlight rebounds off the land in each of the four quadrants of DAR. For example, Melanthia's skin color is olive green, reflecting the generations of farmers in her family. The land is so green and fertile that not only does her skin color emulate this attribute, she occasionally sprouts seedlings on her skin!" exclaimed Lady Antonia.

"Like the eyes that grow out of a potato?" Aelish asked astonished.

"Exactly! Each month, she removes the seedlings that grow on her skin and sends them to her family to be replanted," explained Lady Antonia.

"That's amazing! I think if she had shown my parents her seedlings, my father would have perished right then," chuckled Aelish. "Has there ever been a famine in DAR, like on Earth?" asked Aelish.

"Thousands of years ago, one of the other magical realms destroyed all the crops grown in the S.W. Quadrant by using the fire of dragons. The famine it caused was an act of war, similar to the way famine is intentionally caused on Earth—to weaken or destroy the people of another country. To intentionally starve a Human or magical being, in my opinion, is an act so heinous, so savage, that it evokes feelings of revenge and retaliation. I'm not proud of my reaction, but it is so depraved, I can't help but feel this way," stated Lady Antonia.

"I remember England using famine against Ireland when I was very young. There is nothing more cruel or abhorrent than a child dying of starvation," agreed Aelish.

They flew along in silence, both disquieted by the recollection of famine used as a weapon.

Breaking the silence of their unpleasant memories, Aelish asked, "Why are so many DARlings a beautiful blue color? And they seem to have small fins on their backs."

"Very observant, Aelish!" exclaimed Lady Antonia. "You've only been here a day and you've already noticed this?"

"I did," smiled Aelish.

"A DARling with blue skin color is derived from how the sunlight reflects off the ocean, located in the N.E. Quadrant. Our best fishing is done in these waters. The families from this area of DAR have lived amongst marine life for so long, they've actually appropriated some of the same traits. Many have fins, gulls, and the ability to breathe underwater. DARlings from the N.E. Quadrant are very peaceful. We think it's because they have been imbued with the calm rhythm of the ocean's tides," explained Lady Antonia.

"Oh, my goodness. To be able to breathe underwater!" exclaimed Aelish.

"Many can, indeed," said Lady Antonia. "In the N.W. Quadrant, where the sun is the least strong, DARlings most resemble the porcelain color of our skin, before it turned lavender. The N.W. Quadrant has a gray and dismal climate—very similar to the weather in England.

"Interestingly, all the beings in the magical Kingdom of Yasteron have English and Irish porcelain skin color. Yasteron borders the N.W. Quadrant across the sea from DAR. They are Humanoid in appearance, with one exception—they *all* have blonde hair. They do not couple with magical beings from any other realm, as they feel it would change the purity of their makeup, both physically and magically. They want to keep their hereditary lines pure—similar to the way Humans of noble birth only marry other nobles, whereas DAR is completely the opposite.

"Depending on the type of magical creature a DARling couples with—be it a Selkie, a Troll, or the Alfar—mixed beings are created. Some DARlings subsequently have pointed ears like Drummond, or excessive hair on their bodies, or even a tail! The genealogy of a DARling's heritage results in many varieties of DARlings."

"Why is Thagar's skin color bronzed?" asked Aelish.

Lady Antonia flashed a knowing smile. "Ah! Here in the S.E. Quadrant, the sun is the strongest in DAR. The command center of the military is located in the S.E. Quadrant. Therefore, since most military operations are still practiced outdoors, this results in military families having bronzed, brown, reddish, or black colored skin. Black is the most revered skin color in DAR, as it reflects the centuries these families have devoted to serving and protecting the commonwealth. Black skin color is akin to bravery, courage, and the willingness to make the ultimate sacrifice."

Has Thagar lost family members?

"Ah! Look Aelish! We are entering the main part of the city—be prepared to land in a minute," said Lady Antonia.

Aelish looked down at Bencarlta. She had never seen such a beautiful place—not in books, paintings, or in real life. The Great Rotunda of Peace sat on the highest peak of the mountaintop, accompanied by three additional buildings. The structures were all made of marble or limestone and had Grecian pillars astride their front entrances. Above the entrances were words carved into the structures that reflected the principles and beliefs of DAR.

"Oh, my goodness, the entire city sparkles. Is it because the streets and structures are marble and limestone?" asked Aelish. "Or is it from magic?"

"During the daylight hours, the sun thoroughly drenches the buildings and streets. This enables Bencarlta to continue sparkling, throughout the night, without magic," remarked Lady Antonia. "It's just a magnificent city."

"I realize what Bencarlta resembles—I remember it from my lessons with Miss O'Boyle—Ancient Greece, yes?" asked Aelish.

"You are correct," smiled Lady Antonia. "When Ancient Greece was built, DARling architects and builders visited Earth to observe it firsthand. Upon their return, they convinced the

Head Council to redevelop Bencarlta to mirror the beauty of what they had seen. Ancient Greece was renowned for its architecture and marble structures. Many buildings, such as the Acropolis, remain standing to this day, thousands of years later."

"It's just stunning," Aelish said in awe.

They landed a few blocks away from the Rotunda and Aelish realized they were in the shopping district of the city. Blocks and blocks of gorgeous marble and limestone shops lined the marble streets. Each shop had a distinctive name. The name was either carved into the edifice or hanging from a colorful banner, identifying what could be obtained inside. Aelish had never seen such an assortment of shops—not in Dublin nor in London. There were chocolatiers, apothecaries, sweet shops of every kind, haberdasheries, dress shops for ball gowns, dress shops for daytime frocks, and *magic* shops! Aelish headed toward one of the magic shops, but Lady Antonia steered her away.

"You'll be ready for the advanced level of magic these shops have to offer, only *after* you have completed your education at the Institutum de Magicae. If you venture inside at this point, you will only get yourself into a heap of trouble," laughed Lady Antonia. "Come, let's walk to the Rotunda."

When they reached the Rotunda, Aelish could not believe the sheer size of the structure. The dome at the top was so high, she felt it must touch the stars at night. She stood in front of the great wooden doors and was transfixed by an engraving directly above the entrance doors. It read:

Those Who Choose Not To Accept And Respect
The Differences Of Others
Doom Us All To A Life Without Dignity

"Who wrote that?" asked Aelish. She turned to see Lady Antonia smiling at her.

"It is from the Doctrine of DAR," replied Lady Antonia, "and was collectively written by the Head Council, many years ago. It represents everything we believe in. The engraved precept contains the words that DAR's acronym represents: Dignity, Acceptance, and Respect. Each time I come here, I always make a point of reading it."

"It's absolutely profound," said Aelish.

As Aelish began walking closer to the enormous wooden front doors, they slowly began to open. Six soldiers on each side of the double doors emerged in full military dress. They gazed straight ahead, as they marched in step, alongside the entrance to the Rotunda. Aelish examined the soldiers, noticing at least half were female. She searched their clothing for weapons, but found none.

She walked over to Lady Antonia and whispered, "They don't have any weapons or forms of protection."

"Oh, but they do," smiled Lady Antonia. "They have the instantaneous ability to restrain or destroy any being that seeks to cause harm to the Rotunda. Their offensive magical abilities are unparalleled in the commonwealth, which is why they were chosen to be the Guards of the Rotunda. Whilst there has never been a direct attack on the structure, the Guards are nevertheless, always at the ready. These soldiers would give their lives for DAR in the blink of an eye. They are also protecting the Rotunda through information being sent to them telepathically from the POD."

"The POD—what is that?" asked Aelish.

"The POD is the building to the left of the Great Rotunda, just there," said Lady Antonia, pointing down the marble street.

Aelish followed the direction of her finger to a magnificent building with nearly one hundred marble steps leading up to a landing supported by too many Grecian columns to count. Aelish knew the building had been replicated from the Parthenon.

"POD stands for the Protection of DAR. It is where the military defense of DAR is located," explained Lady Antonia.

"Incredible," remarked Aelish. She began walking toward the POD and noticed two additional buildings down the street. "What are those other two buildings?"

"The one to the left of the POD is the Breanon. It is where all doctrines, spells, and documents, pertinent to the commonwealth of DAR are kept. Imagine all of the books in your lesson room at Brólaigh Castle and multiply them times one billion. Melanthia is one of the few DARlings who has read nearly everything in the Breanon, other than the Keepers, of course," said Lady Antonia, with pride for her Oraculi. "I think the knowledge she obtained in the Breanon made her an exceptional Oraculi and now, an exceptional Head Council Member."

"Who are the Keepers?" asked Aelish.

"The Keepers are DARlings who devote their lives to archiving the history and spells of DAR. There are secrets and magical spells inside the Breanon that other magical realms would kill for—literally. The Keepers are academic masters of magic. As I explained earlier, their particular magical gifts propel them to serve DAR in this manner. It is what they were born to do," explained Lady Antonia.

"Can any being go inside the Breanon?" asked Aelish.

"Certain areas are open day and night for DARlings to access information. But other areas require a very high level of POD clearance, magical attainment, or position, such as those who serve on the Head Council. You will be exposed to the public areas during your magical education at the Institutum de Magicae, which is the building to the left of the Breanon."

"*That* is where I will have my lessons?" asked Aelish.

"Yes. In fact, your orientation begins next week," Lady Antonia said brightly.

"Oh, my goodness. I can't believe I start next week at the Institutum . . . what is the name again?" asked Aelish.

"The Institutum de Magicae, which is of course Latin, but we all simply call it the Institute," stated Lady Antonia. "I'm so excited to see where you will excel in your magical abilities. All right then, shall we go inside the Rotunda?"

"Absolutely," said Aelish. She followed Lady Antonia to the entrance, as the soldiers remained at attention with that same steady gaze.

"Don't bother speaking to them. You can't distract them from their duties," advised Lady Antonia. "And I can see by the mischievous look on your face that you want to bait them into breaking their gaze. Trust me, you won't be able to."

Aelish started laughing as Lady Antonia wrapped an arm around her shoulder. They respectfully walked past the soldiers and entered the Rotunda. It was as if a force were pulling Aelish's head upward. She stared at the marble ceiling. It was covered with artistic renderings of legendary DARlings and magical creatures. She had never seen artwork like this before. The marble was carved and somehow colored, as if it were a painting.

"Many depicted have served on the Head Council," whispered Lady Antonia. "The magical creatures portrayed represent DAR's commitment to inclusion. These beings did not originate in DAR, but are graciously welcomed. Beautiful, isn't it?"

"I could come here every day and not tire of looking at this," said Aelish. Her neck was back and she spun in a circle examining all the carvings. On the walls she noticed more precepts, some in English, others in Latin. Along one of the walls, she saw something astonishing. She walked over to it and just stared.

"It is simply called, Humanity," stated Lady Antonia. "The artist who did your mural created this."

Before them was an enormous sculpture of a female DARling,

sitting on a block of marble. She was unclothed, cradling the Earth in her arms, with one side of her face against the orb. Her long hair hung loosely around the Earth. Her eyes were tightly closed, as she protected the orb from DAR's enemies, depicted in a circular pattern around her. One in particular caught Aelish's attention. It was a huge creature whose upper half was a king cobra and whose lower half was the body of a rat.

"There are no words to describe the emotions this artwork evokes within me, but *that* creature terrifies me," said Aelish.

"That is King Gidius. He is the King of Komprathia," stated Lady Antonia. "The Kingdom is made up of those who are half king cobra and half rat, and others who are entirely rat."

"Rat? Like rats on Earth?" asked Aelish.

"Exactly," answered Lady Antonia. "The rats are referred to as drone rats. Despite the Komprathians being half rat, they treat the drone rats as slaves. The drone rats can speak, think, and reason, but their magical abilities are stunted, as they are not permitted an education. They live in fear every day of being summoned by the rulers of Komprathia, who readily sacrifice them in magical experimentation of new spells, but most often, when testing out new magical warcraft.

"Before our modern warcraft was created, bodies of dead drone rats were always on the battlefield. Komprathia used them as scouts and imbued them with deadly warcraft. Our soldiers had to kill them, as the drone rats were often armed with magical explosions and had killed too many of our soldiers.

"The drone rats are used subversively to serve the desires of King Gidius. He created the atrocious policies toward the drone rats, hundreds of years ago. Their oppression has lasted so long they are incapable of freeing themselves. To witness their enslavement evokes sympathy," said Lady Antonia.

"No way," blurted out Aelish, "rats are disgusting. I couldn't possibly picture them in a sympathetic light."

"DAR teaches us many things, Aelish," stated Lady Antonia. "Always keep your mind open and try not to prejudge, based on your Earthly upbringing. You are going to learn so many new things."

Aelish could not rid herself of the unpleasant taste in her mouth from the Gidius rendering.

"Do you see what's behind the Humanity sculpture?" asked Lady Antonia.

"The Doctrine of DAR," Aelish read aloud. "Are these the rules of DAR?"

"The Doctrine represents the belief system of DAR—our tenets and principles of what dignity, acceptance, and respect, truly mean. You will study the Doctrine, in depth, at the Institute. It is an amazing document and something the Earth would surely benefit from following," stated Lady Antonia.

"Where is the enormous dome?" asked Aelish.

"Come," instructed Lady Antonia. She led Aelish away from the Humanity sculpture toward two more enormous wooden doors on the wall opposite the Rotunda entrance.

Aelish assumed Lady Antonia would need magic to open doors of this enormity, when they slowly began to open on their own. Soldiers emerged in the same formation, as the front entrance doors.

"Are we allowed to go inside?" whispered Aelish.

"Come, dear," beckoned Lady Antonia.

As they entered the Chamber, Aelish looked up at the marble dome towering above her. The sheer magnitude and height of the dome left her speechless, her mouth agape. Hand-carved historical scenes covered the dome. The scenes depicted legendary figures, many with black skin. She assumed they had most likely given their lives for DAR. The renderings were extraordinarily high, yet the craftsmanship of the carvings was so fine; it felt like the figures were alive.

The dome soared above countless circular rows of marble benches. She had never seen inclined seating like this, except in her schoolbooks. Her schoolbooks had included drawings of the amphitheater in the Plaka of Ancient Greece and the Coliseum in Rome. But the Rotunda was different. Circular walls surrounded the numerous rows of marble benches, but unlike the ancient theaters, which were open to the sky, the dome protected the attendees.

Down below at the forefront, was a raised U-shaped dais with magnificent hand-carved wooden chairs. Aelish instantly knew those chairs were reserved for the Head Council of DAR.

"Amazing, isn't it? The U-shaped dais is called The Arc of Leadership and is, of course, where the Head Council sits. Let's relax for a moment on one of the benches," suggested Lady Antonia.

They selected one of the upper rows and sat in silence together, as Aelish looked at everything around them.

"Antonia, this is incredible. Is it grander than King Henry VIII's throne?" asked Aelish.

"Beyond grander," answered Lady Antonia. "Had he seen something like this, he would have bankrupted all of England to build it."

"May I go down toward the dais?" asked Aelish. " I want to see what the dome looks like from there."

"Go ahead, but do not walk upon the dais. The Rotunda Guards and the soldiers in the POD are watching us. It is a sign of disrespect to be upon the dais unless you are a member of the Head Council," answered Lady Antonia.

"How are they watching us from the POD?" whispered Aelish.

"Inside the POD," explained Lady Antonia, "there is a command center about the size of this Chamber that allows those in charge of the protection of DAR, to observe the entire commonwealth. They have active spells that allow them to see inside structures, such as the Rotunda, or outside areas that border other magical realms. I have seen it only once, during my military training, but I will never forget the level of magical attainment necessary to be in control of such an observatory. As Commander of the S.E. Quadrant, Thagar is responsible for the command center."

Aelish felt her stomach flutter, as her mind wandered to Thagar. She had not grasped that Lady Antonia had said she'd received military training.

"You will be shown it as well, during *your* military training," said Lady Antonia.

Aelish snapped out of her daydream and exclaimed, "My *military* training? I'm going to train as a *soldier*?"

"Yes, dear," said Lady Antonia. "All DARlings are required to spend at least two years in the POD and many discover they have a magical affinity for defense. The training is both magically and physically rigorous."

"When do I begin that?" asked Aelish, growing anxious. She never imagined herself a soldier!

"The years of military training are interwoven with your studies at the Institute. As your magical education is expanded through lessons at the Institute, the POD further enhances your education in ways you could never imagine. It's a brilliant method of instruction," stated Lady Antonia.

"I can't believe I'm going to have military training," said Aelish, shaking her head.

"DAR will open your world in ways you never dreamed possible, Aelish," smiled Lady Antonia. "All right then, go and explore."

Aelish walked down the aisle that separated the row where

Lady Antonia remained, from the row across the aisle. She noticed that the flooring had some sort of covering—like a fabric—as she could not hear her footfall. It was so unique. She assumed the fabric on the aisles prevented unnecessary noise from disrupting Head Council meetings. As she descended, she continued to observe the dome getting higher. By the time she reached the bottom, she looked up and could still make out the figures depicted in the dome, but not as keenly.

Aelish faced the dais, which was quite imposing. She felt like she should curtsy in reverence. She wondered if she would ever serve on the Head Council. How she wanted to share this experience with her mother and father. Her father had loved architecture and would never have believed something like this could have been constructed.

She turned and looked back up toward the top rows. She saw the Rotunda Guards standing against the wall on either side of the now closed doors, sealing the Chamber. They continued to stare straight ahead and were so quiet; she'd forgotten they were inside. She located Lady Antonia, who had become quite small, due the distance that now separated them. She began walking back up the inclined aisle to resume sitting with her.

"Did you enjoy it?" asked Lady Antonia.

"There really are no words to describe it," said Aelish. She was out of breath from the climb back up to the bench. "Standing before the dais is extremely intimidating. I felt like I should curtsy."

Lady Antonia threw her head back laughing.

"It does inspire respect for the Head Council, but a full bow or curtsy is absolutely *forbidden* in DAR—too monarchical," explained Lady Antonia. "After all the curtsying I had to do at Court, I'm thrilled it is not allowed in DAR, where it is *actually* deserved."

"Can females serve on the Head Council?" asked Aelish.

"Oh, I'd need to start at the beginning to answer that question," said Lady Antonia, patting the marble bench for Aelish to resume her seat.

20

THE RISING

"THE CONCEPT OF a magical world like DAR was created by the original females that inhabited this dominion a long, long time ago," began Lady Antonia. "Their magical skills and enlightenment had always been superior to their male counterparts. In fact, the females' magical abilities were superior to any other magical being, throughout the entire magical world. And they were certainly *not* sources of evil, as Earthly women of magic have historically been depicted.

"Despite their extraordinary magical aptitude, the original females, unfortunately, chose to follow the Earthly model of power and leadership. They ceded ruling capabilities to their male counterparts. In all other areas, females served equally alongside males, but only *male* DARlings could serve on the Head Council or be Chair," said Lady Antonia.

"Really?" remarked Aelish.

Lady Antonia nodded. "When the horrific outbreak of plague occurred on Earth, in the 1300s, killing millions of people, Earthly women who practiced the white magic of healing were blamed for the pandemic. As the outbreaks continued, these women were hunted and burned. Female DARlings began to take notice. Thus, began the Rising.

"What is the Rising?" asked Aelish.

"For centuries, prior to the outbreak of plague in the 1300s, there had been a movement stirring in DAR. Females wanted to take back the power the original females had ceded. Male DARlings had always been in positions of leadership and DAR was endlessly embroiled in war. To quell the Rising, the all-male Head Council considered they might need to be more open to the option of having females serve alongside them. But they miscalculated the level of support that existed for the females."

"How?" asked Aelish.

"I arrived in DAR in 1537. Two weeks after my arrival, Melanthia arranged for me to provide testimony before the Head Council, about King Henry VIII's Court. It went on for months— there wasn't an empty seat in this Chamber—standing room only," gestured Lady Antonia with a sweep of her arm.

"Weren't you frightened to speak before the Head Council? And weren't you only sixteen years old?" asked Aelish.

"Yes. I had just turned sixteen," nodded Lady Antonia. "At first, I was terrified. But I was brimming with rage over my father's beheading and my mother's subsequent, premature death. Once I found my voice, I realized all that I'd been suppressing. The words came out like a purge.

"I described in great detail the brutality of King Henry's Court. Keep in mind, Henry ruled England for another ten years after my arrival in DAR, until his death in 1547. I told the Head Council everything I had witnessed—especially his mistreatment of women—be they Henry's wives or the women he burned for witchcraft. I discussed the consequences of male primogeniture and how King Henry changed the religious belief system of an entire country in his pursuit of a male heir. The patriarchal society of England was only one example of Kingdoms throughout Earth that behaved similarly. I think the beheading of Anne Boleyn affected the males on the Head Council more than anything."

"Why?" asked Aelish.

"I don't know the exact reason—maybe the sheer brutality? I think they felt guilty," said Lady Antonia. "The all-male Head Council was arrogant and presumed their leadership was greatly superior to Earthly Kings. They viewed themselves as more evolved. But after listening to my testimony about the savagery of King Henry and his persecution of women accused of practicing magic—it was an affront to the magical abilities of the females in DAR," said Lady Antonia. "Beheadings for practicing magic? This resonated with the Head Council and gave them pause."

Aelish looked up at the dome. "What happened after you finished testifying?"

"A few months after my testimony concluded, the Head Council decided they needed to put a referendum before the citizens of DAR. It was time to ask the citizens if females should be afforded the opportunity to serve alongside males on the Head Council. What they never anticipated were the protests and demonstrations in Bencarlta regarding the *language* of the referendum," said Lady Antonia.

"What do you mean?" asked Aelish.

"Females involved in the Rising were joined by other female and male citizens. Demonstrations in the streets were raging and grew to unprecedented levels. Those protesting wanted the language of the referendum to be changed to ask the citizens whether *only* females should comprise the Head Council," said Lady Antonia.

Aelish gasped. "Oh my! What a deep-seated change that would be."

"Somewhat like having a Queen, instead of a King?" asked Lady Antonia. "Worded in this manner, the Head Council knew the referendum would not pass and they could put the entire issue and their guilty feelings to rest. And when it came time for the citizens to vote, the Head Council did just that—the Referendum of 1538 was worded:

Do you believe only female DARlings should serve on the Head Council of DAR?"

"I can't believe they changed the wording," said Aelish.

"They did, indeed. But their gamble backfired," said Lady Antonia.

"How?" asked Aelish.

"Because the referendum passed!" laughed Lady Antonia.

"Good God!" exclaimed Aelish.

"It not only passed, it was overwhelmingly supported by a huge majority of both male and female citizens. The result exemplified how entrenched male privilege had become in DAR. The Head Council could not fathom how it had passed and demanded a recount. Some went so far as to accuse the DARlings who tallied the vote, of sorcery and manipulating the count," said Lady Antonia.

"Oh, how awful," said Aelish. "What a dark time for DAR."

"Very dark. The Head Council had been certain the referendum would fail. They gambled on the language, wanting to put an end to the debate, once and for all. The males never *truly* wanted to relinquish their power. The passage of the referendum reflected how out of touch the Head Council had become with its own citizens.

"The populace had grown weary of the endless warfare

that accompanied patriarchal leadership in both the Human and magical worlds. The citizens decided to put their faith in the extraordinary magical abilities of the females and convert to a matriarchal society," stated Lady Antonia. "Out of the darkness, came the light—it was truly incredible."

"Did you get blamed for the change in leadership?" asked Aelish.

"Oh, yes. I have indeed been held responsible for what happened. It's been twenty-six years since the Referendum of 1538 passed, and certain males removed from the Head Council, to this day, blame me for instigating the matriarchal change. I believe my testimony about the brutality and insanity of King Henry VIII's Court, vividly demonstrated the dangers of a patriarchal society. When King Henry had his fifth wife, Catherine Howard, beheaded on February 13, 1542, those involved in the Rising felt vindicated. For me, the change in leadership was a redemption for my parents' deaths—they no longer died in vain."

"And now Queen Elizabeth I rules England!" exclaimed Aelish. "DAR ended up being first in handing power over to females."

"The irony of King Henry boggles the mind," said Lady Antonia, shaking her head. "After all the atrocities during his reign, by his own hand, through his last will and testament, he enabled his daughters to sit on the throne. And in his heart, he died a Catholic. He never fully embraced the tenets of the Church of England, which he created. The entire change of religion began so Henry could annul his first marriage, in order to secure the perpetuity of a male heir—but it was not to be."

"I think one day the pendulum will swing back toward the middle and both males and females will serve together on the Head Council," stated Aelish. "What do you think?"

"I think you are already showing an affinity for policy and leadership," declared Lady Antonia.

"Which females were chosen to serve on the Head Council after this revolution?" asked Aelish.

"Many came from the Rising, but several Keepers from the Breanon also joined the Head Council," said Lady Antonia. "Their knowledge and magical abilities changed DAR forever."

"How?" asked Aelish.

"Since the change in leadership, DAR has become a peaceful, prosperous place. It was the extraordinary vision of the new female Head Council that allowed this to happen."

"Why? What did they do?" asked Aelish.

"The new females on the Head Council decided to finally harness all the *evil* magic that had been studied for centuries," stated Lady Antonia.

"Good God!" cried Aelish, who heard her own voice echo off the dome.

"Their strategy was so clever," said Lady Antonia. "The Breanon contained all the knowledge necessary to create the most heinous, evil magic. But it had never been produced. The female Keepers, who chose to serve on the new Head Council, possessed the knowledge and decided to venture to the N.W. Quadrant to create it. The N.W. Quadrant is where new and potentially dangerous spells are experimented with, as it is the furthest Quadrant from Bencarlta.

"The evil magic has the power to destroy the entire magical world as well as the Earth. The original females that inhabited what is now called DAR were always committed to peace and the protection of Humanity. The newly appointed females of the Head Council decided to honor that legacy by entrusting themselves and DAR with the most evil of magic. They deduced that if they could produce and control this horrific magic, it would act as a deterrent to all other magical kingdoms—and it worked.

"What a risk," remarked Aelish.

"Truly. They were unbelievably brave. With the exception of Komprathia, the wars have ceased—no sensible magical world wishes to risk annihilation. Subsequent to this heroic and dangerous strategy, DAR began to put into practice the inclusionary belief system written in the Doctrine that had been long forgotten. Beings from throughout the magical world journeyed to DAR. Those who came wanted to live in peace. They wanted to follow the philosophies of the original females and live in the only matriarchal magical dominion. And DAR welcomed them with open arms," smiled Lady Antonia.

"Oh, that's why there are so many varieties of DARlings," said Aelish.

"Exactly," replied Lady Antonia.

"But why hasn't the strategy worked with the Kingdom of Komprathia?" asked Aelish.

"Because King Gidius is insane," stated Lady Antonia. "His desire to destroy DAR and Humanity outweighs his fear of Komprathia being annihilated. His subjects suffer because of his madness and his misogyny. He is of the opinion that weak females now rule DAR—especially since the Head Council initiated a mandate that all citizens must take the Oath of Peace."

"The Oath of Peace," repeated Aelish.

"You will take the Oath in about six months," smiled Lady Antonia.

"But how does one reason or deal with this type of enemy?" asked Aelish.

"You thank God for the steadfast magical ingenuity of our most revered military strategist, Bathwick. She is now Director of the POD. Before becoming Director, she served as Commander of the S.E. Quadrant when the Head Council was all male. They hold her in the highest regard. The newly formed, all-female Head Council promoted her.

"As Commander of the S.E. Quadrant, Bathwick established a magical perimeter on the border between DAR and Komprathia. Through the use of innovative spells, she devised amazing magical warcraft, such as the invisibility wall, on the border," stated Lady Antonia.

"An invisibility wall?" asked Aelish.

"It's incredible. The invisibility wall magically projects images of vast battalions of DARling soldiers in battle. Additionally, her renowned magical sound waves create the illusion of false locations of battle, including the sounds of bombs and fierce magical explosions. The invisibility wall has been impenetrable to date, and diverts Komprathia away from DAR. The DARling soldiers are entirely an illusion. She has saved so many lives. DAR allows Komprathia to waste their resources, day in and day out, as King Gidius refuses to stand down and live responsibly. He will never stop warring with DAR, as long as he thinks he can destroy us. Through Bathwick's brilliant magical diversions and deflections, she maintains DAR's Oath of Peace, while at the same time, keeping the Komprathians off our border.

"There had been other magical warcraft methods used in the past, but Gidius and his military tacticians penetrated them. Thus, we now have multiple magical strategies working in concert. You will learn all about them during your training at the POD.

"Suffice it to say, Komprathia thinks they are winning battles when in actuality there are *no battles* being waged in DAR. The command center in the POD is in constant control of the warcraft spells. Additionally, there are *actual* battalions of soldiers spread throughout all four Quadrants of DAR, in the event the invisibility wall ever failed, which is highly unlikely," smiled Lady Antonia. "She is perhaps the most brilliant Commander in the history of DAR."

"Bathwick sounds extraordinary." Aelish sat there absorbing

all the information from the day, as she stared at the legendary figures on the dome.

Would I be willing to give my life for DAR?

"I fear I have given you too much information," said Lady Antonia. "Shall we go shopping and get you some new frocks?"

Aelish immediately came out of her introspection. "Yes, please!"

21

THE RIDDLE BOXES

"**WAIT! HOLD ON!**"
"Shh, we don't want to wake your family, Isabela,"
cautioned Aelish.

"What do you *mean* DAR created enough evil magic to destroy the Earth?" asked Isabela. "What if DAR is taken over by Komprathia and they obtain the evil magic and use it against us, here on Earth?"

"You need to let me finish the story for you to better understand how unlikely that is. Further, it has already been almost five hundred years since it was created, and all is well, Isabela," calmed Aelish. "Do you worry about the weapons of mass destruction that have been created by Humans? There are enough weapons to destroy the Earth and subsequently DAR, one hundred times over, and you live with that knowledge every day. You're just not used to the idea."

"Hmm, I suppose that's true. I feel the use of science for destructive means is an affront—all this knowledge, so we can destroy ourselves? It's ridiculous," stated Isabela. "How is the evil magic controlled and who controls it?"

"Only fifteen DARlings know the location of the evil magic.

Five reside in the N.W. Quadrant, five serve on the Head Council, and five are Keepers in the Breanon."

"How complicated is it to release the evil magic? Is it similar to the steps the United States has to go through to discharge nuclear weapons?" asked Isabela.

"Far more complicated and many more steps are involved."

"Do *you* feel safe in DAR knowing such powerful evil magic exists?"

"Completely," answered Aelish, "because DAR controls it."

"Okay," sighed Isabela. "There's just so much danger on Earth. When I think about it, I get very upset. Considering that the magical world could now destroy us too, is terrifying."

"That's a natural reaction, Isabela. But once you better understand DAR, and its commitment to Humanity, your fears will be allayed."

"I understand," said Isabela. "But it's going to take me a little time to get used to the idea."

"Let me tell you about the Riddle Boxes," said Aelish.

"The Riddle Boxes?" asked Isabela. "What are those?"

"When we become citizens of DAR and are ready to take the Oath of Peace, that is the one and only time we are shown the Riddle Boxes. There are three Riddle Boxes—one for each letter of DAR. The boxes contain the magical knowledge of DAR, with the exception of the evil magic," explained Aelish. The guardians of the Riddle Boxes are called Shepherds—as they *shepherd* the boxes to different locations, every hour."

"Every hour?" asked Isabela.

"Yes. There are many safeguards in place for the Riddle Boxes, as many magical kingdoms would destroy DAR to possess them. The three small boxes contain all the magic in DAR, comparable to the volumes of information found in the Breanon. It is similar to how music is digitally stored on Earth—instead of having thousands of vinyl records, you can store thousands of songs on one device. The Riddle Boxes is the same concept—they are like the digital version of all the magical information contained in the Breanon."

"You are familiar with the devices we use here on Earth?" asked Isabela.

"Oh, yes, DARlings have playlists in their heads."

"What? Tell me!" exclaimed Isabela.

"We have an entire entertainment center in our brains that, for lack of a better word, is installed, once we become citizens of DAR. We have playlists of songs, movies, books, video games, television shows, and we can share any of the items stored with other DARlings, telepathically. It's really fun. We access it through a variety of different spells."

"Can *I* hear it?" asked Isabela.

"Sure, if I put it on a speaker setting—listen." Aelish put her hand against the right side of her head and a piano concerto by Mozart suddenly filled Isabela's room.

"Oh, my God," smiled Isabela.

"New and dangerous spells are created in the N.W. Quadrant, but it is also where music is composed. DARlings, who devote their lives to the ever-expanding repertoire of spells, find music very relaxing during the arduous task of experimentation. But to be honest, we all prefer the music created on Earth. Our favorite is hip-hop and rap because the cadence is most similar to spell recitation. We are aware the lyrics sometimes can be offensive and misogynistic, however, DARlings understand the struggle. Classical is the second most favorite. I'm sure you would find it hilarious to witness DARlings creating new spells with the music of Tupac Shakur or Biggie Smalls, loudly playing throughout the N.W. Quadrant," laughed Aelish.

"You've got to be kidding me!" laughed Isabela. "No way!"

Aelish began quietly rapping and dancing all around Isabela's bedroom. Isabela fell off her chair in hysterical laughter.

"I'm pretty good, right?" asked Aelish.

Knowing the song, Isabela joined in and they began rapping together. Isabela dropped to the floor and began spinning on her back. She flipped upward and then back to the floor and finished in a freeze position.

"That's amazing!" exclaimed Aelish, clapping. "When I get back to DAR I am going to work on that—what is it called?"

"Breakdancing," said Isabela. She came out of her freeze pose and stood up out of breath. "I learned how to do it in L.A. It's starting to make a comeback."

"I can't wait to work on my breakdancing and show it off at our next gala."

"There are galas in DAR?" asked Isabela.

"We have festivals to celebrate things every day and there are galas with specific themes every month. Some are masquerade balls, and others are held just to see who can design the most original ball gown—they are so much fun. Life is good in DAR. We have a lot of fun," answered Aelish.

They both sat down on the edge of the bed, catching their breath.

"Oh! I almost forgot—how do the Riddle Boxes open?" asked Isabela.

"First, all three boxes must be in the same room. Second, there are twenty-five steps to open each box. But—only the Shepherds know which initial of DAR starts the sequence.

"For example, you may be able to magically answer the riddles the box is programmed to ask you. But if you select the first letter in the wrong sequence, you have to start all over. The D, the A, and the R, are constantly rearranged and sometimes they are repeated. It's never only three initials—sometimes the D is repeated twenty times.

"As for the twenty-five steps, not only are you asked riddles, you have to magically manipulate the boxes, turning them in different directions, in order for them to unlock. The Shepherds are the only DARlings that are apprised of the sequential combinations, which as I said before, change every hour. And don't forget, the boxes are also relocated and separated from each other every hour. The magic is very safe," explained Aelish.

"Why can't you capture, imprison, and torture the Shepherds, in to disclosing the combinations?" asked Isabela.

"Because no one knows *who* they are."

"But don't you see who the Shepherds are when they present the boxes?"

"No. When the Shepherds present the boxes, they are completely covered. They wear hooded cloaks. The only exposed part of their cloak is the narrow mesh netting over their eyes. The three Shepherds are the same height and weight and you can't tell if they are male or female. They look identical. It is a secret society and no one knows how many DARlings serve as Shepherds. Further, even the Head Council and Chair could not tell you who is a Shepherd."

"I find this very dangerous. What if a Shepherd turns evil and aligns themselves with a magical world who wants to destroy DAR or the Earth?" asked Isabela.

"They would need, at the least, two other Shepherds to work in concert with them—because everything is sequential, even the Shepherds. The combination and sequence depends on which Shepherd is handling which specific initial of DAR. Therefore, even if a Shepherd were to turn against DAR, they would need the cooperation of two very specific Shepherds, in the correct sequence, and before the sequence changes, in the next hour.

"It still sounds risky to me," said Isabela.

"I will leave you with this—there are many in DAR that feel the boxes are actually empty," smiled Aelish.

"What!" exclaimed Isabela. "Then where is all the magic stored, if not in the Riddle Boxes?"

"The Riddle Box conspiracy theorists feel that the magic is stored inside the brains of specific DARlings, and that the Riddle Boxes are nothing more than a ruse."

Isabela rubbed her chin with her hand.

"You are now thinking, calculating, and plotting how to solve this mystery, which is exactly the purpose of the Riddle Boxes. They keep magical beings guessing, off-balance, and unsure, which in turn keeps the magic of DAR secure."

"Whew! This is exhausting to think about, let alone to solve," laughed Isabela.

"Precisely," smiled Aelish. "Now, can you imagine how many precautions are in place for the *evil* magic?"

"Okay, I get it," agreed Isabela.

Aelish could see Isabela was no longer worried about the evil magic and was relaxed again.

"I would like to tell you about a very special place in DAR—it is called the Sanctuary. I discovered something there that changed the course of my life," said Aelish.

22

The Sanctuary

Aelish had been in DAR for six months. She was greatly enjoying her classes at the Institute, she had already begun training at the POD, and last week she had taken the Oath of Peace. It was an amazing ceremony and the Riddle Boxes presented by the Shepherds, sparkled like everything else in DAR.

She was acclimating to her new life and surroundings, but she had a nagging sense of loneliness. She couldn't clearly identify where the loneliness emanated from—was it her parents, Brólaigh Castle, her life on Earth? She knew she would always miss her parents, but she loved her cottage in DAR, and her new life was full of purpose. Between her educational studies and her military training, she couldn't grasp why she had a constant pit in her stomach. Most days she just ignored it and moved about her day, but at night when she lay in bed, the loneliness was most profound.

One evening, she returned to her cottage and Drummond had the front door open. She smelled the delicious meal he was preparing, as she began climbing the steps to the porch. When she looked up, she saw him standing in the doorway with his right arm fully extended. In his hand was a sealed note.

"I don't like sealed notes," he said to Aelish. "Please open it and let me know if all is well. It was dropped off early this afternoon, but I didn't want to bother ya' during yer classes. The Sylph that delivered it didn't appear agitated or upset, but I worry nonetheless."

"Hmm . . . Antonia usually sends word to me telepathically, so it most likely is not from her. Let me just open it," said Aelish.

"I will be preparing the meal if ya' need me," stated Drummond. He walked back toward the kitchen area.

Aelish dropped her flypack on the porch and sat on the swing to read the note. The front of the note simply had her name and the seal was navy blue. She broke the seal and unfolded the single sheet of paper. It read:

Dear Aelish,

I know you've been very busy adjusting to your new life in DAR. I hope your studies at the Institute are going well. I know from my staff within the POD that you have been enjoying your military training and are demonstrating a magical aptitude for defense. I wanted to congratulate you on taking the Oath of Peace and hoped to celebrate this milestone by taking you someplace extraordinary.

Please let me know if you will be free one week from tomorrow, as I would like to show you a very special place in DAR. If this sounds agreeable, I suggest you obtain a suitable ensemble at the Broadmoor Shop in Bencarlta, as our destination is a bit rugged. Tell them you will be going to the Sanctuary in the S.E. Quadrant and they will provide you with the proper accoutrements.

Please send your reply to my attention at the POD and I hope this will be amenable to you.

Warmest regards,

Thagar

And just like that—the pit in her stomach was replaced with eager anticipation. Her arm dropped to her lap, her hand still grasping the note, and she stared at the sparkling Rotunda enveloped by the dusk.

"Drummond!" she called out. "Can you please bring me my best stationary, quill, and ink?"

She could hear the clomping of his heavy shoes running throughout the house and within minutes he was on the porch in front of the swing breathless. In his hands, were all the materials she'd requested. He even remembered to include a writing tablet for her to lean on. She could, of course, magically send her reply, but she decided to mirror Thagar's proper decorum by responding with a handwritten note.

"Is everything all right?" asked Drummond. "I confess to having the collywobbles in me stomach."

"All is well, Drummond, set your mind at ease. I may be having a male caller next week," replied Aelish, blushing. "He is offering to take me to a place called the Sanctuary—are you familiar with it?"

"I'm positively chuffed for ya'!" exclaimed Drummond. "Ah! The Sanctuary—haven't ya' been yet?"

"No, I haven't. What is the Sanctuary?" asked Aelish.

"I'll not spoil it by describing it to ya', but all I can say is—ya' sure haven't seen any place like *this* before!" laughed Drummond. He handed Aelish her writing materials. "I'll leave ya' to it, then—holler if you need anything else. I'm going to finish preparing the meal."

Aelish started laughing as she watched him skip back inside. She situated the writing materials on top of the tablet, which she placed on her lap. She began composing her response.

Dear Thagar,

How lovely to hear from you. I am delighted to accept your

invitation and accompany you to the Sanctuary one week from tomorrow. I will do as you advise and seek the proper accoutrements at the Broadmoor Shop in Bencarlta.

I am looking forward to the day and hope this note finds you in good health and spirits.

Best wishes,

Aelish

She addressed the note to Commander Thagar at the POD and sealed it with her personal "A" waxy seal. She summoned a Sylph who arrived almost immediately. She took the note from Aelish, batted her eyes three times, and Aelish could have sworn the Sylph wore a knowing smile! But she was gone too fast for Aelish to confirm it. She headed into the cottage with her writing materials and flypack, very happy.

‡‡‡‡

A week later, which felt more like a month, Aelish was up before the sun and began to get ready for her day at the Sanctuary. She went to her wardrobe and pulled out the items from the Broadmoor Shop. The shopkeeper told her very little about the Sanctuary, as like Drummond, he too said, "I don't want to ruin the surprise for you."

She began dressing, layering all the items of clothing, including *pants*, which she had never worn in her life. They were very tight on her legs and were made out of a slippery, yet warm fabric. She had a long sweater to wear over them and heavy boots that laced up to her knees. She had a warm hat that went over her ears and an odd coat, which was quite long, ending right above her ankles. The coat was made of a similar fabric as the pants. It had lines of thread, dividing sections of the coat that were stuffed like a pastry with a substance that provided additional warmth.

She put the whole ensemble on and began profusely sweating wondering where in the magical world was Thagar taking her?

She immediately began taking everything off and threw the garments onto the bed. Aelish kept on the pants, the boots, and the fitted, long-sleeved shirt, which was also made of the same fabric as the pants.

Whew, that was hot!

She fiddled with her hair and decided on a practical fishtail braid. She gathered everything up from the bed and threw it all on the bench in the front entryway.

"Yer probably wondering what ya' will be needin' all that for," laughed Drummond, as he wiped flour off his face. "Ya' will see, soon enough. Come, let me show ya' what I've prepared for ya' to take."

Drummond had packed up a veritable feast for the day, but it also included some of the oddest items she had ever seen on a kitchen table. There were glowworms, fireflies, and other small insects flying about in a glass jar. In another pouch were nuts, hay, and oats. And another pouch contained raw meat! She stared at Drummond who threw his head back laughing, his conical hat falling to the floor.

"What *is* all of this?" asked Aelish. She also began laughing because Drummond's laughter was infectious.

"I thought yer male caller might be hungry for a hearty breakfast," teased Drummond. Aelish cocked her head to one side, pursed her lips, and lifted an eyebrow.

"You are very naughty this morning," chuckled Aelish. Their jocularity was interrupted by two firm knocks on the front door.

"Go, go! I will pack it all up," said Drummond. He motioned for her to answer the door with his eyes. "I've also made ya' a proper breakfast and lunch for two."

"Thank you, Drummond," smiled Aelish. She headed toward the front door.

Before opening the door, she took a deep breath and realized the clothes she had left on were too tight and revealing, completely improper. She grabbed the long sweater, threw it over her head, and pulled out her fishtail braid. She looked back toward the kitchen area and saw Drummond staring at her. He nodded, trying to give her the confidence to open the door.

The early morning sun bathed Thagar's bronzed face. Slivers of sunlight peeked through his black curly hair, which framed his face—its length, ended at the base of his neck. He was as tall and fit as she remembered. Besides his hair being longer, he had also grown a beard since she'd last seen him. His attire was the same as hers. On his back was a flypack and in his hands was a beautiful gold, medium-sized box with a glittering gold bow.

"Hello, Aelish."

"Good morning, Thagar."

"I brought you a little housewarming gift."

"How thoughtful, won't you come in?"

Once inside, Aelish noticed how Thagar's tall, muscular frame dwarfed the cottage. It somehow seemed smaller than a minute ago. Thagar spotted the clothing scattered on the bench in the hallway and chuckled.

"A bit warm for the S.E. Quadrant. I should have told you to shrink it all into your flypack."

"Come, let's sit on the settee," suggested Aelish. "May I open my gift?"

"Of course. Your cottage is lovely, though a bit smaller, I think, than what you are accustomed to?" teased Thagar.

"I actually prefer it and find it very comfortable," she replied, smiling. They sat down side-by-side on the settee.

"This is to commemorate your recent Oath ceremony. I hope you like it," said Thagar. He handed the gold box to Aelish.

She eagerly tore off the bow and opened the lid of the gold

box. Inside were three handcrafted replicas of the Riddle Boxes.

"These are absolutely stunning," said Aelish. She took one out of the box and examined it. The Riddle Box replica was made of a rich mahogany and had a blonder inlaid wood carved in a checkered pattern. In the front was an "A" recessed into the wood made of abalone stone. The abalone shimmered, making the "A" more pronounced.

"It's abalone, yes?" asked Aelish. She ran her finger over the "A" for a moment.

"Abalone has always been one of my favorite stones and it is said to having a calming effect," said Thagar.

A calming effect! My heart feels like it's going to pop out of my chest.

She took out the remaining two replicas and organized them on the table in front of the settee, until they spelled D-A-R.

"Ohh," she whispered.

"Do you like them?" asked Thagar.

"Very much. The Oath ceremony was one of the most memorable days of my life and now each time I look at these beautiful replicas, I will remember the day. Thank you, Thagar."

With their heads turned toward each other, they were lost for a moment in each other's eyes.

"Well, shall we pack up, then?" asked Thagar, breaking the trance.

"Yes. Come see what my Brownie, Drummond, has prepared. We have a proper breakfast and lunch, but he has also included some of the oddest things." They stood up from the settee and walked over to the kitchen table.

"Ah! So he has been to the Sanctuary?" chuckled Thagar, picking up the pouch of raw meat.

"Yes, he has. I can't imagine what these items could possibly be for," laughed Aelish.

"You will see," smiled Thagar. Aelish realized she had never really seen Thagar fully smile before—it lit up the room!

"The Sanctuary is a long way off, therefore we need to use the Transporting spell. I assume you are now able to execute it?" asked Thagar.

"I can. It was the first spell I learned at the Institute," Aelish said proudly.

"Excellent," said Thagar. "Let's shrink all of these items, including the clothing on the front bench into our flypacks, and we can depart from here.

After everything was packed up, she closed the front door and they stood on the porch together.

"Since you do not know where the Sanctuary is, you will need to hold my hand to transport with me. Will that be all right?" asked Thagar.

Aelish's stomach flipped. "Of course."

"Off we go, then," said Thagar, taking hold of her hand.

‡‡‡‡

Aelish looked around and saw a magnificent forest in front of her, thick with every type of tree and brush imaginable. She saw a sign that read: WELCOME TO THE SANCTUARY. She also noticed it was a bit chilly and was glad she had transported with her sweater on. A female DARling waved to them from the entrance, beckoning them to come forward.

"Good morning, Targo," said Thagar.

"Commander Thagar, it's an honor and a privilege to host you and your guest today," said Targo, smiling at Aelish.

"It is a pleasure to see you again. Have you been well?" asked Thagar.

"We've been very busy and we have a new addition to the

Sanctuary that I think you will be pleased to see," said Targo.

"Ah! Wonderful!" Thagar smiled broadly.

Good God! That smile!

"May I suggest you start in the coldest section and work your way back to the temperate climate?" suggested Targo. "You can simply transport to that area directly. If you should need anything during the day, send me a telly message and I will be there at once."

"Understood, thank you," said Thagar.

"Of course, Commander," replied Targo.

Thagar turned to Aelish. "I suggest we don our warmest clothes before we transport. I know you are used to cold Irish winters, but the first place we are going rivals the coldest place on Earth."

They put their flypacks on a nearby bench, took out their heavy clothing, and bundled up. They put the remaining items back inside their packs.

"I brought an extra pair of gloves for you," said Thagar. He handed her a thicker pair than the ones she had obtained at the Broadmoor Shop. "They will slip right over the ones you are already wearing. I find these to be superior in warmth."

Aelish slipped on the gloves and they both put on their flypacks. Thagar extended his gloved hand and Aelish grasped his hand. She noticed he held it more tightly than before.

"Brace yourself, it's going to be very cold," said Thagar.

They transported to a freezing, snowy mountaintop, with blizzard-like conditions. The wind howled, as it fiercely blew around them.

"Whoa!" exclaimed Aelish, who stared at Thagar in shock. She noted he was thoroughly enjoying her reaction. Though his thick hat obscured most of his face, Aelish saw him smiling brightly at her.

"Welcome to the Himalayas of DAR!" shouted Thagar. "Through magic we have replicated everything about this glorious mountain range, which includes the tallest peaks on Earth. We have altered the climate so we can breathe, as we are extraordinarily high."

Aelish spun in a circle trying to capture everything. She was cold, but the warm clothing made it bearable. She could not believe she was still in DAR. They hiked up the mountain and Thagar pointed to something approaching them from the right side.

Aelish gasped. *It couldn't be!*

"Are they real or magical figments?" she shouted to Thagar.

"They are real!" he shouted back. "This is what Targo was excited for us to see. The SLEW's have been trying to figure out a way to get them from Earth to DAR for ages. I suppose they finally figured it out!"

"What is a SLE . . . Good God, Thagar! Two of them are coming straight at us!" yelled Aelish.

"Get the fresh meat out of your pack—now!" shouted Thagar, more like a command than a suggestion.

Two Yetis, standing ten feet high, had come out of their mountainous snow cave and were approaching Thagar and Aelish, warily. Their hairy bodies were pure white and they had long claws at the end of their hands. Their feet were enormous and Aelish remembered why these mythical creatures were called Big Foot.

"Do you have the meat, Aelish?" yelled Thagar over the wind.

Aelish was frozen in place and not from the cold.

"Aelish! The meat!" yelled Thagar, more urgently.

She snapped out of shock and yelled, "Got it!"

As the Yeti's approached, Aelish realized one was male and the other female, as the female had twisted her whiskers into intricate curls. The male approached them first and stood approximately five feet away.

"Throw the meat, but leave it in the pouch so it doesn't get lost in the snow!" shouted Thagar. "Do it now!"

Aelish threw the pouch. She silently thanked God the wind was behind her, which propelled the pouch further through the air. It landed right at the male Yeti's enormous feet.

"Nice throw," complimented Thagar.

The male Yeti began smelling the pouch and ripped it open with his claws. He began devouring the fresh meat. He turned to his mate and offered her some from his enormous hand. Aelish and Thagar watched them enjoy their meal, which took about thirty seconds to be eaten. The Yetis looked at Aelish and Thagar and began peacefully heading back to their cave.

"They were hungry," chuckled Thagar. "Let's transport—take my hand, Aelish."

Now that the terror had passed, she realized she had never felt more alive. She grabbed Thagar's hand and smiled at him, as they transported.

Aelish smelled ash and fire and turned to see an active volcano behind them.

"Good God, Thagar—look!" she shouted. She pointed at the volcano, which was actively spewing molten lava over seventeen hundred feet into the air.

"Take off your hat and coat and leave them on the ground, but leave on your sweater for protection from the burning ash. It's going to get very hot when that lava gets closer," stated Thagar.

She stared at him in disbelief. They both discarded their warm clothes and began walking away from the volcano. Aelish suddenly stopped and pointed toward the ground about three feet away.

"What is *that*?" she asked.

"That's the Six-Legged Salamander. They are rare creatures

found in the magical world, although some Humans have also reported seeing them on Earth. Be careful of his venomous milk when you feed him," warned Thagar.

"When I *feed* him?" asked Aelish.

"Take out the glass jar of insects. The little male is going to love it," laughed Thagar.

"Thagar, I would hardly call him little—he's two feet long and nearly a foot high and he doesn't seem friendly, despite his beautiful yellow and black skin color," remarked Aelish. "Why does he have six legs?"

"Some believe one set of legs had formerly been wings."

"How can they live in such an inhospitable environment?" questioned Aelish.

"Think of it from a defensive standpoint—not many other creatures would venture near *that*," answered Thagar, pointing to the volcano. "Also, their venom can extinguish flames. Their hatched newborns enjoy the warm ashes. I think he likes you because he's heading your way."

Despite her trepidation, she was greatly enjoying Thagar's playfulness. She took out the glass jar filled with glowworms and other insects. They were all still alive. She knelt down and the Six-Legged Salamander approached with his long tongue extended.

"Empty the jar right onto his tongue," instructed Thagar.

"He won't shoot his venom at me?" asked Aelish.

"It will be fine," soothed Thagar.

She began bending her knees, slowly lowering herself to the ground. Aelish emptied the jar onto his tongue. The creature instantly snatched up the insects. Searching for another meal, the Six-Legged Salamander began to crawl up onto her knees and stared at her. Aelish didn't move, afraid to startle him. He stared at her for another moment and then scurried away.

"I can't believe he crawled up on you!" exclaimed Thagar,

slapping his leg, laughing. "You're a natural with these beasts. Here comes something you don't see every day. Turn around."

Aelish turned her body and realized she was about six feet away from a beast she could not identify. It was spewing flames from one of its three heads, which resembled a ram. Another head was that of a serpent, with its long tongue extended, and its third head was that of a normal lion, which matched its body. But it had a lizard tail.

"We don't want to feed the Chimera," offered Thagar. "I suggest we make haste, before *we* are breakfast—take my hand!"

Aelish took Thagar's hand and they next transported to a beautiful open plain surrounded by a pine forest. The weather here was kinder, but the screech of something flying overhead made Aelish look up. It looked like a flying rooster!

"Hmm . . . the Cockatrice is quite deadly and pretty much eats anything," said Thagar. "I suggest we find a more suitable location to have our meal."

"Is it a form of dragon?" Aelish asked staring, as it continued swooping and circling them.

"The Cockatrice is about the size of a baby dragon. It amazes me how deadly they are for being only three feet long. Look at its clawed feet," said Thagar, pointing toward the sky.

Suddenly, a new screech could be heard.

"Look there, Aelish!" Thagar said excitedly. "I have wanted to see one forever—it's a Roc, also in the dragon family." The Roc was at least fifty feet long and twenty feet high. It resembled a gigantic eagle and it appeared to hunt the same way.

"They are *both* in the dragon family?" cried Aelish. She was terrified that at any minute, the beasts would begin shooting fire at them.

"I wonder why the Roc is hunting here, I don't see any game," remarked Thagar.

"There!" exclaimed Aelish. "A herd of rhinoceros!"

The herd thundered past them in a stampede, desperate to avoid the Roc, but it was not to be. The Roc swooped down and clutched one of the rhinos in his enormous claws. The Rhino wailed at its own death, as the Roc flew back to its lair. The herd continued stampeding until they were out of sight. Even the Cockatrice had disappeared. Suddenly, it became very quiet.

"Let's take this moment of silence as an opportunity to transport to a more tranquil place—take my hand," said Thagar.

They arrived on another plain surrounded by a typical forest.

"I'm famished," declared Thagar. "I assume your Brownie packed a blanket. May I suggest we have a picnic?"

"What is a *picnic?*" asked Aelish.

"It is a meal taken out of doors and quite often, sitting on the ground. Look inside your pack and see if we have a blanket."

Aelish looked inside and saw a red and black plaid swath of fabric. She tugged on it and by the time it was out of her pack, it was large enough to put on her bed at home.

"Ah! Wonderful! You have an excellent Brownie there," smiled Thagar.

He began setting up for their picnic, retrieving all the necessary items out of Aelish's pack. When he was finished and was sitting cross-legged on the blanket, he extended his arm and reached for her hand.

"M'Lady? Would you care to join me?" smiled Thagar.

Aelish blushed. "No one has called me that since I left Earth." She plopped down onto the blanket. They began their delicious meal in peaceful silence with one another.

"You mentioned a word earlier—SLEW—what is that?" asked Aelish.

"SLEW stands for Sanctuary Learning and Educational Worker," explained Thagar. "SLEWs are DARlings that devote their lives and magical abilities toward the protection of endangered mythical and magical beasts found in both the Human and magical worlds. They created the Sanctuary for all forms of creatures that are mercilessly hunted and are near extinction. Through their magical gifts, they create the environmental habitat for each creature necessary to sustain life and hopefully, procreate the species. They are exemplary conservationists. Beasts that would ordinarily eat one another are, of course, separated through magic. They've experienced a few missteps along the way, but overall the Sanctuary is positively thriving."

"What an admirable use of magic," remarked Aelish, "although I did feel sorry for the rhino."

"Part of the natural order," said Thagar. "It gave its life so an endangered creature could survive. Through my visits to the Sanctuary, I've learned a lot about the behavior of these beasts, as well as ordinary ones. The Sanctuary's reference library is exceptional. Through my research, I've also learned a lot about rats."

Aelish's head snapped up from her food and she stared at Thagar, whose eyes were downcast.

"*Rats*? What about them?" Aelish saw he was struggling to meet her eyes. "What is it? Please tell me."

Thagar deeply sighed. "When Sartaine and I came with Antonia to Earth, to assist you with your parents, we were also on a reconnaissance mission to study the rats in London."

"The rats in *London*? Why?" asked Aelish.

"I'm deeply sorry for the loss of your parents, Aelish," Thagar said mournfully. "I think about what you endured, quite often." He finally lifted his head and met Aelish's eyes.

"Thank you," said Aelish. "I appreciate your condolences, but that's not all you want to tell me, is it?"

"No, it's not. Prior to the Head Council becoming all female,

Director Bathwick was Commander of the S.E. Quadrant. I was fortunate enough to serve as her Lieutenant Commander. From the command center inside the POD, she and I began observing intermittent migration patterns of Komprathian drone rats. During each episode of migration, the drone rats would head toward the Portal to Earth, but we would lose sight of them, shortly before they should have reached the Portal. We instructed Tengstaad, the previous Gatekeeper, and the current Gatekeepers, Hamish and Artagán, to keep a watchful eye out for this situation. But to date, none of our Gatekeepers have ever seen drone rats near the Portal," explained Thagar.

"I don't understand," said Aelish. "Why the focus on rats?" She was getting upset and frustrated.

"Since the migrations were sporadic, it took many years before we could put forth a hypothesis that there was a correlation between the pandemics of plague on Earth and the Komprathian drone rat migrations," explained Thagar. "During our reconnaissance mission, Sartaine and I collected deceased and diseased rats. We brought them back to DAR to be studied. Nearly a year after the 1563 outbreak of plague that killed your parents, the Environmental Commission issued a report.

"After conducting in-depth magical examinations on the rats we brought back from London, the Commission coupled their findings with historical studies on plague outbreaks, since the 1300s. They concluded that the one thing all plague outbreaks shared, was the presence of rats, whether on land or on ships. Based on their examinations of the deceased rats from London, they determined some sort of pest infects the rat by sucking their blood. After the pest kills the rat, it then bites Humans, infecting them, and that is how the plague is spread," said Thagar.

"Good God, but there are rats everywhere! If this is true, how could the plague ever be stopped?" asked Aelish.

"By stopping the Komprathian rat migrations," said Thagar.

"But rats have always existed on the Earth," stated Aelish, shaking her head. "I'm confused."

"Based on the findings of the Environmental Commission," began Thagar, "they concluded that the biological composition of Earthly and Komprathian drone rats are nearly interchangeable. However, the slight variation between the two, indicates that ninety percent of the rats on Earth are from Komprathia and only about ten percent are Earth born."

Thagar paused and looked at Aelish. "Komprathian drone rats are secretly being sent to Earth to intentionally spread the plague, Aelish."

Aelish gasped.

"Shortly before your arrival in DAR, Director Bathwick created a task force within the POD to further study this devastating situation. We've subsequently discovered that Komprathia established a series of tunnels that run parallel to the Portal. These tunnels enable the drone rats to pass through the dimension to Earth, undetected, which is why the Gatekeepers have never seen them.

"King Gidius figured out centuries before we did, that the pests biting Earth born rats, were also spreading the plague to Humans. Gidius deduced he could use his greatest natural resource, his own drone rats, as weapons against Humanity. The drone rat's main function is procreation, so he has a never-ending supply of his new weapon. He is using his own kind to kill Humans," stated Thagar.

"This cannot be true!" exclaimed Aelish. "My parents were intentionally killed by Komprathia? But why?"

"King Gidius is aware of DAR's devotion and vow to protect Humanity," said Thagar. "But Director Bathwick felt this was an inadequate explanation for his visceral hatred of Humans.

She ordered the POD to capture and interrogate Komprathian soldiers to better understand Gidius' motivations. Let me ask you something, having grown up on Earth, would you agree that Humans despise rats and kill them whenever possible?"

"Of course," scoffed Aelish. "They are disgusting vermin that serve absolutely no purpose, except to bite babies and kill them in their cradles!"

"There—right there," said Thagar, pointing at her. "That disgust, that repulsion by Humans toward half of the beings in Komprathia and *literally* half of what King Gidius is— encapsulates his hatred of Humans. Despite the abhorrent treatment of his own drone rats, he nevertheless despises Humans for hunting, trapping, and systematically exterminating what he views, as his own kind. He cannot fathom their disdain, especially since Komprathia has never provoked Humans."

"But . . . they are . . ." stammered Aelish.

"The plague presented Gidius with an incredible weapon against Humanity," stated Thagar, "as the only magic needed was for the creation of the secret, invisible tunnels. Our interrogations of Komprathian soldiers yielded crucial intelligence. We *now* know the Kingdom of Yasteron created the invisible tunnels for Komprathia. We do not yet understand why the Kingdom of Yasteron has allied with King Gidius.

"Gidius timed his drone rats' departures with naturally occurring outbreaks of plague on Earth. By using his unlimited supply of drone rats, King Gidius simply sent them to Earth to procreate and spread the plague. The sheer multitude of excessive rats spread the plague faster and farther, killing millions. You have to admire the brilliance of the tactic."

"Admire the *brilliance*!" yelled Aelish. She abruptly stood up from the blanket and began pacing. "My parents were effectively murdered, Thagar. The plague has already morphed into different forms. God only knows what form it will take next. But I know this, if DAR doesn't stop the Komprathian drone rats, Humanity is doomed. The plague has already killed nearly a quarter of the Earth's population!"

"Forgive my insensitivity, Aelish. I was thinking like a soldier, and not like a DARling who has lost their parents," apologized Thagar. "Will you please sit back down with me?"

"No, I am too upset," said Aelish. She continued pacing. "Why didn't Antonia tell me all of this?"

"Because the Environmental Commission's report and the POD's task force findings remain classified, until next week. I wanted you to hear it directly from me and not in some cold classroom. We failed to protect Humanity from something as simple as Komprathian drone rats because we are unable to dismantle the Yasteron spells that control the tunnels. It is a terrible defeat," sighed Thagar.

"All I want to do is destroy Komprathia," Aelish said through gritted teeth. "I am telling you here and now, I plan on making it my mission to stop Gidius."

"I understand how you feel, but you must remember your Oath of Peace, Aelish. It will guide you toward the appropriate methodology to defeat King Gidius. When I was ten years old, I lost my mother in a battle with Komprathia. I couldn't join the POD until I came of age, at sixteen. All I wanted was revenge. For six years, I spent my sleepless nights devising ways to destroy the entire Kingdom," said Thagar.

"You lost your mother in battle?" Aelish asked softly.

"Yes. King Gidius discovered how to penetrate the magic of DAR's earlier military strategies, which are no longer utilized. It was the bloodiest battle within DAR and is simply remembered as the Proelium. My mother was in command of all the ground forces in the S.E. Quadrant, and was killed alongside those who served under her," replied Thagar.

Aelish could see he had become distraught. She finally calmed, and sat back down on the blanket next to him.

"Loss of a family member is very difficult, Aelish," said Thagar. "It brings great suffering to the survivors. But that is what we are, survivors, and in their memory, we must always remember how they would have wanted us to live out the rest of our lives. They would not want us to waste our lives in vengeful bitterness. You can utilize your grief in a productive manner. Of that, I am certain. I'm so sorry we failed you and your parents, but at least now we have the knowledge to effect change. Do you understand?"

"I understand," sighed Aelish. "Some days I fear I will never be over my grief. It consumes me. I suppose time will help, at least that's what I've been told."

"There's a truth to time being a healing agent, but I believe a specific purpose is the only way out of grief. I am still not over the loss of my mother," sighed Thagar.

"Is your father living?" she asked.

"Yes, he is. I am the youngest of four sons. After my mother was killed, my father stayed in the S.E. Quadrant until I came of age and could join the POD. He then returned to the N.E. Quadrant, to the generations of fishers that comprise his family. My three brothers followed in his footsteps and also reside in the N.E. Quadrant, whereas I followed in my mother's."

"Is your father's skin blue?" asked Aelish. "And can he breathe underwater? Antonia told me some DARlings from the N.E. Quadrant have appropriated marine life qualities. Does he have gills?"

Thagar chuckled. "He does indeed have blue skin and we can all breathe underwater. But my father and eldest brother, are the only ones with small gills on their backs."

"You can breathe underwater? That's incredible to me," said Aelish, shaking her head. "Why is your skin color bronzed?"

"My mother's skin color was black, reflecting the generations of her family who served the POD. I am the only one in my family with bronzed skin," explained Thagar. "My brothers all have blue-black colored skin."

"Do you see your father and brothers, often?" asked Aelish.

"My father has a new family with young DARlings. They, along with my brothers and their families, all live on their individual fishing boats. It's a peaceful existence, but not one I could ever embrace. I visit whenever I am able."

Aelish moved closer to him on the blanket and touched his hand. He looked up into her eyes and pulled her against him, kissing her lips. Aelish felt warmth run through her body. Thagar pulled away and looked at her, while his hands gently caressed her face.

"That was as sweet as I imagined it would be," he said to her. He reached for her again, this time kissing her more deeply. He lowered her in an embrace onto the blanket where they lay for some time kissing, laughing, and at ease with each other during the quiet interludes of their conversation.

As the sun began its descent, Thagar sat up and extended his arm for her to rise.

"There's one last thing I want you to experience before we leave the Sanctuary—Gryphon!" he yelled out. "Get out the pouch of nuts, oats, and hay."

As she reached into her flypack to retrieve the pouch, Aelish heard the sound of mighty wings flapping toward their direction. A Gryphon landed right in front of her. She couldn't believe it. She had read about these beasts in books, but thought they were only legends.

"You may pet his wings," encouraged Thagar. "Empty the pouch and he will eat the contents from your hand."

"Really?" she asked.

Aelish tentatively stood up and walked over to the Gryphon. She began petting one of his wings. She heard a low murmur of pleasure from the beast. She put the items from the pouch, onto the palm of her hand. She watched him greedily eat, despite the fact that Gryphons normally favor meat. When the Gryphon was finished, the beast looked down at Thagar.

"Ready for a ride?" smiled Thagar. He mounted the Gryphon, as easily as one would a horse. He extended his arm toward Aelish. The Gryphon lowered itself further, so she could mount the creature. Once she was situated, she wasn't sure what to hold on to.

"Put your arms around my waist, Aelish. Enjoy the ride, as from this vantage point you will be able to see the entire Sanctuary."

The Gryphon rose gracefully into the air. Aelish pressed her body against Thagar. All her feelings of rage and vengeance were left on the ground, as they soared upward on the Gryphon.

"Thank you," she whispered into his ear.

23

WILLIE

"**I TOLD YOU**! I knew it!" cried Isabela. "I knew one of the evil, magical Kingdoms would find a way to kill Humans."

"But Komprathia did so without the use of the evil magic. The magic you feared the most did not cause the death of millions of Humans. By using undetectable tunnels running parallel with the Portal to Earth, created by their ally, the Kingdom of Yasteron, King Gidius used his own drone rats as weapons. He waged a war against Humanity, that in the end, was so simple."

"Using his own beings as weapons—that's beyond horrible," stated Isabela, shaking her head. "Absolutely horrible."

"It's been done many times on Earth. Soldiers forced to fight, under the threat of death, for a cause or ruler they despise. Innocent civilians used as Human shields to stop an enemy from bombing their country. The concept is not new. King Gidius took a naturally occurring disease on Earth, spread by rats and other rodents, and was smart enough to realize his own drone rats could spread the disease much faster. The sheer multitude of hosts he supplied from Komprathia spread the plague with such an intensity, it allowed the plague to morph and evolve into different, deadlier strains."

"But you haven't explained how the plague finally stopped. I know it occurs sporadically on the Earth to this day, but we don't even get vaccinated for it. How did it stop?" asked Isabela, clearly frustrated.

"Let me begin at the Gala for DAR. This is the most elaborate gala in DAR and is held once, every one hundred years. My first Gala for DAR was in 1665 and coincided with the conclusion of my military and educational studies," said Aelish.

"Wait! You were in school for *one hundred years?* Didn't you start school in 1564?" exclaimed Isabela.

Aelish burst out laughing. "Yes, I was. But not everyone chooses to stay in school that long. Lady Antonia, for example, completed her education in twenty-five years, approximately two years before I came to DAR. Education is highly valued in DAR. Since I knew that I wanted to serve DAR at the highest levels of policy and leadership alongside the Head Council, that pursuit requires a lengthy education. It's similar to obtaining a medical, legal, or scientific degree on Earth.

"But it also didn't *feel* like one hundred years. Remember the age disparity and the time continuum. At the time of the gala in 1665, approximately one hundred years after my arrival in DAR in 1564, my body hadn't aged from the time I left Earth. I was still eighteen years old. After arriving in DAR, my aging process came to a halt for a long, long time. It had to catch up to how our age is calculated. In 1665, I had lived a total of one hundred nineteen years or six percent of my total, two thousand year lifespan. According to the formula, I would have only been six years old! Therefore, I remained eighteen at the time of the Gala for DAR, in 1665. My age didn't move until after I had lived three hundred eighty years, which is nineteen percent of two thousand years, making me nineteen years old. That didn't happen until the year 1926!

"Remember, we take the cumulative number of years we've been alive and divide that by our total lifespan of two thousand years. I was born in 1546 and it is now 2018, so I have been alive, four hundred seventy-two years. Four hundred seventy-two years is twenty-three percent, give or take, of my two thousand year lifespan. The percentage of years lived, becomes our age. Therefore, I am twenty-three years old.

"As I explained earlier, those born in DAR mature rapidly for the first three hundred years of their lives to age twenty-eight. But then their age holds for the next three hundred years, or until they have lived six hundred years. For example, Thagar was born in 1350. It is now 2018, which means he has lived six hundred sixty-eight years or thirty-three percent of his two thousand year lifespan. He is currently thirty-three years old. But in 1665, at the time of the gala, I was still eighteen, and due to the rapid maturation of Thagar's first three hundred years, he was twenty-eight years old. He's always been ten years older than me. Do you understand?"

"I get it," smiled Isabela. "It's insane, but I get it."

"Thank heavens you are so intelligent," said Aelish.

"But wait!" exclaimed Isabela. "I just figured something out. If Lady Antonia arrived in DAR at age sixteen, and her age held for a long time like yours did, she was actually *younger* than you, when you arrived in DAR. Oh, my God, she wouldn't have passed your age and turned nineteen until 1901, three hundred eighty years after she was born in 1521! That's when your twenty-five year lifespan difference returned because you didn't turn nineteen until 1926! That's insane!"

Aelish threw her had back laughing. "Isn't that such a hoot? And believe me, she never lets me forget she was younger than me, for a few hundred years. We really are like sisters; she being my slightly *older* sister."

Isabela started laughing.

"It always takes me a moment to calculate my age," said Aelish, shaking her head. "Okay, so to get back to where we were, are you ready to learn how the plague ultimately stopped?"

"Finally," said Isabela. "Yes, come on, I want to know!"

"All right, then," smiled Aelish. "Get comfortable because it's a very long story."

‡‡‡‡

Aelish's back was aching after spending all night in one of the private study rooms at the POD. She was furiously trying to finish her academic thesis. As she was working on the last citation, Lady Antonia burst through the door, breathless.

"Aelish, dear—it's happening again."

"What is?"

"The plague."

"Oh, no. Good God! As bad as when my parents died?"

"Worse. It has the potential to kill at least three times more people than the plague of 1563. One hundred sixty-five residents of London are dying each day, and it has spread to Ireland, Aelish."

"Ohh, Declán's descendants—his grandchildren at Brólaigh Castle. Will the plague never cease, Antonia? It kills from one generation to another, enveloping families in its ghastly, black shroud."

"I know, dear," Lady Antonia said softly.

"And here I was trying to concentrate on my final citation, but I kept losing my focus thinking about my gown for the gala tonight."

"Of course, dear, you had no idea. Is it pretty?" asked Lady Antonia, smiling.

"It's beautiful. It has numerous ruffles throughout the body of the gown and it has delicate, ruffled cap sleeves. Oh, and the fabric is new; it is called chiffon. How can I be talking about a stupid ball gown? Antonia, those poor families," said Aelish, as she put her face in her hands.

Lady Antonia waited for Aelish to lift her head up before giving her a handkerchief to dry her eyes.

"I'm so sorry I upset you, dear. I was actually coming to bring you some treats to keep you going," said Lady Antonia.

She reached into her flypack and placed an assortment of snacks on the study desk.

"As I was coming down the hallway," she continued, "my dear Oraculi, Melanthia, sent me a telly and told me to sit down, as she had a lot to tell me. We spoke for over an hour. As we were nearing the end of our conversation, Melanthia received a Head Council alert about the plague. Ten minutes later, I heard a commotion in the hallway and ended my conversation with Melanthia. Everyone was in a state of alarm having just learned that the plague had returned. I ran down the hallway to find you, as I didn't want you to hear about it, other than from me."

"I understand. You had my best interests at heart, as usual," smiled Aelish. "Isn't it awful knowing firsthand the misery that is happening on Earth, as we sit here in this room?"

"We have to go on living, Aelish."

"But of all the days for this to have been discovered—the day of the gala? It seems the plague will simply never end, Antonia."

"I suggest then, you remain focused on finishing your thesis. Perhaps you may get to put the theory into practice," said Lady Antonia, slyly.

"What do you mean? What aren't you telling me?"

"I think the timing of the plague, your thesis, and the gala, all intersecting at the same time, may provide you with an incredible opportunity," said Lady Antonia. "Also, have you heard about the newest Head Council Member? She was appointed last week and is incredibly controversial. You will get to meet her tonight."

"No, I've been completely absorbed in my thesis," said Aelish. "I've barely been home, I haven't seen Thagar in a month, and I haven't listened to any of the news feeds. Who is this controversial new Council member?"

"Her name is Wilhelmina Von Etzenbach, but everyone calls her Willie," said Lady Antonia. "She was born to a tenant farming family in Bavaria and lived through the worst plague outbreak in the mid-1300s. Her entire family died by the time she was twelve. She disappeared from our sights, right before her Oraculi, Leraza, was directed to bring her to DAR.

"Leraza grew up with Melanthia in the S.W. Quadrant. But unlike Melanthia, who could not commit to the lifestyle of a Keeper, Leraza did. She's a brilliant scholar of magic. But as time went by, Leraza expressed a desire to be outside the tombs of the Breanon. Melanthia helped her transition from Keeper to Oraculi. This was Leraza's first assignment as an Oraculi, and the female vanishes?"

"How awful—and Wilhelmina's skin turning lavender with no one to help her. Why did it take so long to locate her?" asked Aelish.

"Her entire village had died and there was no food anywhere. She wandered the countryside alone for over four years. After she turned lavender, she tried concealing her exposed skin with mud and cut her hair like a boy, hoping it would help keep her safe. She discovered *on her own* how to change her lavender skin back to Bavarian porcelain. By the time Leraza located Willie she was sixteen years old! She had already gained significant control over her magical abilities, most specifically, her gift of being a shape-shifter."

"Really? Such a rare magical ability," remarked Aelish.

"Willie changed her form constantly into a variety of different animals. She hunted prey, as they did, to keep from starving to death. That's why Leraza couldn't find her. Some in DAR feel Willie has been imbued with the Norse legend of the skin-walker, as she can transform into many animals including a bear, a wolf, a deer," Lady Antonia paused, "and even a creature as small as a rat."

Aelish gasped. "A rat?"

"Her magical abilities are extraordinary. Willie shape-shifted into a rat shortly after we realized the drone rats were bypassing the Portal. She is the original DARling to discover how the Komprathian drone rats were getting to Earth."

"Good God! She's who discovered the tunnels?" exclaimed Aelish.

"Indeed. She followed the drone rats over an extended period of time and discovered all their secret tunnels. She even went with the drone rats all the way to Earth," said Lady Antonia.

"That's incredible," remarked Aelish.

"Willie has worked closely with the POD ever since," said Lady Antonia. "She has provided invaluable information over the last one hundred years. I'm surprised Thagar hasn't told you about her."

"Hmm . . . that is odd," said Aelish, with a sudden pit in her stomach.

Why didn't he tell me about her at the Sanctuary, when he told me about the tunnels?

"Melanthia told me that Leraza has worked relentlessly, as her Oraculi, to quell Willie's desire to war with Komprathia. Melanthia is aware of her radical views, but is nevertheless, looking forward to serving with her on the Head Council.

"In light of the new plague outbreak, Melanthia just told me that Council Chair Sukaaja has revised the entire agenda for next week's Head Council meeting. The agenda will now be focused entirely on the plague. Melanthia also advised that Willie will be giving a presentation on her vision of how to stop the Komprathian drone rats . . . "

Aelish did not interrupt Lady Antonia, who had momentarily paused.

" . . . and I told Melanthia that you have a presentation of your own that you would like to present to the Head Council. So you are now, also, on the agenda," stated Lady Antonia.

"You did *what*?" cried Aelish. She stood up so suddenly, her chair toppled backward.

Aelish began pacing the small study room trying to analyze her feelings. She was terrified, excited, and furious all at the same time. She'd stop pacing and try to speak, but nothing would come out. She watched Lady Antonia sitting calmly in her chair, while Aelish wanted to scream at her.

After about five minutes, she realized her anger was somewhat misplaced. The pit in her stomach, that began after she realized Thagar had never told her about Willie, had become a full-blown gnawing. She began massaging her abdomen, as she continued to pace. Further complicating the situation was the fact that she had not told Thagar anything about her thesis, fearing his disapproval.

Aelish righted her chair and finally sat down, still unable to look at Lady Antonia.

"You are angry with me," said Lady Antonia.

"A little."

"But I think you may be more angry with Thagar," said Lady Antonia. She reached across the desk and gently patted Aelish's clenched hands.

Aelish began shaking her head.

"I haven't even gone through the Commencement ceremony, Antonia. How could I possibly present my thesis in front of the Head Council? Especially in light of the recent appointment of this new rising star, who actually discovered the tunnels? I am only a student."

"It is natural to be intimidated, but I believe it is Thagar that has rocked your confidence."

"Why wouldn't he tell me about her?" asked Aelish. "She sounds amazing. Do you think he's in love with her? I can't think of any other reason he wouldn't tell me."

"Have you discussed your thesis with Thagar? Has he asked you about it?" asked Lady Antonia.

"No, I haven't discussed it with him because I know he will disapprove and I fear it will come between us. And yes, he has asked me about it and I always manage to change the subject."

"Hmm . . . so Thagar is not the only one withholding information. I think any speculation on our part, about why he hasn't told you about Willie, is useless at this point. You need to ask him directly, Aelish. Trust is the most important foundation between intimates and he may feel he does not have yours."

Aelish looked into Lady Antonia's eyes. She realized her thesis had been the most important thing in her life ever since Thagar had told her about the Komprathian drone rats in the Sanctuary.

Her education and military studies had of course consumed her, but throughout her studies she had been methodically fine-tuning her thesis. In fact, she had been doing so, for the same length of time Willie had been working with Thagar in the POD.

But Lady Antonia had forced her hand. Thagar would know soon enough about her strategy of dealing with Komprathia. She couldn't believe she was on the agenda for next week's Head Council meeting!

"You're ready, Aelish. You know you are, dear. Let me allow you to get back to your work," soothed Lady Antonia.

"I don't think I can concentrate anymore."

"Struggle through, I will see you at the gala tonight."

"This is certainly going to be an interesting evening," chuckled Aelish. "I think it's safe to say, I will always remember my first Gala for DAR."

Lady Antonia laughed and gave her a hug, as she left the study room.

Aelish returned to the last citation, but decided instead to read her thesis from the beginning. She found herself editing her writing to reflect a different voice; one that she could now hear in front of the Head Council.

24

BEFORE THE GALA

AELISH WAS RECEIVING a telepathic message from Thagar, letting her know he had just returned from the N.W. Quadrant. He relayed that he was getting dressed and would be at her cottage shortly. He wanted them to fly together to the gala.

Aelish sat down on her bed. For the first time in her life, she was experiencing the downside of having Human traits. Ever since Lady Antonia had told her about Willie, she found she was experiencing jealousy. It was an extremely uncomfortable feeling that flummoxed her ordinarily rational thought process. Coupled with her anxiety about attending her first Gala for DAR, it had become unbearable. An expression her mother used to say, whenever she was very nervous, suddenly popped into her head.

'I'm plankin' it, Aelish, I've got ta keep me alans on.'

Her mother used to get extremely anxious before an event with the wives of the other Earls. Remembering it, Aelish burst out laughing at the thought of her mother being so nervous that she had to grab hold of her undergarments.

Thanks, Ma. She momentarily calmed thinking of her mother.

She knew Thagar had been in the N.W. Quadrant for the last month overseeing a new experiment. But all Aelish could think about was if Willie had accompanied him. She stood up from the bed and began forcefully flouncing the ruffles of her ball gown, her nervous energy coming out through her fingertips.

For heavens sake, Aelish, keep your alans on! She burst out laughing again.

Her hair was in an intricate up-do, accentuated by a glittering tiara that matched the jewels on the belt of her gown. She gazed at her reflection and was pleased with her image. She reached for the matching jeweled shoes, with straps that climbed from the top of her foot to the base of her calf. She sat back down on her bed and began putting them on.

She examined the height of the heels, as she fastened the straps. *I hope I don't fall and break my neck!*

Aelish considered this possibility and decided death would be preferable to falling on her backside in front of the all dignitaries that would be in attendance this evening. The Gala for DAR was a veritable who's who of the commonwealth.

The guest list included the Director of the POD, the Commanders and their Lieutenants from each of the four Quadrants, plus either their mates or intimates. Being intimates with Thagar was how Aelish had secured an invitation.

Besides the military leaders of DAR, the guest list included: the entire Head Council, including members of all the various Commissions that reported directly to the Head Council; Master Keepers from the Breanon; the Director of the Sanctuary and high level SLEWs; legendary Masters of Experimentation, as well as famed musicians and songwriters from the N.W. Quadrant; Agricultural Leadership from the S.W. Quadrant; notable artists such as the DARling that created the Humanity sculpture; famous fashion designers that had previously been honored; Oceanic Masters from the N.E. Quadrant; the Director and longstanding professors from both the Institutum de Magicae and the POD, including some of Aelish's most recent professors; and living legends of DAR that she had previously studied, but who would now be standing before her.

Drummond knocked on the door of her bedchamber, as she magically finished fastening the last buckle of the shoe straps. She stood up from the bed and opened the door. She found her Brownie staring at her with his mouth agape.

"No good?" asked Aelish.

"You look like the bloody Queen of England!" cried Drummond. He dramatically bowed, his conical hat falling to the floor.

Aelish began laughing so hard she had to sit back down on the bed.

"I came to tell ya' that yer fella's here and he's waiting for ya' on the front porch. He looks positively dashing," said Drummond. He leaned closer to her and whispered, "And he's shaved off all his whiskers and his face looks as smooth as a baby's arse."

"Oh, Drummond!" cried Aelish, grabbing her waist, doubled over in laughter. "What would I do without you?"

"Let's hope we never find out," he smiled. "Ya' best be going now and have a jolly good time tonight! I'm going to retire now if that's acceptable to ya', Aelish."

"Of course," said Aelish. She gestured with her hands for him to go.

"Oh! I left a tray of spirits on the porch so you two could get a little jingled before the gala," winked Drummond, as he turned to go back under the cottage.

"Thank you!" Aelish cried out after him.

Aelish slowly got up from the bed learning to balance on her heels. She gingerly walked toward the front entryway. She stood there for a moment and took some deep breaths before opening the front door.

Thagar's back was to her. He was leaning against the porch rail staring up at the lights of the Rotunda. She closed the front door, which made him abruptly turn around.

"Oh, my!" he said, staring at her. "You look positively stunning, Aelish."

He moved in for a kiss and Aelish felt the smoothness of his face against her lips. She pulled her head back and ran her hands across his cheeks.

"Do you like it? I felt like I needed a change," smiled Thagar. His black curls framed his beautiful, bronzed face.

"Aside from your hair being longer, you look as you did when I snuck a peek at you from behind the tapestry, in Brólaigh Castle. A little wiser around the eyes perhaps—I've missed you," said Aelish. She kissed him tenderly.

"I've missed that," said Thagar. He ran his thumb across her lower lip.

"Care for a spirit on the swing before we leave?" asked Aelish, eyeing the beautiful tray Drummond had left for them.

"That sounds wonderful. I could use one," said Thagar. He lifted his arm for her to take it as he guided her over to the swing. "You seem a bit wobbly. What are you wearing on your feet?"

As they sat down on the swing, her gown lifted up in the front and Thagar eyed her jeweled, high-heeled shoes.

"Whoa! Are you sure you're going to be all right in those all evening?"

"I was considering using the Balance spell to help me stay vertical," laughed Aelish.

Thagar chuckled, "Well, you sit m'Lady and allow me to pour you a spirit."

She took the small crystal glass from him with her white-gloved hand. "Thank you."

"It's nice to be back in the S.E. Quadrant," said Thagar. "The N.W. has never been my favorite. It's not so much the cold, but you can feel the eyes of the Kingdom of Yasteron on you at all times. If we were not aided by the magical beings in the sea between DAR and Yasteron, I fear they would overrun us. The sea creatures caught two of Yasteron's spies a few days before I left. It truly is amazing how their appearance is the most similar to us, out of all the magical realms. They could easily pass for DARlings, with the exception of them *all* having pale beige skin and yellow hair. They have such exceptional intelligence and auditory skills. I suppose that's why they are so gifted in developing the most sophisticated listening devices, surveillance techniques, and detection grids."

"And tunnels," added Aelish.

"Oh, the tunnels," said Thagar. He began rubbing his forehead, as if the mere mention of the topic made his head hurt. "I cannot disclose much about the experiment I was overseeing, but suffice it to say, it involved the tunnels, and yet again, we were unsuccessful. We simply cannot break down the spells used to create them. We think we are close and then we fail. It is maddening."

His use of the word *we* alerted Aelish. She debated asking if Willie had accompanied him, but she was not emotionally prepared for an affirmative answer.

"We know from our interrogations with the spies we've captured from the Kingdom of Yasteron that they do not share Komprathia's ideals," said Thagar. "Sometimes I think the only reason they ally themselves with Komprathia is to demonstrate to DAR their magical superiority, for example, with the tunnels.

"Their spies have infiltrated and escaped the N.W. Quadrant so many times we've lost count. They take our newest spells with them, and can execute the stolen spells with the same precision. They care nothing about our tenets and principles of peace, nor our devotion to protect Humanity. They choose not to utilize their evil magic against us, knowing it would be mutually assured destruction, yet they assist a barbaric Kingdom like Komprathia. I believe they do it just to play with us," stated Thagar, clearly frustrated.

Aelish could see he was exhausted. She was champing at the bit to ask him about Willie, but she remained quiet.

"Long ago, under the command of Bathwick, we sent a team to Yasteron to try and infiltrate their experimentation room. We hoped to garner the secrets of their spying and surveillance spells, as they are superior to DAR's.

"It took years to orchestrate and the intelligence sent back allowed us a glimpse inside the Kingdom. They are handsome beings, but the females are not entitled to the same level of leadership as the males. King Nevuna is not cruel, but he maintains strict control over his Kingdom and none dare cross him. He has ruled for centuries and is grooming his son, Cardissius, to ultimately replace him. Cardissius is far more ruthless and *very much* wants to control DAR—most especially our females, due to their exceptional magical abilities. In my opinion, Yasteron would be the Kingdom most capable of discovering how to attain the magic in the Riddle Boxes. As for our evil magic, they are satisfied with their own, but only because they are unaware that DAR's is superior," said Thagar. He poured himself another spirit.

"What happened to the team that was sent?" asked Aelish.

"They were ultimately captured and executed," sighed Thagar.

"Oh, how tragic," said Aelish, as she reached for Thagar's hand.

"Despite being tortured for months," continued Thagar, "they gave up very little intelligence. We simply could not rescue them because of Yasteron's exceptional detection grid. The grid locates any attempted penetration into Yasteron's borders. It is the same field of magical knowledge that allowed them to create the tunnels.

"After our team was executed, Yasteron sent their remains back to DAR. As the mission was still classified, we could not disclose what they had died for, but they were given a state funeral. It was of little comfort to their families. Since that epic failure, we have never utilized that tactic again." He leaned forward with his head hanging downward.

It was a rarity for Thagar to open up about current or past missions. What he did not know was that he had inadvertently provided Aelish with crucial pieces of information that she needed for her thesis. She was mentally including the placement of the information, when Thagar interrupted her strategizing.

"You are so quiet, Aelish," said Thagar. "I apologize for being so maudlin on such a festive occasion as your first Gala for DAR. I fear I am a bit weary from so many weeks in the N.W. Quadrant, only to have failed, yet again."

He stood up and forced a smile reaching for her hand.

"Shall we go then, my love?" he asked.

"Let's ascend," replied Aelish.

She was feeling wretchedly guilty for withholding so many things from Thagar, but she said nothing. They lifted upward, holding hands, and began flying toward the direction of the Great Rotunda.

25

THE GALA FOR DAR

As AELISH AND Thagar approached the Rotunda, she could see the lights of the gala from miles away. Because of the risk of having so many important leaders of DAR in one location at the same time, security was exceptional. There were soldiers and weaponry guarding the gala both on the ground and in the air. Security forces in the air saluted their Commander and directed and accompanied Aelish and Thagar through an aerial entranceway.

As they descended, they landed at the security checkpoint entrance on the ground. Aelish observed that Thagar had brightened somewhat from his mood on the porch.

He must certainly be proud of his staff's orderly security process for arriving guests.

She pushed the guilty feelings she experienced earlier, to the back of her mind, and focused on the sheer magnitude of the gala.

No wonder they only do this once every one hundred years. This is nothing like the smaller galas!

They passed through a variety of magical searches, finally arriving at the enormous arched entrance pergola, draped with hundreds of flowers and greenery. Above it was a lighting installation that illuminated the pathway ahead, with the three letters D-A-R.

She walked under the entranceway pergola and looked up at the thousands of tea lights that framed the invisible tent, shielding the guests from potential inclement weather. The tea lights came to a point at the center of the tent, high above the Lawn. The Lawn, as it was known, was an open green space used for various auspicious occasions, but none more so, than the Gala for DAR. The Lawn was over five acres of land situated between the Breanon and the Institutum de Magicae.

Once she was under the tent, she could no longer see the aerial security forces high overhead, protecting the venue. Instead she saw hundreds of floating crystal chandeliers illuminating the tables and there were stars on the floor. The floor was a deep blue color with so many stars, it was as if the guests were walking on the midnight sky.

The chandeliers were also adorned with flowers and greenery and there were floral arrangements floating throughout the tent. The tables were rectangular and draped with iridescent tablecloths, creating a surreal experience. Candles provided low light for the tables, and like all the other lights, were lit through magic and were not actual flames. Silverware and crystal aligned each place setting, along with the most unique plates. Each one had a different design, reflecting each Quadrant of DAR, a legendary scene of heroism, or portraits of former Head Council Members.

Mr. MacSweeney would have been amazed by these place settings!

Translucent menus floated above the uniquely designed plates, which were stacked accordingly for each dinner course. At the back of the invisible tent was an orchestra playing the classics of DAR.

The dance floor appeared to go on for infinity, as beneath it was a body of turquoise water, the same color as her cottage front door. The light emanating from inside the water, underneath the dance floor, made Aelish uncertain where one ended and the other began. She couldn't wait to have her first dance on it with Thagar.

The entire scene was one of enchantment. The males were either in full military dress or elegant formal wear. Many females were also in full military dress, but the females that weren't, wore ensembles she could never have imagined. They wore hats with live animals resting in them, crowns, and tiaras similar to her own, and some of the gowns had trains as long as twenty feet. They would undoubtedly be bustled during the dancing. The gowns were all original and magnificent. She was pleased with her own gown selection after reviewing the other designs, and felt that her ensemble was appropriate for her age and status in DAR.

"Would you care for a spirit or a starter?" asked Thagar. He took a crystal glass from a floating tray, filled with a bubbling liquid. "Or perhaps a cheese-filled pastry puff, my love?"

Aelish watched how a second floating tray appeared, next to the one filled with spirits. She had never seen anything like *this* at the smaller galas. They had all been buffets, where the guests helped themselves.

"Where are the servers?" asked Aelish, utterly fascinated.

"In DAR, no one is relegated to serve," replied Thagar. "The culinary masters are working to outdo each other in their kitchens, and the food is magically sent to the Lawn."

"When we dine at the tables, how do we select our options, and how are they then served?" asked Aelish.

"You simply review the menu options, make your selection, and telepathically send your order. The culinary masters prepare what you have chosen and the food is presented in timed courses, magically appearing on the neatly stacked plates. Once you have completed the course, the plates simply vanish. Be sure you have finished, because the plates are pressure sensitive to your silverware touching them. If you leave your food unattended for too long, it will disappear," laughed Thagar. "Ah! Antonia is furiously waving us over. Let's join her."

Aelish located Lady Antonia, and she and Thagar crossed the star-laden floor to greet her. After many kisses all around, Aelish began to pet the white teacup poodle asleep in Lady Antonia's hat.

"This is little Suzanna," remarked Lady Antonia. "Well, what do you think of the gala? Is it not magnificent?"

"What a production this is! It is a marvel," exclaimed Aelish. She felt flushed from the gala's bubbling spirit. It was making her far tipsier than the spirit Drummond had left for them.

"Would you both excuse me for a moment," said Thagar. "I see Sartaine and need to discuss something with him. I will return shortly."

Aelish and Lady Antonia smiled and nodded.

"It's amazing to see all the legends here. Let me point out a few for you," said Lady Antonia.

Aelish followed Lady Antonia's gaze throughout the tent as she gestured toward specific dignitaries in attendance. Aelish had studied the history of so many of them. To see them in real life was extraordinary.

"Ah! There is Director Bathwick, Aelish," stated Lady Antonia, gesturing across the room. "She has never mated, choosing to devote her first one thousand years to serving DAR in the POD. She recently retired, but will continue to serve as an advisor to the Head Council."

"Good evening, Antonia, Aelish," said Melanthia, behind them.

"Don't you look lovely!" exclaimed Antonia, turning around to kiss Melanthia on both cheeks.

"I wanted to introduce you to my dear friend, Leraza," stated Melanthia. "Leraza, this is my dear, Antonia, who is now Oraculi to Aelish."

"It's wonderful to finally put a face to the name, Antonia," said Leraza. "And I've heard only good things about you, Aelish. You both look lovely this evening. Melanthia tells me you've been greatly enjoying your role, Antonia, as Aelish's Oraculi."

"I have, indeed, been savoring my role as Aelish's Oraculi. You've been an Oraculi for some time now. Does it still bring you satisfaction? It must be so entirely different from your previous responsibilities as a Keeper," said Lady Antonia.

Aelish chuckled inwardly at the machinations of her Oraculi. She knew Lady Antonia was aiming to garner information for her on Willie.

"It has been extremely challenging, since the very beginning, when Willie was lost to us," sighed Leraza. "Since her discovery of the tunnels, I have worked tirelessly to quench Willie's thirst for war and vengeance against Komprathia. Her opinions are well known throughout the commonwealth. I'm sure you are both aware that Willie has been appointed to the Head Council. She will be giving a presentation on the plague and the Komprathian drone rats at her very first meeting. I'm as nervous as a parent sending their DARlette off to their first day at the Institute."

Aelish sensed Leraza's kindness and great depth of feeling and commitment toward Willie. She watched Lady Antonia and Melanthia comfort this gentle Oraculi.

"She has such amazing magical talents," continued Leraza, "but I fear my academic mastery, as a former Keeper, may not be enough to thwart her desires, when it comes to Komprathia. Willie still harbors a great grief over the death of her entire family. Couple that with her scrappy and daring characteristics, I fear her presentation may go off like a loose cannon, now that the plague is once again raging on Earth."

"Hello, Leraza," said Thagar. "It's wonderful to see you again."

"Hello, Thagar. How are you, dear?" asked Leraza, as she embraced him in a hug.

Aelish glanced at Lady Antonia and noted she had also observed the closeness between Willie's Oraculi and Thagar.

"Your cheeks have an orange glow to them Aelish, perhaps too many spirits before dinner?" Thagar teased, still holding the arm of Leraza.

"Did you get to speak with Sartaine?" asked Aelish. She was desperate to change the subject and deflect her blushing upset over his ease with Leraza.

"Ah! Here comes Director Bathwick, Aelish," winked Lady Antonia. "You will finally get to meet her."

Thank you for the distraction, Antonia!

"Director Bathwick," greeted Lady Antonia, "it is my great pleasure to see you again."

"Good evening, Antonia, Melanthia, Leraza, Commander Thagar," smiled Bathwick. And who is this lovely creature?"

"This is my Aelish," Thagar said proudly. "I can't believe you two have never met before."

"It is a pleasure to finally meet you, my dear. Thagar has told me only good things," smiled Bathwick. She extended her hand to shake Aelish's.

"It is an honor and a privilege to meet you, Director Bathwick. Your reputation precedes you and Thagar speaks so highly of you," smiled Aelish, shaking Bathwick's firm grip. Aelish was momentarily blinded, as the light of the chandeliers reflected off the medals on Bathwick's chest.

Bathwick put her arm around Thagar and asked, "And how is my protégé doing—I fear perhaps exhausted from the last month in the N.W. Quadrant? I hope the new Director is treating you well?"

As Thagar and Bathwick chatted, Aelish observed the deep

affection they held for each other; they were more like a mother and son, than Commander and Lieutenant Commander. She instantly liked Bathwick.

"Antonia, you look lovely, and with a teacup poodle in your hat!" laughed Bathwick, gently petting Suzanna. "Good thing my fashion sense is safely tucked inside my uniform." She turned toward Leraza. "I understand Willie has been appointed to the Head Council. Congratulations! And she is to give a presentation on Komprathia? You must be very proud and very nervous."

"I am, indeed," replied Leraza.

"Well *that* certainly is news," said Thagar. "I'm away for one month in the N.W. Quadrant and it feels like I've been in one of the other magical realms. The Head Council—*really*? Has she discussed the details of her presentation with you, Bathwick?"

Aelish could see he was anxious about Willie's presentation, which vexed her.

"No, she has not. But knowing Willie, as you do so well, I'm sure we will all be in for a surprise," chuckled Bathwick.

Aelish felt the bubbling spirit flip in her stomach at Bathwick's pronouncement of Thagar knowing Willie so well.

Did she say that because they have worked closely together on the tunnels or because they have been intimates?

Aelish didn't have to wait long to receive an answer. She saw a lavender-faced female approaching them in a magnificent, black, glittering ball gown. Her beautiful, long blonde hair was in an elaborate up-do, accentuated by a black-netted, birdcage veil that stopped just short of her chin. She instantly knew it was Willie.

"Good evening, Leraza," smiled Willie. "Director Bathwick, Melanthia, Commander Thagar, and I believe Antonia, yes?"

"Yes, indeed," smiled Lady Antonia. "It is a pleasure to meet you. Allow me to introduce, Aelish."

"Ah! The infamous Lady Aelish. The pleasure is all mine," Willie said slyly. And to the astonishment of everyone present, she deeply curtsied, in front of Aelish.

The group froze—they were so stunned by Willie's brazen disregard for curtsies being forbidden in DAR, no one seemed able to find their voice. Aelish quickly scanned the group and noted Leraza looked horrified, Melanthia rolled her eyes in utter disapproval, Bathwick's mouth was agape, and Lady Antonia looked like she was going to smack Willie across the face. Even little Suzanna sat up in Lady Antonia's hat and let out a small yip. But it was Thagar's reaction that shocked her most of all—he was embarrassed—*for* Willie.

Seeing that it was going to be left up to Aelish to put Willie in her place, she returned the curtsy, as if she were back in Ireland, greeting a nobleman's daughter. Lady Antonia gasped and Thagar was so taken aback, Aelish was certain he wished he had remained in the N.W. Quadrant.

"I understand your father was Earl of Brólaigh in Ireland. Tell me—how did he treat his tenant farmers?" asked Willie, baiting Aelish.

Aelish responded, "With kindness and respect, I hope. If your family had farmed my father's land, I'm sure we would have known each other. I would have been most grateful to have had someone to confide in that was experiencing the same challenges of our lavender skin color. I'm sorry we did not get that opportunity."

It was like a collective exhale could be heard from the group, but Aelish wasn't finished.

"Your magical abilities are renowned and may I offer my most sincere congratulations on your appointment to the Head Council. I continue to grieve for my family killed by plague, as

I'm sure you do, for yours. You have my deepest sympathies. Perhaps over time we will find concurrence on how to stop Earthly families, be they nobles or commoners, from the suffering we have endured," Aelish said graciously. "I look forward to hearing your presentation at the Head Council meeting next week."

Aelish noted Willie raised one eyebrow. Aelish took great satisfaction in her surprise. She had not only returned her disparaging curtsy, she had retorted Willie's veiled insult about her father.

"Aelish will *also* be presenting at the same meeting," stated Lady Antonia, smacking Willie's face with words, instead of her hand.

"You *are*?" asked Thagar. Aelish observed he was visibly shaken by the entire exchange between she and Willie.

"Yes, she is," remarked Melanthia. "The Head Council has decided to encourage varying points of view on how to deal with Komprathia and the outbreak of plague occurring on Earth. We are greatly looking forward to hearing your thesis, Aelish. You will be the first DARling to ever present in front of the Head Council, prior to their Commencement ceremony. It is quite an honor."

Aelish knew the encouragement and compliment from Melanthia was more for Willie's sake than for her own, but she was appreciative, nonetheless.

Just then a trumpet sounded, announcing the guests should take their seats to begin dining. Aelish knew this was going to be the most uncomfortable evening she had ever spent with Thagar.

Based on Willie's disparagement, she knew for certain Thagar was currently or had previously, been intimates with Willie. And conversely, he now knew she would be presenting the thesis she had refused to share with him, to the Head Council next week. It was as if their secrets had collided to create the perfect storm.

26

AFTER THE GALA

AELISH TRIED HER best to enjoy the rest of the gala. The food was exceptional, but she had lost her appetite after the altercation with Willie. The music was romantic and soothing, but dancing with Thagar felt like she was dancing with a complete stranger. They had lost their easy banter and had become oddly formal and polite with each other.

When the gala was over, Thagar stayed behind under the guise of overseeing the wrap-up of the event's security. They both knew it was a falsehood, but Aelish was relieved to depart on her own. She needed to get home to process what had happened and ruminate over Willie and Thagar.

Before she flew home, Lady Antonia embraced her, whispering in her ear, "All will be well, Aelish. Don't worry."

At the time Lady Antonia had whispered those words, she could not imagine how that would be possible. And it had been two days since the gala, and she continued to feel the same way.

Even Drummond could not cause a smile. He had made all her favorite dishes and sweets in an effort to cheer her, but they both knew there was only one being who could do that.

She spent her time between two things: editing her thesis for presentation to the Head Council and ruminating about Willie and Thagar. She felt much more confident about her thesis after the revisions, but felt totally disheartened about what was to become of her and Thagar.

In the late afternoon of the second day, a Sylph appeared with a note carrying the same seal as the invitation to the Sanctuary. The Sylph batted her eyes three times and flew off somewhat wearily. It was as if the perfect storm, created by their secrets, had cast a murky gloom over all the magical beings around her.

She went into her bedchamber and climbed under the covers, her head included. She created a small beam of light, by which to read Thagar's note.

My Dearest Aelish,

If acceptable to you, I would like to bring food from your favorite establishment—Jovan's—so that we may dine together this evening at your cottage. I feel it would be best if you dismiss Drummond early, so we may have complete privacy whilst we discuss the issues that have come between us. I will also bring spirits and sweets, so you may relax until we meet at say, seven o'clock? Please send me a telly message informing me whether or not this is acceptable to you. I hope that it is.

Yours,

Thagar

Aelish began sobbing under her bedcovers, with the note crumpled in her hand. She did not know if the outcome of the proposed evening would be a new beginning or the beginning of the end.

She closed her eyes and sent him a one word telly: *Come.*

As the hour approached, it began to pour. She opened her front door and saw that the street had become a river, encroaching the first step to her porch. The weather reflected the tears she had shed for the remainder of the afternoon. She closed the door and went to set the table, and saw that Drummond had already done so. It was the first time she had smiled in two days. She sat in the salon on the settee and waited.

Promptly at seven o'clock, she heard Thagar's signature knock. She rose apprehensively to open the door. He stood there laden with delicious smelling packages. His black curls were dripping from the rain and his smile was surrounded by growth from a new incoming beard.

"Oh, you are soaked!" cried Aelish. "Let me take these so you can dry off."

She took the packages and walked them to the kitchen to try and quiet her nerves. By the time she returned, Thagar had magically dried off. He reached out to draw her into a kiss, but she hesitated and touched his new scruff.

"Growing it back again?" she asked.

"I'm hoping it will lift the tumult between us," he replied.

She could see the sadness behind his eyes. After they briefly kissed, she began massaging her lips.

"I forgot how scratchy it is at this length," she chuckled wanly. "May I suggest we eat right away?"

"Of course, but would you mind pouring us a glass of this first?" asked Thagar. He produced a bottle of his favorite spirit from the inside pocket of his long coat.

After some spirits and a sumptuous dinner, they brought a tray of sweets into the salon. Aelish sat on the couch and Thagar sat across from her in one of the chairs. He reached for one of the sweetcakes set on the table between them.

Before putting it into his mouth he asked her, "Are you

nervous about your presentation?"

"I've been working on revisions over the last two days and I'm feeling more confident."

"You do realize, Aelish, that you've never shared one piece of it with me? Every time I ask you about it, you manage to change the topic—deftly, I might add, but I know when you are avoiding me, dearest."

"I will be right back," said Aelish. She abruptly got up from the settee and left the salon.

"Are you all right?" Thagar called out after her.

"Yes, I'm all right—one minute, please."

She returned with a bound document in her hand.

"I'm due to present this in five days. I think it's time you should read it," said Aelish, handing him her thesis.

"Why haven't you wanted to share it with me after all this time?" asked Thagar, taking the document from her.

She sat back down on the settee, braced for his reaction, and said, "Because there is an element of war in it, but not in the way you presume."

Aelish felt like a twenty-pound rock had lifted from her chest. She rested her head against the back of the settee and exhaled a deep breath. Thagar's reaction, however, made her relief instantly evaporate.

"Oh, Aelish, no," said Thagar. "Then you have not changed how you feel about Komprathia since I told you about the tunnels at the Sanctuary? All this time, Aelish, you have kept this from me? Why?"

"Because I knew you would disapprove and I didn't want it to come between us. But apparently, it has anyway," she said, gesturing toward the disapproving look on his face.

"But your Oath, Aelish. We commit to a life of peace in the harshest of circumstances. Is this because of the current outbreak of plague?"

"No, Thagar. It is because of *all* the outbreaks of plague. You haven't read the thesis, so you're unable to understand the context of how I propose to utilize the art of war. It is not how you think."

Thagar took a long pull of his spirit and placed his glass on the table. He sat on the edge of the chair with his legs apart and sighed.

"You asked me once, if I trusted you," said Aelish. "Do you trust *me*? Do you have faith in my abilities to maintain my Oath, while at the same time, offering up a solution to free the Earth from the Komprathian drone rats that continue to spread plague with abandon? I have taken my Oath and my studies at the POD and the Institute very seriously."

"And all the while, your focus has been solely on this one issue, yes?" asked Thagar.

"The plague has killed millions of people, Thagar. Should we wait until it has killed them all? Our Oath is for peace, but the Doctrine demands we protect Humanity. I believe I have found the delicate balance in my thesis to do both. Will you please read it before I present it?"

"I think after all this time, I would like to hear it firsthand through your voice along with the Head Council," stated Thagar. He tucked the thesis between the cushion and the arm of the chair. "Perhaps being mired in the responsibilities of my position as Commander has prevented me from developing new and alternate ways to combat the drone rats. I have spent one hundred long, unsuccessful years trying to penetrate the spells of the tunnels. I fear I have grown weary."

He slumped back against the chair and ran his hands through his hair, clearly troubled.

"And you've worked with Willie on the tunnels these last one hundred years as well, correct?" asked Aelish.

"I was a fool to think your paths would never cross," said Thagar.
"Are you in love with her?" asked Aelish. "I understand how a shared focus could cause you to have feelings for her." She rubbed her hand against her churning stomach.

"What happened at the gala was entirely my fault," admitted Thagar. "I fear I miscalculated the hurt I caused Willie when I ended our relationship, which resulted in her disparagement of you at the gala. I should have been completely honest with you from the moment I told you about the tunnels at the Szanctuary."

"So you *have* been intimates? May I ask for how long?" When he did not answer right away, Aelish pressed him further. "Do you still love her, Thagar? Was she in the N.W. Quadrant with you during the last month?"

"Oh, Aelish," sighed Thagar. "How long have you been worrying about this?"

"Since the day of the gala. Please tell me, Thagar. I need to know."

"Yes, we have been intimates, and no, she was not in the N.W. Quadrant with me during the last month. I am not in love with her. In fact, when I came to London when your parents died, I knew then, that I had *never* been in love with her."

"Can you please start at the beginning?" asked Aelish.

"When I first met you at Brólaigh Castle, you were a small DARling. Willie and I had recently become intimates. She and I were born during the same time period of the mid-1300s, whereas you and I, were born two hundred years apart."

"I am aware of the difference in our lifespans, Thagar— please, go on."

"When Sartaine, Antonia, and I returned to Earth, years after first meeting you at Brólaigh Castle, I was focused on our reconnaissance mission regarding the rats. What I was not prepared for, was what happened to me when we aspirated inside that horrible house in London."

Aelish was paying close attention. She had never before heard Thagar refer to the borrowed house in London as horrible.

"You were standing with your back to us on the balcony, gazing at the chaotic scene on the street below. When you turned and ran into Antonia's arms, nearly collapsing onto the floor, my heart seemed to break open. Since the death of my mother, I'd kept my heart firmly shut and closely guarded for fear of it breaking irreparably. The DARling I saw in front of me was not the small DARling I had met at Brólaigh Castle. You had grown up so lovely, Aelish. I couldn't reconcile the former with the current one in Antonia's arms. It was as if I had never met you.

"While Antonia comforted you, Sartaine and I did a quick inspection of the house and we found your parents dead of plague. When I realized you were completely alone, in a strange city, with your parents lying dead, ten feet away, I was overcome with emotions I did not recognize. There was sadness, of course, but there was something else. Your anguish did not overpower your determination in seeing your mission through—getting your parents out of London, with a proper Catholic burial, in the middle of an outbreak of plague. It was a strength I have only ever seen in battle and my respect and admiration for you transformed into love. It enveloped my heart, all on its own. By the time the boat docked in Ireland, I had fallen in love with you."

"But Willie endured even worse circumstances brought on by the plague. Her magical gifts are unparalleled and she is stunning. Why me and not her?" asked Aelish.

"You're asking me to describe the intangible mystery of love, Aelish. I wouldn't even deign to try," chuckled Thagar. "I felt like a being had put a spell on me. I *hoped* a being had put a spell on me. Then I could rid myself of the agony I felt, being in love with you.

"When I returned from London, I was honest with her. I told her my feelings for you and how they were different from my feelings for her. I told her you knew nothing of these feelings, and regardless of whether you and I were ever together, I could no longer continue our relationship. The glaring light of love had clearly illuminated that I had never been in love with Willie, or any other being for that matter. And that is why Willie treated you so harshly at the gala."

Aelish remained quiet, listening to every word.

"After I ended the relationship," said Thagar, "it was extremely difficult, as Willie and I had to maintain our professional relationship. We had to remain focused on our work regarding the tunnels. Many times she tried to reconcile with me, but I was adamant. I remained chaste and alone, Aelish— I was waiting for you."

"Why didn't you tell me this at the Sanctuary?" asked Aelish.

"I didn't think it appropriate to bring up a previous intimate, however relevant it was to our conversation about the tunnels. It would have been unseemly and undignified. As time went by, you were involved in your studies, and I in my work. I mistakenly concluded that it was unnecessary to ever tell you. It was me she was trying to hurt at the gala, not you. I hope you can forgive me, Aelish."

Aelish stayed silent.

"I along with others born in DAR, find the Human traits of DARlings born of the Earth, confounding," said Thagar. "These traits, more often than not, propel Earth born DARlings to have more empathy and more kindness toward others—you *feel* deeper than we ever could. I have tried to understand it, but fear I never will.

"In the beginning, I was drawn to Willie's passion and wildness. But I saw how easily that wildness could turn into recklessness—she can even seem unbalanced. The gala was not the first time I'd seen her behave in this manner, but it has gotten much worse since I ended our relationship.

"Leraza has tried to intervene, help her cope with the end of our relationship, and thwart her desire to war with Komprathia. I cannot imagine the humiliation Leraza endured after witnessing her *curtsy* in front of Melanthia and Bathwick. She's on the precipice of taking a seat on the Head Council and she embarrasses her Oraculi and herself, all for my benefit—to demonstrate the hurt I've caused her.

"I hope in time you will forgive me, Aelish, for having put you in such a situation, with no forewarning. I did not protect you and allowed you to be blind-sided."

"I think the Earth is a much harder place to grow up in, than DAR," said Aelish. "I think that Willie cannot forget the scrappy girl starving in the Bavarian countryside. Despite her extraordinary magical abilities, she still could not save her own family, nor all the other families she witnessed dying of plague."

Thagar gasped. "After all that I have just told you, I certainly was not expecting an empathetic reaction. It appears you have already forgiven her for the ill behavior she demonstrated toward you at the gala. This is a *perfect* example of how Human traits confound me—I shall never figure it out," said Thagar, shaking his head. "I hope you have some empathy and forgiveness for me, as well."

"Of course, I do," said Aelish. She was still evaluating everything Thagar had revealed.

"May I join you now on the settee, my love?"

Aelish patted the place next to her.

"And shall we agree, then, to never keep secrets from one another, from this point forward?" asked Thagar, as he sat down beside her.

Aelish did not answer him. He lifted her chin and held her face in his hand. Aelish kissed him, to intentionally avoid answering his question.

"Shall I take that as a yes?" asked Thagar, still holding her face in his hand. "Why do I get the feeling you are still not telling me something?" He groaned and pulled her into an embrace. "It's a good thing I love you, Aelish. Tell me when you are ready."

Her mother had always said that lying by omission was the same thing as a direct lie, but in this moment, she could not lose the warmth of his embrace.

27

AELISH

AELISH SAT ALONE at the presenter's table in front of the Head Council. The citizens had all departed with the exception of Lady Antonia, Thagar, and Sartaine who sat in the front, side row. The doors were locked and the Rotunda Guards stood against them on either side preventing any entry into the Chamber.

Aelish had requested a closed session with the Head Council. It was extremely rare for them to do so, wanting total transparency with the citizens of DAR. Aelish had met with Melanthia two days ago and explained that if she discussed her thesis in open session, it could potentially jeopardize the lives of certain magical beings. Melanthia remained quiet for some time after Aelish's request. But the bond they forged so long ago at Brólaigh Castle was strong. Melanthia supported Aelish's request and convinced the Head Council.

Council Chair Sukaaja, her black skin reflecting generations of military sacrifice, had finally calmed down after the open session. Willie's presentation had called for the complete annihilation of Komprathia—her loose cannon had indeed gone off. Sukaaja had threatened to resign on the spot, if a motion was made to bring Willie's proposal for a vote before the Head Council. No members made such a motion.

But to Aelish's surprise, the audience in the Chamber was evenly split between cheers and boos over Willie's proposal. She had never witnessed the commonwealth so divided. There was unrest brewing and the clock was ticking for the Head Council to take bold action against Komprathia. The plague was killing thousands a day.

"You have requested a closed session and I would like the record to reflect the age and student status of our next presenter," stated Sukaaja. "Are you ready to begin?"

"I am, Council Chair," stated Aelish.

"You may proceed."

"For the last six months, I have been transporting into Komprathia behind DAR's invisibility wall, in order to have clandestine meetings with an asset I have cultivated."

She heard Lady Antonia cry out. She saw Thagar shoot up from his seat and Sartaine stand and put his arm around Thagar. What he said to Thagar was inaudible to Aelish, but it made Thagar sit back down. The Head Council Members began speaking across and over each other until Sukaaja slammed down the gavel and called for order.

"Who else knows about this?" asked Sukaaja.

"No one, except my Brownie, Drummond," Aelish took a long pause, "and the two families from Komprathia, I found living in my garden."

She heard Lady Antonia gasp. Thagar again stood up from his seat. She heard Sartaine pleading with him to sit down. She knew her relationship with Thagar was already over, but she held on to her convictions. She remained outwardly unaffected by the reactions of those she loved.

"And who is your asset in Komprathia?" asked Sukaaja.

"His name is Cagélét and he is the Minister of Security for Komprathia. He reports directly to King Gidius' brother, Obredón," stated Aelish.

"Do you understand your actions constitute the most egregious crime against DAR and that you have endangered the entire commonwealth? You have conducted clandestine meetings with a high-ranking official from an enemy Kingdom, one that we are currently at war with, and you have aspirated into said Kingdom with no authorization. Do you know the penalty for such actions?" asked Sukaaja.

"Yes, Council Chair. Banishment from DAR for life, to another magical realm of the Head Council's choosing."

"And knowing this, you continued on this course of action, regardless of the consequences? What if you had been captured?" asked Sukaaja.

"I was prepared to utilize the Exterminate spell and destroy myself," answered Aelish.

She heard a male voice cry out and knew it was her beloved, Thagar. She saw Melanthia put her hand across her chest, as if unable to breathe.

One of the Head Council Members blurted out, "Wasn't that spell made illegal after the Rising?"

With tears in her eyes, Melanthia indicated to Sukaaja that she wished to respond to the question.

"You may answer, Melanthia," stated Sukaaja.

"No, it is still legal. Although, in my opinion, I feel it should be abolished. However, it is buried deep inside the Breanon. It had formerly been available in the public access area, but I had it moved to the secure area, once I joined the Head Council. How did you discover it, Aelish?" asked Melanthia.

"I was searching for a spell like this, as I knew my mission was a tremendous risk. One of the Keepers in the Breanon told me that the spell was kept in the secure area, not accessible to students. Subsequent to my conversation with the Keeper, I located it buried amongst other books in the *public* access area, after I received a note at my cottage, telling me where to look."

"Does this Keeper know anything about your meetings with Cagélét?" asked Sukaaja. "And further, would you be able to identify this Keeper?"

"No, Council Chair. The Keeper knows nothing about my meetings. And yes, I would be able to identify her. As I stated earlier, the only life I was willing to risk was my own."

"And all of DAR!" yelled out another Council Member. "There often isn't *time* to utilize the Exterminate spell when captured. And after Komprathia tortured you until DAR's magical abilities were compromised, what was to become of your commonwealth?"

"You are out of order," admonished Sukaaja. "But I appreciate the question and would like you to answer it, Aelish."

"The father of one of the Komprathian families living in my garden is the Deputy Minister of Security. His name is Seratus. He has spent years orchestrating his family's escape, along with the family of Komprathian drone rats he found hiding in his garden. He refused to leave the drone rat family behind, as he is fiercely opposed to the policies in Komprathia toward their drone rats. Seratus helped orchestrate my meetings with Cagélét. We agreed that each time I transported into Komprathia, if I had not returned within twenty-four hours, he was to find me in Komprathia and kill me on sight. If captured, he would tell King Gidius that I had held him prisoner in DAR."

Lady Antonia began crying.

"Wouldn't he have endangered his own life by returning to Komprathia?" asked Sukaaja.

"Quite possibly, Council Chair. But Seratus was willing to give his own life and terminate mine, to protect the magic of DAR."

"And what if he was unable to reach you?" pressed Sukaaja. "What if DAR had caught him trying to return?"

"I prepared for that eventuality by learning how to manipulate the Exterminate spell as a timed-event."

"Can you explain that in more detail?" asked Sukaaja, intrigued.

"I would cast the Exterminate spell on myself prior to transporting into Komprathia. I learned how to control it through a time-activated spell, which would destroy me within seventy-two hours. I could not get the time frame any tighter and that is the only reason I allowed Seratus to put himself in harm's way. I hoped I could survive the torture for seventy-two hours, should Seratus not be able to reach me, without compromising the magical intelligence of DAR."

Aelish heard Lady Antonia trying to calm down Thagar and one of the Head Council Members utter, "That's incredible."

"I think we need a short recess," stated Sukaaja. "Guards, please encircle the presenter."

Ten Guards aspirated around Aelish. They were dressed differently from the ones guarding the doors. They encircled her while she remained seated. When she tried to send a telepathic message to Lady Antonia, she was unable. She realized her magical abilities had been rendered immobilized by the Guards. She tried to glance over to where they were all sitting, but the Guards blocked her view.

After fifteen minutes, the Head Council reconvened. They wore troubled looks on their faces, as if there had been discord among them.

"Guards, allow us to see the presenter," commanded Sukaaja.

They separated just enough for the Head Council to see Aelish and for Aelish to see the Head Council. Aelish desperately wanted to test out her magical abilities, but she was afraid any magical movement on her part, would further compromise her already precarious situation.

"Let the record reflect that the Head Council has decided to let Aelish continue with her presentation," stated Sukaaja. "We wish to hear your explanation for such reckless and thoughtless behavior toward your commonwealth. Choose your words very carefully. This may be the last time you are allowed to speak before you are permanently banished, since you have already confessed your actions."

Aelish could not let herself think about never returning to her cottage. She had waited for this moment since Thagar had told her about the tunnels in the Sanctuary. There was nothing left to do, but speak the truth.

"My Human mother once told me, 'never underestimate the depths of the broken female heart.' And mine, Council Chair, has been broken since the day my Human father, Cian Carrigan, Earl of Brólaigh and my mother, Saoirse Mulcahy Carrigan, Lady of Brólaigh, drew their last breaths in London, England, killed by plague, one hundred and two years ago.

"Six months after I arrived in DAR, I learned that the Kingdom of Yasteron had built secret impenetrable tunnels, bypassing the Portal to Earth, for their ally Komprathia. Komprathia then used those tunnels to force their own drone rats on a suicide mission. The drone rats were sent to Earth to catch and spread the plague, as weapons against Humanity. Upon learning this, I decided to devote my magical education and attainments toward stopping the drone rats.

"Commander Thagar and Head Council Member Wilhelmina Von Etzenbach have worked tirelessly for decades, trying to break down the tunnel spells, in an effort to destroy them. But even if the tunnels were destroyed, wouldn't Yasteron simply relocate and rebuild them? In my opinion, a successful military strategy must include not only the destruction of the tunnels, but also the destruction of the *relationship* between Yasteron and Komprathia. DAR must forever isolate Komprathia from the advanced magical abilities of Yasteron.

"The commonwealth of DAR is growing restless. The citizens have tired of Gidius' endless assault on Humanity through the use of plague. One of your own Head Council Members, only hours ago, called for the annihilation of Komprathia, violating her own Oath of Peace. But the Doctrine of DAR clearly states we must protect Humanity. Are the Oath and the Doctrine not equivalents?

"I grew up in Ireland, under the oppression of England and its monarchy. I assumed there was another heir to the Kingdom or an advisor close to Gidius that wished to overthrow him and stop his madness against the drone rats. Since learning of the tunnels, I prayed to God for a way to combat Gidius' incomprehensible evil. When I found the Komprathian families in my own garden, I knew God had answered my prayers.

"It took a long time for me to gain the trust of Seratus, but I discovered that his love for DAR was equal to my own. His place of refuge means more to him than it does to the average DARling; he does not take it for granted.

"I learned that Seratus and Cagélét were very close and like-minded. They both wished to free Komprathia from the tyranny of King Gidius. So, they made a pact. Seratus would escape and locate a DARling willing to go to Komprathia and meet with Gidius' younger brother, Obredón. Obredón wants to overthrow his brother and stop the murder of the drone rats, which he considers citizens. This in turn, would slow the spread of plague on Earth."

"How many times have you met with Cagélét over the last six months?" interrupted Sukaaja.

"We have met on twelve separate occasions in Komprathia."

"But you have never met with Gidius' brother, Obredón?"

"No, Council Chair."

"Why not?"

"Obredón knows I am here today, before the Head Council to secure DAR's support. Without it, there is no point in meeting with him and endangering his life."

"Let's hypothetically say we commit to that support. We would of course need to know more specifics, but what then?"

"I would have Cagélét arrange for me to meet with Obredón. Each time I met with Cagélét in Komprathia, I changed my appearance from a DARling to a Yasteron. I did this for his protection. If our clandestine meetings were discovered, Cagélét would simply be meeting with an ally of Komprathia.

"Did you transport as a female from Yasteron only for his protection, or were there other reasons, as well?" asked Sukaaja.

"There were other reasons. Cagélét informed me that Gidius rarely lets Obredón conduct meetings without him. Gidius is obviously wary of the second in line to his Kingdom. Thus, Gidius would most likely be present at the proposed meeting with Obredón.

"The pretense of the proposed meeting would be to improve Komprathian security. I would be posing as a security expert from Yasteron. While I am now fluent in the languages of Komprathia and Yasteron, I do need further training on Yasteron's surveillance and detection grids, to convince King Gidius. When Obredón begins the coup, I want Gidius to remember it occurred *subsequent* to this meeting. I want him to clearly understand that Yasteron deceived him and pledged their support to his brother."

"So that, has been your ultimate goal?" asked Sukaaja.

"Yes. I want to destroy the relationship between Yasteron and Komprathia in perpetuity."

"And how will you attain the intelligence needed to destroy

the tunnels?" questioned Sukaaja.

"DAR must not only support Obredón's coup, but we must also provide him with the magical warcraft necessary to protect the Komprathians who choose to stay and fight King Gidius' soldiers. Only then, will Obredón release the spells of the tunnels to DAR.

"Komprathia has existed under tyrannical rule for a long time. They are a magically backward society. DAR need not provide them with complex warcraft spells. Those we no longer utilize would be sufficient. With DAR in control of the warcraft, we could reduce the loss of life on both sides of the Komprathian civil war, by nearly ninety percent. We could, therefore, maintain the balance between our Oath of Peace *and* the tenets of our Doctrine.

"Once we possess the tunnel spells, we would destroy them. With Gidius' trust of Yasteron severed, he could not rebuild them. The drone rats would be stopped. Gidius would now be embroiled in a civil war against Obredón. He would soon forget about Humans, as his focus would be on regaining control of his Kingdom. He will ultimately be defeated, but only with DAR's assistance.

"Finally, once we have the tunnel spells, DAR can rebuild them leading *away* from Komprathia, into DAR. As evidenced by the families living in my garden, they are already trying to escape. DAR should assist the refugees of Komprathia through various programs focused on education, resettlement, and vocations. When the civil war is over and Gidius is no longer a threat, they can return home to what will hopefully be a peaceful, prosperous Kingdom that is now an ally of DAR," concluded Aelish.

The Chamber was completely quiet.

Sukaaja cleared her throat and asked, "Aelish, how did you manage to go behind enemy lines without the POD ever noticing, twelve times in the last six months?"

"I had several classes in the N.W. Quadrant on stealth techniques, taught by an ingenious Professor. Professor Quentin showed us the magic of a new stealth fabric he is working on that would allow DAR to secretly penetrate the detection grid of Yasteron. He explained that the fabric was a prototype and not complete. He taught us that the detection grid in Yasteron was far superior to anything developed in DAR, to date.

"I asked him if I could take a small piece of the fabric as a souvenir from my time in the N.W. Quadrant. He was most flattered to part with it, knowing it was harmless for me to have. He explained that the spells woven into the fabric needed many improvements to surpass the detection grid of Yasteron.

"When I returned to the S.E. Quadrant, I used a spell to create yards of the fabric to fashion myself a tight-fitting suit. The first time I transported into Komprathia, I expected to be stopped by DARling soldiers, but nothing happened—not departing DAR or reentering DAR. The stealth capacity of the fabric worked. It bypassed the spells of our own detection grid and the invisibility wall on the border between DAR and Komprathia. Our detection grid obviously needs improvement and Professor Quentin is quite close to completing a stealth fabric that will be able to bypass Yasteron's detection grid."

"So, by using your student status, you manipulated a trusting Professor in to giving you one of our greatest military secrets?" asked Sukaaja.

"Yes, I did."

"I have two questions, Aelish," stated Sukaaja. "Why have you risked your life and your freedom? And why have you *intentionally* violated the laws of DAR?"

"Until the Komprathian drone rats are stopped, my grief over the deaths of my parents will not end. My grief only worsened after learning they were, in effect, murdered. Losing my life or my freedom, to honor my parents, is an easy sacrifice to make."

Sukaaja threaded her hands together and rested her chin on them. She stared at Aelish. "Do you have any remorse for violating the laws of DAR?" she asked.

"No. Laws are merely guidelines of societal behavior. When they begin to prevent a society from acting boldly to stop a tyrannical ruler like King Gidius, those laws then contradict their original intent and purpose. To be able to violate them with a clear conscious, as I have, demands they be redressed. The laws are not only failing the society that enacted them, but they are also failing those the society swore to protect."

"Do you have any regrets regarding your actions?" asked Sukaaja.

"Yes. In order to protect those I love the most, I was deceitful and dishonest. In my selfish quest to stop the plague and rid myself of the unending grief I suffer from, I fear I have lost their love forever."

Sukaaja took a deep breath. She looked from side to side at her fellow Council Members.

"Does the Council have any final comments or questions for Aelish?" asked Sukaaja.

Willie motioned to the Council Chair. Aelish knew Sukaaja most definitely did not want to hear from Willie again this day, but the rules of order forced her to allow it.

"You may proceed," stated Sukaaja.

"Council Chair, as an Earth born DARling," began Willie, "I would like to convey to Aelish and the Head Council that I not only understand her unending grief, but I suffer from it, as well. Watching thousands die of plague, with our magical abilities powerless to stop it, affects those of us with lavender skin for a lifetime."

Aelish weakly smiled and nodded at Willie.

"Do any other Council Members wish to speak?" asked Sukaaja.

The Head Council Members remained quiet; they were somber and pensive. Melanthia looked devastated.

"Very well, then. Let the record reflect that until the Head Council has reviewed Aelish's case in its entirety, she is now a prisoner of DAR. Aelish, you are to be confined in the N.W. Quadrant Detention Center. You will be held for a period of no more than six months, without a final determination of your status. The Guards will process and transport you to the Detention Center this evening. Do you have any final questions?" asked Sukaaja.

"Yes, Council Chair. Will my magical abilities be restored during my time in the Detention Center?"

"No, they will not—for your own protection," stated Sukaaja.

Aelish knew she was referring to the Exterminate spell and simply nodded her head.

"Guards, please escort the prisoner to the processing center," commanded Sukaaja.

One of the Guards motioned for her to rise and the ten Guards encircled her freedom. As she was escorted out of the Chamber, she heard Lady Antonia sobbing. Aelish looked up at the dome and wondered what the legendary figures thought of her actions.

28

PRISONER 1415988

AELISH STOOD LOOKING through the grate of the small window of her cell. The sun was rising, but the color of the sky was like a continuation of the gray wall color of her ten-by-ten cell. During the last six months, she was allowed no visitors and had not even received the representation of a solicitor. She deduced that since she had told the Head Council everything, there was no reason for a solicitor.

Prison was awful. It was reminiscent of her weeks of confinement at Brólaigh Castle when her skin color began changing. But mostly, it reminded her of how she felt locked inside the house in London by the Watchmen. She found it interesting how confinement, and her fear of it, had been a constant theme in her life.

The monotony of prison was the worst aspect. Every day was the same: the same schedule, the same food, and the same activities, day after day. Days bereft of her magical abilities left her emotionally barren. If not for her faith and the rosary provided to her by the Detention Center, she knew her sanity would have left her after a week. It was hard to keep track of the days, as they rolled one into another, but she knew today was six months to the day of her imprisonment. She was anxiously awaiting the outcome of her fate.

She lay down on her cot trying to calm herself and fell into a dream about the first time she had transported into Komprathia. She arrived behind DAR's invisibility wall and was standing behind enemy lines and the war zone. The trees were charred and void of branches, their stumps stood as monuments to past battles. Cagélét had given her the coordinates for transporting into the safety zone, yet she was still close enough to observe the Komprathian troops setting up weaponry to try and penetrate the invisibility wall protecting DAR. To see it from this side was extraordinary. The soldiers were furiously working to set up warcraft that was completely unnecessary and useless. Without the actual spells, the soldiers could never physically destroy the wall.

What a legacy for Director Bathwick.

Her inventions and creations had saved so many DARling soldiers and citizens, while at the same time, exhausting the resources of Komprathia's military. Aelish could see there were no deaths amongst the soldiers, but their faces were weary with defeat, from the endless and fruitless battles.

They must do this day after day after day. For a moment, she pitied them.

Unable to use any of her magical spells for fear of alerting DAR's detection grid, she continued walking away from the war zone to the rendezvous point arranged by Seratus and Cagélét. The brush was high, but the color of everything was muted. The Kingdom was devoid of vivid color anywhere. The trees were a bit fuller here, but their leaves seemed dead despite remaining on the branches. Hues of brown and dull greens marked the landscape along with gray stone structures.

She could see small horizontal openings along the upper portion of the stone structures. She assumed they were windows in the stone structure homes of the Komprathians. They were less like homes and more resembled bunkers—bunkers she had seen in the N.W. Quadrant of DAR used to protect and store supplies for magical experiments. In DAR, however, the bunkers were both above and below ground. She wondered if it was the same in Komprathia.

As she continued on her way, drone rats would occasionally scurry over her boots on the way to their nests. She saw families of Komprathians outside their bunkers doing daily chores and preparing meals, but the entire Kingdom felt scorched. And it smelled burned. It reminded her of the Irish countryside after British troops had burned the crops to induce famine. The Kingdom had that same smell of death.

So far, the camouflage spells transforming her appearance from a DARling to a Yasteron were holding. The hooded suit she had fashioned from Professor Quentin's magical fabric covered her entirely with three exceptions—her pale beige face, her pale beige hands, and the remaining portion of her yellow hair, not covered by the hood, which hung loosely over her breasts—even her boots were encased by the suit. She had transformed her appearance, prior to transporting, as she was terrified any use of DARling magic on this side of the invisibility wall, would set off DAR's detection grid.

The Komprathians she passed did not look at her with suspicion. She looked like any other young, female Yasteron. While the suit appeared effective in allowing her to remain undetected, she kept looking behind her waiting for the soldiers of DAR to capture her.

"Prisoner 1415988."

Aelish instantly awoke, but was briefly disoriented. She realized the commanding voice was that of her favorite Detention Center Guard. Her cell gate clanged open and the Guard entered holding a bag in both hands, like she was carrying a tray.

"You are free to go," said the Guard. "Here are the clothes

and belongings you came in with."

Aelish shook her head and pinched her arm through her prison uniform to make sure she was not still dreaming. She sat up on the side of the cot and looked up at the Guard trying to find her voice.

"I am not to be banished, then?" asked Aelish. She stood up slowly from her cot, feeling as though her legs would not support her.

"Apparently not. In fact, you are the new hero of the commonwealth. We have not seen this much unrest in DAR since the Rising. Bencarlta has had nothing but demonstrations for months, the citizens all clamoring for your release," stated the Guard.

Aelish stared at her in disbelief.

"You will see when you return to the S.E. Quadrant. There are new shops in the district that have opened up over the last six months. They offer a variety of items such as cups, plates, shirts, all with your image on them; your image is now everywhere."

"Good God, that cannot be true," said Aelish. She sat back down on the cot holding her bag of belongings, feeling faint.

"The Guards were forbidden to tell you anything about it until the Head Council made their final decision about your status."

Aelish put her face in her hands and began to weep.

"May I say, Prisoner 1415988, that the Guards are all in agreement—we have never guarded a more elegant, gracious prisoner in the history of this Detention Center. You don't belong here and we are all happy to see you released."

Not knowing what else to say, Aelish softly said, "Thank you."

"Get dressed and I will escort you to the exit. There's a being already waiting for you outside," smiled the Guard.

As Aelish dressed, she tried to comprehend what could have happened that allowed her to regain her freedom. Other than being allowed to read books from the Detention Center, all prisoners were isolated from the events of the outside world. Deprived of their magical abilities, they could no longer access DAR's telepathic news feeds.

The Guard returned for her. Aelish was now dressed and smelled the mustiness of the gown she had worn before the Head Council. She planned on burning it. As she stepped outside her cell and began walking with the Guard, she heard the sound of the cell gate lock behind her. She hoped she would never hear that sound again in her life. They headed down a series of stairwells and hallways, until she and the Guard came to a steel door.

"Are you ready?" asked the Guard.

"Will my magical powers be restored?" asked Aelish, petrified of the answer.

"Yes. As soon as you clear the confines of the prison property and have gone past the fence, you will have a clear signal. You might be a little rusty, but all will be normal in about a week's time. Good luck to you, Aelish. Thank you for what you did for DAR," said the Guard. It was the first time the Guard had used her actual name.

Aelish nodded and weakly smiled, unsure of anything. The Guard briefly closed her eyes, magically opening the steel door. Despite the grayness of the sky, the sunlight behind it momentarily blinded Aelish. As her vision settled, she saw Lady Antonia standing on the other side of the fence, furiously waving at her. She was jumping up and down, crying and smiling.

Aelish walked through the door of the fence that opened on its own and she collapsed into Lady Antonia's embrace.

"Aelish, dear!" cried Lady Antonia. Her face was wet with tears. "Let me look at you." Lady Antonia pulled away and examined Aelish's appearance. "Were you physically hurt in any way?" She inspected Aelish from head to toe.

"No. They were distant with me, but as kind as one would expect from prison Guards."

"You are so thin, Aelish and your skin color is so faint," said Lady Antonia. She reached behind Aelish's head for her signature fishtail braid that was no longer. "They cut your hair, then. Nothing that can't be fixed with a little time."

"I want to go home, Antonia. Can we take the long way and fly home? I want to see the world again before I see my cottage. Do I still have my cottage?"

Antonia hesitated.

"They took my home away, then," Aelish said resigned.

"No, dear. You still have your cottage. But are you strong enough to fly? We could simply transport back to Bencarlta."

"Let's try, if I get too tired we can always transport."

Aelish was oblivious to how heartbreaking her depression and exhaustion was to Lady Antonia.

"Shall we ascend?" asked Lady Antonia, with false cheerfulness.

"I hope I still can," said Aelish.

At first nothing happened and her head began to ache, but then slowly, she began to lift.

"Good God! My magic is coming back!" exclaimed Aelish, crying, as she lifted into the air. "That was the most horrendous part, having no magical abilities."

"Are you sure you are strong enough to do this, dear?" asked Lady Antonia.

"I think so. It feels so good to ascend again," said Aelish, floating a few feet off the ground. Aelish could see Lady Antonia was internally debating their decision to fly.

"All right then, dear, slowly at first," cautioned Lady Antonia. "The N.W. Quadrant is not as populated as the S.E. Quadrant, so there are not many beings flying. Let's proceed slowly. We can take our time."

Aelish lifted high into the air and began to fly side by side with Lady Antonia. She began to emotionally brighten, feeling the wind on her face. She had never flown with short hair; it felt very strange. They flew together in silence until they reached the intersection of all four Quadrants, precisely in the middle of DAR.

"Let's rest for a bit," suggested Lady Antonia. "There is an establishment near the intersection where we can get something to eat. You must be starving."

"I am a little hungry, now," said Aelish.

As they approached the establishment, Lady Antonia said, "Oh good, they have tables outside that are not crowded."

They chose a small table under the bough of a beautiful tree and Aelish sat down, closed her eyes, and put her head back. The warm weather approaching from the S.E. Quadrant began to restore her. Lady Antonia went inside to order their meals and Aelish looked around at the vegetation and mountains in the distance. She quietly thanked God for her deliverance. She reached into her gown pocket for the prison rosary and made a mental promise never to part with it.

Lady Antonia returned and relayed that the food would be at their table shortly.

"How are you feeling, dear?" asked Lady Antonia, sitting down.

"A bit better," answered Aelish.

Their meal magically arrived and from the first bite, Aelish ate like a starving peasant in Ireland. She didn't stop eating and drinking until the whole meal was devoured, saying nothing. She was unaware that Lady Antonia had begun to weep, until Aelish looked up, after finishing her food.

"Please don't cry," said Aelish. "Thank you. That was the most delicious meal I have ever eaten and I will never forget it."

Lady Antonia had eaten nothing.

"Please eat, Antonia," coaxed Aelish.

"All right, dear," said Lady Antonia. She wiped her face with a handkerchief and began to eat.

When Lady Antonia was finished, they sat together in blissful silence, until a group of females between young and grown approached the establishment.

"Is that *Aelish*?" asked one of the females to the others.

"Oh, my DAR, it is!"

Aelish, who was clearly startled, looked up at the group of DARleens, who now stood around their table.

"Is it really you?" asked one of the females to Aelish. "Can we capture your image with us?" They all gathered behind her and flashes of light kept going off, disorienting Aelish.

"Will you sign your name to our schoolbooks?" asked another.

"All right, now," smiled Lady Antonia. "Aelish has just been released from the Detention Center and is too tired to sign your books. But you can tell all your friends that you were the first DARlings she met after being released from prison. Now, off you go," said Lady Antonia, her hands in a scooting gesture.

"Wait! Are you Antonia, her Oraculi? Oh, my DAR! It's Aelish's Oraculi!" screamed the females all together, jumping up and down.

"Here," said Lady Antonia, "take my information and feel free to send me a telly if you need guidance." She put her hand to the side of her head and telepathically transmitted her contact information to the DARleens. They all screamed with excitement after receiving it.

"No one is going to believe this—we *have* to take an image with you," said one of the females to Lady Antonia.

"Very well, then. Gather round and take your images," said Lady Antonia. She smiled broadly for the females. "Excellent, now off you go."

The females walked into the establishment giggling, laughing, and shouting to one another.

Within two minutes the owner of the establishment walked outside and said to Aelish, "Oh, my DAR, is my food the first you have eaten since your release today?"

"Yes, it was absolutely the best meal I've ever eaten," answered Aelish. She extended her hand to the owner. "I am Aelish. What is your name?"

"Oh, I am no one, I mean my name is Ella, owner of the establishment," she fussed, stumbling over her words. "But of course, I know you are *Aelish*! Thank you for what you have done for DAR. My mate will never believe you were here; he is going to kick himself for being lazy and not helping me out today."

Aelish observed that the DARleens were watching the entire exchange from behind the establishment's glass window. They were still laughing and continuing to jump up and down.

"It's been an honor," Ella said smiling broadly. "We will all leave you in peace now. Stay as long as you like. I know you don't live here, but I hope you will come back and visit us again."

"Of course," said Aelish.

When the owner went back inside the establishment, Aelish stared at Lady Antonia and asked, "What just happened? And since when do you give out your *information*?" asked Aelish, with one eyebrow raised.

"Well, that's why I wanted to stop before we entered Bencarlta," said Lady Antonia. "You're quite famous now, Aelish, and being your Oraculi . . . well . . . I, too, am now famous. You are the new hero of DAR, Aelish," stated Lady Antonia.

"That's what the prison Guard told me right before I left. I forgot all about it. What is going on? Help me, Antonia. Why am I a hero? I thought I was going to be banished today," said Aelish with tears in her eyes.

"Well I'd have to start from your presentation in front of the Head Council. Are you sure you're up to hearing what happened in the aftermath?" asked Lady Antonia.

"Yes, I need to know what is going on," said Aelish.

"Very well then, dear. I will try my best to remember everything."

29

THE AFTERMATH

LADY ANTONIA BEGAN:
"As we were waiting for your presentation to begin, I asked Thagar if he had read your thesis. He indicated that although you had given him a copy of it five days before, he had decided to wait and hear it through your voice, in front of the Head Council.

"From your first statement, when you disclosed you'd been transporting into Komprathia, we all knew your chances of walking out of the Chamber that day were highly unlikely. Thagar shot up from his seat to stop you from further self-incrimination. He knew the penalty of your first statement was banishment from DAR. But Sartaine, one of the most levelheaded members of the military I have ever known, convinced him to remain quiet. He told Thagar to sit down or he would be immediately detained in light of your being intimates. When Thagar shot up again after your second statement, Sartaine advised that we had to listen to the whole presentation. Only then, might we be able to help you regain your freedom.

"I actually don't know how the three of us made it through till the end. Watching helplessly as the Guards encircled your freedom, leading you to the processing area for the Detention Center; it was one of the darkest moments in my life, Aelish.

"But we had no time to absorb it. After you were escorted out of the Chamber, Sukaaja told Thagar and Sartaine they were both relieved of their commands forthwith. They were to be detained in the Military Detention Center of the POD, otherwise known as the MDC. Twenty more Guards appeared. Thagar began resisting his detainment and was floated out, after the Guards magically rendered him unconscious. Ten Guards encircled each of their freedoms and led them to the MDC. I did not see either of them again for over four months.

"The Head Council did not believe you could have transported into Komprathia, without Thagar or Sartaine's assistance. The investigation penetrated every level of the POD for weeks. The Head Council was not convinced Professor Quentin's fabric was sufficient to allow you to slip in and out of Komprathia, unseen. They assumed the detection grid of DAR, as well as the invisibility wall, were being deactivated for your clandestine meetings with Cagélét. DAR's most revered POD leadership, from every Quadrant, was questioned for weeks. The fact that literally no one knew anything, actually made it appear *more* like a conspiracy.

"I don't know what would have happened to Thagar, if Bathwick had not been his Commander. She became intricately involved in his interrogation sessions, after the first month. It was very hard for her to treat him as a suspect, but she needed to make sure he had not done anything untoward to DAR, because of his love for you. She saved his life, Aelish, in every way, as well as his command, which was restored within four months. Thagar and Sartaine spent three months in the MDC. They forged a bond greater than brothers. Sartaine was also reinstated as Lieutenant Commander. I didn't think either of them would ever want to serve the POD again. However, their devotion and commitment to DAR goes back so many generations, it flows through their veins.

"I was not detained, but was ordered to appear at the POD for interrogations, fourteen hours a day, for the next two weeks. It was frightening, Aelish—to be under suspicion and treated as though you are guilty, when you are innocent. I felt I had failed you in every way imaginable, foremost as your Oraculi, but most painfully, as your friend. I berated myself for not fully recognizing the agony you lived with, day in and day out, over the deaths of your parents.

"When I first came to DAR, my testimony before the Head Council about King Henry VIII's Court and the subsequent matriarchal change in DAR healed me, as it redeemed the deaths of my parents. I realized, during your first hundred years in DAR, there had been no such redemption for you.

"After listening to your presentation, I knew you had protected me from being implicated through ignorance. I now knew why you had never let me fully read your thesis, only choosing to share certain concepts.

"Here I was the Oraculi, who should have been protecting you, and you ended up protecting me. I should have done more to help you overcome your grief—to stop you from becoming reckless with your own life. My God, Aelish, the Exterminate spell? And you fashioned it with a time-activated spell? You took all these precautions to ensure your own death, to protect DAR. The sacrifice, the bravery; I did not feel worthy to be your Oraculi. I was certain the Head Council would strip me of my position. I deserved to be stripped of it.

"The Keeper you mentioned in your presentation was identified within the Breanon. She was subsequently relieved of her duties for providing you with the Exterminate spell. She became the first to publicly protest against the Head Council, on your behalf. She cared nothing about her legacy as a Keeper and applauded your actions.

"Willie seized on the sentiment of the Keeper and became your greatest supporter. She galvanized the social unrest in the streets to obtain your freedom. There were demonstrations and chants every day outside the Rotunda and on the great Lawn:

'Free prisoner 1415988—free her now, before it's too late'

'Free Aelish'

'Free the hero of DAR'

'Free the brave female—the Head Council is wrong—they're doing nothing for Humanity—save the Earth'

'Save the Humans from the plague—bring our Aelish back again'

'She broke no Oath, she did no harm, she fought for Earth, sound the alarm'

"The protests and demonstrations continued for the duration of your confinement in the Detention Center. Now that you are free, the Head Council is concerned about further unrest. They are taking measures to calm the citizenry, in order to regain control of the commonwealth.

"Business is booming for the new and existing shops near the Rotunda; your image is on every imaginable item, Aelish. Throughout Bencarlta, there are banners, posters, murals, and new art installations. DAR's most famous artists created them, to help you regain your freedom. You need to prepare yourself before we get there, because you have never seen anything like it. Despite no longer having your signature fishtail braid, you'd still have to change the color of your hair to get around the city unnoticed.

"But who held up the process in substantiating that your presentation was truthful—Drummond! I wanted to throttle him. You forewarned Drummond that you might not return to the cottage, and when you didn't, he followed your instructions to the tee.

"He hid the Komprathian families, far outside the valley. We couldn't find him for a month! He wouldn't answer our messages.

Finally, his sister Drusilda advised me that in an emergency situation, there is a secret Brownie spell utilized to contact another Brownie. She told him she was dying from the mayhem and wanted to say goodbye—and it worked—he came out of hiding. He never did get to see Drusilda. When he arrived at my house, soldiers immediately detained him. It was pitiful to watch him resist his confinement—his tiny legs kicking, his conical hat falling to the ground. I still feel guilty, but I had no choice.

"The Head Council had ordered the POD to locate the families in order to corroborate your presentation. The interrogators told Drummond they would banish you forever, if he did not give up their location. For you, Drummond gave them up. The Komprathians were not treated unkindly, but they were of course, terrified. Seratus corroborated everything you had presented and that was when the tide began to turn. Drummond is once again living with me. He has been a nervous wreck with worry about your detention, and has been slow to recover from the trauma of having his own freedom detained. Living with Drusilda again has further exacerbated his condition.

"But who *legally* gained your freedom? That honor went to the Head Council Member, who years ago should have become a Keeper—my beloved Oraculi, Melanthia. She was devastated by your detention and remembered reading a very old law that could legally free you. But she could not find it. Melanthia is not easily deterred by a challenge, especially when it comes to research. She spent months searching in the tombs of the Breanon, until she found it.

"The Law was written over five hundred years ago and states:
§§DARC 215815: Any DARling may use subterfuge and violate the existing laws of DAR in an effort to prohibit the creation of a tyrannical ruler in a magical realm or free a magical realm from tyrannical rule.

§(A) The law does not provide DARlings a way to escape prosecution of existing laws simply by claiming their intent was to prevent a tyrannical ruler or free a magical realm from tyrannical rule.

§(B) Thus, the law is applicable when the facts demand it and the Head Council finds it to be so on a case-by-case basis.

§(C) The law is especially applicable when said tyrannical ruler is causing the murder of his own beings/subjects within the magical realm and when said realm is warring with DAR.

§(D) The end justifies the means—if the result is freedom in the magical realm from tyrannical rule and the actions undertaken by the DARling in question was with the intent to create a peaceful alliance with DAR.

§(E) The law applies if the DARling in question has not violated his/her Oath of Peace. No DARling shall be prosecuted or banished for crimes against DAR when this law applies. If the Oath of Peace has been violated, the law does not apply.

"I don't know how she found it. Five hundred years ago, the all-male Head Council wrote the law, long before the Rising. Once the rumor about the law began to permeate throughout DAR, males who had served on the Head Council joined the protests—some had served over a thousand years ago. They came out in droves to demonstrate, along with the citizens Willie had previously galvanized. Once Melanthia located the actual law, banners were made with the wording of the law and the signatures of the all-male Head Council that had created it. When the males realized a law they had enacted might actually free you, they weren't about to miss their moment of vindication.

"Melanthia presented the law only two days ago at an emergency meeting of the Head Council. The crowd spilled over from inside the Rotunda, past the Lawn, onto the streets of Bencarlta. The size of the crowd was becoming dangerous. In an effort to encourage DARlings to stay in their homes, the Head Council magically amplified the hearing throughout the city. Citizens could simply open their windows and hear the meeting, as it was happening. That had never been done before in the history of DAR—not even during the Rising!

"The entire situation was a first for the all-female Head Council. They now understood what the males had endured during the unrest of the Rising. The Head Council and Council Chair Sukaaja knew that after all the investigations, after all the interrogations, after detaining you for six months; this long-lost law had rendered the actions described in your presentation, as perfectly legal. Although the interpretation of the law, and how it pertained to your actions, was still up to the discretion of the Head Council, they knew you had to be freed. This only happened two days ago, Aelish, forty-eight hours before we all knew you were to be banished. Oh, Aelish, thank God!" finished Lady Antonia. She was sobbing, yet smiling, as she reached her hand across the table to hold Aelish's.

30

KING GIDIUS

"**G**OOD GOD, WHAT I put everyone through," said Aelish, weeping.

"Aelish, you challenged the tenets of DAR and you freed Komprathia," smiled Lady Antonia.

"*What*?" asked Aelish.

"Despite your imprisonment and inevitable banishment, the Head Council knew your thesis was a brilliant covert operation and military strategy. But before they could attempt to implement it, they first had to determine if any other DARlings had conspired with you. That's why Drummond hiding Seratus became so dire—we needed Seratus to corroborate your presentation.

"Once Seratus was found and he confirmed that Cagélét and Obredón were indeed awaiting your verification of DAR's support, the POD put your entire thesis into motion. Truer words were never spoken when you stated: 'Komprathia is a backward magical society.' It took DAR two weeks to finish what I imagine you thought would take years to accomplish."

"Two *weeks*!" exclaimed Aelish.

"Yes, Aelish. The tunnels were destroyed and there was no need to rebuild them. Once the Komprathian soldiers realized the King's brother was staging a coup, they put down their weapons and our soldiers peacefully entered Komprathia. Obredón did indeed keep his word. He provided DAR with the tunnel spells along with new intelligence on Yasteron's surveillance and detection grids.

"Obredón and Cagélét had King Gidius arrested and he is currently awaiting his sentence. He has actually been brought to the MDC in DAR," stated Lady Antonia. "And with the tunnels destroyed—the current outbreak of plague is almost at an end, Aelish."

Aelish gasped and stood up, but her legs gave way. She collapsed onto the ground, sobbing. She could not believe it had worked.

Would the destruction of the tunnels finally end the devastation from the plague?

Lady Antonia sat on the ground with her until she could regain her composure. Once they resumed their place at the table, Lady Antonia reached across and held Aelish's hand.

"Now do you understand why you are the hero of DAR, Aelish?" asked Lady Antonia. "And why the DARleens requested my information? My counsel is now sought after. You have made me famous by proxy, Aelish," chuckled Lady Antonia. "I am presently the most renowned Oraculi in all of DAR."

Aelish smiled at the outcome for Lady Antonia.

"There is, however, one final piece of business that requires your attention," Lady Antonia said tentatively.

"What? What is it?" asked Aelish.

"King Gidius has requested to meet you, prior to his sentencing," stated Lady Antonia.

"Good God! Why?" exclaimed Aelish.

"I have no idea why, Aelish. And you do not have to do this. But if you wish to see him, we must go today. He is being sentenced tomorrow, after which I imagine he will be executed for crimes against his own kind."

"Have I been granted *authorization* to see him?" asked Aelish.

"Yes, you have been granted authorization by the Director of the POD and the Head Council."

"What a difference twenty-four hours makes," Aelish stated with rancor.

"If you wish to do this, I would like to transport to the MDC prior to your going home. I suggest you finish this last thing, so you may begin to put all of this behind you. Additionally, there is to be a festival in your honor, later this week," smiled Lady Antonia.

"Good God—a festival—in my *honor*? Two hours ago I was in a cell with no magical abilities, cut off from DAR, from Earth, and from everyone I ever loved," said Aelish. "I get the sense this festival is being held more to calm down the citizens, than it is to honor me."

"It's going to take some time for you to get over your confinement, Aelish," said Lady Antonia. "It's natural for you to feel bitterness and continued mistrust, but I disagree with you. The festival is not more for the citizens, than it is for you. The Head Council wants to demonstrate to DAR and to you, the brilliance of your thesis. And there is a being very anxious to meet you."

"Who?" asked Aelish.

"Obredón," smiled Lady Antonia. "He will be in attendance along with Cagélét, Seratus, and other dignitaries from Komprathia. For the time being, Obredón will continue to serve as King, until such time as the realm rehabilitates their form of government, abandoning a monarchy. Aelish you freed a realm from tyranny. This is an amazing moment. After centuries of war, DAR and Komprathia are at peace and are forming an alliance. The festival is to celebrate all of this. Do you understand, dear?"

"I can't believe my theory worked. There were so many

variables," stated Aelish.

"You deserve this, Aelish. Look upon the festival as redemption for the actions you took to honor your parents. These last one hundred years did not abate your grief. It is my hope that the festival will begin the healing process," assured Lady Antonia.

Aelish looked at her and felt tears spill onto her face.

"Perhaps," sighed Aelish.

"Well, have you decided whether to see King Gidius? I feel it is fitting you are dressed in the same gown you wore for your presentation to the Head Council," chuckled Lady Antonia. "I suggest after today you may want to dispose of it."

"I am going to burn it," Aelish said rather forcefully. She saw her own bitterness reflected on the distressed face of her Oraculi.

"I am worried about your mental health, Aelish. Do you think you can manage going inside a different detention center after having just been released from another, only two hours ago?"

"I don't know. I think I should try."

"All right, then, dear. Let's transport directly inside the MDC. I will send a telly to the MDC Director that we are imminently arriving. Ready, then?" asked Lady Antonia.

"Yes," said Aelish, " but could you hold my hand, like the first time I went through the Portal?"

"Absolutely, dear," said Lady Antonia, reaching for Aelish's hand.

‡‡‡‡

They arrived in a dank hallway of the MDC. Aelish saw the same Guards that had detained her freedom, lined against both sides of the hallway. She felt panicked. But then, they saluted her!

Good God! This is unbelievable!

Aelish could not bring herself to return their salute. She opted for a modest smile and nod, as she and Lady Antonia walked past them down the hallway.

They began to hear animal sounds. They turned left at the end of the hallway and entered a massive room with a huge cage, detaining one prisoner. King Gidius' enormity was commanding and impressive. His cobra head shot upward and the hood of his cobra neck flared, turning red with rage at seeing them.

Lady Antonia gasped, but Aelish felt oddly calm. She had learned how to remain calm when facing fear, during her confinement. She also recognized the familiar look of isolation and frustration on the beast.

His dark, evil pools of eyes, stared at them. His cobra hood was enormous and his body was at least eighteen feet high, ending in a thick rat's tail. He had small rat arms coming out of his chest area. He was menacing.

After twelve missions, Aelish was used to the appearance of Komprathians. But King Gidius was truly a marvel to his own kind. He swung his mammoth cobra-rat body around and moved closer to the side of the cage where she approached him. Lady Antonia stayed at the entrance to the room. Aelish knew she was terrified.

The Guards began to shout, "Back up and behave, Gidius!"

Gidius glowered down at her. She was so small compared to him.

He spoke English and asked her, "You did this to me? A small, ugly, purple female with hair the color of a demon? I don't know you. Why did you come after my Kingdom and turn my brother against me?"

The Guards did not admonish him and remained quiet.

"Because you killed my parents."

"So, what? Who were they to me? I assume they were Human

based on the putrid color of your skin? It brings me great joy to know they are dead. I hope they died of plague, spread by my drone rats. It seems fitting, since Humans so inherently despise all rats."

Aelish scoffed. She could definitely feel her Irish getting up.

"Interesting turn of phrase—Humans inherently despising rats—and what of their King? Their King, who murders his own drone rats because of his unquenchable hatred for Humans."

Aelish paused and waited for him to respond, but he said nothing.

"Humans will always have the protection and power of DAR behind them, whereas you chose to endlessly war with DAR. You chose to methodically murder Humans by systematically using your own kind as weapons, murdering them as well. You killed your own subjects by using them to spread the plague in a crime against Humanity. You are not a King, you are nothing but a murderer."

Gidius continued to stare down at her. Aelish saw he was trying to understand how this diminutive being before him, had destroyed his life.

"I'm sorry you won't die the horrible death of plague like my parents," said Aelish. "It seems fitting you should die in this manner, considering you are already of a diseased mind. I feel sorry for you. You are nothing but a pathetic tyrant, who has lost all of his power."

"Have I?" he shouted. His booming voice echoed off the walls. "You obviously don't understand Komprathians at all, you stupid female. We are the closest in makeup to Humans, which is *why* we are able to catch and spread the plague. Even *I* can catch the plague!

"This entire time, all your ignorant, arrogant, peace-loving realm had to do to defeat us, was release plague-ridden drone rats into Komprathia. Fools, all of you! Did you not think drone rats sent to Earth tried to return to Komprathia? Some even made it all the way back, infected with plague, but I had them instantly killed, as they exited the tunnels. *All* Komprathians can catch the plague you *masters* of magic!" he hissed sarcastically.

Aelish had never considered the notion of the poor drone rats trying to get back home. He was a ruthless, merciless beast. He was not only willing to expend the lives of his drone rats, he was also willing to risk his entire Kingdom becoming infected with plague, from their possible return. All of his abhorrent and gruesome strategies were in place, to further his quest to destroy Humanity. He was insane.

"And since Komprathians are the most similar to Humans, we also have Human traits, as I imagine you do, having been born of Human parents. So that makes you and I very similar," he hissed with his cobra tongue. "You and I carry the traits DARlings despise the most in Humans—warring, hatred, greed, and jealousy."

Aelish felt her stomach flip, remembering her bout of jealousy over Willie and Thagar. Gidius was beginning to disquiet her and he was starting to pollute her mind.

"You think my brother Obredón and his side-kick Cagélét won't ultimately betray DAR, as they feast on your food, steal your magical spells and warcraft, and pretend to care about your commonwealth? He has coveted my power his entire life as the second-born. And in the end, his thirst for power will not be enough to satisfy him, like most Humans. He will want more and more and will ultimately betray the goodwill DAR has bestowed upon him, because your realm so blindly believes they can make him their ally. Ha! An *ally*!" he yelled.

King Gidius swung his massive body the other way. With his back now to her, his hood began to flare again. Aelish moved closer toward his cage and grabbed the iron frame.

"That may be," said Aelish, "but a savage, heinous being, such as you are, will always be remembered as nothing more than a murderer. That's your legacy, Gidius."

She was so focused on the disrespect he had demonstrated by turning his back to her, that what she didn't see coming, was the small rat he produced from inside his long robe. He swung his body around and held up the squealing rat, so she could clearly see it.

"Tell Seratus to look no more for the young male of the drone rats he stole from me. I put a spell on him that has delayed his infection of plague—until today!"

She instantly recognized the young son of the drone rat family she harbored, but before she could utter a word, Gidius bit off his head and devoured the entire creature.

"Nooo!" yelled Aelish.

The Guards all saw what he did, but were ordered to stand down, and let Gidius perish by his own hand. There was nothing they could do anyway; the disease-ridden, young drone rat was already eaten. How he had conjured the young drone rat that had escaped with Seratus from inside his cell, became in that instant, the mysterious legacy of King Gidius. No one ever figured it out, not in DAR nor in Komprathia.

"You DARlings are impotent. You forget the power I have always had over my drone rats, even in confinement. You think I would let DAR kill me? *I* kill me and I will be dead of plague, as you requested, within two days. I wanted to make sure I granted you your wish. I hope the manner of my death haunts you, as I'm sure the manner of your parents' deaths haunts you, hopefully, till the end of your days."

Aelish wanted to strangle him with her bare hands, but the plague was already doing it for her. King Gidius let out a deafening scream. He began wildly shooting his deadly venom throughout the room, as he began dying. But the soldiers were quicker and put up a magical shield to repel the venom. He began groaning and collapsed onto the floor, all eighteen feet of him, curled in a circle. He lifted his head and hissed at her one last time, waiting for death.

Knowing he was too weak from plague to harm her, Aelish spat in his face.

"I hope you die in agony."

She turned toward Lady Antonia who looked like she would, without a doubt, never ever, be the same.

Aelish put her arm around her and said, "Let's leave this filth and go home."

As they walked briskly toward the exit of the MDC, they nearly collided with Sartaine.

"Aelish!" he exclaimed. He embraced her in a heartfelt hug. "What are you doing here? The POD was aware you were released this morning, but we were not informed you had chosen to see Gidius."

Aelish pulled out of the hug to look at his face. "It's so good to see you, Sartaine, you look wonderful," she said with a weak smile. How she wanted to ask him about Thagar and why he wasn't here. "It was my understanding that I had permission to speak with King Gidius before his sentencing, and that it had been authorized by the Head Council and the Director of the POD?"

Lady Antonia, who was still shaking asked, "Didn't the Director of the MDC inform the POD that Aelish was coming to see King Gidius? I sent him a telly right before we arrived."

"No, we never received such a message," said Sartaine, clearly upset. "Ever since Gidius has been imprisoned, we've noticed our telepathic frequencies are experiencing interferences, and messages are not getting through. We fear he has put a spell on our communications to cause further mayhem. Had I known, I would have met you both here, to ensure your safety."

Aelish tried to ignore the fact that Sartaine had said *he* would have met them at the MDC and not Thagar. It was further confirmation to her exhausted emotions that Thagar was lost to her.

"Well, Gidius will be dead in two days," stated Aelish. "The interference in telepathic communications should return to normal by then."

"But what has happened? Why will Gidius be dead in two days?" asked Sartaine.

"They will tell you all about it inside," fussed Lady Antonia. "I can't relive what we just experienced. I fear I will never get it out of my head."

Aelish could see Sartaine was concerned over the lapse in communication with his command, but he graciously did not delay them any further.

"I will deal with it inside," he said. "And I look forward to seeing you both at the festival."

Aelish noticed Sartaine quickly said something to Lady Antonia before he began running down the dank hallway toward Gidius' cage.

"What did Sartaine just say to you?" asked Aelish.

"Something about a surprise for you at the festival. Can we please get *out* of here?" she asked, distressed.

"I could care less about this stupid festival!" exclaimed Aelish. "All I want to do is go home and sleep for a month."

"I understand," nodded Lady Antonia. "But let's quickly fly over Bencarlta, Aelish. I want you to see it all."

31

THE ARTIST'S HOUSE

"Let's stop up ahead for a minute," said Lady Antonia.
"Okay," agreed Aelish.

Once they had landed, Lady Antonia asked, "Well? Have you ever seen anything like that? I was here at the height of the Rising, but it pales in comparison."

"My image is everywhere and so many of the buildings are defaced with writings on them," said Aelish. "To see oneself in such a light is surreal. I don't like this notoriety."

"Too late for that, dear," chuckled Lady Antonia. "Each morning they magically clean up the defacement of the buildings, and by the next day, they are all back again. It has been an indescribable time in Bencarlta."

"Why have we stopped?" asked Aelish. "I thought we were going directly to my cottage?"

"There is one more stop we need to make before we get to your cottage. Do you think you are strong enough? I don't think *I* am strong enough after what that despicable beast did," stated Lady Antonia. "I shall never forget it! And the loss to the drone rat family—absolutely appalling."

"Is it important we make this other stop? I am exhausted," sighed Aelish.

She was still processing what Gidius had said to her about their shared Human traits. It was too disturbing and she was too raw; she had no emotional defenses left to protect her own rationality. As for the young drone rat, she could not bear to think about it.

"The artist who created the Humanity sculpture in the Rotunda has created something in your honor that will be unveiled at the festival. He just sent me a telly and asked if you could stop by his house to examine it. He wants to make sure you approve, before he puts the finishing touches on it. He's running about fifteen minutes late and said you should make yourself at home, look around, and that you can't miss the sculpture. This way, you can give him your feedback when he arrives, and leave straightaway," stated Lady Antonia. "I hope I heard him correctly, in light of the issues we are having sending messages. That hideous beast!" yelled Lady Antonia.

"I can't believe there is going to be a festival in my honor— and with an unveiling of a sculpture by the most famous artist in DAR? I feel so disoriented," said Aelish.

"Aelish, dear, you are exhausted."

"After what Gidius said about Obredón," Aelish said, "I confess to questioning my judgment and trust in Cagélét, Seratus, and in freeing Komprathia."

"Aelish!" exclaimed Lady Antonia. "You've just been let out of detention and were made to witness the murder of the young drone rat you'd grown fond of. Of course you are feeling flummoxed! If you were not, I'd be very concerned about you. Watching him rip the poor young drone rat's head off—Good God—I nearly collapsed, it was so reminiscent of my father's beheading. I will have to go to the hot springs in the N.E. Quadrant to restore myself after the festival." Aelish noticed Lady Antonia's hands were shaking from a seemingly new nervous disorder.

"The artist's house is not far from here. Shall we ascend, then?" asked Lady Antonia.

"All right," Aelish acquiesced.

They flew a short distance and landed in front of the most beautiful house Aelish had ever seen in DAR. It indeed looked like the house of an artist. It was made of limestone, had soaring glass windows, high flat rooflines, and was situated perfectly on the mountaintop just below the higher mountain where the Rotunda sat, capturing the majestic views.

"This must be amazing at night, to see the lights of the Rotunda with such proximity," marveled Aelish.

"While you go inside to inspect the sculpture, I am going to your favorite dressmaker to get you a new frock. For heaven's sake—that gown!" cried Lady Antonia.

"But don't you want to see the sculpture? We can shop together tomorrow," said Aelish, whining a bit.

"I've already seen it," stated Lady Antonia. "I don't want you to enter your cottage wearing that gown." They had always shopped together for frocks, but Aelish was too tired to argue.

"You'll come back here and fly with me to my cottage afterward, yes?" asked Aelish.

"Of course, dear" stated Lady Antonia, smiling. "All will be well, Aelish. Go and enjoy the moment. It's not every day you get the most famous artist in DAR to make you a sculpture!"

Before Aelish could protest any further, Lady Antonia ascended and was gone.

Aelish climbed the marble steps to the front veranda. There were marble balustrades and the veranda floor was made of small, iridescent, glass tiles. The entrance double-doors were at least fifteen feet high and made of hand-carved, mahogany wood.

Knowing no one was home she gently lifted the iron latch of the door handle. She pushed open the right side of the double-doors. The entryway was two stories high with a balcony all across the upper level. The entrance hall was the size of her cottage. It was surrounded by exterior windows and had a black and white marble floor. While it was very grand, it did not have an old-world, traditional feel. She had never been inside a house like this before.

Not knowing which way to go, she decided to head down a wide hallway off the main entrance hall, toward the back of the house. She froze when she noticed that inside a grand bedchamber, off the hallway, was the same mural in her own cottage of Brólaigh Castle.

She stepped inside the bedchamber and stared at the two-story rendering of her ancestral home. Above her was a floating chandelier similar to those at the gala and there were wooden beams across the ceiling that reminded her of the great hall in Brólaigh Castle.

This is incredible. She was confused as to why the artist would want to wake up every morning to the same mural he had created for her, in her cottage bedchamber.

There was artwork everywhere—paintings, sketches, and sculptures. Off the wide hallway, toward the back of the first floor, was a circular open area. The area contained a towering curved staircase that led to the second story. It also led to the remaining rooms on the first floor. And there she found the sculpture.

It depicted Aelish in her signature fishtail braid, forcing an iron spear into the belly of King Gidus with her right hand, while she held the orb of Earth in her left hand. Her left arm was extended backward, away from his reach. Gidius was so lifelike she felt an irrational fear. It was an astonishingly accurate rendering of what they both looked like. His hood was flared and red, as he glowered down on her small frame, as she slayed the twenty-foot high beast.

Good God!

After staring at it for a few minutes, she became anxious. She decided to venture back toward the bedchamber with the Brólaigh Castle mural to settle her. On her way back, she noticed a diploma from the Institutum de Magicae hanging on the hallway wall. Before she had time to examine it, however, she heard the heavy boots of a male's footfall coming from the back of the house. After running covert missions and being imprisoned over the last year, her instincts kicked in and she remained silent against the hallway wall listening.

Who else would know I was coming to this house? Antonia would never lead me into a trap.

She tried to quell her fear, which she blamed entirely on her frayed nerves from the events of this unbelievable day. She began stealthily heading toward the direction of the footfall, which had ceased.

When they saw each other, Thagar fell to his knees trembling and whispered, "Aelish."

She ran to him and embraced his head against her breasts. His shoulders racked against her, as he sobbed.

She ran her fingers through his long black curls and whispered, "Thagar, it's all right, my love. I'm all right, or I will be, if I still have your love?"

"Aelish," he whispered over and over as he sobbed.

Aelish inhaled his smell allowing it to restore her. As she held him, she looked toward the direction from whence he came and realized that the end of the hallway ended in an observatory at the back of the house. The extraordinary glass windows from floor to ceiling captured the sunlight that drenched the room. The sunlight began to spill into the hallway, as the sun fell lower over the Rotunda.

He pulled away and looked up at her, as she wiped his tears with the sleeves of her gown.

"Can you stand, my love?" she asked gently.

He began to rise and he embraced her tightly, as though he could not believe she was real. He pressed her against his chest and felt for her braid. He began furiously trying to locate it, finally realizing, it was no longer there.

"They did this to you? They cut off your hair?" he seethed.

"It's nothing, it will grow back." She heard him inhale a deep and angry breath as he pulled her closer to him.

"I failed you. First with the rats which killed your parents, and then with the grief you suffered from, after their deaths," he said, not letting her go. "I should have done more, Aelish. I did not protect you."

"Thagar, you did nothing wrong. You could not free me from my own mind. I had to do that for myself. My life trapped me. I couldn't move forward and I couldn't go backward. I was in some kind of purgatory, with no way out of the grief I brought with me, all the way from Earth to DAR. You told me in the Sanctuary that I needed to find a purpose, one that wouldn't violate my Oath and, in turn, that purpose would free me. When I found the Komprathian families in my garden, I knew what that purpose would be. Please forgive me for what I've put you through."

Thagar gazed at her and began deeply kissing her. She felt warmth course through her exhausted body. He led her into the observatory, which was like a glass castle, yet had total and complete privacy—the mountain landscape preventing any being from peering inside. The floor was covered with a deep fur-like covering.

They knelt on the floor embraced in each other's arms. Thagar began unfastening her gown and lowered it down to her waist exposing her breasts. He gently took one into his mouth and she remembered. She arched her head backward and ran her hands through his hair. He gently guided her to the floor, the setting sun reflecting the glow of their lovemaking.

When they were spent, he grabbed a small throw from one of the settees in the room and gently covered her. He situated himself under the throw, allowing her to lay her head on his muscular chest, which felt like tufted pillows. She listened to the sound of his heart in unison with her own. They fell asleep, and awoke after dark, to the light reflected off the Rotunda. Aelish had never slept so peacefully.

As she sleepily ran her fingers through the hair on his chest, she felt a hairless spot with a scar—a scar that had not been there before her imprisonment.

"What is this, my love?" she asked, sitting up on one elbow.

She magically created a small beam of light to examine it more closely. She noticed there were three more additional hairless patches with scars, similar to the first.

"Good God! What *are* these?" exclaimed Aelish.

"They are from my interrogations. They hurt no longer."

"They were not respectful of you during your detention?"

"They treated me even harsher because of my rank as Commander. A betrayal to DAR at that level is not taken kindly."

"I did this to you! Good God, Thagar," she cried and began weeping over his chest. Small rivers of tears rolled off his scars down to his waist and fell onto the floor. It was as if her tears were trying to wash away the scars and restore him to his former self.

"They tried every interrogation technique we have ever been taught," he said quietly.

She did not want to hear what he was about to tell her, but knew she had to listen to what he had endured because of her.

"The physical pain, although horrible, was nothing compared

to the mental anguish they inflicted. They lied: they told me you'd been banished; they told me you went back to Earth; they told me you were dead. I was so sleep deprived and exhausted from the physical pain that I did not have the ability to see through their lies. Yet, I had nothing to tell them.

"There are two reasons I am here with you right now; I left the copy of your thesis in your cottage, and Bathwick came to one of my interrogations about a month after my detention. I don't think I've ever heard her speak in such a manner. She nearly lost her mind when she saw what they were doing. I owe her my life. But had they found your thesis in my possession, I don't think even Bathwick could have saved me or my Command."

"Why do you still serve DAR?" asked Aelish, feeling nauseated.

"A crime of this nature is rare in DAR. I am also trained to interrogate in such a manner, when treason is suspected. But having experienced it firsthand, I know the techniques are ineffective. We train for it, but when it is actually happening, it is entirely different. You will say anything to make it stop and if you know nothing, you will invent a story. Since the restoration of my Command, I have been methodically rewriting the rules of interrogation for not only accused citizens of DAR, but also for enemies from other magical realms. We are too evolved a commonwealth for such barbaric treatment of any being, whether guilty or not. It will not be done again."

"One needs a strong moral compass not to torture a being such as Gidius," stated Aelish. She gazed at Thagar with the deepest respect. "I went to see him this afternoon with Antonia."

"I know. Sartaine sent me a telly after he ran into you and Antonia at the MDC. Why did you decide to go?"

"I needed to see the being that murdered my parents and millions of Humans. I thought it might help me heal," sighed Aelish.

"But Gidius set a trap for you, didn't he?"

"Yes, he did," stated Aelish.

"Gidius is a horrible, cunning creature," stated Thagar. "He likes to gain access to your inner thoughts and make you doubt your own senses."

"Yes, he did exactly that," said Aelish. "Gidius told me that he too had Human traits and that he and I were more alike, than you and I are alike. It was very disturbing and made me question my mission in freeing Komprathia. Killing the innocent, young drone rat was ghastly, but implanting doubts in my mind, was the trap. I told him I wished he could die of plague. He said he wanted to grant me that wish and then he magically produced the young son of the drone rat family, I had grown so fond of. He devoured him right in front of me—it was all done to torture me. He told me that he hoped his death would haunt me, as he knew my parents' deaths haunted me. I have never encountered such evil before, Thagar. Knowing he is actively dying of plague is of some comfort, but it's a convoluted comfort," stated Aelish.

"I am so sorry, my love. I would have been there for you had I known you had decided to see the beast."

"Antonia sent a telly alerting the MDC to our imminent arrival," explained Aelish. "We were unaware of the havoc Gidius had wrought on telepathic communications. When I did not see you at the MDC I assumed you could never forgive me for my deceitful behavior. In truth, I felt I had lost your love during my presentation to the Head Council and suffered with that loss throughout my confinement."

"You never lost my love, Aelish," said Thagar. "Your keeping the mission covert, even from me, was the only way to run the operation. Had you told me what you were doing, I could never have sanctioned it without going up the chain of command within the POD. And the Director of the POD would've had to bring it to the attention of the Head Council. But you knew all of this, from your military education and training. It would be untruthful of me to say I was not devastated that you didn't share it with me. But I also understood the single-minded focus a mission of this nature required, as well as the deception.

"But the part of your thesis that was unbearable to hear, was how you planned to utilize the Exterminate spell. You prepared for all contingencies: first, the arrangement you orchestrated with Seratus to reenter Komprathia to kill you; then, if he was detained, captured, or killed in the process, you manipulated the Exterminate spell to activate after seventy-two hours; and finally, you hoped you could endure the torture, as you waited for death from the spell.

"I was in awe of your magical abilities, your preparedness, your bravery, and your devotion to DAR. But your acceptance in sacrificing your own life to complete your mission to obtain retribution for your parents' deaths meant your objective overrode your love for me. Had you been forced to utilize any of the methods you devised to bring about your own death, conversely meant, I would have been forced to endure the rest of my life without you. It was painful to hear, Aelish."

Aelish could not meet his eyes. She allowed what he said to penetrate the wall she had built around herself, brick by brick, since her parents died in 1563, over one hundred and two years ago. She may have freed a Kingdom, she may have redeemed her parents' deaths, she may have even stopped the plague, but she had mangled and tortured Thagar's love. She'd severely hurt him and was ashamed.

She tried to explain. "Each time I transported into Komprathia, I waited for the soldiers of DAR to take my freedom. I just prayed it wasn't your face I'd be looking at when it happened," said Aelish. "It made me sick to deceive you for so long, but the alternative was equally unendurable. If I didn't at least try to stop the drone rats, I would never have a chance at becoming whole again. The contingencies I planned for in the event I was captured were all orchestrated to prevent me from betraying DAR. Once I presented to the Head Council and my deception was revealed, I accepted that I would lose your love forever.

"You once told me you thought DARlings born of the Earth were capable of great depths of feeling, but I think it is actually the other way around, Thagar. DARlings born in DAR are the ones who feel, love, and forgive more generously. You are the embodiment of that fact, my love," said Aelish, as she softly kissed him. "Please forgive me."

"I am incapable of not loving you, Aelish, and I forgave you a long time ago. I am a soldier and I understand the conflicts that can arise between a mission of this magnitude and the ones you leave behind, in order to execute it. If you had put my love ahead of your objective, you would have failed.

"Do not allow what I have suffered or the insanity of Gidius to rob you of your victory. The fact that he chose to kill himself in front of you, clearly demonstrates that you had become his nemesis—you were the catalyst that made him lose everything, including his life. You vanquished an enemy of DAR and of Humanity, and you did it all without taking lethal action. You freed a Kingdom from tyranny and never broke your Oath," said Thagar, shaking his head in admiration.

Aelish tried to absorb all that Thagar was saying.

"You are now a living legend, Aelish. The artists are working on your image on the dome of the Rotunda, as we speak. You may have single-handedly stopped the plague on Earth. At the least, you gave Humans a fighting chance if it ever comes again. The amount of rats able to spread the disease has been reduced by ninety percent without the Komprathian drone rats. And you saved the lives of the drone rats as well.

"I only wish you could have been present in the command center when we destroyed the tunnels. When I think of the years spent trying to dismantle the spells of those tunnels—all of our attempts unsuccessful—until you devised a successful military strategy, coupled with the art of diplomacy. You orchestrated an arrangement with an enemy realm to release the tunnel spells, plus we acquired a multitude of new intelligence on Yasteron's surveillance and detection grids from Obredón. Your entire operation is at the level of Bathwick's warcraft and I have never said that about another DARling, Aelish. You know how I revere her. What you need to understand is that you are now revered in the same way—by me, and by all of DAR.

"The Kingdom of Yasteron is of course furious with DAR for convincing Obredón to disclose their most coveted military spells. But Yasteron's complicity in killing the drone rats of Komprathia will never be forgiven by Obredón—the alliance is permanently severed. I have never seen two brothers so different from one another. Obredón despised the alliance Gidius made with Yasteron's King Nevuna. Obredón has been working for decades to stop the annihilation of his own beings, sacrificed to satisfy his brother's unending quest to destroy Humanity. He is very anxious to meet you. Yasteron has become a grave concern for DAR, but that is for another day.

"Do not heed what Gidius said about Obredón and Komprathia, and allow it to pollute your mind with the seeds of doubt. Komprathia will become a great ally of DAR, regardless of their Human traits. But we must always remember that they are the only magical beings in the magical world that can catch, spread, and die of plague, or any other Human illness. That weakness could once again be exploited to harm Humanity and we must never forget it.

"It will take some time to overcome what you have been

through during the isolation of your confinement, bereft of all magical abilities. I am still experiencing the consequences of my own confinement. But it will get easier, it will get better—I promise, my love," said Thagar, as he gently stroked her face.

"Well, I have already experienced a change in the POD's attitude toward me," said Aelish. "When Antonia and I transported into the MDC this afternoon, the same Guards who had encircled my freedom were lined up in the hallway, and they saluted me! It was beyond bizarre."

"They'd have better saluted you!" exclaimed Thagar. "They would have found themselves severely reprimanded, if they had not. You don't yet fully understand what you have accomplished for DAR and for Komprathia," smiled Thagar. "Did Antonia take you through Bencarlta? Your image is everywhere."

"I saw. It is surreal and frankly, uncomfortable for me," said Aelish.

"When I was finally released from the MDC, I flew over Bencarlta and observed the unrest over your imprisonment. Every day there were demonstrations and your image was everywhere, but you were not. It made your absence all the more painful for me."

Tears began to form in his golden eyes.

"I tried to stop you from incriminating yourself, after the first line of your presentation, but Sartaine restrained me. He told me I would be immediately detained if I did not remain quiet. He advised that we needed to listen to the entire presentation, to be in a better position to help you regain your freedom. We were naïve not to realize we would also lose our freedom that day. As you continued, I knew they were going to banish you. Once I was freed and had my Command restored, I was determined to spend the rest of my life searching for you, so I could follow you there. If not for Melanthia, only two days ago . . ." his voice trailed off, as a tear fell down his cheek.

Aelish gently wiped it away with her fingertip.

"When the Guards encircled your freedom Aelish, a part of me died inside. I try to keep that moment at bay, but it infects my dreams," said Thagar.

Tears fell from his eyes, as he ran his hands through his hair. He gazed at her and in his eyes she saw his unqualified love and his forgiveness for what she had put him through. It was in this moment that she finally began to understand the depths of his love for her during all the years they had been together. What he had endured for her—and to love her still—it was unfathomable.

Aelish realized the strength of his love had been sustaining her since he arrived in the house in London. He had always been her rock, her foundation by which she tackled everything these past one hundred and two years, since the loss of her parents. Losing her life during the mission, her imprisonment, and forthcoming banishment, she now realized, were all less frightening than actually losing his love. She made a mental promise to never abuse his love again. It would be an affront to God to disrespect the blessing he had bestowed upon her, in having Thagar's love.

He gently stroked her face. "You have a rare gift for combining diplomacy and covert military strategy—very impressive for one barely out of her military training and educational studies. But you are the embodiment of the female DARling—your exceptionalism and bravery is why DAR is so incredible. Have you seen your diplomas in the hallway from the Institutum de Magicae and from the POD?"

Aelish gasped. "*My* diplomas? Oh no! I just remembered—I was supposed to meet the artist here who created the sculpture in the back hallway. Oh, Thagar, we've been in his house all this time!"

Thagar threw his head back laughing.

"For such an astute DARling, I'm surprised our ruse

actually worked."

"What do you mean? We have to get out of here—the artist must have been delayed," said Aelish, horrified they had been intimate in the artist's house.

"This house," said Thagar, gesturing with his arms, "was given to *us* by the Head Council. Sartaine, Antonia, and I conspired to trick you into coming here."

"What? I don't understand—*our* house? But I have my cottage and you have your house," said Aelish, completely confused. "This home is so grand, we don't need all of this."

"Well, apparently the Head Council feels that the newest legend of DAR, and her newly restored Commander of the S.E. Quadrant, *do* need a house of this size. I actually feel the size is reflective of the guilt they feel over our treatment. But it does happen to have amazing views," he said, continuing to laugh at her.

Aelish stared at him trying to absorb what he was saying.

"Would you agree that we are now finally finished keeping secrets from each other?" asked Thagar.

"Yes, Good God, yes," agreed Aelish.

"Well in that case, since the Head Council was generous enough to bestow this grand house upon us, no matter their motivations, I thought perhaps we might begin living together. And in turn, perhaps that might lead to our becoming mates. After all that has happened, I think I need to keep a more watchful eye over you," teased Thagar.

"Are you asking me to make Commitments with you? Good God, only this morning I thought I had lost your love forever," said Aelish.

"Yes, I am Aelish. But you also need to decide on whether you even like this house. May I suggest, when the sun comes up, you see the views from every room. But for the time being, let's start with the grand bathing room attached to the grandest bedchamber I have ever seen."

"That's why the mural of Brólaigh Castle is in it!" exclaimed Aelish.

"My poor, Aelish, you truly are not yourself. But I think I have something that might help you," he said. He easily picked her up, the throw blanket falling to the floor. She began squealing with delight.

He gallantly carried her to the largest bathing room Aelish had ever seen. In the middle of the room, was a huge bathing tub filled with steaming water. Thagar gently lowered her into the warm water. He grabbed a stool from beneath one of the two separate washbasins, as well as a large scrubbing cloth, and a beautifully scented bar of soap.

"I know I'm not the prettiest lady-in-waiting, but would m'Lady mind if I washed her?" he asked, in a mocking British accent. "Nothing would give me greater pleasure."

Aelish burst out laughing and decided to play along with his theatrics. She rested her head against the enormous tub and said, "Certainly, m'Lord, but wouldn't you rather get into the tub *with* me?" she asked, naughtily.

"Do you think there is room for both of us?" he asked, feigning ignorance.

"I think there is room for a small village in here."

"Well . . . if you don't think it will be too crowded," said Thagar, as he climbed into the tub. "But I still insist on giving m'Lady a proper bath."

"But, of course," said Aelish.

As soon as Thagar began soaping up the scrubbing cloth, she began giggling ridiculously. By the time they were finished washing each other, there was water all over the marble floor and Aelish could not remember a time when she had laughed so hard.

When they were both clean, Thagar lifted her up and

magically dried them off as he carried her through the air to the most beautiful bed in the gorgeous bedchamber with the mural of Brólaigh Castle. He magically turned down the covers and gently lay her down on one side of the bed. The linens were beyond luxurious and felt like silk against her bare, newly washed skin.

He dropped down beside her and covered them both with the bedspread. He magically lit the fireplace, more for romance than for warmth, and dimmed the chandelier floating above the wood beams of the ceiling.

"So . . . I never did receive a definitive answer earlier to our making Commitments," said Thagar. He nestled into the bed with her, each lying on their side, facing each other. "Are you agreeable then to making Commitments with me?"

"Of course, my love," smiled Aelish. "You are the only being I have ever loved."

"Well, in that case, it is customary for us to seal our Pre-Commitments with a jewel."

Aelish watched as he opened his hand. He was holding two identical amethyst stone amulets.

"I chose this stone because it matches my soon-to-be mate's beautiful skin and I would be proud to wear your skin color around my neck, always. I would like us to mate for the rest of our lives, Aelish, long as they may be," smiled Thagar.

"Are you sure? DARlings usually have several mates, due to our protracted lifespans. Won't you tire of me?"

"I am helpless to love you, Aelish. I have already loved you for a thousand lifetimes. So no, I will not tire of you. Do you feel you will tire of me?" asked Thagar, tentatively.

"I feel as though I have loved you since before I ever met you, growing up on Earth—like I was waiting for you. I fell in love with you from the moment I laid eyes on you, hiding behind the tapestry in the great hall of Brólaigh Castle," admitted Aelish.

Thagar reached across and gently kissed her. He pulled away from her with a beaming smile.

"Now, you see here—how the amulets are missing their tops?" he asked.

He created a small beam of light and directed it at the top of one of the stones. He pointed toward the top edge of the stone and took her finger and ran it over the grooves located there. Aelish could see something was meant to attach to the grooves.

"When we make our Commitments, we magically store our vows inside the amulet and we seal it forever with a small top. We do not have access to the tops until after we make our vows to one another. After our vows, the stone magically produces the tops so we may seal the stones at the ceremony. Until then . . ."

He lifted the beautiful iron chain and put the amulet around her neck.

"Now, you put this one on me," he guided.

Aelish reached up and slid the iron chain over his curls until it lay at the base of his neck. She looked at the stone around Thagar's neck and then down at the one around her own neck.

"They are so beautiful," she said.

"Of course, they are. The stones are the color of you, Aelish," said Thagar. He kissed her tenderly and then asked, "Would you like to make love telepathically?"

"Telepathically?" asked Aelish, confused. "I don't understand."

"It is usually reserved for after the Commitments, when we have taken each other as mates. But I feel we are already there and it may infuse your heart with much needed magic, after six months bereft of all magical abilities," explained Thagar.

"I never knew there was such a thing," said Aelish.

"I have never done it either," said Thagar, "but I've been researching the art of the DARling Rapture."

"The DARling Rapture?" asked Aelish. "What *is* that?"

"Well, besides my own research, I've also asked some of the males at the POD with mates about it. They said the Rapture is best done at night, as it leaves you in a splendid sleep," chuckled Thagar. "We can save it for after we have taken our Commitments if you are not ready, my love."

"No, I want to try it," said Aelish, enthusiastic. "The worst part of losing my freedom was having no magical abilities. If you think it will help restore me, let's try it."

"All right, as long as you are sure."

"I'm sure," smiled Aelish.

"Only through the Rapture can we create life together, so unless you wish to make a DARlette with me, we first have to use the Prevent spell, and then we can begin," explained Thagar.

"Ohh . . . that's why I've never become . . ." said Aelish.

"Of course, my love. I would never have put you in that position without our discussing it first. DARlings can only procreate through the Rapture," reassured Thagar. "I can't believe Antonia has never told you anything about this."

"Perhaps because she has not yet mated, and was unaware you were intending to ask me? She's also British, Thagar, they are very proper," laughed Aelish.

"Well, no matter. I get the honor of telling you, and soon, showing you," said Thagar. His beautiful smile illuminated the bedchamber. Aelish could see his greedy anticipation, but that he was also a bit nervous. She reached across and fervently kissed him.

"As delicious as that was, during the Rapture we do not physically touch each other," explained Thagar.

"Ohh," said Aelish, intrigued.

"We simply lay facing each other, as we are now, but we need to be only a few inches apart," he instructed, moving closer to her. "All right, now. Close your eyes, my love."

Thagar began reciting the Prevent spell, which was beautiful. She felt a peacefulness come over her. Slowly as their minds joined, Aelish began to experience the manifestation of ecstasy. She felt euphoric as they shared the Rapture's melding of each other's love for one another and she experienced the depths of his adoration and love. It was no longer anything she ever had to wonder about. He opened her heart and she reciprocated, as they soared to a place reserved for the highest level of love, between two DARlings.

As the Rapture began to recede, Aelish and Thagar had experienced the true depths of each other's love for the first time.

"I did not know you loved me that much," said Aelish, with tears down her face.

"Nor did I know the expanse of your love for me," smiled Thagar. He embraced her and began passionately kissing her. Entwined, they fell into the deep slumber foretold by the males at the POD and slept until the sun was directly overhead.

‡‡‡‡

Aelish began to stir and instinctively reached for Thagar who was no longer in the bed. She opened her eyes and saw the mural of Brólaigh Castle. Slowly, she began to remember where she was and what had transpired during the night.

She reached for the amulet around her neck and rubbed it between her fingertips and recalled the Rapture. She smiled and stretched her whole body. As her senses awakened, she became aware of a very familiar aroma.

She jumped out of bed and looked in the bedchamber armoire for something to put on. She saw that Thagar had brought over most of her clothes from her cottage. She also saw a beautiful new white robe emblazoned with an "A" on the top pocket, hanging on one of the armoire doors. Floating next to it was a note:

Dearest Aelish,

I hope you like it. It is almost as soft as you are.

Love,

Thagar

She reached for it and slipped the robe over her bare skin. She tightened the belt into a bow.

Oh, this is soft!

She pattered barefoot on the limestone marble floors toward the wide hallway. The marble floors were oddly as warm as the wooden ones in her cottage. As she entered the hallway, she realized she did not know where the kitchen was. She followed the delicious smells and eventually found Thagar sitting alone at a magnificent, long mahogany table, having tea.

She sneaked up behind him and wrapped her arms around his neck. He laughed and turned his head sideways and reached up to kiss her.

"Good morning, my love . . . or should I say good afternoon?" he chuckled. He was already washed and dressed.

"How long have you been awake?" she asked.

"Not very long. The males were right—that was an incredible sleep—it felt like a being had put me under the Slumber spell. I don't think I have ever slept so soundly."

"The whole night was beautiful," said Aelish, kissing him, "and this robe is just lovely. Thank you for everything, my love."

"I'm so glad you like it," he smiled. "Come, sit and dine with me."

She sat down on the chair to the right of the one he occupied at the head of the table and gazed out the glass window at the landscape. The kitchen faced the valley where her cottage was.

Thagar reached across and gently held the amulet around her neck in his hand.

"Any second thoughts, then?" he asked.

"No, my love. None," smiled Aelish.

"Good," he said, smiling broadly.

Aelish looked at the feast on the table and took a bite of a biscuit she had generously buttered.

"There's only one being in the world that makes these," she said with her mouth full.

"I've already eaten four of them. And he makes the butter without magic?" asked Thagar.

"Incredible, right? Wait! Is he *here*?" exclaimed Aelish.

Thagar called out, "Drummond!"

Aelish heard Drummond answer from far away. "Coming, Sir! It takes me a wee bit longer to get out of me dwelling under this house—it's so big!"

Drummond entered the kitchen and froze when he saw her.

"Aelish!" he cried out, as he ran to her. "Oh, no—what has happened to your hair?"

Aelish got up from the table and dropped to her knees to give him a heartfelt embrace.

"I did everything you told me to do, Aelish. I still feel ashamed I gave those horrible soldiers the location of the Komprathian families—and now the young son is gone," cried Drummond, his Brownie tears falling onto her robe.

"It's all right, you did wonderfully. Thank you, my dear, sweet, Drummond," she said consoling him. "Everything will be all right."

"It was my stupid sister, Drusilda, who tricked me. She sent me the secret Brownie message only to be used when we are literally dying. I came looking for her and soldiers then surround me! I was so scared Aelish, but I didn't tell them where the families were for another two whole days," stated Drummond, proudly.

"Yes," said Thagar, glaring at them from the table. "He followed your instructions so well, we couldn't find him or the refugee families for an entire month."

Drummond who was still partially embracing Aelish, whispered into her ear, "I don't think he likes me anymore, Aelish. He more *commands* me than speaks to me, the way we do with each other."

Aelish whispered back, "That's because he *is* a Commander, Drummond. But I will speak to him. Don't worry. He's been through a lot because of what we did."

"All right, Aelish," he whispered back.

Thagar stared at the two of them and Aelish could have sworn she detected a wry smile.

Drummond eyed the depleting feast on the table over Aelish's shoulder and said, "Let me get some more biscuits, as Antonia said she will be dropping by this afternoon."

"And don't forget my favorite spirit, Drummond!" yelled Thagar, after him.

As Drummond was exiting the kitchen, he turned around, looked at Aelish, sand pulled a face behind Thagar's back, which conveyed: *see what I mean?*

Once Drummond had left the kitchen, Aelish sat back down and took Thagar's hand in hers.

"My love, you must not command him; you must ask him, with a please. He's a member of our family, not a servant," Aelish scolded sweetly.

"*Our* family?" teased Thagar. "I like the sound of that."

He half stood up from his chair and reached across the table and kissed her adoringly.

"I promise to be kinder. You know how fond I am of the little male," laughed Thagar.

"You're impossible," said Aelish, trying not to laugh.

As Drummond reentered the kitchen, Thagar's favorite spirit and a bounty of food in tow, Thagar said stiltedly, "Thank you,

Drummond. I am most appreciative." Aelish wanted to pinch him, but she didn't want Drummond to know he was being insincere.

"You are most welcome, Sir," said Drummond, smiling and genuinely happy.

Thagar downed his spirit in one shot and said, "Well, I'm off to the POD for a few hours. Give Antonia my best and do take a minute to gaze at the views from every room. I want to make sure you are truly comfortable here, my love."

"I will," said Aelish. She walked with him to the front door.

As they passed the sculpture of Gidius, she shuddered. "We have to get that thing out of this house, if I am to live here."

"Oh! I almost forgot to tell you," said Thagar. "Some art handlers from the Rotunda are coming by later to take it out of here. They are bringing it to the festival, before it is finally placed in the Rotunda. Oh, and they also want the gown you wore before the Head Council. They are going to frame it as part of the art installation, honoring you."

"Good God! I wanted to burn that gown," said Aelish, distressed.

"Well, perhaps you best retrieve it from the observatory where you left it last night," teased Thagar.

"You are so naughty today," said Aelish, as she reached up to kiss him goodbye.

"Just happy, my love."

After Thagar left, she and Drummond had a chance to talk and she could see he was already returning to his usual, affable self. She instructed him to go rest and told him that no matter where she and Thagar chose to live, he would always be with her.

She took a thorough tour of the house and decided it was gorgeous. Thagar was correct—the views from every room were uncompromising. Once the sculpture was removed, the house would feel like a home.

She was upstairs looking out one of the bedroom windows, when she heard a thunderous knocking on the enormous front doors. She assumed it was the art handlers from the Rotunda come to take the sculpture and her disgusting gown. But when she opened the door, Lady Antonia was standing there.

"Why didn't you just come in?" asked Aelish.

"Well, I felt it only proper since Thagar might also be living here and . . . Good God!" exclaimed Lady Antonia, eyeing the amulet around her neck. "Are you Pre-Commitments?"

Lady Antonia nearly knocked Aelish over with a hug, already knowing the answer to her question. She pulled away from Aelish and looked at her face. She inhaled a huge gasp and whisper-yelled, "And you have done the Rapture!"

Aelish opened her mouth, but nothing came out, which made Lady Antonia burst into hysterics.

32

ISABELA MUST DECIDE

T HEY WERE BOTH sitting cross-legged on Isabela's bed facing each other—Isabela's hair, long since finished.

"But hold on," said Isabela. "If King Gidius was responsible for previous pandemics, but he died *after* The Great Plague of 1665, what caused the third pandemic or the Modern Plague of the 1850s that lasted well into the 1900s?"

"I knew you'd catch that," laughed Aelish. "We all thought the legacy of King Gidius would be how he had magically conjured the young drone rat, infected with plague, and murdered him. But Gidius was more cunning than we ever could have imagined.

"When a new outbreak of plague began in the Yunnan province of China, in the early 1850s, the Head Council thought perhaps it would be a contained, naturally occurring outbreak. As we discussed earlier, these outbreaks occur to this day. But it spread to Hong Kong and Guangzhou killing tens of thousands of Chinese citizens. Since both cities were major coastal shipping hubs, just as in the 1300s, the disease followed the trade routes. There was plague in Bombay, India; Cape Town, S. Africa; Guayaquil, Ecuador; and San Francisco, California and Pensacola, Florida in the United States—all port cities throughout the world."

"I know, it killed over fifteen million people worldwide," said Isabela.

"It was terrible. It was like the sun stopped shining over DAR," sighed Aelish.

"And Komprathia was now a peaceful, evolving commonwealth," said Isabela. "Was there a traitor in Komprathia? Had someone betrayed Obredón?"

"About a year after the plague began raging, Obredón received a message, hand-delivered by one of his staff members. The parchment of the message was at least two hundred years old and bore the seal of King Gidius. Obredón did not break the seal, but instead began searching for its origination point.

"Ultimately, the original Komprathian that had received it was located. He indicated the message had arrived in the normal course of daily correspondence. He had simply gathered it up with the regular daily delivery and the message eventually arrived on Obredón's desk.

"Obredón, of course, suspected one of his advisors of committing treason, but he wisely turned the message over to DAR, before opening it. The message was sent to the N.W. Quadrant, where it was thoroughly examined through magical experimentation. The only oddity of the message was a ticking sound. It could only be heard when put through a specific sound wave experiment," explained Aelish.

"Like a ticking clock—like a bomb?" asked Isabela.

"Exactly. It was very faint and barely discernable," stated Aelish. "Obredón was immediately contacted and it was suggested the message be opened in the N.W. Quadrant, as a safety precaution for DAR and Komprathia. Obredón traveled there, as did Thagar, who was now Director of the POD; Melanthia, who was now Council Chair; Bathwick, who served as a consultant on all warcraft; and myself, as Policy Director for Earth."

"I would have been so nervous," stated Isabela.

"Trust me, when it came time to break the seal, the full gamut of emotions was experienced by all in attendance," said Aelish.

"Who actually broke the seal?" asked Isabela.

"A very brave magical experimenter. We were all behind an impenetrable magical wall, watching and waiting," said Aelish.

"And?" Isabela asked anxiously.

"And . . . nothing. It was an ordinary message, except for one difference—it had a time-activated spell on it. That was the faint ticking sound. The spell caused it to be delivered whenever there was another pandemic of plague. It just so happened to be nearly two hundred years after King Gidius wrote it in 1665."

"Ah! Like your time-activated Exterminate spell?" asked Isabela.

"Much more sophisticated," stated Aelish, humbly. "Let me get the exact phrasing of the message for you." She put her hand to the side of her head, closed her eyes, and began reciting King Gidius' message:

My Dear Brother, Obredón,

I imagine if you are reading this message, I am dead, and you have stolen my Kingdom from me. I congratulate you on a successful coup.

I hope a respectable amount of time has passed for you to have ruled, gained the trust of the allies you forged in overthrowing me, as well as the trust of Komprathia, before I released hell upon DAR's precious Earth, one last time.

How I wish I could see your face and the faces of those, that I'm certain are standing alongside you.

During London's Great Plague of 1665, I magically transported tens of thousands of my drone rats along the trade routes of the second pandemic in the 1300s. I situated them in secure nests close to the sea. This way, when they awoke from my time-activated spell, magically sensing the next outbreak, they would be ready to die for me, one final time. I imagine by this point, they have killed millions of Humans utilizing my favorite weapon, the bubonic plague, and all of its fabulous mutations.

Consider this my congratulatory gift on your new position as ruler of my Kingdom.

In admiration, your brother,

Gidius

"Oh—my—God!" exclaimed Isabela. "He is *horrible*. From the grave, he caused the deaths of millions of Humans?"

"Oh, it was humiliating," said Aelish. "We all stood there, no one saying anything for quite some time. Hearing his message read aloud by the brave experimenter was as if Gidius had returned from the dead. It was so cunning, so shrewd, so, exquisitely evil. Although no one ever said it out loud, there was admiration by everyone behind that magical wall, for what he had done. Once we returned home, Thagar and I talked about nothing else for weeks," said Aelish.

"But looking back on it now, you must be so proud of your accomplishment in defeating him, right?" encouraged Isabela.

"It took me a long time to recapture the feeling of the success of my mission."

"But if you hadn't done what you did, can you imagine what other things he had in store for Humans?" asked Isabela.

Aelish gently nodded.

Isabela stared at Aelish and said, "I mean, I am looking at the being that literally stopped the plague."

"I had a lot of help, Isabela," said Aelish.

"Not really. The whole concept was yours and yours alone," stated Isabela. "And you were put in prison because of it!"

"The Detention Center was an experience I can never forget, no matter how many years pass," sighed Aelish.

"How did you survive it?" asked Isabela, shaking her head.

"I survived it by accepting from day one, that I would be banished and by never doubting my actions. The simple rosary given to me by the Guards, along with my faith, allowed me to stay calm in the face of so many unknowns."

"Did you think they would send you back to Earth? That's where I would have wanted to go," said Isabela.

"They don't banish to Earth. The Head Council feels it is too fragile a place for a rogue magical being who defies their authority," said Aelish.

"What happened between the Kingdom of Yasteron and DAR? Did they retaliate against DAR?"

"Very astute question. Interestingly, in the last three hundred and fifty years since Gidius' death in 1665, there's been relative peace throughout the entire magical world. Yasteron has been exceptionally quiet. If I'm being completely honest, it has left me unsettled. I feel as if we are missing something."

"Because they are the ones you never see coming?" asked Isabela, using Aelish's own words.

"Exactly," chuckled Aelish. "We anticipated their retaliation to occur soon after Komprathia was freed from tyrannical rule, but it never happened. For the last three hundred and fifty years, I have worked closely with the POD, the Keepers in the Breanon, and the Institute. In my role as Policy Director for Earth, I report directly to the Head Council. All of this time, I have felt we are missing something, and I have been searching for answers. Is Yasteron truly living peacefully alongside us, or are they stealthily exacting their revenge on DAR? The answer eludes me," said Aelish.

"What happened to Komprathia?" asked Isabela.

"Komprathia has become a jewel in the magical world. It was an exceptional experience to have had a role in their becoming one of the more evolved and peaceful magical dominions. Komprathia's government now reflects that of DAR's, in that it is also a commonwealth. Females have equal roles with males and the drone rats are positively thriving. After receiving the full rights of citizenship, including an education and the right to vote, the drone rats also now serve in leadership roles within the newly formed commonwealth. The change from when King Gidius ruled to now—well, other than the fact that the Komprathians look the same—the commonwealth is almost unrecognizable."

"But after such a legendary accomplishment, isn't being an Oraculi a step down?" asked Isabela. "No offense, but it just seems so boring after what you've accomplished."

Aelish burst out laughing. She adored Isabela's directness. For a brief moment, she hesitated to reveal the entire truth of her mission as Isabela's Oraculi, but decided to proceed.

"While serving as an Oraculi is a very esteemed position in DAR, comparative to my mission in Komprathia, you are correct—it is not on the same level. Yesterday, on Sunday morning, before the Head Council, I officially became an Oraculi," smiled Aelish.

"*Yesterday?*" asked Isabela.

"Yes. When Melanthia congratulated me on becoming an Oraculi, the audience got a real kick out of it. I was literally standing before the Head Council under a hand-carved depiction of myself in the dome of the Rotunda, alongside other legendary figures of DAR. But serving as an Oraculi to an *Earthling,* has never been done before."

"What? Are you serious? I am the first person?" Isabela asked astonished.

"You are the first. You are also the first Human, not related to a DARling born of the Earth, who has been told of DAR's existence. As Policy Director for Earth, I created the initiative of mentoring a potential Human scientist. If you accept, we will be the pioneers of this new policy. The most dangerous aspect of the initiative was, of course, revealing the existence of DAR. We have never openly intervened in the affairs of Earth, but the situation has grown dire, Isabela, we are running out of time. The Head Council instilled their faith in my abilities and encouraged me to try."

"So, if I don't agree to this, I will cause your new initiative to fail? Oh, my God, that's so much pressure," Isabela complained.

"Don't let that impact your decision. I will find another way to pursue a positive outcome for DAR and Earth," assured Aelish. "Your intelligence demanded honesty, so I told you the truth."

"But what if I am the wrong person? What if my life yields nothing of great importance? What if I'm an abject failure? Maybe I want to be an actress instead of a scientist?" asked Isabela, in a panic.

Aelish raised one eyebrow, cocked her head to one side, and chuckled.

"Well you certainly are beautiful enough. Go look in the mirror and tell me if your hair is appropriately styled for the actress you want to become," laughed Aelish. She gestured for Isabela to look in the mirror.

"Oh, my God, it's so shiny and straight!" exclaimed Isabela. "Abuela is never going to believe I did this on my own and I never lie to her. What am I going to tell her?"

"What do you think would happen if you told her the truth?" asked Aelish, testing her.

Isabela sat back down on the bed with her head downcast.

"Go ahead, run through an imaginary conversation with her.

She's going to see your hair in another two hours," said Aelish.

"I think if I told her the truth, it would upset her, and she would think I'd lost my mind," said Isabela, looking up at Aelish.

"Do you think it would be fair to burden a Human of normal intellect with the truth—that you encountered a magical being? I mean no disparagement toward your grandmother, but knowing about me and the magical world where I come from, could not only rock her faith in God, but could also potentially rock her well-being. Do you understand?" asked Aelish.

"But I've never lied to her before," stated Isabela. "Maybe by omission, but not directly to her face."

"My mother used to say there was no difference. But sometimes not divulging the truth is in another person's best interests. You would be keeping a secret for your grandmother's benefit," said Aelish.

"Like you did with Thagar?" smiled Isabela.

"You had to make me feel it, didn't you?" chuckled Aelish. "Yes, like with Thagar."

Aelish could see Isabela wrestling with the notion of deceiving someone she loved so dearly. She knew the conflict very well.

"Earlier this evening, you said yourself that your grandmother 'would have a heart attack'—remember? She actually could, Isabela," cautioned Aelish.

"Well, if it's for her benefit, then okay. But only for that reason could I do it," Isabela stated emphatically.

"We are entrusting you with the secret of DAR's existence, Isabela. The majority of adult Humans wouldn't believe you regardless, but children would, and you could inadvertently endanger our world. You and I must make a pact that DAR has to remain a secret whether or not you agree to move forward. You cannot reveal this information to anyone, not only to protect DAR, but also to protect yourself. You'd find yourself in a psychiatric hospital," Aelish said seriously.

"But I don't want this responsibility. I didn't ask you to come here. My mother is going to die and I am going to be a wreck when it happens, as will the rest of my family," said Isabela. She began crying. "How can I possibly handle responsibilities for DAR, when I'm dealing with the impending death of my mother? It's not fair of you to expect me to deal with both things."

Aelish could see she was frightened.

"I understand your hesitation and your reluctance. I, too, experienced what you are feeling, when I was your age. My skin color began changing and I morphed into a magical being. I wanted no part of it. I wanted to be like every other person in Ireland."

Isabela looked up and wiped her tears.

"You must come to this decision of your own free will, Isabela. We are not forcing you to help us, but your extraordinary aptitude in science is rare. Your mother's situation, awful as it is, has brought you into this body of knowledge because of the love you have for her. And no matter the outcome for your mother, Isabela, you have to bear it and stay focused on reaching your greatest potential. Females are the strongest beings in both the Human and magical worlds. You must honor that legacy, as well as your own mother, by not allowing her outcome to derail you. I say this with empathy, as I have lived through it, and what I am asking, will not be easy," soothed Aelish.

"I don't want to care about DAR or the Earth. I can barely cope with what has already happened to my family. Besides, you've already saved Humanity from the plague," pleaded Isabela.

"You've done a lot of scientific research for your mother and you know another event like the plague is coming, Isabela. The atmosphere is heating up; the glaciers are melting; ice shelves are breaking off; the permafrost is disappearing; Arctic ice is melting;

and Antarctic ice is melting underwater at an alarming rate.

"You and I both know what's in that ice—greenhouse gases, bacteria, and viruses that have been buried for centuries. If the ice abruptly thaws, it will release methane and carbon dioxide into an already compromised atmosphere, accelerating climate change. Additionally, ancient dormant bacteria and viruses could spring back to life. This would increase the chance of an old or new, deadly disease developing organically. At this point, it may all be inevitable. But DAR needs young scientists on Earth to be ready for what's coming."

"It's all so depressing and hopeless. Like it's already too late," stated Isabela, defeated.

"We can't give up, Isabela," said Aelish. "What would have happened if Jenner, Fleming, Salk, and Haffkine had given up?"

"I understand everything you're saying. But watching my mother die has made me so angry," said Isabela. "By this time, why *can't* we cure cancer? I feel like true science has no place in our world anymore. Why have we allowed climate change to accelerate like a runaway freight train? Why aren't we actively trying to stop it? What is *wrong* with us? You say Humans have the gift to cure illness, but we don't! We don't care about anything. We just let people suffer and die."

"You are not wrong, Isabela," said Aelish. "But you need to ask yourself *why* Humans don't do more. Are the Leaders on Earth not paying attention or do they simply not care? Do they actually understand the consequences of Human negligence, yet, choose to ignore it? Do they only care about appeasing their wealthy benefactors, in order to retain their positions of power? Is there a cure for cancer that has been stymied because there is more money to be made from sick patients, than from cures? Any one of these scenarios portends disaster for Humanity.

"Corporations, both private and public, are attacking and

ravaging the Earth's natural resources with unprecedented callousness. They drill, they frack, they pollute with abandon, and the Earth is finally beginning to weaken. In thirty years, Isabela, the oceans will have more plastic in it than marine life. And that's assuming there will still be any marine life. The oceans are heating up forty percent faster than was previously thought.

"Climate events that were once rarities are now occurring on a regular basis. Wildfires, droughts, rising sea levels, and flooding are already causing major economic impacts. Once world economies become threatened and food and water shortages occur, famine and poverty will bring about wars and cause untold upheaval. Add a raging infectious disease into the mix—my God, Isabela— Humanity will be decimated," said Aelish, upset.

"I know, I know. Everything you're describing is true. It's a horrible time to grow up," stated Isabela.

"Climate change on Earth has already begun to impact DAR's food supply, Isabela," sighed Aelish.

"What? Seriously?" asked Isabela. "But you're magical beings. Can't you just magically create food?"

"Remember earlier, when I told you that all our food is grown in the S.W. Quadrant? How Melanthia sends home the seedlings that sprout out of her olive skin? We *grow* our food, Isabela. We use magic to harvest and care for the crops, but the seeds of what we grow, cannot be magically created," explained Aelish.

"Oh, my God! What are you saying? DARlings could starve?" asked Isabela. "Why is this happening from climate change on Earth?"

"Clouds," said Aelish.

"Clouds?" asked Isabela.

"Yes," said Aelish. "Clouds have an enormous impact on the Earth's climate. Clouds have traditionally reflected about one-third of the total amount of sunlight that hits the Earth's atmosphere, back into space. DAR survives on that sunlight reflected off the Earth.

"Because greenhouse gases from burning fossil fuels has become trapped in the Earth's atmosphere, this has led to either an increase in clouds or an absence of clouds. Prior to the last two hundred years, the S.W. Quadrant always had the perfect balance of sun, rain, and shade for the crops to flourish. The farmers used minimal magical intervention to produce abundant harvests. But once the industrial revolution occurred on Earth, the farmers in DAR experienced more and more challenges in combatting the repercussions from the altered state of Earthly clouds.

"Excessive cloudiness on Earth causes an *increase* in reflected sunlight in DAR, which burns the crops. Conversely, the lack of clouds on Earth causes a *decrease* in reflected sunlight altering the process of photosynthesis for the crops. The decrease in sunlight has also resulted in the formation of thick, moisture-laden clouds, which cause torrential rains, subsequently drowning the crops. Further, the melting Arctic ice is also causing less reflected sunlight from the albedo effect."

"I can't believe DAR is experiencing climate change, and it's caused by *us!*" cried Isabela. "This is really upsetting!"

"Our worlds are interconnected, Isabela," said Aelish. "Part of my responsibilities in DAR is to create progressive leadership policies for the Head Council to implement. I am very proud of initiating the first seed vault, two hundred years *prior* to the industrial revolution. My original intent was to protect our seeds from potential magical enemies. I never considered the possibility that the Earth would become the greatest threat to our food supply. The Seed Vault for DAR, known as the SVD, is of course protected by magical spells, but we located it in the N.E. Quadrant, as the ocean provides topographical protection. The SVD has proven invaluable."

"Oh, my God! Like the Global Seed Vault envisioned by Dr. Cary Fowler in Svalbard, Norway?" asked Isabela.

"Yes!" chuckled Aelish.

"I was so excited to learn he was born in Memphis just a few months before we moved to Tennessee," said Isabela. "He's amazing! One night I stayed up until six o'clock in the morning because I couldn't stop reading about the Global Seed Vault," said Isabela.

"Tell me," encouraged Aelish.

"Well, it's sometimes referred to as the doomsday vault. While there are over one thousand seven hundred gene banks around the world that have seed collections, they are all vulnerable to war, natural disasters, etcetera. So the first part of the vision was *where* to build the Global Seed Vault, what country? I found it fascinating that the United States was not chosen as a safe haven for the seeds. Of course the climate of Svalbard on the Norwegian island of Spitsbergen is superior to any place in the United States for preserving the seeds at zero degrees, but I don't believe that was the sole reason.

"In 2003, Dr. Fowler who is a scientist, a conservationist, and a biodiversity expert, began to envision a backup storage facility where all the world's seeds could safely be stored, both from natural and man-made disasters," said Isabela. "Ultimately, Norway was chosen because it is respected and trusted globally when it comes to the issue of biodiversity. And the climate conditions in Svalbard are almost perfect. The facility stays naturally frozen without the aid of mechanical equipment. Can you imagine thinking up something like this?" asked Isabela.

"He sounds extraordinary," Aelish said smiling.

"Oh, he is," agreed Isabela. "In 2008, his idea became a reality. The facility was built and carved through nearly five hundred feet of deep permafrost inside a mountain in the Arctic Circle. Svalbard is located halfway between the main part of Norway and the North Pole. Inside the mountain, the permafrost naturally keeps the temperature at twenty-three degrees. The seeds are further frozen mechanically to zero degrees. But the fact that the mountain is already below freezing, makes it much easier to maintain the zero degree temperature needed to safeguard the seeds.

"Although the Global Seed Vault was never intended to reseed the world after a worldwide catastrophe, like a nuclear disaster," explained Isabela, "it was designed to safeguard Humanity's food supply. You see the seeds' value lies in their being a genetic source in breeding plants. Did you know nearly ninety percent of historic fruit and vegetables have disappeared in the United States?"

"That's an astonishing statistic," said Aelish.

"The seeds in the Global Seed Vault are used to assist scientists who breed plants and are working on developing new crop varieties for farmers. Think of the seeds as a collection of Human traits," chuckled Isabela.

Aelish burst out laughing. "Oh no, not those."

"It's like picking out the best traits and crossing them with existing plants to create crops that can resist disease, pests who eat them, drought, or plants that can grow in extreme heat," explained Isabela. "Dr. Fowler explained in one site I read that the seeds in the vault are duplicate copies of collections housed in other seed banks around the world. If something happens to one of those facilities and the seeds are destroyed, there is a backup copy in the Global Seed Vault. There are currently nearly one million packets of seeds in the vault. How cool is that?"

"Very," said Aelish.

"The Global Seed Vault was created to stop the extinction of various crops. If it's in the Seed Vault, it is supposedly safe. But then the Seed Vault flooded in 2016!" exclaimed Isabela. "I was doing my homework and came across an article that explained soaring temperatures in the Arctic caused an unexpected thaw in the permafrost, which caused flooding in the entrance tunnel of the Seed Vault. Thankfully, the water didn't reach the actual seeds, but the permafrost in the mountain had previously been viewed as failsafe protection against natural or man-made disasters and it begins *melting*? Like, are you kidding me? I couldn't believe this happened. But Norway, who used its own money to build the vault in the first place—I think it cost like nine million dollars—has already committed another thirteen million dollars to create new waterproof walls and reinforcements to prevent future water intrusion. I think they chose the right country to house the Seed Vault."

As she sat there listening, Aelish decided not tell Isabela that she and two Agricultural Masters from the S.W. Quadrant had attended a lecture, years ago, given by Dr. Fowler. They came to Earth to learn how Humans were genetically breeding crops that could withstand extreme climate conditions, as DAR needed to take action against the destruction of its crops, caused by climate change. The lecture provided them with crucial information that ultimately led to the creation of the Magically Modified Seed Project, otherwise known in DAR as the MMSP. And he was, indeed, *amazing*.

"You are very inspired by Dr. Fowler. Would you agree, then, that there are other Humans that share your passion for real science?" asked Aelish.

"I suppose, but he really is exceptional," replied Isabella.

"You have a strong moral compass, Isabela and there are other Humans who share that trait with you." Aelish reached inside her flypack and handed Isabela a flash drive. "And they do care about climate change."

"What is this?" asked Isabela. "You have *flash drives* in DAR?"

"Today, a report from the United Nations Intergovernmental Panel on Climate Change, entitled: **Global Warming of 1.5°C,** is being released worldwide."

"How in the world did you obtain a forthcoming report from the IPCC?" asked Isabela, astonished.

"Magic, of course," smiled Aelish.

"I know they've been meeting all week in Incheon, South Korea," said Isabela. "I set a reminder on my phone to check on the status of their conclusions. I can't believe you have this!"

"On that drive," said Aelish, "is not only the press release, and the summary for policy makers, but the entire report, along with other internal documents from the scientists who worked on it. I thought it would be helpful for you to not only read the report, but more importantly, to see how many Humans care about science. The report was written and edited by ninety-one scientists, from forty different countries, who analyzed more than six thousand scientific studies. Like you, they believe in science, and agree that the status quo cannot continue if Humans are to avert the catastrophic impacts of climate change. The report is grave and projects that by 2030, the effects of climate change may be irreversible."

"Oh, my God! But that's in only *twelve years*!" exclaimed Isabela. "And today's the eighth of October, so it's more like only *eleven* years!"

"I know, Isabela. Humans must urgently begin to change their global environmental policies, but more importantly— their attitudes—they must stop living in denial. Throughout the history of the Earth, Humanity has always triumphed, so far.

"The question you need to answer is, do you want to become a leader whose focus is to ensure Humanity's survival, or do you want to walk away from it all? You have to decide that for yourself, Isabela. I am only your lowly Oraculi," Aelish teased.

Isabela chuckled and shook her head at Aelish. She got up from her bed and began pacing. Aelish could see she was calculating, theorizing, and strategizing.

"I can't believe how dire the report is—2030, *seriously*? It feels like it's already too late," said Isabela, who had momentarily stopped pacing.

"It may be already too late, Isabela," said Aelish. "But if you give up and stick your head in the sand, there will be many more Isabelas and Aelishes coping with the loss of those they love the most. Wouldn't you rather be on the frontlines of science trying to save Humanity?"

"If I agree to you being my Oraculi, will I ever encounter other magical beings?" asked Isabela.

"Besides myself—yes, from time to time," stated Aelish. "When you encounter a magical being or a moment you know derived from magic, you must have your wits about you. You need to deflect the conversation and change the subject. Humans are easily distracted and often doubt their own senses. Whereas, *you*, must not discount your senses and believe in what you see and hear. You will grow accustomed to magic sporadically being in your life," explained Aelish.

"But I won't be able to speak to anyone about it?"

"Not at this point, but perhaps in the future," stated Aelish. "We don't want you to feel isolated. And please know, I will always be here for you for the rest of your life."

Isabela remained quiet and continued pacing.

"You need to take some time to think about this commitment, Isabela. I know I am asking a lot," said Aelish.

Isabela sat back down on the bed and stared at Aelish.

"Dawn is approaching and it's time for me to leave," said Aelish. "I am going to put a Deep Sleep spell on you that will make you feel like you've slept for eighteen hours, when in fact, you have less than two hours before you need to get up for school. There is one more thing I want to give you."

She reached inside her flypack and took out a metal object in the shape of an egg. She allowed Isabela to hold it.

"This little gadget will allow us to communicate with one another," explained Aelish. "After you've given it some thought and decide you don't want any part of this, simply turn the center portion of the egg to the left. If you decide you want to move forward, then turn the egg to the right. Both directions will allow your message to reach me in DAR. If we move forward and you urgently need to see me, turn the egg two clicks to the right. But only manipulate the egg at night, when you are certain no one will come into your room."

Isabela begin to physically examine the egg and Aelish quickly put her hand over Isabela's.

"Do not experiment with this and do not turn it until you have decided, understood?" asked Aelish. "I'm going to put this on your desk, on my way out. No one else will be able to manipulate the magic out of the egg. It has already been imprinted with your fingerprints. If your grandmother or someone else in the house picks it up from your desk or tries to fiddle with it, nothing will happen. It will only recognize your fingerprints. Now, let's get you tucked into bed. You have a big day tomorrow and your first class with Dr. Rios."

"Oh, I almost forgot," smiled Isabela, as she nestled under the covers, lying on her back.

"I remember my first day at the Institute. I was so excited," said Aelish.

She tucked Isabela into bed and arranged the covers so that her hair would remain smooth and in place. Isabela would then awaken from the Deep Sleep spell, in the same position she was currently in.

"Let's say goodbye for now, then," said Aelish, as she gently kissed Isabela on the forehead. "The metal egg and the flash drive will be on your desk."

"If I decide not to do this, will I ever see you again?" asked

Isabela.

"Probably not, sweetheart," soothed Aelish. "But we will always remember each other, won't we?"

"Yes, always," Isabela said softly, already falling asleep.

"Go to sleep. All will be well, Isabela," whispered Aelish. "And remember, if you are ever on an airplane, especially at night, look toward the southeast. You might catch a glimpse of the lights in Bencarlta."

Isabela smiled and fell asleep.

Aelish put the egg and flash drive on Isabela's desk, shut all the lights, and made herself invisible before leaving the room. She needed to do one more thing before she left.

She went into Isabela's parents' bedroom and stood over Isabela's mother asleep in the hospital bed. Aelish instantly felt tears begin streaming down her face. She had, of course, seen the condition of her mother through her Viewer. But to see her up close was entirely different. She was so ill, so frail. Aelish put several No Pain spells on Isabela's mother, which would last for the first two months of her new treatments.

She then gingerly removed the yellowed, linen pouch from the bodice of her gown. She carefully pulled out the rosary given to her by the Detention Center Guards and gently placed it over Isabela's mother's heart.

Aelish kissed her forehead and whispered, "Please survive, Marisol."

33

FIRST DAY OF SCHOOL

MONDAY, OCTOBER 8, 2019 7:00 AM

ISABELA WOKE UP and immediately remembered Aelish. She did, indeed, feel like she had slept for eighteen hours. She reached up and felt her hair and smiled—the room still smelled of lilacs.

She sat up on the edge of the bed and began mentally reviewing everything Aelish had told her during the night. She saw the metal egg on her desk and sighed.

She began making her bed, trying to think of what to tell Abuela about her hair, when Abuela suddenly burst into her room. She was holding a clothing item on a hanger under a garment bag. She took one look at Isabela and dropped the hanger onto the floor.

"Izzy, how does your hair look like this? Did you do your own hair last night?" asked Abuela. She picked up the hanger from the floor and slung it over the back of Isabela's desk chair.

"I watched a tutorial on the Internet, but it took me forever," said Isabela, evenly, leaning against her bed. And there it was. The first direct lie she had ever told Abuela. What surprised her was how easily the lie had come into her head.

Abuela came over and began stroking Isabela's hair feeling the straightened smoothness of the new texture.

"It looks really nice, Izzy. I'm proud of you. Maybe you can do it by yourself from now on," teased Abuela.

"I don't ever want to do this again by myself," said Isabela, her eyes downcast.

Isabela felt guilty after Abuela had said 'I'm proud of you,' but she remembered what Aelish had told her. *'Knowing about me and the magical world where I come from, could not only rock her faith in God, but could also potentially rock her well-being.'*

Isabela hugged Abuela.

"What was that for?" asked Abuela, pulling away from Isabela.

"I just want you to know how much I love you," said Isabela, staring at Abuela.

"You look so grown up, Izzy, like the actresses in my telenovelas," laughed Abuela. "Maybe when you grow up, you will become an actress?"

"Ha!" Isabela laughed nervously, as she remembered saying those exact words to Aelish only two hours ago.

She could hear Aelish's voice in her head. *'Deflect the conversation and change the subject.'*

"What's under the plastic on the hangar?" asked Isabela.

"Ah! Your mother and I have a surprise for you," exclaimed Abuela. "We went online together and picked out—this!" Abuela lifted up the garment bag to reveal a beautiful short brown leather jacket. "And, we also bought something else to go with it."

Abuela headed toward Isabela's closet and reached down to the closet floor. She picked up a box, which had been hidden from view. Abuela lifted the lid of the box and held up a beautiful pair of short, brown, suede boots.

"Oh, Abuela," said Isabela, "the jacket is gorgeous and the boots are so cool. I hope they fit. Thank you."

"Try everything on and meet me in your parents' room, so we can show Mom," Abuela said happily.

"Okay, go, go. Let me get dressed," said Isabela.

After she finished dressing, Isabela walked into her parents' bedroom where everyone was waiting. Her father was the first to say how beautiful and grown-up she looked; her mother had her hand over her mouth, the happiest Isabela had seen her in months; Javier gave her a thumbs-up sign; and Abuela was beaming.

"I look okay?" asked Isabela, still needing confirmation from her family.

"Gorgeous!" they yelled in unison.

"Come on, kiddo," said Javier, "you don't want to be late. I'm driving you to school today. I'll wait for you in the garage."

"Oh, awesome," said Isabela.

"I have to go too, Izzy," said her father. "You're hair looks amazing like that."

"Thanks, Dad," said Isabela.

She reached up and kissed her father goodbye. She wished him good luck in his new position and watched him leave the bedroom. She could hear her father and Javier laughing together, as they both headed toward the garage.

"How are you feeling today, Mom?" she asked. She bent over the hospital bed rails to give her mother a kiss on her forehead.

"Izzy, your hair and your outfit—you look so grown up—so beautiful," said her mother. "Oh! Look what I woke up with today, over my heart." She held up a wooden rosary. "I feel so good today. I have no pain, it's really weird. I'm going to keep this rosary next to me, always. Do you know where it came from?"

Isabela knew immediately that the rosary was the one given to Aelish in the Detention Center. As she held it in her hands, she could see the wood worn down from Aelish's fingers. She knew what that rosary meant to Aelish. She could not believe she had given it to her mother.

"I found it on my bike ride yesterday, cleaned it up, and left it on you last night after I gave you your medicines," Isabela lied. *Another lie.* It was disturbing how easily they came out.

"You don't have any pain today, Mom?" asked Isabela, making sure she had heard her mother correctly.

"No. I haven't felt this way since . . . well, I can't even remember when, it has been so long," chuckled her mother.

Isabela knew Aelish had put No Pain spells on her mother similar to the ones she had used on her own parents, as they died of plague. Spells to ease their suffering. She felt tears spill down her cheeks at both gestures of love Aelish had demonstrated for her mother. Isabela reached down and embraced her mother.

"Don't cry, mi amor," said her mother. "It's good I feel this way. It will help me on my first day of the new treatments."

I know. That's why Aelish used the spells.

"Ay, you better go, Izzy. Javier needs to get back in time to take your mother," said Abuela.

"Okay. Good luck today, Mom, and know I will be thinking of you all day," stated Isabela, wiping her tears with the back of her hands.

"Have a great first day," said her mother. "And remember, on your worst day, you're smarter than everyone else on their *best* day." Her mother started laughing, a sound Isabela hadn't heard for a long time.

"I love you, Mom," said Isabela, blowing her a kiss, as she

left the bedroom.

"Don't forget your lunch! I left it on the kitchen table!" yelled Abuela.

"Got it! Love you!" yelled back Isabela.

‡‡‡‡

Isabela stood outside the door of her homeroom and looked through the glass. She saw her homeroom teacher Ms. McQuire speaking with Dr. Rios as her classmates settled into their seats. For a moment, she was paralyzed with fear and couldn't turn the doorknob. But then Dr. Rios saw her at the door, burst into a huge smile, and began waving for her to come in.

Isabela opened the door.

EPILOGUE

I SABELA SAT AT her desk and picked up the metal egg remembering the first time she had used it.

Everyone in her family was in bed, but she couldn't sleep. It had been a month since Aelish's visit. She was still adjusting to her new school; her Dad was acclimating to his new position; Javier, always the trooper, had become a barista and methodically took her mother for her treatments, never complaining; her mother was handling the new treatments very well and was still experiencing virtually no pain; and Abuela continued to care for the entire family and was cautiously optimistic about her mother.

But Isabela was worried. How long would the spells on her mother last? She remembered analyzing the situation. Was that reason enough to allow the magic of DAR into her life? What was Aelish really asking of her—to study science? She had always intended to become a scientist. Yet, the question of whether she could remain focused *if* her mother died, was still a real concern. But there was one thing Aelish had said that kept replaying over and over in her head: '*There will be many more Isabelas and Aelishes coping with the loss of those they love the most.*'

She remembered picking up the metal egg and turning it over and over in her hands. Finally, she turned the egg to the right. The egg had made a whooshing sound and opened on its own. She saw the top disconnect from the bottom, still held together by two small hinges and a small creature flew up. She had almost fallen off her chair she was so startled.

She now knew the creature was a Sylph and Isabela remembered her encouraging smile.

All Isabela could manage to say was, "Hello."

But the Sylph was patient and sweet, batting her eyes and smiling at her.

Isabela hadn't known what to do, so she simply asked the creature, "Am I supposed to give you a message for Aelish?"

The Sylph had batted her eyes three times.

She'd taken that as a yes, and remembered taking a deep breath before telling the Sylph, "Please tell Aelish that my answer is yes—I want her to be my Oraculi."

The Sylph again batted her eyes three times, vanished as quickly as she had appeared, and the metal egg had slammed shut.

How she had agonized over her decision. Looking back on it now, she couldn't even imagine Aelish not being a part of her life. She smiled and put the egg back in its special spot on her desk and picked up her phone to text Aelish.

Can we meet tomorrow for lunch? It's important. xoxo